THE QUICK OF THE SUN

CAMERON LAMBRIGHT

THE QUICK OF THE SUN

Cameron Lambright

-INCANDESCENCE PRESS-

This is a work of fiction. FICTION! The old adage applies: "Please don't sue, he's not talking about you." Names, places, etc... resemblance, etc... entirely coincidental, etc, etc.

INCANDESCENCE PRESS
www.incandescencepress.com

Original Cover Art by: Soheil Hamidi Tousi

For those who seek redemption and stumble into transcendence.

C H A P T E R [1]

SAMSON FORD WAS IN SPACE. He floated easily, drifting in any direction he wanted. He could see nothing and it receded into the distance wherever he looked. Above him, below him. There was nothing, but the nothing was not nothing. It was greyness or mist, it was air, or something like air, his sight could dimly perceive the distance of it and that it went on. He flew forward, slowly and then faster, until the nothing rushing past his ears sounded deafening. It was air, he decided. He couldn't quite remember exactly what air was, but that didn't matter. He felt conviction that it was air. As he flew forward, the air coalesced and diffused at the edges of his vision, without ever really changing, and he realized that it would be impossible to go back to where he started. There was no compass or landmark here, only his body and the endless, endless air. He flew like that for days, or whatever days were.

Eventually, he came to a wall. It had levers and wheels and sliding panels on it and extended endlessly in all directions. He did not know why the wall was there, or what was behind it, but he felt that he must go through it to proceed. There was a woman, a shadowy figment of a woman, who haunted his mind, black haired and dark eyed. He did not know who she was, only that he should return to her. That he needed her. He didn't know why. It was as if the need were intrinsic to him. He shifted the levers and moved the sliding panels on the wall, and turned the wheels, but nothing happened. He flew along its length and breadth for many periods of time and the wall was always the same, always stretching out into the distance farther than he could see. The face of the woman seemed to smile at him, half in disappointment. He flew back into the nothing, the air, fast, faster, turning and spinning about without orientation, enjoying the freedom of flight.

The air rushed over his body and he could again see nothing in every direction. He turned loops and pirouettes, then flew straight for days and days. Or whatever days were.

Eventually, he came to the wall again. It was the same wall, with the same levers and panels, although he was sure he had flown in a new direction. He switched the levers again and slid the panels back and forth, and turned the wheels, which made the wall emit peculiar sounds but accomplished nothing. He plunged back into the nothing again, and flew faster than before, faster than light, faster than he could think or perceive, away from the wall. The woman's face seemed to envelop his mind and he despaired that he might never reach her. He must get around the wall to reach her. She was so regal in the shadows of his thought. The rushing air pushed against his face painfully and seemed to prick the surfaces of his skin. He might obliterate himself on the wall if he came to it again. He wouldn't see it. He might explode through the wall or find that he had worked his way around it. He didn't care. It felt good to fly so fast; it was comforting to imagine hitting the wall, or finding its edges, or finding the other side of it. She might be on the other side. He felt that his skin was leaving a faint mist of blood trailing through the air, adding something to the nothing, almost infinitesimally. He smiled.

He flew on like that for days, or whatever days were. Eventually he was in front of the wall again, he didn't know how.

CHAPTER 2

ᔑAMSON'S BRIGHT, WHITE RACER FLASHED in a blur across the finish line at the Solar Regatta and faded toward the distance, never slowing.

"He's the first across the finish line, but... he's been... disqualified," the announcer said, voice trailing at the end of the sentence as it became less relevant to the racer shrinking on the screen and threatening to disappear from view. "Uh, this might be a problem folks, Samson Ford is not slowing down. He might be in trouble. We've lost all feedback and communication from his ship."

Stephanie de Rothschild got onto the phone immediately, giving pursuit orders to her rescue ships. She instructed them to be the first on the scene and to bring back Samson and his racer at any cost. She sent warships too, as a precaution.

"How unfortunate," Phillipe Bloodworth said quietly.

He stood up from his chair in the Bloodworth executive suite at the Solarium and looked from the glimmering ceiling to the door. The assembled executives in the room, Bloodworth's favorites, all either stared at him or looked down.

"I'll be leaving immediately," he said, and walked out.

MEDIA COVERAGE OF THE RACE and its aftermath was frenzied. Hourly news updates about the location and status of Samson's racer continued on some popular holo-stations for weeks. In the days and nights immediately after the race, coverage was 24/7 everywhere.

"I'm just saying he won the race, that's all I'm saying," said a famous retired racing pilot with smooth, alabaster skin.

"But you can't win the race if you are disqualified, Humphrey!" said a female host with deep, golden skin and black hair. "He was disqualified, whether people agree with that decision or not. Those are the rules of the competition. Chang is the winner. Samson Ford was not a finisher, and considering the fact he is probably needlessly dead now, maybe there is a good reason for that. His engineer was banned from racing."

"Well, I don't agree with that," the old racer said.

"I don't agree with that at all," chimed in one of the co-hosts of the show. "He was disqualified on a pretext, so what? You and I and everyone know that the real winner of the race was Samson Ford. He competed in the race the same as everyone else, and he crossed the finish line first. He didn't break any rules during the race! You can write whatever you want in the record books, but the history books will remember Samson Ford as the deserved winner. Even Chang himself has said he considers Ford the winner of the race."

"But he was disqualified, it's a fact!"

"Fact, shmact. The disqualification was a pretext of discrimination against Ford because of him being a natural born. It shouldn't have happened, and as far as most racing fans are concerned it doesn't count."

"But Iwahara was banned!"

"Ok, Iwahara was banned, but did Samson Ford know that? It's only grounds for disqualifying him if Samson Ford knew. And everything that has come out so far indicates that Samson Ford didn't know. And Iwahara was only banned for fixing races. It's not like they cheated in some way. There is no allegation of that. Ford won the race fair and square."

"You don't know that he's dead," the old racer, Humphrey, said.

"Ok, we don't know, but let's not get bogged down in that."

"I mean, it's absolutely possible he is still alive. You don't know that he's dead. And I hope he's still alive."

"We all hope that, Humphrey."

4

"No, this is all thanks to Bloodworth's twisting and maneuvering things in the background."

"Oh no, 'He Who Shall Not Be Named'."

"Don't start that, Humphrey. We don't want to talk about Bloodworth."

"Yeah, we don't get paid enough to talk about rumors like that on this show. Not the last time I checked."

"Haha, not even close. Don't start talking about 'He', you've said too much already."

"The truth is the truth, and this is just a bunch of bullshit!" the old racer said.

"Haha, calm down, Humphrey, calm down. Let's go to a commercial and we'll talk more about the race in a few minutes."

POPULAR OPINION IN THE FOLLOWING weeks held overwhelmingly that Samson Ford's disqualification was directly attributable to Phillipe Bloodworth. A massive boycott of Bloodworth businesses ensued and the tide of public favor turned back in the direction of the naturals. On Earth, the ban and relocation of natural born humans was reversed and several districts opened criminal prosecutions against individuals who had been involved in the extra-legal rounding up and deportation of them. The result of this was growing chaos, not stability. As Bloodworth had understood, once broken it was hard to put the egg of human society back together again.

Samson's racer ran out of fuel half-way to the asteroid belt and Rothschild ships began working to slow it down. Media vessels and other would-be-participants swarmed about like fireflies, as much as such a thing was possible around a moving object deep in space. Not all of the Rothschild actions of control and intimidation were legal, and Stephanie made sure her warships were ever present to exercise object authority over the rescue operation. She rejected any suggestion that Samson was dead; he needed to be protected.

When the call finally came back to Stephanie that her crews had captured Samson's ship, she breathed a deep sigh of relief and then held her breath. There was a long pause as the admiral in charge of the rescue operation stuttered on the line. Stephanie almost passed out and had to consciously remind herself to breathe again.

"Well?" she said finally. "Have you opened up the racer yet? Is Samson alright?

She knew he must be dead. She had not acknowledged her despair to others, but as soon as Samson's ship failed to slow down at the finish line she had known it. The admiral was too afraid to tell her. He was dead.

"Just tell me the truth, in simple words."

"I'm sorry, Mistress," the man said. "Mr. Ford is– Something's happened to him."

"Is he dead?" Stephanie almost screamed.

"We– It's–," the man stuttered again.

Stephanie felt a deep rage burst out from inside her, of a character that she had never experienced before. If she was holding a gun and the man had been in front of her she would have killed him immediately. No, she wouldn't have. But many people weaker than her would have, and she could understand it now.

"DON'T MINCE WORDS!" she screamed. "Is he dead?"

"I'm sorry, Mistress. We can't tell."

CHAPTER 3

SAMSON'S BODY WAS TRANSLUCENT AND radiated a strange aura. If you touched it, you could run your hand through it and feel a texture like gelatinous gas. It gave Stephanie shivers to touch it. His body was not affected by such touches, or other physical actions taken upon it, and did not observably change over time. Doctors and scientists were mystified.

They suspected that what had happened to him was in some way a consequence of the relativity effect, which was likely to have been experienced from Samson's reckless acceleration at the end of the Solar Regatta, and which the matter in Samson's ship had clearly undergone. Complicating the equation was the fact that Stephanie and Kenichi had installed Samson's ship with something similar to the protective ring that she had always worn, that was supposed to put Samson's body into a preservative quantum phase change in the event of imminent biological failure. The device could not explain the state Samson was in now, but it *had* activated. It was probable that the unique state of matter Samson's body had become was attributable to an interplay between the unpredictable relativity effect and the shifting quantum phase state that the protective device had activated. Stephanie had an entire laboratory retooled and assigned with a round-the-clock schedule to study Samson's body and try to understand what had happened to him. Her most prestigious expert on the subject of the relativity effect, Dr. Rajesh Nguyen, was placed in charge of the lab and given an unlimited budget.

IT TOOK TWO WEEKS TO HAUL the racer back to Rothschild, the small artificial planet that was the Rothschild's Corporation's home. During this time it took Stephanie great effort to think of anything else, although she didn't have a choice. Since her identity had finally been exposed to the public, her responsibilities as the head of Rothschild's were now unavoidable and overwhelming. She had to act and be seen to act in order to stabilize her empire. Her father had viewed it as an empire, although the word was impolite. It was accurate. Thoughts of Samson were pushed back in her mind during the day, but lingered and haunted her at night. She slept little.

She wished that she didn't feel such strong emotions about Samson, and couldn't understand why she did. He was a racing pilot, he was bound to die, she knew that. She didn't accept that he was dead. Intellectually, she knew that he must be, but could not accept that it was true. Intellectually, didn't seem to matter. It was like what believers said about religion, about the god. As if there was a deeper truth than simple reality. She didn't know how she could live without Samson in her life. How long had she known him? It wasn't long. Yet it was as if he had become a part of her, an organ that she depended upon to stay alive. She believed it was childish to feel this way. The image of his face and the sound of his voice, his laugh, echoed over her thoughts.

What was love?

She needed him to be alive. He had become an untouchable, apparition-like thing. Both more and less than a corpse. If his body could be brought back, if it had been perfectly preserved, then he too might be brought back. He might live again. Like the legendary Jesus of Israel. She assigned physicians specializing in resuscitation to Samson's lab, so that one was awake and on call there at all times. She paid them enough to keep them there contentedly, which was a lot. Even then, they argued persuasively to her that their skills were being wasted. She felt guilty, but it was the only way. If she failed to do everything possible to bring him back she would not be able to live with herself. If he came back, hurt but not dead, and there was nobody there to save him.... Five minutes could be the difference. She needed Samson to talk to her again, she needed him to hold her. Billions of people depended on her, so it wasn't a waste of resources if it could accomplish something that she needed so badly. The logic was selfish intellectually, but emotionally undeniable. She did everything she could, and the faint hope, the distant shadow of the faintest flicker of hope, that a dead man, an ephemeral corpse, a human body whose matter had undergone a change of phase in some way that physics could not currently explain – that the corpse could come back to life – was the only thing that held the pieces of her shattered heart together and allowed her to keep moving forward.

SIMON OKUNLE SAT WITH STEPHANIE in her private breakfast room. She ate bacon, a vegetable omelet, and small pancakes at a little nook with an obsidian topped table. The windows of the room opened onto idyllic gardens that almost seemed to spring inside. He rested his palms on the perfectly smooth, glassy surface of the table, thinking of what to say to her. She could be such a frustrating person, and he was so glad that she was the person she was. She was everything she needed to be, if only a little too kind, if only too emotionally keen. But those were qualities that would protect her from the ravages of power. And they would make power painful to her. She was exactly what one would expect the Baron's daughter to be. Perfect even in her imperfection.

"I'm terribly sorry about Samson, Mistress."

"I know you are, Simon," she said quietly.

"I'm glad that you know, because what I need to say to you will sound harsh."

"That's ok."

"You can't bring a corpse back to life."

9

"He's not a corpse."

"It can't be done, and all of medicine in the past 300 years confirms this."

"We don't know that he died, his body is in an altered state. If we can bring his body back to its normal state in space-time it might not be dead, he could be in a kind of stasis, trapped out of time." Simon looked at her sadly as she said this. "It is possible, Simon!"

"Nobody understands what happened to his body, but what you are talking about is like hoping to reincarnate a person from a photograph. An image of him is left behind, a ghost; it's not a person, it's not even a corpse. You have to be stronger than this and carry your load, which is *heavy*, forward. You cannot set it down."

"So you think I should just give up on him?"

"Give up on the idea that he's not dead, yes."

"Just close the lab and bury that ghost of him in a coffin?" Stephanie's voice cracked.

"I'm not saying close the lab, or even stop studying him. But you have two of the best doctors in the world who specialize in saving people's lives, and they're not saving any lives! That's wrong."

"I'm not calling off the doctors," Stephanie said.

"You should."

"I will not do that."

Even perfect people are fallible, Simon thought, pained to see Stephanie so traumatized.

KENICHI IWAHARA WAS SUMMONED TO a meeting with Stephanie. As he approached it, he marveled, as always, at the overwhelming luxury of Rothschild Palace. Throughout the Solar System, people often called the little planet Rothschild, 'Rothschild Palace', but he now understood that those who actually lived here reserved that name for the palace itself. Kenichi had only spoken to Stephanie once since the Solar Regatta, in the immediate aftermath of the race. It had been hard for him not to be ecstatic after his racer had won. It had also been hard for him to realize that Stephanie did not consider him a friend. He continued living on Rothschild, as before, and did not know what the future would bring. Even now, he had heard about Samson's body but had not yet been able to see it for himself. There had still not been an official news announcement, but most people understood that Samson had died.

It made him sad to think that Samson had died. Not that he would miss Samson, exactly. He liked Samson, and Samson had liked him, but it was not an emotional attachment. Rather, the Solar System would be a little bit less beautiful with Samson dead. That was why it made him sad, Kenichi thought. "The good die young," was an ancient saying that often seemed true. Although, statistically, the bad had a much higher chance of dying young. I should live forever, Kenichi thought, abstract tongue in cheek, being equal parts bad and good.

A security officer met him at the palace front entrance and escorted him through the interior. They rode an automatic floating platform most of the way. They passed through field scanners that were not explained, but which he understood to be automatic code and electronics scanners to detect any miniature robot or other potentially weaponized device crossing into the inner chambers of the palace. The security on Rothschild was exceptional, and had been steadily augmented in the weeks leading up to and after the Solar Regatta. As they crossed one courtyard, a large battleship circled the sky high above them. There were battleships on constant patrol now.

In another sunny courtyard, he waited as directed at a wooden table shaded by a large tree. He heard quick footsteps

11

clacking on paving stones, then Stephanie strode through the courtyard to greet him. She was as beautiful as ever, tall and elegant. She was more self-possessed than he remembered her, even from just weeks before. She seemed regal now. She had always had that quality, but it was subtle in the past, concealed. Kenichi admired her body as she crossed the courtyard and regretted how old and awkward he was and that she didn't consider him a friend. Her black hair shimmered in the sun. He stood to greet her.

"Please sit down, Kenichi," Stephanie said.

They sat down across from each other at the table and she watched him appraisingly for a few seconds before speaking again.

"I'm sorry that I have not been able to keep in touch better. I hope you have been well?"

"Yes," Kenichi said, "I'm well. I always imagined if Samson won we would all celebrate together, but it didn't happen that way."

"No."

"How are you, Stephanie?"

"Very busy. I was insulated from my responsibilities as the head of Rothschild's for a long time, but now I am not." She paused and smiled, "I won't get to work on spaceships anymore."

"And Samson? All I've heard are rumors."

"That's one of the two things that I needed to talk to you about. Let's talk about that in a moment. First we need to talk about your situation."

Kenichi twisted in his seat as Stephanie watched him imperiously. A lot of the softness had gone out of her. She sat bolt upright, as if made of steel. He looked past her at the empty courtyard around them. It wasn't a particularly nice courtyard, or in a special location, it seemed random. Her eyes didn't let off of him. He made brief eye contact with her and twisted his fingers.

"I would like to stay here and work on race engineering," he said, glancing indirectly at her. "You know how valuable my work is, and I don't have anywhere else to go. I'm grateful for your hospitality so far, and if possible I would like to make it a permanent situation. I have a lot to contribute."

"Ok, this isn't a job interview, Ken," Stephanie said, "you can relax. I fully appreciate how valuable you are and how much you contributed to our Solar Regatta project and Samson's success. We're friends in a way, aren't we?"

"Yes," Kenichi said quickly, thrilled that she did actually think of him as a friend, even if "in a way".

"I'm not trying to beat about the bush," Stephanie said. "The fact is that you cannot leave Rothschild even if you want to. As you must know, after being publicly outed during the Solar Regatta, you are now being sought by the authorities on Earth and face what will amount to a life prison term if captured. What you probably have no way of knowing is that they are pursuing your case with unusual vigor and have assigned a special investigations team to track you down and bring you back to Earth.

"Bloodworth has enormous influence on Earth and he has apparently taken a personal interest in you."

"That's...worse than I realized," Kenichi said.

"We can only protect you from arrest and extradition here on Rothschild. But we're happy to do that. I absolutely want you to stay here on a permanent basis and work for me."

"Done!" Kenichi said.

"Good. That brings me to Samson's situation. Samson, as I'm sure you've heard, is dead. We are going to make a public announcement about it soon. But what has actually happened to him is... more complicated."

"What do you mean?" He stared wildly at Stephanie, forgetting to feel intimidated. "Is he alive?"

"At the end of the Solar Regatta, or soon afterward, his body experienced an unusual phase change, suspected to be a consequence of the relativity effect. It is almost as if he is gone, but a ghost of him has been left behind."

Kenichi's mouth hung open as he tried to imagine what Stephanie was saying and fit this news into his understanding of life and the universe.

"That doesn't make sense, was the matter in the ship changed by the relativity effect?"

"Yes. But wait, let me take you to the lab where we have Samson and you can see things for yourself. This is the second reason I needed to speak with you today. I want you to act as a special consultant, to work with my lead researcher, Rajesh Nguyen, in understanding what happened to Samson. We are trying to find out if there is any way that we can reverse the effect on his body, to bring him back into phase, so to speak."

Stephanie stood up and was suddenly very distant again. A security agent seemed to materialize at her elbow. She led the way to the lab, which was on the grounds of the palace, and discussed with Kenichi what had happened. The entire time that he was with her, she never betrayed a hint of emotion in regard to Samson.

LATE THAT EVENING, FAR LATER than she had planned, Stephanie sat down at her desk and wrote a letter to Samson's brother, Theodore.

Dear Theo,

As you must be aware by now, we recovered Samson's ship from space in the aftermath of the Solar Regatta. I am inexpressibly sorry to inform you that Samson did not survive the aftermath of the

14

race. His body was severely impacted by the relativity effect, to the extent that it has taken our best scientists some time to determine...

Her tears stained the keypad she was using. Some of them were angry tears. If Samson had not been disqualified, perhaps he would not have pushed so recklessly at the end to win. One man, Phillipe Bloodworth, had torn her life apart and was tearing the Solar System apart. He had killed Ben. The image of Bloodworth's face floated in her mind until she felt sick inside and wanted to lash out. She had lived with no desire to fight, but he had forced it upon her. The fight would devastate millions, or more, and she was forced to lead it. She would be forced to destroy him, but to destroy him would mean destroying others. It would not be enough to kill him, she would have to dismantle what he had built, the manifestation of him. She had to protect her family of billions, and she had already failed to protect the person dearest to her. Rothschild's and Bloodworth's were at war already, lives were being crushed by the battles being waged, but their trade war could easily ignite into an actual military conflict. The whole Solar System would be sucked in and millions would die, at a minimum. And all of it would sit on her shoulders, and all of it because of Phillipe Bloodworth, a detestable piece of human trash who had wormed, bullied, and stolen his way to power. Samson would likely still be alive... and Ben too... She had no choice but to destroy him.

She could feel Samson's arms around her for a moment. A brief moment. The absence of his touch began to feel like pain. She needed him to hold her. Now there would be nobody to hold her, perhaps ever.

C H A P T E R⁴

L ISA MAUI BEGAN RECEIVING CALLS and messages within
minutes of Samson crossing the finish line. They trickled
in at first.

"Hello?"

"This is Morty Abrum from Giant Newspaper, I'm trying
to reach Lisa Maui."

"What do you want?"

"What do you think is going through Samson's mind
right now?"

"What?"

"You dated Samson Ford, right?"

"Wh– Only a couple of times. Look, I don't have time
to talk right now."

She hung up the call. The next one came two minutes
later and was more of the same. They kept coming. Over the
next hour the trickle turned into a constant, steady stream.
Lisa's card glowed and she tried to ignore it. The aftermath of
the Regatta was chaotic and it was all she could do to keep up
with the work being thrown at her. All any of the interns could
do was keep up. For that matter, it seemed to be all anyone
working anywhere in the Solarium could do. The directors
were beside themselves.

She hoped, as she ran through the corridors of the Solarium, that Samson was alright. It wasn't a fervent hope, or
grounded in deep emotion, but a simple hope and wish. Too
many pilots had died at this Regatta. And Samson was a friend.
Even Gideon Killian had almost died; she happened to pass
one of the landing docks as they were loading him into an
ambulance transport. He was far away and didn't look at her.
He didn't look at anyone. He was probably not dead. Chang
was fine, standing on the victor's platform, receiving lukewarm

applause from the spectators, punctuated by rounds of boos. The audience liked him, he had done nothing wrong, but he was also not the winner of the race. They were booing the race directors, or whoever they thought made decisions about the race; they were booing the fact that Samson was not accepted as the official race winner. He had really won. It was amazing.

LISA'S WORK AT THE SOLARIUM finally slowed down a week later, and her contract term as an intern also came to an end. More than usually swamped after this Regatta, the Racing Board begged her to sign a new contract and stay on, but racing had become sour for her. She didn't even know why, exactly, but she wanted to get away from the Solarium and never come back. Media were everywhere still and more aggressive than normal, people said. They wanted to know exactly how the decision had been made to disqualify Samson. They wanted to know who on the Solarium had been where and said what when during the race. They wanted to know where Kenichi Iwahara had been and where he was now. They wanted to know everything about everyone, just in case it fit into their story somehow. Samson's finish, disqualification from the race, and current unknown status while hurtling mutely through the Solar System in his racer was the biggest news story of the decade. Of course they wanted to talk to Lisa, she had actually known Samson personally, and in the recent past, which turned out to make her rare. As soon as her contract ended she caught the first available transport back to Earth.

A man on the transport sat down next to her. He was tall and handsome, well engineered. His skin was smooth and pink. Lisa watched the stars outside through the big windows of the transport lounge. Space was so distant and so on top of them at once. She always felt a current of exhilaration from it. Even now, faintly, behind all her other overwhelming emotions and

17

fatigue, that current of exhilaration was there. It was fun to imagine the distant stars, and to dream of some day traveling to them, traveling beyond the Solar System. Of course, that was impossible, but it was fun to imagine it. The people were fun too, on a transport. If you ever got tired of looking out the window into space, you could shift your gaze and watch the people around you. Everyone has a story to tell. If you got tired of the people you could ignore them and look back out into space.

"You're Lisa Maui," the man said. "I've been trying all week to contact you."

"Are you a reporter?"

"That's right."

"I haven't had time to talk to any reporters," Lisa said. "And I'm not sure I want to, anyway."

"Why don't you want to?"

"Because— Why do you guys want to talk to me so bad?"

"You were close to Samson Ford."

"We weren't that close."

"I read that you dated him."

"We went on two dates, is that what this is about? His girl-friend is Stephanie de Rothschild, why don't you talk to her."

"Is? So you think he is alive?"

"I hope he is. Can't you talk to some of Samson's other friends? There must be loads of people who know him better than me."

The man knitted his fingers absently and slid deeper into the cushion of his chair, completely relaxed.

"Well, that's the thing, there are very few people on record who were close to Samson. Especially recently. His partner, Ben Johnson, is dead apparently. And his engineer, Kenichi Iwahara, is on the run. Stephanie de Rothschild, of course, is completely inaccessible."

"I forgot that Ben was dead," Lisa said.

"I'm sorry. Maybe you can tell me about Ben, too. Samson's career as a racer, although he was winning races and moving up through the circuits – it is only very recently that he became famous, per se. His private life has been very private. A few old girlfriends have been dug up, but they knew him only brief amounts of time and had not been able to keep in touch with him afterwards. You dated him recently, so you are the girl that everyone wants to talk to right now."

"I'm lucky to have been on the Solarium this week, where there was so much crazy stuff to occupy the press," Lisa said.

"Very much so. If you were at home on Earth, for instance – I read you were from Earth – there is no way you could have gotten on board this transport, or even left your house, without a herd of journalists following you."

"What do you want from me?"

"Only to interview you," the man said, sitting up straighter.

""Why should I give an interview?" Lisa yawned.

"Well, money for one thing."

"I don't need money that bad."

"Ok. Although let me say in passing, it would be a lot of money. But there are better reasons than that. Look at what is happening in the world, the discrimination against natural born people, herding people up on Earth, Bloodworth using his power to stop Samson from winning the Solar Regatta – you can have a say in those things. You can have an influence! What you say about Samson, what you know about him, what you think about him, what you feel about the ending of the race and how he has been discriminated against – those things will be heard all over the Solar System. Your voice can have power because of this, power for good. Did you think about that yet?"

Lisa had not thought about that. She thought about her

19

grandparents at home on Earth, and how much she wanted to be sitting and eating dinner with them. Listening to them talk and perhaps telling them some of her stories, and having the time to quietly think while they talked. But she gave an exclusive interview to the reporter who had sat down next to her on the transport.

Five weeks later, after Samson had been brought back to Rothschild, a large holo-tv broadcast into a luxurious board-room on Earth and Lisa Maui was on its screen. She was talking with a male and female talk show team about Samson and the latest developments to his situation, which were few.

"He wanted to win the Solar Regatta more than anything," Lisa said. "And now he has won it."

"Lisa, you were good friends with Samson," the male host said, "you even dated him. What would he think about the situation right now, with everyone in the Solar System following his story and waiting on pins and needles to find out what happened to him? But all of us being kept in the dark."

"I think he would want people to know where he was and what had happened to him," Lisa said. "I'm sure he wouldn't want it to be a secret."

"Do you miss him?"

"Yes, I miss him. He's such an amazing person. He's probably the best pilot in the Solar System, and one of the best men that I've ever met. I wish I was closer to him now. Now that I can't contact him I wish I had tried harder to be closer to him when I could. He doesn't let a lot of people into his life, but I didn't know that before."

"You keep speaking about Samson in the present tense, Lisa," the female host said, "but don't you mean to say he WAS one of the best men that you've ever met? You don't believe he's still alive, do you?"

"Yeah," Lisa said, "that's true. It just doesn't seem real that he's gone, because we never got to see him die. He just won the race and then Rothschild's took his ship, and then that was all. There wasn't even a funeral. And nobody can find out what happened."

"He's dead you stupid bitch!" Phillipe Bloodworth screamed at the holo-screen.

He switched it off and folded his hands palm down on the table, giving his genetically perfect executives a challenging look. Bloodworth was shorter and fatter than any of his executives.

"That was Samson Ford's former girlfriend, Lisa Maui," he continued, "one of several people stirring up the media and striving to become the new figurehead of the naturals movement. She, of course, is herself genetically advanced."

"Ford was a statistical anomaly that can't possibly be replaced," a woman with grey, cloud-like skin said.

"Are we completely certain he's dead?" Bloodworth asked the room.

"Absolutely certain, sir," an unassuming man with neutral features and dark, neatly trimmed hair said from the back of the room. "One of our people there has been able to view his corpse."

"Do we have video?"

"Not yet, sir."

"Public pro-naturals sentiment in the wake of Ford's appearance in the Solar Regatta and the ongoing war with Rothschild's has galvanized our enemies at the worst possible time," Bloodworth said. "Margins are down 46%, and revenue down 15% across all industries. We need to step up our public relations campaigns and plan for a fight to the death with Rothschild's. That means a fight that could easily continue for another ten years."

21

"We need to make our sponsorship of the racing leagues dominant and extremely visible," said a man with soft cream eyes and buttery, chocolate skin. "We should be the face of racing all over the Solar System, so that the Bloodworth Corporation becomes seen as almost an equivalent of the sport. Samson Ford was one thing, but there is another race each month, and another Solar Regatta in four years, there will be new drama and new champions that everyone will want to talk about. By being willing to invest more than our competitors, we can hijack the public love of racing and convert it into positive public sentiment for Bloodworth's. And for us it is essential, because otherwise our current negative public image vis a vis racing will fester and leave a lasting ulcer weakening the company."

"Good," Bloodworth said. "I'm placing you in charge of that, Cereus. Keep me in the loop and use whatever resources are necessary."

"We should reinvigorate our advertising and promotion of Oberon," the cloudy skinned woman said. "It's a decent planet, and we can make it seem so appealing that it almost feels shameful for people to talk about relocation to Oberon in negative terms. We can show that people relocating there are happier than they have ever been, and underline the fact that you have given this as a gift to natural born citizens completely for free. And at the same time, we should step back from the efforts at forceful relocation and achieving a quarantine; let that alone for a while until public sentiment calms down and becomes less inflammatory."

"It's too late for that," Bloodworth said, "we're committed to it."

"Nevertheless, promotion of Oberon and hammering in that message of what an amazing place it is can play an important part in winning the public mood."

"I agree with that. I'll put your company in charge of the new public relations campaign. Good work."

"I'll have to be the troublesome one here, Phillipe," said one of the oldest men in the room. "We need Camilla for this."

The man was unusually tall and had softly metallic, subtly golden skin and color shifting eyes. He had straw white hair with a long, intricately coiffured goatee.

"Camilla resigned," Bloodworth said shortly.

"She's the best public relations mind on the planet!"

"I can't get her, Frank! I want her, but I can't get her. You were there at the Solar Regatta, you saw what happened. I know I was wrong, but she won't work for me anymore."

"Have you even called her to apologize?"

"I don't want to apologize," Bloodworth said and stared at the man, an edge creeping into his voice.

"Phillipe, we need her."

"What about Plan B?" asked an icy woman with green eyes and blonde hair.

"Not everyone here is party to Plan B," Bloodworth said. "Our work progresses, but it's not yet to a stage of implementation."

"I think we should prioritize our resources and energy into Plan B," the woman said.

"Noted. Give me other ideas."

The meeting continued for hours.

C H A P T E R 5

$\int$ AMSON FLOATED IN THE AIR in front of the puzzle that blocked his passage through the wall. He had been here a long time and made no progress. The puzzle had seven large switches, three wheels, and eight panels that slid back and forth. Each mechanism appeared to be binary. The switches could be switched either up or down. The panels could be slotted into place on either the left or the right. The wheels, when spun, would turn a few rotations and then stop with a resonant 'bong'. That was as far as the wheels would turn in one direction, so that to move them again he would have to turn them in the opposite direction. Each wheel, when it had spun, bonged with a distinctive tone, so that between the three wheels that could each turn in two directions there were a total of six tones that could be produced. The mechanism also consisted of countless gears, various pipes and whistles, rivets, screws, and compasses that spun lazily in various directions. He had manipulated all of the levers, wheels, and panels thousands of times already, hoping to find the perfect combination that would open the 'lock', or at least to understand the puzzle better. There was nothing else he could do.

After trying a few thousand more combinations without noticeable success, Samson floated back onto his back (relative to the wall) and stared up into the nothing. He stared at the nothing for a long time, trying to think of what else to do. He understood that he had to get through the wall, that this was the path to the woman whose image floated in his mind, and that whatever there was to be found, whatever meaning and illumination could exist for him, could only be found by reaching her. There was only one path forward.

He tried to calculate the number of possible permutations of the lock. If it was simply a matter of getting each binary station (each lever, wheel, or panel) into the correct position then the calculation was simple. Seven switches, three wheels, eight panels made 18 binary stations and therefore a total of 2^{18} possible combinations. Multiplying on his fingers, he calculated that it was approximately 262,000 combinations. This was a tedious number, but meant he could realistically solve the puzzle through a systematic trial of all combinations. So far he had simply been trying things at random.

However, that first calculation assumed that the puzzle could be solved, or 'lock' opened, simply by getting every binary switch into its correct position. It would be an entirely different calculation if the order in which the switches were switched mattered at all, that is to say if the solution to the puzzle were sequential in any way.

Assuming that the puzzle was simply sequential, that each binary position needed to be switched only once but in the correct order, and that which position the switch was flipped to didn't matter but only that it was switched, then the number of possible combinations would be 18! or $18*17*16*15*14(...)*3*2*1$. Calculating this on his fingers was harder. He simplified the calculation by roughly approximating it to $(20^3)(10^{10})(5^5)$. 20^3 was 8,000, 5^5 was 3,125, 10^{10} was 10,000,000,000. 10,000,000,000 * 8,000 was 80,000,000,000,000 or 8 with 13 zeroes after it. 8 with 13 zeroes after it times 3,000 (he simplified), made 24 with 16 zeroes after it. 240,000,000,000,000,000. Roughly. Give or take a few zeroes. Under the circumstances, he could not realistically solve a puzzle of that magnitude by trying all possible combinations. If the puzzle was sequential and the position that the stations were switched to mattered, then it was even worse: something like 36!, which was a lot.

It was also obviously possible that the puzzle code was more complicated than that. It might require, for example, adjusting the sliding blocks into the correct arrangement, then turning the first wheel clockwise into position, then adjusting the blocks into a new correct position, then turning the same wheel counter-clockwise into its opposite position, then moving the blocks to a new arrangement, then switching one of the switches (the correct one), then turning the second wheel clockwise into its rest position, changing the positions of the blocks to a new combination, turning the second wheel counter-clockwise, etc., or some 'combination code' along those lines. He decided against trying to use a systematic approach and began manipulating the switches, blocks, and wheels again at random, hoping a pattern would emerge.

EVENTUALLY, AFTER TRYING A FEW thousand more random combinations, Samson became frustrated. If the puzzle couldn't be solved, perhaps it could be broken, and perhaps the wall could thereby be broken through. This was counter-intuitive, because the switches and panels and wheels of the puzzle looked as solidly built as a block of granite. He wrenched and pried at the switches and wheels until it bruised his hands, but they were every bit as intractable and impervious as they looked. He tried to kick through the sliding blocks with his feet, to no effect. He had pounded and tested the wall itself, which was connected around the edges of the puzzle with great plates and bolts, many times already and found it to be even harder and denser than granite, and seamless. He flew away from the puzzle, several body lengths, and then back toward it feet first, crashing with a jolt that hurt his ankles. This had no effect. He flew back again further and accelerated faster at one of the sliding panels, crashing into it with tremendous force and pain. His feet split and bled from the impact, but the puzzle was unaffected. He floated back and stared away into empty space again, dripping blood into the nothing. Which way was up? It could have been any direction, but somehow the blood fell. Not toward the wall, but parallel to it.

After some time passed, Samson redoubled his efforts at manipulating the puzzle, whistling and singing while he worked. Finally, after a great deal more trial and error, a pattern began to emerge. He found that if he set the wheels a certain way and switched a particular switch, the puzzle emitted a pleasant tone. If he then followed by switching any station other than one particular panel, a discordant tone sounded. But if he followed by switching that particular panel, a new pleasant tone sounded. In this way, following the 'music', he gradually worked out a pattern to the puzzle.

Samson felt certain that he had 'cracked the code'. As more and more correct steps were uncovered, the 'music' revealed itself to be a beautiful song and, finally, after spinning a wheel to sound the sixth possible wheel tone, the whole puzzle rumbled and began to play music continuously, of its own accord. Samson shook with anticipation and watched it without blinking, but after playing its song the machine stopped and nothing else happened. He tried several times again, with the same result, but could make no further headway. The song itself was pleasant, so when he ran out of ideas he played it again and again for his own pleasure, and with the hope that something else would occur, until even the music began to grate upon his predicament. Then he flew back again into the nothing, without direction, accelerating and twisting angrily in space.

THE NOTHING RUSHED PAST HIM, enveloping and caressing his skin, stinging his eyes. A long time passed. At some point, without trying to, Samson came to the puzzle again. He began switching the different stations, imagining the woman's face as he worked and singing a plaintive song. He had always

27

liked to sing, especially when he was alone during the day and working. He put the switches back into place to begin his 'correct' solution, the one that played music. As he threw the first switch of the 'correct' solution into place the puzzle emitted its pleasant hum and the hum created a harmonic with the song that Samson was singing. The puzzle began to vibrate and glow. Samson continued the steps of the combination that he had already found, while singing in relation to the sounds of the puzzle machine at the same tonal interval that he had coincidentally discovered. It took several tries to get it right, but with each successive step the puzzle machine reacted more and more dramatically, until finally, at the end, a great symphonic crash resounded through the air. The blocks all slid apart with a flood of blinding light, opening a hole in the wall, and Samson flew through the hole as quickly as he could.

He dimly perceived another man floating in the sky near him, who gradually came into focus. Samson blinked his eyes against the brilliance of a bright blue sky. The other man was covered in white feathers and had a straight, white horn protruding from his forehead. His fingers and toes were punctuated by hooked, pink claws. He shrieked and swooped at Samson.

CHAPTER 6

In Magdalena, Theodore Ford sat reading Stephanie's letter on his card. His brother was dead. The card seemed so small and fragile in that moment, how could such an insignificant device wield such power over him? It was not a shock to learn that Samson had died. Even on Magdalena they had been informed of the outcome of the race. A teardrop fell from his face onto the card, which was quiet and blank, and the card seemed as nothing. A clump of nothing in his hand. Some part of him, some buried part, had expected Samson to die for a long time. Some part long pushed down under his consciousness. Even without the race the letter wouldn't have surprised him. His brother was dead.

Theo stood up quietly and moved to walk out of the room, then grunted and kicked the open door to the room off of its hinges.

"Theo?! Theo, what's happening?" His wife, Maria, rushed in. She caught her breath and hugged him. "It's Samson?"

"I'm sorry," Theo said. "I'm sorry."

The children stared timidly at him from the hall.

"Yes. He's dead," Theo said quietly to his wife, so that the children could not hear. "At the end of the race. Relativity effect. Stephanie wrote to me."

"I'm sorry, honey."

"I'm sorry," Theo said again, and picked up the door.

Late that night, after the children had gone to bed, Theo and his wife lit candles in front of the cross altar and prayed to God together until morning, for Samson's soul.

The next day, Theo was called to an audience with The Prophet, the leader of the Church of the Magdalena Revelation.

"Welcome, Theo," The Prophet said, his body sunken a

little in his robes but his grey eyes beaming out of them as Theo kneeled to kiss his hand. "I am told that you have news of Samson."

"Yes, Holiness," Theo looked down, "as we were all afraid of, he perished from relativity sickness at the end of the race."

"I'm so sorry, child," The Prophet said, looking at him with gentle pity.

"Thank you, Holiness."

"We must have a prayer procession to celebrate your brother. And the elders and I have also been in discussion about a new holiday to celebrate Samson."

"Th-thank you, Father."

"Sit with me, Theo," The Prophet motioned to a plush couch. "It may surprise you to learn that there is actually a different reason why I have called you here today."

The Prophet sat down on the sofa and motioned again, indicating for Theo to sit down next to him. Theo sat down and a priest appeared with tea. He could not think of what to say and thanked The Prophet again. The Prophet smiled at him with the gentle, enigmatic smile that was his particular expression.

"These are troubled times," he said. "What happened to Samson is a symptom and a sign. Natural people are not going to be allowed to live in peace. The new, artificial people are determined either to enslave or destroy us. Their blasphemy against God is not enough in itself, they must destroy all who love God. They are compelled to make this world truly theirs, truly of themselves, truly without God. This is all as I have prophesied and foreseen."

"Can none of them be saved, Father?" Theo asked quietly.

"Very few, my child. These may be the ends of times. When God is completely renounced from this world, this world will cease to exist. The godless souls that were here will be cast into the outer darkness, the great nothing where they will become not. We still hope to turn back this tide and reap the beautiful bounty of life from this world we have been given, but it will be hard. I have foreseen that a great war will soon come to Magdalena, a great and terrible war."

The room was silent, and Theo felt disoriented. He kept hoping that The Prophet would say something more, but The Prophet seemed to be waiting for him to respond.

"Is there no way to prevent it, Father?" Theo finally asked.

"They will come to destroy us and we will be forced to fight," The Prophet said. "This is not a war of our choosing, but we must prepare to defend our land and our beliefs. We have already been pushed here, to the outskirts of the Solar System. Our efforts to create an interstellar travel have yielded no fruit. I have foreseen the battle, after they come for us. We must prepare for a great and terrible war."

"How shall I prepare, Father?" Theo asked.

"I am convening a council of war to lead our preparations. I need for you to be an observer on the council, lend to them your insight and assistance in whatever ways you can, and report back to me when I call on you about their activities. You will not have a vote on the council, but you will have a voice."

"Of course, I will do whatever you ask of me, Father."

"You have an important role to play, Theo. You are an invaluable resource for us. Because of your work in recovering our lost sheep, you have more knowledge and insight into the other societies of the Solar System than almost anyone else in Magdalena. You have walked among them without being corrupted. And you have been friends with one of their most powerful leaders, Stephanie de Rothschild. That connection could prove to be essential. I want you to know what is happening, and to be able to offer input about it. I need you as a personal advisor and trusted resource on the council."

31

"This unexpected for me," Theo said in his meekest possible voice. "I was hoping that I might journey to Rothschild to pay my respects to Samson. But I am honored to be of service and will do whatever is necessary, Father."

"I'm sorry, Theo. God's timeline is, unfortunately, often not the timeline of man. The next council meeting is in an hour. You may refresh yourself in the meantime, then I will take you there and introduce you."

CHAPTER 7

$\int$ AMSON DODGED AWAY AS THE unicorn being swooped, snatching at him as it flew past. It had short, pink claws on its fingers and toes that were hooked and sharp. In the bright blue of the sky, it turned and flew at him again, slowing as it neared this time. Samson tried to ease away from the creature, but it was fast and did not want to let him flee. It kept shrieking unintelligibly, and finally got close enough to grab his ankle with a clawed hand. He kicked it with his other foot and the two of them grappled in the air. The creature was strong and its feathers felt soft and alien against Samson's skin. He held its face away to prevent it from biting him. Being in the air, neither of them could gain much purchase with which to leverage their opponent. They twisted and tumbled together.

A vast, brushy desert stretched out on the ground below them, as far as the eye could see. The wall that Samson had expended so much effort to pass through had disappeared somewhere behind them, somewhere beyond them and this sky.

As Samson and the creature fought, more unicorn men began to appear, soaring in from various directions. They did not interfere in the fight, but approached closely to watch, as if they were hostile spectators, some with arms folded, some with hands on hips. Samson tried to keep an eye on the new audience, and in his distraction the creature got its mouth around his arm and bit down into it. With his free hand, he gouged at the creature's eyes.

Blood ran from Samson's arm, but, for that matter, he was bleeding all over, being cut up by the creature's claws. It twisted to disengage and he let it go. Then the creature spun abruptly and tried to bury its horn into his chest. The horn tore across his skin, just missing as Samson shifted from its path. He planted a kick into the creature's face as it went past him, crushing its nose into a bloody pulp.

The unicorn creature held its hand to its crushed nose and stared at Samson. The other unicorn men, or people, although they seemed like men, that surrounded them in the air, shrieked and hooted approbation. All of them looked very similar to the first one, to Samson's combatant, but with various coloring of greys and browns in addition to the white. They seemed to be intelligent, and Samson wondered if he could somehow become friends with them.

Finally, the original creature shrieked at Samson with something like derisive anger and began to fly away. The other creatures followed it, and Samson chased them. The brushy desert stretched on and on below them as they flew, with hardly a landmark, and the endless blue sky was bright overhead. No sun could be seen in the sky, but sunlight seemed to radiate from everywhere, bathing Samson's body dripping blood. His wounds healed quickly, though. He did not wonder at this. He followed the unicorn men for hours, or whatever hours were, but they gradually drew away, until he couldn't see them anymore. Then he was again alone.

THE LAB THAT NOW HELD Samsons's body had walls and a floor that were patterned in large diamonds of white and bright, lightly hued green. It was a maze of instruments and display panels, generating an ocean of white electronic noise. The chairs in the office were soft, sealed foam that was easy to sterilize and difficult to contaminate. It was a unique hybrid of digital operating theater, doctor's office, and advanced physics lab. Stephanie sat in a chair near Samson's unsubstantial body, watching it. Kenichi and Dr. Rajesh Nguyen hovered nearby.

"That's not Samson," Kenichi was saying, "it's just matter that has been transposed. There's no blood flow, there's no cellular activity. There aren't even cells, per se. Even though it looks like Samson, what we see is what has become of the atoms that made up his body. It might not even be that, it might be more like a hologram. We're doing everything we can to understand what happened, but we can't perform miracles. Samson is dead."

"We don't understand what has happened to his body," Stephanie said. "This could be a kind of stasis. It could still be possible to bring him back."

"Stephanie," Kenichi said, with real sympathy in his voice, "that's extremely unlikely."

Her face was impassive, but Stephanie's dark eyes had been flashing anger. Although they tried not to react to it, it made both Kenichi and Dr. Nguyen scared. The anger triggered their self-preservation instincts, forcing them to remember how powerful she was, and therefore how dangerous.

"Mr. Iwahara isn't saying anything I disagree with, Mistress," Dr. Nguyen said. "I wouldn't express it as bluntly, but what he said is essentially true. We are doing everything possible to understand what happened to Samson, and I believe we will be able to eventually make sense of it. But it is unforeseeable that we would be able to bring him back to life. To tell you anything else would be to lie to you and deceive you with false hope. I cannot do either of those things."

Stephanie stood up from her chair. She was a tall woman, but seemed even taller than she was. She looked from one to the other of them and then at Samson again. He was so perfectly preserved, all three of them were conscious of it at the same time, such a hair's breadth from being with them.

"I don't accept that," Stephanie said. "Continue your work, but don't do anything that will compromise the integrity of his body."

This last prohibition sounded like a threat, and after it she walked out of the room.

C H A P T E R 8

D R. RAJESH NGUYEN WAS A medium built, physically soft looking man with extremely intense eyes. He had glittery, bronze skin and midnight colored hair. As a young man, he had been one of the Solar System's most celebrated physicists, but his scientific career stalled after he became enamored of the relativity effect and spent the next two decades of his life trying unsuccessfully to decipher its enigma. He was, debatably, the Solar System's foremost authority on the subject.

"This is going to be difficult," Kenichi said to Dr. Nguyen after Stephanie left.

"It was always going to be difficult."

"If she could only set her emotions aside for a moment and think about it rationally, I'm sure she would understand what we are telling her."

"Reason often finds no bearing," Dr. Nguyen said, "when it comes to the people we love."

"That's true."

"Poor Samson."

Kenichi paced in a contemplative circle around the body, occasionally glancing up toward his new colleague.

"I know exactly what you mean," he said, "but I can't feel sorry for Samson, or even sad about his death."

"No?" Dr. Nguyen raised his eyebrows ever so slightly.

"It's not that I don't miss him or wish he was here. Actually, I feel a deep regret over not being able to celebrate the Solar Regatta victory with him. Not being able to celebrate the victory at all, for that matter. I mean – we won! We actually won it. The champions of the whole Solar System. Samson didn't care about celebrating, I don't think. I mean – Samson wanted to die! You didn't know him, so it might not make sense, but – and it's not right to say he *wanted* to die, but he was absolutely ready to die in order to win the race. If it was a choice between dying and winning, or losing and living, he absolutely would choose to die and win. That's how he flew, that's why he was so successful. And that was the choice! He wouldn't have won at the end of the race if he had not accelerated the way he did. He knew the trade-off and was happy to make it. I mean – he won. He got what he wanted. I actually feel happy for Samson. I can't feel bad about the fact that his dream came true. He accomplished his greatest goal and I feel happy for him."

"And you accomplished your goal," Dr. Nguyen said.

"Yes, but– Fuck racing. There were other dreams in my life that I would have died for. At least one. I would rather we had lost and Samson was still alive. Except for his sake, if you can see what I mean."

"I would have liked to meet him," Dr. Nguyen said. "He is missing a wonderful woman. A wonderful life! I would have liked to meet him and see why the Mistress loved him so much."

"At best," Kenichi said, "we can hope to make this body corporeal again and give him a proper funeral."

"At best."

"It's amazing that with all we have studied it – for centuries! And we still don't understand the relativity effect at all," Kenichi said.

"We have been trying for many years. It's a humbling phenomenon."

"You're far braver than I, Rajesh," Kenichi said. "After finding out when I was a child how fruitless the two centuries of research on the phenomenon had been, I never wanted any part of it. Not at all."

"It is that thing," Dr. Nguyen said, "that once you start to really study it, seems to be the only thing worth studying."

"You hunt the biggest game."

"Yes."

"Actually, you're like Samson in a way."

Dr. Nguyen thought about this, but had nothing to say in reply. The two of them sat silently and watched Samson's body for several minutes. The way it affected light was strange, almost as if it glowed, but without glowing.

"Has there been much research into the electro-magnetic sub-channels associated with matter transformed in the relativity effect," Kenichi asked, breaking the silence.

"Of course. The sub-channels are usually slightly distorted, but not in any way remarkable."

"I see."

"Let's set up a sub-channel scan anyway," Dr. Nguyen said. "It's something we haven't done yet."

"You have the equipment here?"

"We can go borrow it. There's a matter-channel acceleration lab not far away. We'll get my lab assistants back in here and set to work on it."

A TAXI-CAB DRIVER FROM VENUS named Salvador stepped out into the bright sunshine of the Arizona desert. This desert was hot, but cooler than the deserts on Venus. It was also lit by a different light. The sun on Earth was weaker, but more direct. It had that intense, over-radiated quality of open skies, compared to the rich Venutian light that poured out of Venus' thick, dense atmosphere. The dust in the air here was different too, grittier. Salvador had never liked the desert, not even on Venus.

"You're free now, get out of here," said one of the guards who had escorted him outside. The man had pale yellow skin that Salvador knew had never been fashionable. Although everything was more fashionable than Salvador's plain, light brown skin.

A few other natural born men stumbled out of the detention center doors behind Salvador. He had no idea why they had held him here longer than almost everybody else. Most of the "detainees" had been released shortly after Samson Ford had won the Solar Regatta. Samson Ford, he was Salvador's favorite man. Every second of the time that Samson had driven Salvador's cab to escape from press that were chasing him in Mamito was treasured in Salvador's memory. Samson Ford had driven with him. Samson's friend Ben was there too, the one they killed. They killed him even though he was an engineered man. They didn't care.

"Get the fuck out of here, or we'll take you back inside."

"Where do you want us to go?" one of the men behind Salvador asked.

"You're free now, go wherever you want. There's a town a few miles up the road. Go there, or walk into the desert. We don't care, you didn't want to be here and now you can't be here. Leave!"

"You took my wallet! I want my wallet back. I want my card!"

A few of the guards began advancing forward from the detention center door. They were like demons of the steel mesh and barbed wire fences that embodied the facility, stretching out for miles.

"We'll bring you back in here if you want!"

Salvador and the other men lifted their feet and proceeded as quickly to the road as they could manage without losing every semblance of human dignity. Salvador was in front and walked in the direction of the town without heeding the other men. They were not his friends.

"Son of a bitch," one of them cursed while spitting on the road. It was an old-style asphalt road. This was a strange place. "They're sons of bitches," the man repeated.

Salvador paid him no mind. These men were not his comrades. He did not like them or trust them. He could understand why they were held behind, they were being punished. They were criminals who should be in jail. They were men who hurt other people in the detention camp. But, for himself, he didn't know why he was kept behind. None of the guards in the camp could tell him why. That was the way the world was, without a why. Life was arbitrary. He had been to Earth to visit his sick grandmother, and he had been picked up on the streets of Buenos Aires. For all he knew his grandmother was dead now. For all she knew he was dead now. When he got to the town he would find out.

He walked faster. The other men were lazy and slow. Salvador could understand why the engineered people hated the natural born. Of course, not all of them did. Like Samson's friend Ben, who was killed. But he could understand it. Natural people were trash. Of course, the genetically engineered people weren't much better. That's just how people were, it didn't matter what you did to them. It didn't matter if they were smart or stupid, tall or short, weak or strong, perfect or sickly. No matter what people did with their technology, with their cleverness, they couldn't change their nature. At least not to make it better. Sometimes he felt like he could understand everyone, that they were all trash and he could understand them. Natural born or engineered didn't matter. Who hated who. On days like that he could smile and it didn't matter what happened. He was happy then. Even with men like the men behind him, he could pretend they were his friends. But today was not a day like that. Today was a day when he was weary. Weary, and walking down an unknown desert road, to an unknown town, without water, without a card, under a hot sun that was already burning his skin. Sweat dripped off his nose constantly.

"Hey Salvador, why are you walking so fast?" one of the men behind him said.

"I walk because I walk!"

The dust here was different than the dust of the deserts on Venus. Salvador hadn't been to them all, but he had been to some of them. He had traveled as much as he could on Venus. He was a cosmopolitan man, although he had not gotten to travel through the Solar System, except to Earth. The dust here was coarser and grittier. The dust of the deserts on Venus was soft and fine. It was so fine that you could breathe it. And if you did that too much you would contract Venutian lung. Everyone on Venus who lived in the deserts did. But it was treatable. This Earth dust, Arizona dust, was thick; it clumped up in your mouth and throat so that you choked on it. It was like tiny rocks, microscopic sand, not like dust. Not like the dust on Venus.

Salvador's clothes were soaked with sweat. The sun was killing him. It was killing them. If the town was only a few miles away they would only just get there before they died. Perhaps. It seemed like they had already walked a mile or two. Was it only a mile? He thought about going back to the detention center. Were they more than half-way? Could he still get back? He didn't know. He became scared. He kept walking, focusing on his feet. The town was only a few miles up the road. There were no turns in the road. Why was there even a road here? He concentrated on his feet. Asking why, was a mistake. The people who asked it in the center— It was hard to understand. Everything was hard. He felt sick and concentrated on his feet. It was hard to lift his legs.

There was a fork in the road and he kept walking. He couldn't stop. There was no sign at the fork in the road, there was nothing to see looking one way or another. There was only road and desert. He glanced both ways but didn't stop. He had

41

a vague sense that the other men were following along behind him. He had a vague sense that one of them was whining, like an animal. He heard a whine escape his own throat and stopped it. He concentrated on his feet.

The last thing that Salvador remembered was crawling on the ground, beside the asphalt, immune to the pain of the burning dirt. He could only focus on a tiny spot straight in front of his eyes. His body kept seizing up and convulsing, throwing him onto his belly, rolling him over. He clawed his way forward. He was sure that he had gone more than three miles. He must have gone more than that. The sun here was so intense, so coldly hot. It was coldly hot. He could feel the cold in the heat. Why had they kept him behind? Why hadn't they released him with the others? Why did they hate him? There were no whys in this world. He concentrated on his hands, with that tiny spot of focused vision, and dragged himself forward even when his hands clenched up into claws. The cold of the heat was like a revelation. He clawed until he couldn't see anymore. At some point he stopped clawing. And there never had been any town.

BACK ON THE SMALL, PARADISE planet called Rothschild, Kenichi and Dr. Nguyen worked late into the night to set up an electro-magnetic sub-channel scan of Samson's body. They didn't like each other, but they didn't dislike each other either, and they worked well together. Kenichi respected Dr. Nguyen, which was more than he usually did, and Dr. Nguyen didn't care what Kenichi thought of him. They both felt free and solved problems quickly whenever they popped up. It took doing, but before the night was over they had every wrinkle smoothed, every hiccup spooked away, and every nanoscopic sensor carefully fixed in its individual place. Dr. Nguyen sat at a computer terminal to monitor the scan while Kenichi monitored the equipment.

The initial scan results were unusual, but only a short sample, and preliminary. Dr. Nguyen and Kenichi worked to adjust their equipment to generate a continuous pattern. The sun was up in the sky by the time their machines were registering the sub-channel feedback live, in real time. As Dr. Nguyen watched the pattern his eyes slowly bulged out from their sockets. He stared holding his breath until a fit of coughing overcame him.

"Look at this pattern," he croaked, and motioned to Kenichi.

"Th– Th– This is–" Kenichi stuttered. "These are like brain waves!"

CHAPTER 9

DR. NGUYEN AND KENICHI SPENT the next week analyzing the peculiar wave pattern emanating from Samson's body. It was an exciting, but mystifying discovery. The waves were anomalous, a phenomenon that had never been reported before, and it was hard to know what to make of them. There was nothing, to Dr. Nguyen's knowledge, that would cause dynamic electromagnetic sub-channel radiation to emanate from static matter, such as what Samson's body had become. Although what kind of static matter, exactly, his body had become was still as much of a mystery as the sub-channel radiation itself.

The waves did bear a resemblance to brain waves, but that was superficial. Neither Dr. Nguyen nor Kenichi wanted to bring the discovery to Stephanie until they understood it better. The pattern could easily be a mere artifact, or the product of a feedback loop or other contamination. What was so exciting about it was the potential to better understand what relativity effect was. There was the hint of possibility that this wave pattern could be a code that would describe the nature of the changes to matter that occurred during the relativity effect.

Finding themselves unable to glean new insight from a passive study of the waveforms, they began attempts to interfere with or manipulate them to see how they would respond. Dr. Nguyen set up an amplifier circuit plugged into a feedback loop to send a strong feedback signal into the ion sub-channels emanating from the body.

"Before we switch this on," Kenichi said, "are we certain we are not taking a risk? What if by interfering with it we damage the phenomenon? Stephanie might interpret it as us having 'killed' Samson. And there is the possibility, however remote, that these waveforms represent a form of consciousness. They are so strikingly similar to the brainwave patterns seen in dreams."

"We can't understand the phenomenon without probing it," Dr. Nguyen said. "All of our research so far has yielded no real insights. We discovered this phenomenon, but we don't know what it is. It could be noise. We have to figure out the impetus of the waveforms. If – in the extremely unlikely event, if – we are dealing with some form of consciousness pattern, this would be the first step toward communicating with it. The Mistress is not irrational. She understands science. If there is any problem, I will accept full responsibility for what we have done."

"That's good enough for me," Kenichi said. "All the monitors are active and being recorded. Let's flip the switch."

"In 3.... 2.... 1...."

SAMSON FLOATED AIMLESSLY OVER THE desert. It was the same everywhere, hot and dry and interminable. It was hard to avoid flying in circles. He couldn't say for certain that he was doing so.

He suddenly felt a great pain of blackness that seemed to crackle through everything. It was as if the universe was dying. He screamed. Then it went away, and it was as if what had happened, the crackling black pain, had never happened. It was as if it had never existed. Although he remembered it. As if it couldn't possibly exist.

"OK, THAT'S ENOUGH," DR. NGUYEN said, switching off the feedback signal. "More than enough. Kenichi, look at this."

"We'll have to get an expert in neurological waveforms to consult with us," Kenichi said. "This looks like consciousness."

"Yes."

"Look at how it fought with the feedback pattern," Kenichi

45

pointed to peaks and troughs in the graph. "This is adaptive. There's no question this is adaptive. It's like we're talking to the universe. Do you know the ancient teachings that were held by the religionists called 'Buddhists'?"

Dr. Nguyen looked white.

"We don't know what it is," he said.

"We have to tell Stephanie."

"We can't go giving her false hope!"

"No, that's true," Kenichi said, "but this could be one of the biggest scientific discoveries of – science. Let's do it again."

"We won't try it again. Not until we study what happened. We shouldn't bring it to the Mistress until then, either. If she comes to check on our progress, then yes, of course we tell her everything we can, but we don't need to disturb her before we have a chance to examine it and think about it."

"Why does this scare you?" Kenichi asked, breathless.

"It doesn't scare you?"

"No, it's exhilarating. I want to shout 'Eureka!', only I don't understand what the discovery is yet."

ON A DIRTY, GARBAGE STREWN street in Neo Vega, there was a dirty, garbage strewn apartment with a holo-tv inside blaring into a mostly empty room. In the center of the room, an enormous man sat watching the tv from a broken-down easy chair. His red eyes were bleary, and several empty liquor bottles had been cast on the floor around him. The room's one window looked out onto another building's wall, but street noise from the city still echoed in. Sirens and screams, engines, screeching air brakes, raucous laughter.

The tv was louder than the noise, and the huge man gesticulated and sometimes shouted at it.

"We still don't know if Samson is alive or dead," a man on the tv was saying. "How can we trust Rothschild's? There was no funeral, no pictures of the body. They might just be holding or protecting him."

"He's dead, you fucker! No one could survive that, fucking idiot. His body's probably too fucked to show—"

"Rothschild's may just want to maintain an air of mystery about what happened to Samson," the man on the tv continued, "to let his legend grow. The more that the life of Samson Ford becomes a legend, the better it is for the pro-naturals movement, which Rothschild's is heavily backing. They may even be detaining Samson to try to use him as some kind of under the table bargaining chip with Phillipe Bloodworth. This trade war is devastating both companies, and some people say that Rothschild's is coming off with the worst of it."

"Fucking idiot."

The huge man changed the channel, picked up one of the cast aside liquor bottles with a long arm, and tilted a few last drops into his mouth.

"It's amazing how well Terry is able to navigate these blind obstacles," a racing broadcaster on the new channel said breathlessly, "as if his mind can instantly compute them and situate them into a mental map. This is why he is the..."

"He gets told the obstacles ahead of time! Fucking morons."

A cracking sound interrupted the tv and the man stood up as two other men came crashing through the apartment's front door. Without a thought, as the first intruder blinked his eyes and waved his gun around, the huge man hurled his liquor bottle directly at the intruder's head. The glass of the bottle exploded from the impact and the intruder flopped to the floor unconscious, his face a mess of blood. Scamp, which was the big man's name, charged forward and stepped on the unconscious man's neck as he went. The second intruder, who was holding a long knife, froze, caught between twin impulses to run or to attack. Scamp's eyes were barely focused. He felt

47

like his movements were being pushed by an irresistible wave that he was delicately balanced on. He caught the man's knife hand and crushed it. The knife fell to the ground and, as a fist swung to hit him, Scamp snatched the man up by the waist and smashed his head and shoulders into the floor three times. It was as if he were swinging a fish and cracking its head upon the ground.

The two intruders were not quite dead. Warm blood sputtered from the second man's lips. The first man's body kicked and writhed gently, as if it were trying to wake up. Scamp carried the men outside and left them in a dumpster.

3/21

Burglars again tonight. I thought word would get around after the first ones. Too much chaos in this city. I don't know if they're dead, I left them in the dumpster outside like before. Mars was better than this. But this— It has its own appeal. This is nowhere land. Samson Ford started here. No wonder he was tough. When I think of how he's dead it makes me get teary eyed now. Strange. I don't understand it. I could have killed him once. Now I feel some kind of guilt. For doing nothing. Guilt for nothing. I saved his life. He started in this nowhere land and I could end here. This city is so full of empty. I should try to cross the desert to Magdalena. Ha, as if they'd take me. I'm worse than genetically engineered to them. Samson's brother even called me a monkey man. Life is a strange thing. I would have killed him then, too. He said that I was part baboon, as if he knew. As if he could have known. That was true. The genetic test showed that. Fucking idiot lab techs, blinking at it. I could have killed them, too.

I don't feel like I'm a man. I want to do something important.

- Scampadorous Maximus

CHAPTER 10

PHILLIPE BLOODWORTH WALKED OUT OF a meeting with his top executives. They were beautiful. They were all beautiful, and brilliant, and perfect. They were even better than he was, although they lacked his insight, his killer edge. They were what human beings should be. It made his blood run faster to be around them. When human beings like these could be created, there was no excuse for imperfection, for trash. There was no reason why every human being couldn't be a human such as these. An elite human should be the standard, the barest minimum, not the bar.

His executives were on edge. They handled it well, but the trade war frightened them. Margins were slashed, if they existed at all. Reserves were being tapped. And there was always the threat of armed conflict. Rothschild's were dangerous. The heir, Stephanie, was soft, but Simon Okunle had ensured that their potential was finely honed. Assassinations could happen, even open physical war. If it came to that, billions would die. The soft one, Stephanie, would do anything to prevent that, and that was their weakness. That and siding with the weak against the strong. Rothschild's were formidable, but Bloodworth Industries were pure killers. There was a good chance that people were going to die. In fact, they were going to. And if Bloodworth industries were defeated – if they were crushed – their executives would not be welcome in the other majors. At best, their careers would be severely stunted. At worst, after the bloodshed, after defeat, whatever executives survived would be hunted down and exterminated. The same thing had happened 100 years ago, when Apple Corporation was destroyed. So everything was on the line, and his executives were scared. Although they handled it well. That's why he was the leader and they were not.

They wanted him to bring back Camilla. They even shouted at him. The temerity! But he liked his executives to have spirit. They were right, too, he needed her. But what would it take to get her back? It might not be possible. He had grabbed her and forced his finger up her ass in front of all the other executives at the Solar Regatta. Humiliation! Loss of face! It was one of his favorite memories. Camilla had been getting too arrogant, too comfortable. She was rubbing off on the others. She had seemed to be moving outside, becoming an island of her own, as if she didn't have Bloodworth Industries completely at heart. It wasn't something he planned, but in the moment it was the perfectly appropriate thing to do. She squirmed! The idea came into his head and then he had to know what she would do after it happened. To see her face and hear the words she would say. Camilla. She was in several ways his best executive, but she didn't understand the politics, the dynamic. He didn't mind apologizing to her. He never minded apologizing, one to one. If it wasn't a show. If no one could sit and salivate or giggle over him being humbled. An apology was just words, like any other words. Sounds coming out of your mouth. Depending on the words you said you got certain reactions, certain results. Words were like a combination code to humanity. Sometimes "I'm sorry" was the right combination to get what you want. Words had power over other humans that he could not understand. Empty words. As if they weren't even people, but only robots looking for certain inputs. He had spent a lifetime studying the inputs. He could use that power when he wanted. Sometimes it was an apology. He didn't begrudge an apology, when it was the right combination. Camilla would know that it was empty words.

He got into his office, sealed the door, and contacted Camilla on her holophone. She had sold her home on Earth and was living in a set of luxury apartments on the Solarium.

The sun glared through a window behind her when she answered the call.

"What do you want, Phillipe?"

"Camilla! It's good to see you! You're a hard woman to track down."

"I don't want you to track me down, Phillipe. I don't want to see your face again, so tell me what you want before I hang up."

"Don't hang up!" Bloodworth thrust his palms out in front of him in a conciliatory gesture. "I need to talk to you. In the first place, we need to talk about what happened at the Solar Regatta. I did something horrible and I don't feel right about it. Let me apologize to you."

"Your apologies are only words, Phillipe."

"No, I mean it, look at me, is my face red or not? What I did was inexcusable."

"I'm hanging up."

"You were my best executive! Camilla, you think I don't know that? You were my best executive and you deserved better than what I did. I regret it. I feel ashamed of myself!"

"Words, Phillipe."

"Look at me, is my face red? I'm a human being, I feel the same emotions as the next man. Just – let me explain something, show you something of myself, of me. Even if you hate me, look – you understand power, Camilla, you see it. You're always the smart one in the room. So how did I get to be so powerful? How did that happen, do you see that? By pushing the goddamn envelope, that's how it happened. By pushing the goddamn envelope until it sometimes burst. You're smart, Camilla, you're one of my own, my great ones. You know how I've done what I've done. I've ridden the edge, the extreme edge, for fifty years. I've ridden the edge of what's permissible, what's acceptable, what's legal! You can't be on the edge without

51

going over sometimes – I have to go over the edge sometimes, that's how I've gotten what I got, that's how I win. Is this fake emotion, Camilla? Is my face red? I have to push at the edge of what's permitted, that's my inner nature, it's who I am! You can't push on the edge – you can't be me! – without getting it wrong sometimes and pushing too far, without getting it wrong sometimes and causing something bad, without doing something that you didn't want to do. You regret, but you are who you are. I can't turn it off and on! I went over the edge with you, way past the edge. That cost me one of my great ones. And I want you back on my team, with us, where you belong. I'm sorry, Camilla. I wish I could take it back, and I'm sorry."

Bloodworth's face had changed from red to white, and a teardrop rolled down his cheek.

"I know you're not sorry, Phillipe," Camilla said, "but thank you for saying that."

"Will you consider coming back to us?"

She laughed bitterly.

"Of course not. Don't think about sending your goons after me, Phillipe, I've put pieces into place to cut your testicles off if you do."

"No one will come after you. I'm apologizing, not attacking. How will you cut my testicles off?"

"Don't fuck with me, Phillipe. Just leave me alone and I won't bother you. But if harm should suddenly come to me, or to people I love, you'll find out what precautions I've set into place. Just leave me alone."

"Camilla, I need you."

"Trade war not going well, is it?"

"You have the best public relations mind in the Solar System. And you're one of us. Everyone misses you, they were screaming at me to get you back. They're scared to be in this fight without you."

"That bad, is it?"

"I'm willing to give you whatever you want."

"Give me back a life where Phillipe Bloodworth never held me down in front of my friends and stuck his finger up my ass, Phillipe! Give me that!"

Her eyes flashed with teary rage.

"I'm hanging up," she said quietly.

"Camilla, wait! I can make you a delegate."

"What?"

"On Earth, I can make you a delegate of the United Earth Congressional Assembly. This year, Camilla, not down the road. I can put you in at the next cycle. You'll have money, power, fame. Protection provided by the Earth Government Special Service. I'll make you a delegate. You can go as far as you want from there. Maybe even crush me, if you're still bitter then. I'll make you a Delegate. Come back to us."

Camilla Rosenberg stared into the holo-screen for a long time, and Phillipe Bloodworth waited silently for her to speak.

"FIND A WAY TO COMMUNICATE with him," Stephanie ordered emphatically.

Kenichi and Dr. Nguyen blinked their eyes at her.

"Wh– wh– wh–, uh– uh–," Dr. Nguyen stammered.

"Find a way."

"Stephanie, that's not–" Kenichi grasped for words. "That's not what this means. This doesn't mean Samson is still alive. This doesn't mean those are brain waves."

"It's him," Stephanie said. "I'm certain it's him."

"That's not what this means," Kenichi repeated. "This is an amazing discovery, possibly a breakthrough in understanding the relativity effect, but those aren't brain waves. They only share a resemblance to brain waves. We don't understand what they are, but there are many things they could be. They seem to be some sort of resistance or feedback from matter or space; from the fabric of the universe, literally. They could be something like the consciousness of the universe, although that wouldn't be consciousness per se. They could be some misunderstood reflection of our brainwaves in this room, or our computers. That wouldn't be uninteresting, because whatever the pattern is coming from, even if the pattern itself is mundane, this avenue of feedback is previously unobserved and likely to have significant implications for how we understand the building blocks of matter-energy."

"Don't patronize me," Stephanie said. "This is not a scientific experiment, it's a person that I love. You can't believe these are an equivalent to brain waves, but that is exactly what I think they are. I'm not asking you to stop doing what you're doing, as long as it doesn't risk harming Samson, but I'm ordering you to make it your chief priority to figure out how to communicate with him. If you give that your best efforts and are unable to make any progress, then we can consider other alternatives."

"Mistress," Dr. Nguyen finally found his tongue. "We don't want to give you false hope."

"False hope? Do you think I believe that we can bring him back? That I will have Samson in my life again? You misunderstand me, Dr. Nguyen. I can't imagine that happening. Nor am I laboring under a false impression that the universe revolves around me. But if your wife was on a ship that disappeared, and years later it was found crashed on the side of a remote mountain, would you go there to search and find her corpse, or quietly content yourself with the fact that she was dead, which you already really knew?"

Stephanie's eyes were fierce, and her face was patches of white and prickly red.

"But Stephanie, you said–" Kenichi began.

"Let me finish! Of course you would do what you could to find your wife's body. Of course you would! You would leave no stone unturned, otherwise you couldn't live with yourself. You couldn't, Dr. Nguyen. Kenichi could, but you couldn't. And why would you need to find her body? Not for hope, exactly, but for the chance. For that tiny, infinitesimal chance that she was there alive, that you were somehow wrong, that the billion to one shot had occurred, the unlikeliest scenario, just for that chance. For hope? No, because to turn your back on that chance, that infinitesimal potentiality, to accept the 'fact' of her death while that tiny chance remained, would be turning your back on the person you loved. You would leave no stone unturned, not for hope. Not something like hope. But for shame. Or the fear of shame.

"Leaving no stone unturned means different things to different people. What it is possible for one person to do depends on who the person is. It is possible for me to do a lot. I don't expect to get Samson back, I don't expect that at all. But I expect to do everything I possibly can. I expect to sleep at night with the knowledge that I did everything I can. I expect to sleep at night like that."

Her eyes glistened with moisture, but Stephanie's gaze was strong. Her back was straight and her bearing unperturbed.

"Forgive my impertinence, Mistress," Dr. Nguyen said. "We will do exactly as you ask."

When Stephanie left the meeting with Kenichi and Dr. Nguyen she walked straight to a meeting with Simon Okunle and her other top executives. She could have used a floating platform, but she chose to walk. She felt emotional and empty, all at once. Jumping out of her skin and also dead. Walking helped to settle her emotions, which was much more comfortable than concealing them. It was exciting, Samson could be

55

alive! For all of what she had said, the feeling inside her was different. She knew it was him, as surely as she knew anything. It made no logical sense to know that, but somehow it was true. It was true beyond needing a justification, inside of her. It wasn't true in some objective, empirical sense, but it was still true. She doubted that it was true, and held no hope in her mind, yet felt emphatically that he was alive. That they had discovered his consciousness, somehow. He was somewhere still, somewhere that was not completely separated or inaccessible. He was alive.

This was what the religions were like, she realized. This is what the people of Magdalena felt who believed in the god. It wasn't that they were ignorant or irrational. It wasn't that they were stupid. They were convicted by a truth. How do we know what is real? What makes something true? We believe in the things we can deduce from the things that are already inside us that we know to be true. Free will. We know when we choose to look up or down, or to think about racing or love, or truth, that we are making a choice. It is the truth inside of us that isn't predicated on anything else, that isn't justified. The people who believed in the god felt such a truth. And Samson was alive. It was true. But Samson must be dead, even though she knew he was alive. It should be impossible to feel something so certain, for no reason. This was how the people who believed in the god felt. She wondered if Samson ever felt that, or what he could be thinking and feeling now. If he did die, she wondered if she would feel his spirit sometimes, with her, like the old legends. Yet, he must be dead. The only thing that she could feel was that he was alive. He must be dead. She wanted to grieve, but she could only believe he was alive.

Outside the conference room where she met her executives, Stephanie stood and tried to compose herself.

"What is the big news, Mistress?" Simon Okunle asked, coming up behind her.

"How can you tell there is news?"

"I've known you since the day you were born. You conceal it well."

"It's something I'll tell you later," Stephanie said, "in private."

Simon opened the door for her and she greeted her executives warmly. The meeting was, as always now, about the trade war and the fight over the rights of the natural born. She found it difficult to concentrate and kept feeling irritated with her executives' stupidity. That was not normal. She had the best team, realistically, that a human being had probably ever had, and was sincerely grateful to have them. The problem obviously must be herself, but today everyone in the meeting seemed to grate with insipidity. She let Simon lead the meeting.

"We haven't been able to find out what it is," said Pavel Williams, Rothschild's current intelligence chief, whose skin was robin's egg blue, "but we're now certain that Bloodworth's are funding a secret project that they call 'Plan B'. The project has something to do with the naturals and is thought to be the company's most closely guarded secret. Our source, who became familiar with the existence of the project – just knowledge of its existence is limited to a very small group – believes there may be only a handful of people in the Solar System who know what 'Plan B' actually is. Possibly only Bloodworth himself and the men working directly on the project. Considering some of their closely held projects that we do know about – illegal experimentation blending animal and human genetics, for example – it is frightening to try to imagine what this Plan B might be."

"What might it be?" Albrecht Durer asked.

"Free form speculation won't do us any good," Stephanie said.

"No," Pavel Williams said, "as the Mistress suggests, we simply cannot say. But our source said Bloodworth's manner was frightening when he talked about Plan B. And our source believes it is so significant that I felt all of you should be informed as well."

"Thank you for keeping us in the loop, Pavel," Simon Okunle said. "Just to be clear, this 'Plan B' is a project that has been in the works for years, so it is not directly related to the trade war?"

"That is our understanding. It is certain the project has been ongoing for several years."

"Thank you, Pavel."

Stephanie found it more and more difficult to concentrate on what they were saying. It was so important, but she could barely hear it. It was worse that they had found something at Samson's lab. It made her life harder. It was so wonderful that they had, and it was worse. She couldn't stop thinking of it and, moreso, it drew a blanket over her brain. She realized that her distracted presence was having a negative impact on the meeting. She would be better, tomorrow. Tomorrow she would be strong. She made her excuses and left the meeting early.

Stephanie's bedroom was her sanctuary. Warm and cozy and clean and familiar. Unbelievably luxurious, which was natural to her. Surrounded by her favorite paintings. Her favorite music and sounds, perfectly rendered. Her favorite books on a shelf. Her favorite scents, or none – often the scent of natural roses, perfectly bloomed and arrayed in some of the worlds' most beautiful ancient vases. Her best friend and maid, Cylla, brewed Stephanie a hot cup of tea and tried to talk with her to cheer her up. She made Cylla leave.

She sat by herself in her bedroom, then lay awake in her

bed late into the night, thinking about Samson and Phillipe Bloodworth. Thinking about the war that was so real, so visceral and affecting to her people, to more people than her people, the billions of individual people, with lives shaken up, awake at night with fear, trying to find a way forward. They were so much reality, and so unreal. As if they were flat and imaginary, as if they were an ancient film. Their imagined travesties. She wanted them to feel real, to be impassioned for them. She wanted to feel guilty, and didn't. She thought about Samson, accelerating at the end of the race, knowing that it would kill him. Did he think of her then? She lay in her bed with her eyes open, staring into a perfect darkness. Feeling that Samson was alive, but knowing that he was dead. Feeling cold, shivering. Feeling cold and totally alone.

C H A P T E R 11

AMSON FLEW ACROSS THE ENDLESS brushy desert, hoping to find the unicorn men. Hoping to find something, anything at all. He flew down and walked along the ground, but there was nothing. Dirt and rocks and bushes. It was exactly as it appeared. Flying was faster, although it was hard to be certain that he wasn't flying in circles. He flew up to see farther, and flew up and up, but the desert stretched on, with no features, until it faded out of sight below him and he was surrounded by endless blue and the omni-sunshine that had no specific source but shone everywhere. He didn't fly far into the blue, but straight back down again, afraid to escape into it and lose his bearings.

The woman was somewhere down below, or at least the path to her lay in that direction. He could picture a face: dark, deep eyes and black hair. A face that was subtle and beautiful. It seemed to hold such moment for him, but he didn't know why. She was important. Everything depended on finding her.

He flew over the desert faster, until it was a blur below him, and eventually an aberration in the blur appeared. He flew lower, and slowed, and the thing loomed up from the ground as he approached.

It was a structure.

As he approached closer, a humming bird appeared in the air beside him. The bird darted in and out around him, flashing iridescent red and green, twittering. Samson felt flattered and whistled at it. The bird darted in and poked his hand with its beak, drawing blood.

"Ouch!"

He tried to shoo it away.

The structure was a kind of temple, a pyramid squared off and rising toward the sky. He squinted against the bright daylight. The humming bird darted in to attack him again and he twisted to avoid it. He didn't know why a humming bird should be here, but he would hate to hurt one. The little bird continued to dart around him angrily. Then two small finches and a skylark flew out of the sky to join it. He wanted to welcome the company – breathing, warm blooded creatures – but they screeched and swooped onto him as they approached, clawing and biting him. He brushed the birds away and looked toward the pyramid, trying to fly faster. It seemed difficult to fly fast with the birds harassing the air around him. The pyramid was tiered, with many square levels. Twenty or thirty levels – it was huge. The air in the distance around it began to appear thick. Samson twisted and turned and swatted at the birds.

As the pyramid came closer, more small birds swarmed after him, and then gulls. The gulls attacked with a single minded fury, slowing him to a near stop, gradually covering his body with cuts and tears. Through cracks between his fingers, which were covering his eyes, he could see that the pyramid had a great ramp on one side that led up from the ground to a dark doorway near the top.

Eagles joined the other birds now – large, formidable creatures. When they swooped into him the heavy bodily impact knocked him and the other birds spinning. He couldn't see the pyramid anymore. He couldn't see the desert or the sky, only a blur of feathers and beaks and talons accompanied by a roar of chirps and shrieks. He had become a cloud of twisting arms and wings, flailing legs, blood and puffs of feathers, pain and indignant fury.

He flew up, away, whatever way seemed away, back from where he came, coughing and choking on the blood running down his head and face. Eventually, gradually, the swarm of birds trailed behind and left him, starting with the eagles, then the gulls, then the smaller birds. Samson flew faster and faster as he got away, his vision a haze of weakness and adrenaline. Where was the pyramid? If he lost it he might never find it again! He turned just in time, shifting course from a line into a broad arc. Just in time. It was still there, a dot on the horizon in the distance. He kept it in his vision, circling it from afar, blinking through red mist. He was still swinging his arms, kicking and twisting against the birds that were no longer there; he brought his body back under control. His two fists were clenched. He unclenched his left hand to reveal a little brown finch, crushed. He turned it out of his hand and watched it fall, lifeless like a stone, to the ground. He unclenched his right fist and there was the little humming bird. Its red and green still flashed and glittered in the light, but brokenly, like a torn up, sequined dress.

Samson watched the little bird in his hand for a long time and wondered what he had done wrong. His cuts and scars healed quickly as he flew, and he did not think that it was strange for them to do so.

On Titan, Saturn's largest moon, a woman named Ariana was walking through rolling fields of grass. The beautiful skyline of the city of Pollonia, completely smog free, loomed in the near distance behind her. She had tears in her eyes and one of them rolled down her pale white cheek, across an elegant scattering of pink pigment dots that were her parents' eccentric nod to the beauty of freckles. The grassy hills rolled on and on, unblemished, with their perfect four inch grass. In the distance in front of her a blue river wound between them like a gentle snake.

Pollonia lay down in the grass and stared up at the sherbet orange sky. It was the height of the day, and the sky was filled with light from Titan's enormous mirrored solar sails which also orbited Saturn. The sun was beautiful here, more beautiful than Earth. It was just as pretty, but less overwhelming. She looked at it until it stung the tears out of her eyes, then closed them.

A car sailed past overhead, slowing to look down at her as it went by. No one walked out here, not this far from the city, not often. She must have walked for ten miles at least. She had it in her mind to keep walking until she reached the river. She didn't have a plan.

After several minutes of laying spread eagled on her back with her eyes closed, the buzz of an engine roused her to sit up. A young man in a float-scooter was riding towards her from the bottom of the hill. When she looked at him he waved.

Of course it was a natural born; they were like rats. Always crawling out from the most unlikely places. Just what she wanted to see today. Of course it was.

The man pulled up at a polite distance from her and idled his engine.

"Are you ok?"

He was wearing goggles and pulled them up onto his forehead.

"Not really."

Ariana didn't look at him directly, but off to the side and up at the sky.

"What's the problem?"

"People like you are the problem, aren't they?"

"Why, because I'm bothering you? I was just worried because people don't usually wander out here by themselves. I live in the house over there, in the distance. See it at the top of that hill? It's a little green house. It's just a little green dot from here. See there?"

"I don't give a fuck."

"Do you need a ride somewhere or something? I don't want to bother you, but I watched you walking across the hills for a long time. You don't have any water. I mean, people don't usually walk out here."

"It's a free planet isn't it?"

"Yes. Sort of."

"I don't need your help. It's people like you who ruined my life."

The young man brought down his scooter to rest on the ground and cut its engine.

"Why, because I'm natural born? Do you mind if I get off and sit with you? It gets pretty boring out here in the hills."

"Do what you want."

"You're pretty," the young man said.

"We all are, to you."

"That's not completely true. I don't think so."

"Why don't people like you hurry up and move out to Magdalena? You can sit around the Christmas tree with Samson Ford's family singing Zippity Doo Day to the god."

"I don't believe in the god. Why would I want to go to Magdalena?"

"You're not going to get into my pants, kid. And I'm sure if you try something I can kick your ass."

"That's fine. I'm not trying to bother you. I was just worried. Do you know that three different people have wandered out and drowned themselves in that river this month? I'll leave if you want me to."

He stood pointing at the blue river snaking along in the distance.

"It's not easy to kill yourself on Titan," the woman said.

"Isn't it?"

"Suppose you jump off of the floor of a tall building, what happens?"

There was an awkward pause in the conversation as the young man looked at her curiously. His natural 'red' hair was long, half down to his shoulders, and unruly.

"I don't know," he said finally, "what happens?"

"The gravity locks on the perimeter of the building activate to break your fall before you hit the ground. You didn't know that?"

"I don't get into the city much," the young man said. "And I probably didn't have as good of an education as you. But that sounds like fun. Why don't people do it all the time?"

"There's still a chance that the fall might kill you."

"Oh."

"And it's illegal to do it for fun."

"I see."

Ariana lay back and stared up at the sky again. The young man was sitting cross-legged a couple of yards away from her. He scooted a little bit closer.

"That would be the fastest way down," he said.

"Yes it would."

"You don't want to kill yourself do you?"

"Is that what you do with your life, watch the hills and try to keep people from killing themselves?"

"I've never done it before, but I thought today I would give it a try."

"No, I don't want to kill myself."

"Good."

"Do you think that anyone who was serious about killing themselves would answer yes?"

The young man stared at the river in the distance.

"I don't know. Wouldn't they?"

"Only people who weren't serious would answer yes. People who wanted your help. People who were serious wouldn't be interested in help."

"That might be true. Although I think suicide is a funny thing."

"What do you know about it?"

"What do you know about it yourself?" the young man returned. "I used to want to kill myself, that's how I know."

"Well my husband was one of the people who drowned themselves in that river last month, so that's how I know."

"Gosh. I'm sorry."

"Are you?"

"Yes."

"What do you care?"

"It's sad. I feel empathy for you and him when I hear that. Isn't that normal?"

"Maybe. But it's this whole trade war that caused him to kill himself, and you know whose fault that is."

"Bloodworth's?"

Ariana's lips released a stifled, bitter laugh.

"Bloodworth's. Bloodworth's just a business man. He doesn't give a fuck. He just wants to make a profit. It's the natural born whose fault it is. The ones shouting 'Samson Ford! Samson Ford! Zippity Doo.' It's the ones stirring up trouble whose fault it is."

"That's rough," the young man said. "I hope you don't think I had anything to do with it."

"How should I know?"

"I don't think natural born people are at fault for wanting to be treated like human beings, are they?"

"Oh, give me a break. Please."

"Bloodworth's was rounding up people on Earth and locking them up, trying to ship them off to the edge of the Solar System. To Oberon. Do you know how small Oberon is? It couldn't hold a billion people–"

"That's Rothschild's fucking propaganda."

"It's true!"

"Bullshit."

"My uncle was locked up on Earth."

"That's probably because he was a criminal."

"No, his name was Salvador, we call him Uncle Sal. He was locked up in one of Bloodworth's detention camps. They wanted to ship him to Oberon, we got word from him a few weeks after the Solar Regatta. We haven't heard from him since then, though. Not even since all the prisoners were released."

"Well he sounds like a real win."

"He was a good man. Why are you being so hateful?"

"I'm sorry about your Uncle Sal, but I know for a fact that almost all that stuff about natural born people being rounded up was Rothschild's propaganda."

"It's not propaganda. How do you know that?"

"It's all over the fucking news!"

"It's not on the Rothschild's news."

"Of course not, that's the whole point."

"Well anyway, I don't have anything to do with the trade war."

Ariana was sitting up again and the two of them sat in silence on the top of the hill while staring in the distance at the river. She realized for the first time in hours that she was thirsty.

"Do you have any water?"

"Yes," the young man said, and went quickly to retrieve it from the saddlebags on his scooter.

"Thank you."

While Ariana drank the water she thought about what to say. She felt bad for being hostile to him, but had recently begun to despise the natural born. She hadn't always been that way. Once upon a time she had even marched in favor of natural born rights. But they were causing too many problems now. They were proving all the things that the people like Phillipe Bloodworth had said were right.

"Do you know what Rothschild's did to us?" she asked.

"What did they do?"

"They cut off all our businesses. We were fresh food suppliers to Rothschild's restaurants all around the city. They cut us off because we were under the Bloodworth's umbrella. We were franchisees! We don't have anything to do with Bloodworth's practices or policies. My husband and I invested all of our savings into our little chain of wholesale grocers, we only started to make any money from it last year. It took eight years before that to get us up and running. Almost all of our customers were under Rothschild's. They didn't have any control either, they felt bad. They didn't want to stop doing business with us. My husband thought if he put all our own money back into the business that he could keep it afloat. He sold our house. We had a nice house. He sold our car. Bloodworth's couldn't save us, because the Bloodworth's restaurants in town already had their own suppliers. We couldn't find new business fast enough. We wrote off the franchise and tried to sell direct to consumers. Rothschild's banks owned our loans and foreclosed right away as soon as we missed a payment! We didn't miss a payment once before that, we didn't miss any payment. The first one, the first one they swooped down. It was all in the fine print that they could do so. Nobody ever does that, or nobody did before the trade war, but they could do it. Friends we know tried to challenge it in court, but that didn't work. My husband and I lost everything. My husband's dead now. They were getting ready to throw us off of Titan, did you know they do that? With your bad education? Did you know they throw you out of this joint? Give you a charity bus pass back to Earth and say don't let the door hit your ass on your way out?"

"I know they do," the young man said.

"Well that's what Rothschild's did to us," Ariana said.

68

"That's what all the trouble about the natural born has done for us. I don't have anywhere to go on Earth. My parents are old. I have to start over, trying to find a job – now. Now? Do you know what it's like to try to find a job right now? I haven't been able to find one on Titan."

"I'm sorry," the young man said.

"I know you are. I'm sorry for being mean to you. It's not your fault you're natural born."

"Is it a fault?" the young man asked.

"Oh, I don't know anymore. Why can't your parents just give you some fucking genetic upgrades like everyone else?"

"My parents couldn't afford it."

"There are scholarships! There's Planned Parenthood."

"It's not as easy as you think," the young man said. "You don't know what it's like to be poor."

"I'm learning," Ariana said.

As SAMSON'S MIND CLEARED AND he continued to circle the temple from afar, he spotted an oasis on the ground. The oasis had palm and fig trees, long grass in bushy patches, and a clean, deep pool. Samson flew down to the pool and lay beside its bank, drinking deeply from its water. Quenched, he crawled into the water and rinsed his flesh, becoming conscious for the first time of his body's fatigue. He climbed back out of the water and lay down in the shade of a low palm. Although he had not been conscious of being hot, the shade felt mercifully cool. He did not move again, or even open his eyes, for a long time.

When he did finally open his eyes, Samson's ears were ringing with the bleating sound of sheep. He awoke to find the oasis overflowing with them. The sheep had exquisite long, reddish-brown and black coats. They were inquisitive and beautiful, which was strange, because Samson had always thought of sheep as particularly stupid and ugly animals. They had glistening black eyes, which he thought was unusual, although when he thought about it he couldn't quite remember how a sheep's eyes were normally expected to be. He shooed one of the more adventurous members of the flock away when it waddled up and nibbled at his hair, and sat up to look around.

There was a man standing among the sheep at the edge of the pool. He was tall and held a long shepherd's crook. He wore the hood of a woven cloak up over his head and Samson could not clearly see his face. The man seemed to gaze at Samson from within the shadows of the hood.

"Hello," Samson said.

"Hello."

The shepherd's voice was baritone and resonant. He turned away from Samson and minded his sheep, and neither one spoke to the other for a time.

"Who are you?" Samson finally asked.

"I come here often," the shepherd said. "Who are you?"

Samson looked at the ground, and up at the unbroken crystalline blue of the sky, and down to the shepherd again.

"I don't exactly know who I am."

"Then neither will I tell you who I am," the shepherd said.

"I came from a place of endless nothing," Samson pointed generally behind him. "And I came through a wall and a lock. An endless wall with a great lock in it."

"I don't know it," the shepherd said.

"I want to enter the temple in the distance," Samson said. "Do you know it?"

"Yes, I know it."

The sound of the sheep lapping at the water, and playful bleating and splashing in the pool filled the clearing. The shepherd began to circle the pool, gathering his flock.

"You will need fire to get past the birds," the shepherd said.

"How will I get fire?"

"How will you be able to see inside the temple without it?"

The shepherd finished gathering his sheep and led them away. Samson felt that it was somehow wrong, or a mistake, to follow. He called after the shepherd several times, but the shepherd did not heed him.

CHAPTER 12

AFTER MONTHS OF STALLING, ROTHSCHILD's finally distributed a video showing Samson's body and explaining in detail what had happened to him. They did not, of course, mention the unusual intra-matter waves that had been discovered emanating from his body and that they were feverishly researching. After the broadcast presentation, sitting at a table at the front of a large auditorium on Rothschild, Dr. Nguyen answered questions from the press. His fingers shook, but his vocal manner was composed.

"So just to be clear," a male reporter asked, "this, that we've been watching on video, this is Samson Ford's corpse?"

"We believe that is most likely, yes."

"Most likely?" the reporter cut in, "Is it or not?"

"Let me finish," Dr. Nguyen said. "As many of us will recall from our school physics, the transmutation of matter that occurs during the relativity effect is quite mysterious and not at all well understood. We believe this is Samson's corpse, which is to say that it is a transmutation of the matter that his body was composed of, but we cannot say so with certainty at the present time."

"But–!"

"Let me finish. Other explanations are possible. Principally, that what we have in our lab could actually be a kind of 'image' of Samson's body that was somehow created as a byproduct of the relativity effect. It seems less likely, but it is possible, that during the relativity effect his body was converted to energy, or in some other way obliterated, and this image or 'reflection' of it was left behind."

"But that means," another reporter cut in.

"Let me finish. Let me finish. Hold onto your horses, I'll call for the next question when I am ready for it and everyone will get a turn.

"Even if the 'body' of Samson that we have in our lab is not *technically* his corpse, the fact remains that Samson Ford was killed by the relativity effect shortly after crossing the finish line at the Solar Regatta. Whether the 'body' we have is actually the corpse or not is a technical, scientific point that generally amounts to splitting hairs, but because I am a technical, scientific person for whom this hair splitting distinction is important in his research, I must do so.

"Next question!"

"How do you know the relativity effect didn't kill Samson Ford before he crossed the finish line?" a young female reporter asked, eliciting several grumbles from the crowd of media people.

"Health and vitality sensors on board his ship show unambiguously that he was still alive when he crossed the finish line. This was also true of the vitality signals transmitted in real time during the broadcast of the race, which everyone who was watching will remember. All evidence shows that he was still alive when he crossed the finish line and no evidence indicates otherwise. However, both the logs found on his ship and the logs transmitted from his racer in real time ceased to function, under the burden of the relativity effect, within the first minute after Samson's racer crossed the finish line, very possibly within seconds of it, in fact. While it is true that he was still alive when he crossed the line, all of our research indicates that he was very near to death by then. It's easily possible that he was not conscious when he won the race."

"So you believe he won the race?" a man in the back shouted.

"I'm sorry, that's just my personal opinion. Your own judgment about that is as good as mine."

"What will happen to his corpse, will you return it for burial to Magdalena?"

"We have no settled plans for what to do with it," Dr. Nguyen said carefully, "other than to continue our research for the time being. We are fully funded and given a free leash by Rothschild's with the goal of understanding in more perfect detail exactly what happened to Samson, and helping to prevent it from happening to other pilots in the future."

"But his people are a spiritual people, and they have rights!" said a reporter in the back, whose plain brown hair and imperfect skin revealed him as a natural born.

"Samson left a will and testament shortly before the race designating Stephanie de Rothschild as his sole heir and executor. And, even though it is a little bit off our topic, let me be clear about this: Some cynical minds have been incredulous at the idea of Samson designating Stephanie de Rothschild as his heir, because she is such a prominent person, but anyone who does any research will find that Stephanie was the person closest to Samson in the months leading up to the Solar Regatta. Samson's long time business partner and companion, Ben Johnson, was killed not long before the race, so it is perfectly normal that Samson would make the other closest person in his life his heir and executor. There is no reason to question this. To my knowledge, it has not been questioned by Samson Ford's family, who were the first to be informed of what had happened to him, which was the reason for Rothschild's delayed initial announcement, nor has it been questioned by any of the other people who were close to Samson near the end of his life – Lisa Maui, for instance.

"We will continue with our research, and when the time comes it will be Stephanie de Rothschild's decision what to do with her loved one Samson Ford's remains. Just as he wished."

"Look," a pale yellow, aged reporter in the front row squeaked, "when you do scans on this body, what does it look like on the inside? Do you see cells and organs and those sorts of things? I mean, what exactly is it composed of?"

"It's an altered state of matter," Dr. Nguyen said, "not previously seen before. I want to underline that this in itself is not unusual; we regularly see unique forms appear when matter has been subjected to a severe relativity effect, these unique material objects are created regularly and sold openly for, albeit, very large sums of money.

"When we scan the body, with magnetic imaging for example, we see an undifferentiated material field, not individual cells and organs. If you touch the body this would not surprise you, as one can slowly slide a hand through it without altering or separating it. It has properties of both solid and fluid, or you might characterize it as something more like a hologram or an electromagnetic energy field. This quality of the matter is unique and one of the most interesting areas of our research."

"How do you move it?"

The questions continued.

"WHAT DID YOU MAKE OF the Rothschild's broadcast and the interview with Dr. Nguyen, Lisa?" the host of a popular, Earth based, news-of-the-day program asked Lisa Maui.

"It's hard to see his body and realize that Samson is really dead," Lisa said. "And not be able to go to a funeral or ceremony. He was a friend to me, but he meant so much to so many people."

"He was an icon."

"Absolutely, and that's the positive thing that we can really take from this: that Samson leaves a legacy behind."

"It's unbelievable what's happened to his body."

"It's eerie," Lisa agreed.

"I hope what's left of him doesn't end up in a museum or something horrible like that."

"Right."

"Was he— Samson wasn't completely comfortable with his fame, was he?"

"No, he wasn't completely comfortable with it," Lisa said. "But if he didn't like it in some way, he wouldn't have been racing. Samson liked to speak through action."

"What action can people take now to honor Samson's legacy?"

"Support natural born rights and legislation. Contact your political representatives and raise your voice about it. I'm the spokesperson for the Natural Born Rights Alliance and we have a site up with a wonderful checklist of things that people can do to memorialize Samson and honor his legacy. For one thing, we're helping to organize special memorial services for Samson in cities throughout the Solar System, to give people a proper chance to say goodbye. We still need volunteers and even organizing help in many cities and it is a wonderful chance for people to be involved in Samson's legacy."

"That's great. That's really wonderful, and I assume people can just look up Natural Born Rights Alliance and find all the information about that."

"Yes, or just go to NBRA on the Rothschild's net."

"And you spoke of political representatives, Lisa, but they aren't even necessarily the biggest players in regards to this issue, are they?"

"That's true, Jon," Lisa said. "The trade war happening right now between Rothschild's and Bloodworth's Corporation is all about the issue of natural born rights and discrimination. Everyone knows that Phillipe Bloodworth hates the natural born, and Bloodworth's Corporation is doing everything in its power to make life difficult for natural born people like Samson Ford. Rothschild's is the opposite, they have been the biggest supporter of natural born rights in the Solar System.

"To give you an example, the drug Rildoxylin is patented

to Bloodworth's Corporation and distributed exclusively to Bloodworth owned pharmacy chains. Rildoxylin is the best available treatment for genotypal dysmorphic rejection, a rare syndrome that causes debilitating lesions on organs throughout the body, including the skin and brain. GDR syndrome is rare in gene woven individuals, occurring in only one per 50,000, but in natural born individuals with genetically engineered ancestry the occurrence is one per 1,000. And what we've recently learned at the NBRA and only today officially confirmed, is that all Bloodworth's owned pharmacy chains have begun to refuse to do business with natural born people, and also refuse to sell Rildoxylin to pharmacies that are not controlled by Bloodworth's Corporation, so that Bloodworth's is actually refusing to allow natural born people throughout the Solar System to have access to this medication."

"That just came out today? That's outrageous!"

"And that's only one example. We have an enormous list on our NBRA site of similar acts of discrimination being perpetrated by Bloodworth's Corporation. And the point is that people can have a huge impact on this issue by patronizing companies that support natural born rights, such as companies controlled by the Rothschild's Corporation, and by boycotting companies that support discrimination against the natural born, such as all companies owned and controlled by Bloodworth's corporation. And we have full lists of those companies on our NBRA site."

"And you don't work for Rothschild's, do you Lisa?"

"Absolutely not. NBRA is a completely independent, nonprofit organization that is funded entirely by donations from private individuals, and I am funded entirely by them. But you are getting to what I think is an important point, Jon, which is that this issue is not *only* about Bloodworth's and Rothschild's. I only focus on these two because they are by far the largest and most committed players on this issue, and the ones with the most influence. There are thousands of other companies that have come out strongly in favor of natural born rights or in favor of discrimination, and we have lists of those on the site, too. But other dominant corporations, such as Nike, have not taken an overarching position on the issue and have been allowing their subsidiary companies to act individually, one way or the other, so in those cases it is often easiest to check with the subsidiary company itself, to see if they have taken a public stand on the issue."

"I can't believe they're not letting natural born people have those medications."

"It's crazy, Jon. But that's why it is so important now for people to stand up and speak up about this issue, and vote with their pocketbooks."

"Thank you for coming on today, Lisa."

"It was my pleasure. Thank you."

The program cut to a commercial, and in Manhattan Lisa Maui's grandfather switched off the holo-tv.

"It's embarrassing to watch you watching me on tv," Lisa said.

"Don't be silly. We watch it whenever you're on," her grandfather said. "We're so proud of you. Always."

"It's amazing how you have become a blossom of the lime-light, Lisa," her grandmother said. "It's not something I would ever have imagined would suit you, but it absolutely does!"

"Yeah," Lisa said, "it seemed really uncomfortable at first, but it also felt good. When I would get done with an interview, it felt good, even though I was nervous. It was weird. But now I love it. It's exciting."

Lisa and her grandparents moved to the dining room and set the table for dinner. Her grandparents' dining room had a big, wrap-around window that looked out on the dazzling lights of the city. Being there felt like being in the driver's seat of the world. And that was also how Lisa felt lately: important and in the center of things. She felt significant and like she was doing valuable work, essential work. She felt righteous and felt like the world had meaning; her life, her story, made sense. She wondered for a brief second if Samson had felt this way, and didn't know, and moved on to other thoughts.

Her grandmother carried in a steaming, candied baked ham on a yellow ceramic platter and placed it at the center of their table. Lisa and her grandparents stood at their chairs and said, "Let us be grateful," in unison before sitting down to eat.

"Where do you think this struggle for natural born rights is moving to, Lisa?" her grandfather asked during dinner.

"Well– What do you mean?"

"What do think is going to happen?"

"Oh. I can't say what's going to happen, but I can hope. I don't think anyone knows what will happen, but that's why it's important to do what we can."

"So you aren't worried about the consequences of this movement?"

"I think what I'm doing is the right thing to do."

Her grandfather rarely challenged her in a direct way like this, and Lisa felt flustered. She had often listened to her grandparents talk, and enjoyed their debates, but they never hectored her or forced her to participate. Now things were different. She was being questioned directly at home, critically and about her personal ideas. Pat responses that she might have given a broadcaster seemed inadequate and inappropriate.

"I think your grandfather is trying to find out if you believe that this naturals movement is going to succeed," Lisa's grandmother said.

"I know. But how can I know if it will succeed? I'm only one person and I do what I can for what I believe in. Samson won the Solar Regatta, so anything is possible."

"But do the people at NBRA believe that Bloodworth's is going to lose the trade war?" her grandfather asked.

"I can't say for certain, but they seem to think so. If you add up the natural born population and the genetic population that is sympathetic to them, it is a lot larger than the genetic population that is against the natural born."

"Do they have an idea about what will happen if Bloodworth's lose?"

"What do you mean?"

"Billions of people's livelihood and wellbeing are tied to Bloodworth's Corporation, and it has tentacles interwoven into the heartstrings of nearly every political organization in the Solar System. Rothschild's is the same, of course. These mega-corps cannot fail without massive social and political upheaval. It has been theorized for more than a century that no mega-corp can fail without actual war. And that would mean the slaughter of millions, at a minimum!"

"Well, a lot of people in the naturals communities are preparing to fight, if they have to," Lisa said. "But at the NBRA we are all really hopeful that it won't ever be necessary. I mean, the NBRA is not getting ready for war, we are working for a political solution. Bloodworth's doesn't have to be destroyed, that's not even a goal of ours, they just have to be motivated to change their position. If some of their workers lose their jobs, they can get new jobs with other companies. The demand that created the jobs in the first place will still be there."

"Phillipe Bloodworth will never compromise on this," her grandfather said. "And neither will Rothschild's. And the natural born *can't* compromise, because for them this is literally an existential battle. All forces of history and personality have aligned themselves against compromise. This day was always foreseen. It is a fight to the death."

Her grandfather's eyes were bright and he was breathing quickly, which was common when he discussed things. He glanced around at the table of food and reached out as if to take something, then stared distantly as more ideas churned through his head, and folded his hands back in his lap.

"I hope that your grandfather is being over-dramatic," her grandmother said, "but this is a dangerous moment in history."

Lisa sat straighter in her chair and served herself some more candied ham. It was bright red and crumbly. She mixed it around in a puddle of gravy that was already on her plate.

"The NBRA is pushing for a political solution," she said. "And that's what I believe in, too. Nobody is going to go to war over a boycott when we live in a really prosperous Solar System. There's no reason for people to fight and die in a war, that would be insane. A lot of scholars have said that in a Solar System like we have now, with so much prosperity, that it wouldn't even be possible to have a war."

"Lisa, your grandmother and I are so proud of you and what you are doing," her grandfather said. "We are in support of you 100%. But you are becoming a figurehead on one side in a dangerous conflict. You have to be aware of the dangers so that you can protect yourself."

C H A P T E R ¹³

D AVID ISCHEWITZ WAS AN AWKWARD man with old style red
hair and very bright eyes. His skin was a creamy, butter
color that had never been in vogue. He was a senior research
associate for Bloodworth's Corporation and had been directing
the development of a special virus product for the past decade.
Only a few people in his lab, including himself, understood
the full scope and nature of the project, and only a handful
of people outside of the lab did. Ischewitz' wife did not know
what he did, although she would have approved of it. The
other scientists in the facility that contained the lab, and their
scientific colleagues throughout the Solar System, his professors
and friends for instance, had no knowledge of his research
either, so that his professional reputation and credibility had
been long in decline. This did not concern him, as his project
was a work of principle, a calling. In his own lab he was king,
and the people privileged to know what he did either feared
or admired him. His project was near to completion.

A tall, perfect man burst into the lab's office as David was
combing through a series of thousands of data graphs.

"He's coming!" the man said frantically and began to
straighten up the office equipment in the lab.

David rubbed his eyes. The man was named Gregory Epitokales. He was the company CEO and David's immediate
superior. He looked at David expectantly.

"It's Phillipe Bloodworth, he's coming!"

"Ok," David said. "What are you so worried about?"

"What am I wo– It's Phillipe Bloodworth!"

"We run the best lab in the Solar System, so whether it's
Phillipe Bloodworth or Baron de Rothschild himself come
back from the dead we can hold our heads high."

"Are you mad?"

Phillipe Bloodworth walked into the room accompanied by the executive in charge of all Bloodworth's health and pharmaceuticals business, Abujani Chan, who was Gregory Epitokales' boss and friend. Bloodworth was dressed casually in cream colored slacks and a pin-striped shirt with polka-dotted cuffs and collar and mother-of-pearl buttons, the shirt-sleeves partly rolled up.

"Hello, hello," Bloodworth said.

"H-hello sir!" Gregory said and bent forward obeisantly.

"Hello Mr. Bloodworth," David Ischewitz said with a wave and a nod. "Mr. Chan."

"Let us show you around the lab, sir," Gregory said. "We run the best lab in the Solar System. All your investment here is now coming to fruition and we are ready to change the face of the world."

"That's what I like to hear," Bloodworth said, "because I need you to be ready."

"What do you mean we're ready?" David asked Gregory.

"Your work, David. The lab's project. It works!"

"David's work is amazing," Abujani Chan said. "The human testing phase has been 100% successful."

"Good, good," Bloodworth said, taking note of David's troubled face.

The two executives gave Bloodworth a fawning tour of the lab, with David in tow. They kept David quiet most of the time, but asked him occasionally to explain technical details or to answer specific questions that Bloodworth had. Bloodworth became more and more excited as the tour progressed, while David became more and more disconcerted. Something had been happening over his head. Eventually, they worked their way back to the main office where they started.

"I'm so proud of you boys," Bloodworth said. "When I first heard about this project it sounded like a dream, but now it has become a reality. I've been working closely with Juan Porovic to prepare delivery systems and vehicles. Everything compartmentalized. We have culturing and propagation facilities completely built and waiting as of a month ago. Mass production will begin immediately, and we expect a broad deployment of the virus as soon as possible. Possibly within days."

"Deployment of the virus?" David said. "What are you talking about?"

"We've always planned to deploy the virus as soon as it was ready. You want it to be deployed, don't you?"

"You have to understand, Mr. Bloodworth," Gregory said, "my colleague doesn't mean to be rude. He's just a particularly cautious person and unaccustomed to moving from lab to production this quickly."

"Of course I want the virus to be deployed," David said. "I've spent ten years of my life designing it for a reason. But it's not finished. It's not ready. If someone told you that then they were misleading you."

"What's he talking about, Abu?" Bloodworth snapped.

"It's absolutely ready. David is a good engineer, but he's a little bit excitable. Every test has been a complete success."

David Ischewitz glared at Abu with angry confusion.

"We're absolutely ready," Gregory echoed. "Don't mind David, he's an eccentric but has played an important role in this project. It's hard for him to let it go."

"We have to deploy now," Bloodworth said. "Later might be too late."

"Mr. Bloodworth," David cut in, "can I speak to you completely frankly?"

"Please do."

"You're causing problems, David," Gregory said through a stiff grin.

"No, let him talk," Bloodworth said.

"You'd have to be crazy to deploy that virus now," David said.

"I don't like to be called crazy."

"It has only been tested on seven human subjects. And that has been in the last month. We haven't been able to observe long term effects at all, and it is a statistical sample of seven. Seven! They might not be representative, they might be outliers. I don't know what my boss or his boss have been telling you, but don't be a fool. If the virus did something unexpected the consequences could be catastrophic."

"In what discipline is your PhD?" Bloodworth asked with a raised eyebrow.

"He doesn't have a PhD," Gregory said, while trying to push David out of the room. "He's the junior scientist on this project. *We* both have PhDs in virology."

"I may not have a PhD," David said, "but this is my lab! If you deploy that virus now you could kill billions of people!"

Abujani Chan and Bloodworth walked out of the office and proceeded down the quiet, empty hallway to the building's entrance. Bloodworth's face was thoughtful and dissatisfied.

"Some people," Abujani said, stopping and turning to face him, "are afraid of the future. They like a big idea in theory, but to bring about the reality of it terrifies them."

"We have to move forward," Bloodworth said. "You said it's solid, so it's solid. Right? The future doesn't wait. Change is change for everyone."

"It's solid, sir."

"What is he afraid of, that everyone might die?"

"He thinks it might be worse than we thought, or even not as bad."

Bloodworth grinned and something about it made Abujani's stomach clench.

"If everyone might die, then it might kill you and Gregory," he said.

"I wouldn't approve it if I had any doubts."

Bloodworth grinned bigger and seemed to be imagining some possible future.

"Imagine if it was really bad," he said.

"Sir, we know what it is, we know what it does, we've mapped the mechanisms and effects down to each individual nucleotide of viral DNA. We've run extensive simulations and tested it both in vitro and in vivo, without a single surprise or even the slightest variance from prediction and expectation. There are no 'ifs' left, that's why Gregory and I have both given the green light. There will be no surprises."

Bloodworth's smile softened.

"Human beings fear change," he said, "almost as much as they need it. That's one of the reasons I always advocate for diminished fear thresholds. Fear keeps us from being everything that we could be."

On Pluto, a woman named Rhea flexed her muscles against the controls of a harvester machine that was extracting ore. Robots couldn't do the extracting here, where the environment was complex and hazardous. Sensors often failed. Ice or water-ice avalanches could be triggered by a myriad of things. So people did the work, which was brutal, and lived hard and were paid well.

Nobody really lived on Pluto to live there. It was a horrible place. You were there to work and you left when you could. Most of the people on Pluto were men. Rhea, who was a natural born woman and not particularly attractive, thus still received more than a normal share of male attention. Which almost half the time she didn't mind.

The controls on the machines were robust and uncivilized.

The control wands in her hands resisted every twist and turn. She was drenched in sweat, under her heavy insulated clothes, and covered in grease. Shrieking steam whistles signaled a change of shifts, and Rhea backed her harvester out and turned it around gratefully. The harvester was 90% full. That was well above average and meant more money in her paycheck for this day's work. Rhea usually managed to be well above average, and felt like she had to be. If she was only average, being a rare woman among many men, everyone would interpret it as crap.

"Hey Sunshine," a male voice called out to her as she climbed down out of her rig.

"Hey yourself."

"You going to the Ice Cooler tonight?"

"I haven't decided yet!"

The rumble of churning rock and machinery drowned out the sound all around and made conversation nearly impossible, which Rhea also didn't mind. The men she spoke to weren't really friends, mostly, although occasionally one of them might be a lover. Pluto was a lonely place. Her real friends here weren't the other hard laborers, but the support staff. The people who worked in the Ice Cooler, the people who worked in the Canteen. She didn't know why she connected more with these people than the ones who did the same work she did. Probably it was just coincidence.

Rhea went into the women's locker room, which was sized for only a handful of women, while the male locker room was sized for dozens. She stripped off her clothes methodically and dialed one of the shower faucets up to a steaming heat. There was almost never another woman in the locker room, and Rhea enjoyed the privacy. When there was another woman, it was Billie, who also worked a harvester, but usually had different shifts. Billie and Rhea were friendly with each other, but weren't friends.

You would think we'd have a lot in common, Rhea thought, as she scoured her skin with a washcloth before stepping into the shower. You would think that, but we have hardly anything in common. All we can talk about is work, but we both do our job and try to forget about it. Who wants to talk about work?

She stepped into the steaming spray of water and it scalded her cold skin, heat penetrating into her bones – it felt magnificent. They always had hot showers here. Really hot showers. It was one of the things that made life here livable.

Rhea heard the door of the locker room open and a few seconds later Billie walked in, stripping off her clothes as she walked through the room and throwing them carelessly on one of the two small benches in front of the lockers.

"Hi Rhea," Billie said, and smiled.

"Hi Billie. Steam feels good. Shift was long. You starting or finishing?"

"I wouldn't take a shower to start," Billie said, and laughed.

Rhea couldn't help glancing at Billie's perfect naked body. Engineered women were all so beautiful. It made her want to shrink into a shell.

"Your eyes, Rhea," Billie said. "Always wandering. Don't tell me you want a piece of me."

She turned on the shower head next to Rhea and stepped into the water herself, looking Rhea's naked body up and down unabashedly as they stood in the steamy water together.

"It's not that," Rhea said. "You're just so beautiful. I'm just jealous a little bit."

"I swapped shifts with Simon Clee," Billie said. "Harvesting over in Gamma Sector. Do you know Simon? He wanted a piece of me last night, and we had some fun, but he wasn't very good. I wouldn't recommend it."

"He wouldn't look at me. He's engineered."

"Of course he would look at you. There aren't a lot of

women here. You're flesh and blood, not like those holo-screens. You can have what you want, just like me."

They showered in silence for a while, and Rhea felt self-conscious as she lathered her body up with soap. Self-conscious was an emotion that Billie seemed completely aloof from.

"Why do you work here?" Rhea asked abruptly, finishing quickly and rushing for a towel. "On Pluto. Why are you here?"

Billie rubbed soapy, steamy lather under her arms, around her breasts, and down her sides.

"The money is good," she said. "I like the men. I like the attention, being one of the only women here. I like being the only engineered woman here. Did you want an honest answer? I don't want to live a deep life. I like to be special here, get attention, play around, have drama, fuck like crazy, work hard, just live a superficial life, without thinking. I don't want to think too much. I work here for three months, and fly across the Solar System for three months, and spend three months at the Solarium buying toy boys and pretending to be rich. Then three months back, and the toy boys here who I don't even have to pay for. I'm special here, you know what I mean? Is that more info than you wanted?"

"You must be special to be a woman and do what we do," Rhea said. "You must be special. Not only here, just special."

"Now I'm going to start again with thinking you want a piece of me. Why are you here, Rhea?"

Rhea had her clothes on now and was applying cosmetics to her face in front of the mirror, with a towel still wrapped around her damp hair.

"I don't know any other way to earn good money," Rhea said. "I don't know anything else to do. I'm kind of proud of myself here, you know? Working a hard job, crushing ore with the best of them. I hate all the attention from the men most of the time, but the other part of the time I crave it. As long as you're not around I'm special. When you're around I'm nobody."

"That's not true."

"Maybe it's because there aren't any other genetically engineered women out here that I like it. Not other than you. You know? I have pride. It hurts to be inferior."

"You're deeper than me, Rhea," Billie said. "And I've got the smart gene package. I think you're great, so don't worry about it."

"You sure take long showers," Rhea said, when Billie didn't appear remotely close to finishing under the tap.

"You bet I do," Billie said, and smiled. "That's exactly the kind of person I am."

EARLY THE NEXT MORNING, PHILLIPE Bloodworth, Abujani Chan, and Juan Porovic briefed Camilla Rosenberg via highly encrypted holo-conference on the details of Plan B.

"Everyone, therefore," Abujani was saying, "without these advanced immunomodifiers, which have been included in all gene weaving packages for the past 95 years and which only occur in humans created through gene weaving, will be rendered permanently sterile. To put it more simply, all natural born people will be made sterile. Anyone who is a product of gene weaving will be unaffected by the virus. A perfect solution.

"And the virus propagates rapidly. Based on our projected zones of deployment throughout the Solar System, 99% of the human population will have been infected within the first three days."

"You aren't planning to just release the virus everywhere, willy-nilly, are you?" Camilla asked.

"We will release it surreptitiously. No one will ever be able to determine where it came from."

"No, no that's all wrong," Camilla said. "You're not thinking clearly. You're lucky you brought me back, Phillipe."

"I know we are, Camilla," Bloodworth said, "so tell us what you think we should do."

"The virus has to be blamed *on* somebody," Camilla said. "No one is going to come to the conclusion that it just happened naturally. You can either let people reach their own conclusions, which likely means they will be blaming you, or you can choose who they are going to blame."

"Keep talking," Bloodworth said.

"Obviously, you need a patsy. And this is what is actually so beautiful about your plan, that you boys aren't even seeing: you can get a group of naturals to unwittingly release the virus and be blamed for creating it. Now they not only are devastated by the virus, but they are not allowed to become victims. They are only victims of their own stupidity, which gathers no sympathy. They become their own worst enemies to fight with amongst themselves. And seeing their dangerous incompetence will make it seem that what is happening to them, the sterility, is actually a good thing."

"Yes," Phillipe said, "I like that. Well, it's true, isn't it. The sterility is actually a good thing for the future of humanity. That's good. But saying it and doing it are two different things. Who exactly, for example, would we blame it on?"

"That's easy," Camilla said, "the Magdalena cult. They experiment with weird technologies and weaponizations. Suppose they unleashed a virus to eliminate natural born unbelievers, but unwittingly infected themselves too. Or make it better, suppose they were trying to develop viruses that would only infect gene woven individuals, but they accidentally released a virus that does the opposite. Suppose they were studying the virus effect differentiation between natural born and genetically engineered humans, and also trying to weaponize viruses, and they made a big mistake."

"Yes," Bloodworth said, "yes, this is what we will do."

"And the whole Solar System can hate them instead of us. We can even help clean up the mess after it's done, and earn credit as humanitarians."

"Yes," Bloodworth said again, eyes twinkling and rubbing his hands. "Yes, yes."

C   H   A   P   T   E   R ¹⁴

SAMSON SAT ON THE BANKS of the pond in the oasis, sweating. He had gathered together an assortment of very dry sticks and was rubbing two of them vigorously against each other, working under the intense light from the sky to maximize the ambient heat. This was how you built a fire – maybe? Like most things that he knew, Samson had a vague conception of building a fire but didn't know why. It was knowledge without context. He didn't know how he even knew what a fire was, he couldn't remember having seen one. But he did know what it was, he could envision a fire. He could imagine how a fire might spread from bush to bush and tree to tree – he could imagine that it would burn him to touch it, that it was dangerous.

He rubbed and rubbed the sticks together, until they were rubbed flat against each other and a thin layer of grey wood dust lay on the ground. The sticks were hot to touch. His muscles and neck and back ached from the work. Only a little bit more. He rubbed the sticks furiously. Only a little bit more. His arms, muscles burning, slowed down of their own accord. He shifted to focus the workload onto different sets of muscles and redoubled his efforts. Only a little bit more and the sticks might flame up, he might be close, only a little more, just a little more, he might be close, it might only take a little bit more effort. He rubbed the sticks together until he could do so no longer, until he could sit up no longer, until he could no longer lift his arms. The sticks were hot to touch, but there was no flame. There wasn't even any smoke. What was smoke? He lay on his back and stared up at the blue sky.

The sticks were dry, they were the type of thing that would burn easily. Rubbing them together would create heat, and they were strong enough to rub together for a long time. If he could rub them together for long enough, if he could raise the heat on the wood high enough, it should start a flame. Without an existing source of flame to draw from, he couldn't think of any other way to acquire it, although he had thought about the problem for a long time. He didn't even know that rubbing the sticks together would work, but it seemed like it should. If he could rub until the sticks got hot enough.

After rest, he tried rubbing the sticks together again. Later, after that, he chose sticks of a different kind of wood and did the same thing with them. His hands eventually worked into blisters and tore, and when that happened he had to wait for them to heal, which didn't take a very long time but made him impatient. It was always the same result, heat but no flame.

Samson searched for different kinds of wood while his hands healed. He found one more branch in the desert from a tree that seemed different from the rest, after a long search. It gave him the idea to rub different varieties of wood against each other. When his hands were healed and his arms felt fresh he went back to rubbing the sticks again.

This time he chose two sticks from different trees to rub together. Perhaps the differential in textures would create more friction and result in more heat. He sat on his knees, bracing one stick between himself and the ground with his thighs, and rubbing the other stick against it vigorously, in a technique he had slowly begun to develop. He rubbed the sticks together sharply and frenetically, as if he were a robot specifically designed for the purpose. When the two sticks grew hot they began to shed off dark powder this time, almost black, as if the flame could come at any second. He rubbed and rubbed, raising a dry 'shisha-shisha-shisha' sound through the clearing. His fingers pinched where he held the sticks, his neck and back contorted with stiffness and pain, his knees and ankles protested under the static pressure of his weight. There was more dark powder, turning to black, and both of the sticks, where they touched each other, turned dark. A little bit more. He rubbed the sticks together until he could no longer move his arms, then fell back again onto the soft earth on the banks of the oasis. More promise, but the same result, heat but no flame.

Feeling that he had gotten close, Samson attempted the exact same technique again, three times in a row, with rests in between. It brought him no closer to his goal. Next he tried different combinations of wood to see which ones might work best. He went through them systematically, taking breaks when needed, searching for new materials or varieties of wood when his hands became too blistered to hold the sticks. Nothing worked better than what he had already found, most things worked worse.

At an impasse, he flew up into the sky and looked at the temple again in the distance. He flew close enough to draw the hummingbird again, or a hummingbird, but kept the oasis also in sight. He spun maneuvers to dodge the hummingbird's attacks, enjoying it as a game at times, but often more complacently, and always casting his gaze forlornly at the temple. She was there, the woman, whoever the woman was. The woman that mattered was there, or the path to her was there. The only path forward was there, the only path ahead for him, the only path to where he needed to go. He was still nowhere he realized. He was still surrounded by endless nothing. Even though the nothing contained things, it was not a thing. It was an emptiness. It was an emptiness that he was trying to escape from. The thought occurred to him that he had been trying to create fire for days, and he wondered why he had thought it, because when he thought about it some more he had to admit to himself that he didn't know what 'days' were.

Later, he flew back down to the oasis and tried again. He

had noticed that the wood at the ends of the sticks was harder than the wood when you felt it from certain sides. This time he rubbed the end of one of the sticks against the soft side of another one, which he had already flattened before with friction. He rubbed the end of the first stick against the side of the second stick furiously and soon black dust formed. It smelled like fire, somehow. A wisp of smoke floated up from between the sticks. Samson caught his breath and rubbed the sticks together harder, and faster. More wisps of smoke rose up. He must be very close to creating flame. He rubbed and rubbed, he must be close, only a little bit more! Eventually, the wisps of smoke stopped coming and he was forced to rest his arms from fatigue. He still had no flame. He tried the same exact technique several times, believing that he was very close, with rests between each effort. But he did not create flame.

He drank from the pond of the oasis, squeezing his fingers into the mud on its bank, then crawled under the shade of a palm tree to lay down. On his back, frustrated, he closed his eyes and let his mind wander, thinking wordless, unformed thoughts. A pale man raced him, sprinting across the desert. His friend died. Someone laughed. The woman he loved had disappeared. He couldn't find her. His brother and his brother's wife played with their children and invited him to join them, although he couldn't move. He was in a house in space, among the stars, flying from one planet to another, with his friend who had died. Space was beautiful. He was bleeding in space, floating, twisting and turning, his blood drifting away in bubbles. A synthcat licked his wounds. On the synthcat's neck was a red collar, with a locket, and inside the locket was a photograph of a woman. She was calling to him. Then the synthcat was gone and the woman was with him, naked, twisting and turning with him in space, between the stars, licking his wounds. She was beautiful. As he tried to look at her, to crystallize the image of her in his mind, bright hot light from the sky above the oasis glared into his eyes. The shade of the trees had shifted, as it did, although the light in the sky had no particular source. His arms felt strong again.

Samson had noticed, in his most recent efforts to make fire, that as the point of the stick whose end he was using rubbed itself into a sort of 'V' shape, the friction of the two sticks worked better and he got more smoke. And it worked even better, and he seemed to get even more smoke, when the 'V' end rubbed out a groove in the flattened side of the stick he was rubbing with it. There seemed to be a 'sweet spot' when the 'V' end and the groove fit together in just the right way. The sweet spot never lasted for very long, though, before the 'V' tip became flattened from the friction or the groove became rubbed too wide. It occurred to him that he needed to create the perfect conditions from the start – to somehow cut or grind a 'V' at the end of one stick and a groove into the side of the other that were exactly the right shape, and while the wood was fresh and not ashy yet. Fresh wood generated the most friction and the fastest heat.

He began searching for rocks. He searched around the oasis and into the desert for a sharp rock that could cut and shape the wood. He smashed rocks together to break off pieces and flakes, looking for something that would break wide, so that he could hold it in his hand, and with a thin, jagged edge that could cut into the wood. He searched for some time and found a type of rocks that shattered sharp. He broke them and broke them until he acquired the perfect shape. Then he took this stone blade back to the oasis and went to work shaping two fire-making sticks. He at least hoped they would be fire-making.

This time, after shaping the sticks carefully, Samson was able to produce a large amount of ash and possibly a brief flame. He thought that he had seen a flicker of flame. He was excited, and cut the sticks down to fresh wood, and tried again. And again. His sticks wore out, so that he had to go into the desert to search for more. He found new sticks, and returned, and shaped them with his stone blade. He tried to make fire again, and rested, and again. And created a flame! A tiny finger of flame!

He caught his breath and held the burning stick up in front of him, afraid to even breathe on it. He held the other stick in the flame and tried to spread the fire. The flame blinked out. He tried again several times, but could not get the flame to keep or spread. He rested and thought about what to do.

He walked around the desert collecting dry leaves and other dusty, crumbly things that seemed as if they would be very easy to burn but were too soft to rub together. He created a little, soft pile of these desert bits and scraps, a nest to hold the flame. Then, after a few tries, he created a tiny flame again, and set it gently onto the nest, and the nest burst up in a rush of heat and red and orange. He balanced sticks over the nest in the heat of the flame, and the sticks began to burn, and then he piled more sticks on the burning sticks, and those sticks burned too, until the flame was large. And he had fire. He could *make* fire. Samson grinned through smoky veins of sweat that were streaming down his face.

SOMEWHERE IN SPACE BETWEEN EARTH and Venus, Killian Gideon sat watching the stars from the cockpit of his space yacht. Space was lonely, but it was also freedom. The stars blinked at him in their endless twinkle of unfathomable emptiness. Space could feel so overwhelming when you were alone. He smiled at the thought. As if anything could overwhelm him. People said that the stars were beautiful, and he understood what they meant. But the stars weren't beautiful. They were just there. Just big explosions stretched out in a vast, endless vacuum. Like tiny pebbles on the beach. They didn't mean anything.

His eyes were a vivid shade of violet that was rarely seen. His skin was perfectly white, hairless, and where it wasn't scarred it glowed with raw vitality. He rubbed at the extensive scarring on his neck and face, and stretched his hands and wrists. The Solar Regatta had torn him up, that was for sure. He should have won, but instead it was Samson Ford who won, who was dead. Which of them was better for it? Surely Samson. Killian would have traded places with him in a second. He rubbed the muscles in his forearms, which were now always tight. Both of their racing careers were over, but Samson had ended his with a win. Well good for him.

Killian felt lonely. He had done his best and didn't have any regrets, it was only luck that allowed Samson Ford to win the race and him to lose. He often felt lonely now, without racing. It hadn't even been that long, but his career was over. Over. That seemed impossible, but his body would never be able to race at a high level again. The twitch reflexes weren't there now, the nerves had been damaged. One day he had been the best and the next day he had been an old man, retired. Although he wasn't old. He had to find a new direction in life, but didn't have any plan for after racing.

So here he was. He should have brought a girlfriend with him. He thought it would be a nice change of pace to relax and cruise through space out here alone. It was boring and lonely. The girls didn't care about his scarred up skin. They didn't care that he was retired, not yet. He was still rich and famous. He was still Killian Gideon. Maybe he would get a job doing commentary for one of the big racing networks now. Bloodworth's, especially, was chasing him. Everyone knew that his racing career was over. He had announced it right away, as soon as he knew. Of course, the girls were stupid, most of them were still secretly hoping he would make a comeback.

He looked out at the stars. The universe was so empty, not full of life. Watching it alone, without a purpose, without a race, was painful. He turned back on some of the communications channels that he had cut at the start of this trip, to make it peaceful. Maybe someone would call him. If they didn't, he'd call someone. Maybe one of his girlfriends. Even though most of them were so stupid and pathetic, he needed to talk to people.

IT WAS EASIER FOR SAMSON to learn to make a torch than it had been to make fire itself. He knew that he needed some way to transport the fire, to carry it. He first used brute strength and his stone blade to tear big greenwood sticks off some of the desert bushes. The greenwood sticks burned slowly, but did not burn well. While cutting sticks off of bushes he found that he could cut open the bulbous stem at the base of certain bushes and collect a sticky resin from inside of it that burned well. He dipped the tips of his sticks in the resin and lit them on fire, but the torches created this way burned out very quickly. To compensate for the quickness of the resin itself burning out, he tried wrapping the tips of the torches in big, green leaves harvested from the oasis and coated in resin (which also acted as a makeshift glue), and these burned strongly for a much longer time.

Samson lit a particularly nice, large torch that he had made in this way and flew toward the temple as quickly as he could fly without putting the fire out. A hummingbird came and began assaulting him as before, then more of them, then larger birds, exactly as had happened to him the first time he approached the temple. The fire from the torch did not keep the birds away as he had expected. Nevertheless, he tried to fight through the birds to the temple, but his body was soon torn up by relentless claws and beaks and his torch snuffed out by the whirling chaos, and as before he was forced to flee.

He flew back to the oasis, full of frustration and anger. He lay in the shade by the water for a long time, and his body healed. His mouth tasted like iron, and he wondered why he tasted, what the point of taste was, and he wondered why he had not noticed it or thought about it before. Water tasted like water, but he had not known that he needed to drink it until he had done so. When he had done so the water had been good. There must be other things like that, things that would only make sense after he did them. His mouth tasted like iron, but he couldn't think precisely of what iron was. This world of his was mysterious and incomprehensible, he realized, but the realization was only in passing and did not perturb him.

The shepherd came to the oasis with his sheep again while Samson was lying there, and Samson asked the shepherd why the fire did not keep the birds away.

"You must go to the temple when it is dark," the shepherd said.

Samson thought about this, and a word popped into his mind – 'night'. He didn't know what the word meant, but felt that it was connected to darkness. He did not understand how the world could become dark, how the light that filled the whole sky and seemed to come from everywhere could disappear.

"But when will night come?" he asked the shepherd, testing the word.

"Night will come when you want it to come," the shepherd said.

CHAPTER 15

T HEO FORD SAT IN ON a meeting of the war council of the Church of the Magdalena Revelation, where senior military officers were presenting a strategic overview of the military powers of Magdalena itself and of other significant forces within the Solar System. A young general led the presentation.

"Nuclear weapons are still a major concern, although they have been less thought about and feared during the past 125 years. As many of you will know, 125 years ago Jackson Botvinnik invented the counter-chain reaction. We ourselves, and all the major military forces in the Solar System, maintain a stockpile of nuclear payloads, even though their utility in war is now questionable. A single advanced nuclear warhead would completely obliterate an area with a radius of 10 miles were it not counteracted by a counter-chain device. The counter-reaction is automatic, and one counter-reaction device can effectively cover an area with a radius of 1,000 miles or more. As some of you may have learned in advanced physics, the counter-reaction device takes advantage of quantum time pairing phenomena, so that it nullifies the nuclear reaction near instantaneously, before any significant amount of energy – that is, an explosion – is released. Some physicists have actually argued that because of a space-time paradox the counter-reaction actually occurs *before* the nuclear event that it is reacting to. But there is always the fear of a malfunction in the counter-reaction device, even though all robust modern systems, like Magdalena's, are filled with overlapping layers of redundancy. And there is also always the fear that a way will be found, perhaps through some new technological or scientific breakthrough, to defeat the counter-reaction defenses.

"To sum up: nuclear arsenals are maintained, but are unlikely to have much utility during a war."

The men around the conference table shifted in their seats as the young general loaded up media for his next subject. Theo watched the other men's faces, which were lined with fatigue and worry. None of the men looked at him, and they hardly looked at each other. It was as if each man held inside of him some secret or special burden that was already too much for him to bear. The feeling in the room frightened Theo.

"Most people," the young general continued, pulling up a new set of charts and images on the holo-projector, "both in Magdalena and on the outside, misunderstand the nature of military power in the Solar System, so this is important to cover. The major powers in the Solar System are not the governmental or planetary body organizations. Let me repeat that, because people often find it a difficult point to accept: the major military powers in the Solar System are not the government or planetary body organizations. The major military powers in the Solar System are the major corporations: Nike, Rothschild's, Bloodworth's, Google, Tintorio, and Samsung, specifically. Between them, these six corporations control nearly all of the military forces in the rest of the Solar System, and the governments and planetary bodies control very little.

"Accept that this is true for a moment, because it is, and I will explain how it came to be that way. Major corporations control the money and capital resources in the rest of the Solar System. Natural resources, currency interest and rates, information and data transfer, travel services, manufacturing, are all completely controlled by corporate powers. Beginning in the 21st Century, public services that had been exclusive to governments, such as military services, were gradually privatized to contractors. These contractors were then gradually conglomerated, until the major corporations controlled virtually all of them. In the rest of the Solar System, everything is this way. The corporations control everything and the governments function as servants of the corporations. As such, governmental posts still can hold a great deal of power, but that is because the government positions are de facto executive posts within the major corporations, not because the governments continue to wield power.

"Getting back to the subject of military power in particular, military contractors are theoretically under the orders and command of government executive officers and political heads, but the mega-corps exercise de facto control over them too."

"What about what happened to Apple?" Theo asked from the back of the room.

The young general and many of the men around the council table seemed surprised at the interruption. Several of the older men cleared their throats and touched the crosses that hung from their necks through their shirts.

"Yes, well, some people used to think that Apple was a special case where the governments of Earth and Venus exercised their authority over the mega-corps," the young general said, "but the newer thinking about that is that other mega-corps were exercising control over the governments of Earth and Venus. Apple lost in the trade war and thereby lost their power within the governments, and the other mega-corps then used the governments to help dismantle and cannibalize Apple."

"It was terrible business for all the corporations," Theo said. "There was a huge depression."

"Not as much of a depression as the masses were lead to believe. A lot of what happened during and after the wars with Apple has been popularly misconstrued. I'll direct you to some books, after the presentation, Mr. Ford, where you can read more about it in detail."

Theo didn't ask any more questions during the presentation, although he often thought of them. He felt that the general did not know what he was talking about.

"Getting back to our presentation," the general continued, "and looking at the current trade war between Rothschild's and Bloodworth's, Stephanie de Rothschild and Phillipe Bloodworth both control substantial government military powers, in addition to the significant private armies that they both, and all of the mega-corps, semi-secretly employ.

"As far as military technologies go, the corporations keep the best of it for themselves. This makes it difficult to know what their true capabilities are, as their most advanced weapons systems and technology are never patented or made public. We have some knowledge through espionage and other efforts, but the extent of capabilities of the private corporate armies is largely opaque. Rothschild, for example, the artificial planet that is the corporation's home, has been rumored to be a planetary battleship, actually a weapon system, capable of transporting billions of people while attacking or defending itself."

"Is that true?" a man with a bushy white beard near the front of the table asked.

"We don't actually know whether or not that is true, but there is no question Rothschild is equipped with substantial military capabilities. It is the base for at least four pinnacle class battleships, for example, each with a complement of 10,000 soldiers..."

Alexander Grumiaux sat and watched the floor of the United Earth Congressional Assembly from a private balcony in the gallery. He had distant eyes that seemed to notice little, but saw everything. Pages, and officials, and custodians on the floor buzzed about in every direction, practicing, preparing, fixing what needed to be fixed. The Assembly only met twice a year, everything had to be put into perfect order to prepare. It was an honor for the people on the floor to be there. When the Assembly actually met, only delegates were allowed on the floor. Of course, many of the votes and deals to be struck were worked out in the weeks and months beforehand. That was a lot of what was happening now. As they moved back and forth, carrying messages, repairing furniture and fixtures, testing the different systems – the sound, the computers, the microphones, the cameras – every single person on the floor occasionally looked up at Alexander. Although he had given up his seat the previous term and was currently a member of the public, he was still the most politically influential person on Earth. That made him the most powerful person in the Solar System, most would say.

He squeezed the small waist of his latest girlfriend, who sat next to him. She was young, intelligent, and had the kind of airy, profoundly naïve mind that allowed her do anything he wanted her to do and believe it was good without hesitation. Her skin and hair were gentle violet hues and she wore tight fitting, layered, beautifully styled clothes. He liked violet girls. His girlfriends and whores were often violet hued. It was a treat for her to be here with him, to visit the Assembly which she had only seen on tv, and she conducted herself very timidly for fear of doing anything wrong.

Alexander knew that he really wasn't the most powerful person in the Solar System, but he wasn't far down the list. The corporate barons, who owned everything, were more powerful than any politician. But the corporate barons still needed the power that the politicians had. And he was the king of that. He would also be a delegate again starting in the next session, which was less than a month away. He loved the Assembly. Leaving it had been a mistake.

Down on the floor, a young page looked up at the famous, powerful man who had been an influential delegate on Earth for eighty years. Alexander Grumiaux didn't look a day over

106

forty and didn't look at all diminished from how he had looked in the videos from when he started. His old fashioned gold and copper skin was surprisingly wrinkle free. Nobody knew what Grumiaux's secret to youth and health was, and it had been decades since anybody asked. Those questions weren't welcome. There were many dark rumors about the man, and among the pages it was received wisdom that Grumiaux held blackmail influence over half the delegates in the Assembly. He could ruin your life, or he could have you killed by someone whose life he could ruin. He was a close ally of Phillipe Bloodworth, with tentacles in everything, like an octopus. It was said that he was one of the men who helped Bloodworth achieve his success. He had been an outspoken critic of the natural born since before Phillipe Bloodworth was born and had taken an active role in the current war, denouncing Rothschild's and drafting legislation against them. Grumiaux's eyes met the page's and the young man shivered. He was glad that Grumiaux liked women. It wouldn't even occur to the young man to be jealous of Grumiaux's gorgeous young girlfriend, with her bright smile and glittering violet eyes of exceptional hue. That would be like lusting after the bride of a mythological devil – too dangerous to be contemplated, even in secret.

SAMSON LAY ON HIS BACK beside piles of dry wood, with the black remains of a fire a few yards off. He stared up at the bright, endless sky. The world must become dark, it must become night, although he could not grasp with his mind exactly what night was. It seemed impossible.

The woman appeared to him suddenly, more clearly than before. He could see her, and more than that he could feel her, as if she were inside his mind. The blue of the sky and the desert around him seemed to fade.

Where are you? I don't understand where you are.

Her voice was in his mind, but he did not need to answer. He did not need to speak. She could feel what he felt and see his sight.

Who are you?
You know me.
I don't.
Yes.

Was she inside of him? Samson sweated, and his heart raced, and briefly he tried to block her out. She was in him, but she was also in a lab, with a body floating beside her. It was as if he could see through her eyes, or not even through her eyes, but could feel the impression of her eyes upon her mind. He wanted to reach to her, to touch her, but this was not that. He didn't know what a lab was, but it was a very clean room with many devices and machines, and for some reason it was a lab. She was happy.

Yes.

He was scared. Terrified.

Don't be.
You are who I seek.
You I seek.
You are me.
No.
Of me.
We were.
Come back.
Where?

Visions of ships and stars and naked bodies made little sense. She was sad and her emotions began to fracture apart. She was afraid.

I'm not.

She was terrified.

He concentrated on the temple in the distance, the pyramid, and it confused her. She was caught in an enormous struggle, she was a leader of the war, and she needed him to help her carry the weight.

No, not that.

It was too heavy for her, but he could not get into the pyramid and the pyramid confused her. She couldn't understand where he was.

I want to.

I am me.

I love you.

She loved him, but she was afraid. She was so important to him and the people around her had not believed her. She was lonely.

I should be lonely too.

Don't be.

But I'm not.

You're alone.

I don't know why.

Then she was gone and the blue of the sky was blinding.

Stephanie blinked her eyes for several seconds in the bright white light of Dr. Nguyen's lab. Attached to her head was a sort of electronic skullcap with hundreds of thousands of thin, protruding wires, like copper hair. Although it was different in appearance, the technology underlying the device was nearly identical to the "mind sharing" arcade devices that were popular at amusement parks and carnivals. She shook her head in a shivering reflex and glanced from Kenichi to Dr. Nguyen.

"I spoke to him," Stephanie said without breath. "He's in there. I spoke to him!"

Dr. Nguyen stuttered, slack-jawed, for words, while the color of Kenichi's face slowly drained to match the whites of his huge, unblinking eyes.

C H A P T E R ¹⁶

ON THE UPPER WEST SIDE of Manhattan, emerging from a big, brass-edged revolving door that was the entrance to a news studio building, Lisa Maui walked out onto the street after recording an interview. The air was damp, but crisp, and the fading light of the late afternoon still bright. She decided to walk down the street for a few blocks before catching a cab.

The Manhattan sidewalks were filled with people, as always, and most of them did not notice her, but many did. The ones who noticed her recognized her, and most of those who recognized her smiled at her. A young couple asked for an autograph, and Lisa smiled and chatted with them for a moment. Several men and women said things like "up NBRA!" or "Keep at it, Lisa!" as she passed. There were others, a smaller number, who did not smile. These often had the most stylish or exotic skin tones, eyes, and hair. They watched her with hate and barely restrained aggression. They glared. Lisa was used to them already, she encountered them everywhere now, and she ignored them.

It had worried her that she might have difficulty catching a cab at this time of day, and there were pedestrians on every corner trying to hail one, but when she approached a curb four empty cabs pulled up.

"This is amazing," she murmured, and got into the first cab. Other pedestrians got into the other cabs as hers pulled quickly away.

"How's it going?" the cabbie asked as Lisa told him her grandparents' address. "Sure, sure."

"I'm doing great," Lisa said.

"Hey, haven't I seen you on tv?"

He shifted through traffic at street level in a mesmerizing way, taking rights and lefts until Lisa stopped being able to follow where they were going.

"You probably have. Are you sure you're going the right way?"

"Trust me, this is what I do. I'll get you there faster than anyone. It must be weird to be on tv, huh?"

"It's not really weird. Why would it be weird?"

"All those people, watching you. It would make me uncomfortable. It would put a cold touch down my spine. Maybe I'm weird, huh?"

"I don't know," Lisa said. "It seems like a big deal to be on tv at first, but then after you do it a few times it just seems normal."

"I see."

The cab wove through unfamiliar streets and seemed to be going north when they were supposed to be going south.

"This isn't the right way," Lisa said. "Where are you going?"

"I'm taking you there," he said, repeating the address. "Trust me."

"I want to get out now. Here."

"Just relax."

"I don't trust you, let me out now," Lisa said in a rising voice.

"Would you just relax? What's the matter?"

"Let me out!" Lisa screamed, now with tears welling in her eyes, while banging on the plastic panel separating her from the cabbie.

"What's the matter? We're almost there!"

"We're not almost there!"

They were somewhere in upper Manhattan, and when the cab stopped again at a red light Lisa tried to get out. The door would not open and the window would not roll down.

"Hey, why won't the door open? Let me out of here!!"

"There's nothing wrong, just relax."

The cab accelerated quickly at the light change. Lisa got out her card to place an emergency call, but it could not get a signal. She shook and banged on the door.

Suddenly the cab turned in to a big, open garage and the garage's automatic door closed behind them. Lisa kept trying to place a call or message through her card. She couldn't understand why it wouldn't work.

Two large men yanked open the car door and pulled Lisa out of the cab.

"Hey! Who are y—"

Before she had time to think, they stuffed a gag into her mouth, clamped headphones on her ears, tied a bag over her head, and handcuffed her hands behind her back with plastic cuffs. In the seconds this was happening, other men attached decals to the cab's windows to give them tinting, removed decals that had been covering its body to change its color, and changed its registration plates. The first two men tied Lisa's legs together for good measure and threw her into the back of a van. She landed painfully and felt the lurch of the vehicle beginning to move.

Reeling from shock, Lisa tried unsuccessfully to gather her senses. Deafening music bombarded her through the headphones. She screamed into the gag what to most human beings, whether engineered or natural born, would have been a nausea inducing scream. If it hadn't been muffled. To the men in the van it just made a funny, pathetic squeaky sound.

CHAPTER 17

SAMSON CONTINUED TO develop his fire making skills, and gradually became a master of it, but night would not come. For no specific reason, he also spent his time building a crude kiln in the earth and using the fire to bake bricks. He didn't know why he did it, and only halfway understood what it even was that he was doing, but he enjoyed doing it, and it seemed like he should. He made the bricks from wet clay and ground up dry husks of plants. With the bricks he could build something. He made a few of them at first, crude lumps of fired clay, then better ones – as he learned to make them better he cast the first inferior ones aside. As his supply grew, Samson began to carry the bricks to an open spot in the desert where he built fires, and stack them up. First hundreds of bricks, then thousands, then many thousands, until eventually he had stacked them into a pyramid of his own, about three stories high, with a flat platform at its top.

He liked to climb to the top of his pyramid and lay on his back, staring up at the sky. Being at the focal point of the structure seemed to focus his thoughts. He could see the oasis down below him on one side, and the endless desert stretching away on every side. The temple was too far away for him to see without being higher. Mostly he didn't look down, but up. His mind would stretch away into the bright, blue, endless nothing. Sometimes the woman would come to him here. She would invade his mind like before and they would exchange confusing communications. He didn't understand where she came from or why, only that she was important. And, more and more, that he knew her. He knew who she was! He couldn't tease the information quite out of his mind, but it was in there somewhere, who she was, like a shadow of a memory, or a word at the tip of his tongue.

Mostly, he thought about night. He didn't understand what night was. He didn't understand what it was supposed to be, but it was darkness that came over everything. He knew that somehow. Night would come when he wanted it. He wanted it! It didn't come. He spent long breadths of time laying on his pyramid waiting for night. It didn't come. That was because he didn't know what it was, to want it. But how could he know what it was if it didn't come? Perhaps the woman could tell him somehow, about night, when she came again.

You are – she said, or expressed, and projected himself at him. His identity. He could not grasp it. He was flight and strength and exhilaration, and vulnerability. She loved what he was, if that was him. If he was still that. The if was from him not from her.

Not if.

You are – who?

She was beauty, and complexity, and vast, vast power. She was trying so hard to show him who she was. Who she was to him, who she would be to him, if his mind could grasp it, not who she was to herself. How could he recognize who she was to herself? She was scared, and trapped, and proud. She was endless with pride.

No.

You are.

He was fractured, stubborn pride, and she was endless crystal pride. She was better than others.

No.

You are.

He knew that she was, he had known it before. She knew it and tried to forget.

No.

He was some kind of hero. He was greatly mourned, when he died.

114

Not.

But.

Not.

Night?

Emptiness and fear and excitement, and time. Passing time. Night was to do with light and time.

Why?

Night?

Why?

Her eyes were dark and impenetrable, for a moment he could see them.

They are?

He saw them from himself, from his mind, not from her. She was afraid and this was difficult for her. She was tired. Exhausted. She was afraid.

Why not you?

It scared her that he was not afraid, but he was not. Why be afraid? Fear seemed absurd, and he understood it, out of all the things he didn't understand. It hurt her that he was not afraid.

She was fading.

Night?

What?

Night?

No, why?

Night?

Dark, cold.

Night?

It was as if her tears were rolling down his mind.

Night?

Then she was gone again, and the brightness of the blue above him hurt his eyes.

In Magdalena City, Theodore and his wife Maria sat down to dinner with their three children. Paul, the eldest, was 12, followed by Judith, 10, and Eve, 6. They held hands around the table, said a prayer of thanks to God, and blessed The Prophet before eating. Theo blinked his eyes open during the prayer to make sure that the children's eyes were closed and they were praying sincerely. His wife's simple, hearty food, most of it taken from the family garden, steamed delicious aromas on the table in front of them. Theo was grateful for his wife, and glad that his new position was keeping him home in Magdalena. As a shepherd assigned to track down and lead back Magdalena's lost sheep in the Solar System, he had spent many periods of months separated from his family. His time with them was lived intensely, in anticipation of when it would be interrupted again. This was the longest stretch he had been able to spend at home in years.

"What did you do at work today, Dad?" Paul asked.

"Yes, what did you do today, Daddy?" Judith and Eve echoed.

"Don't ask your father about work again," Maria scolded. "Just like before, he can't talk about it."

Theo chewed his food and made a smile with his lips at his children. He drank from an icy glass of limeade.

"Why can't he tell us about it?" Paul demanded.

"Yeah, why can't he, Mom?" the girls echoed.

"You just shush and don't worry about it," Maria said. "Tell your father what you did today."

"What did you do today, Paul?" Theo asked, while serving more food onto his plate.

"I got to fly a jet bike in the northwest desert!"

"You did?"

"It was great. Yeah, Jacob's parents took us. I flew so fast, I almost flew into a crow. But I was wearing a helmet. If I wasn't wearing a helmet it would have been bad."

"Did you hit it?"

"No, I didn't, but it was close. I could almost feel it touch my head. Jacob's dad thinks I'm almost good enough to get my license. I'm a better pilot than Jacob, he even says that. But Jacob's good, too. We're both good."

"How high did you go?"

"I flew way up. It was 4,000 or maybe 5,000 feet. I was all alone and I turned a loop in the air."

"A loop?"

"Just like Uncle Samson would have done, I turned a big loop. And Jacob's dad got scared and made us fly slower, but we were fine."

"You just listen to Steven when he tells you that," Maria said. "Good grief."

"You have to go slowly," Theo said, "things like jet bikes are really dangerous. You have to respect them. Your Uncle Samson was an expert pilot, he understood everything about the machines he flew, and he always respected them. That's why he could do what he did. He wouldn't be happy if you weren't being careful."

"Do you think he's looking down on us, Dad? Do you think he could see something like – me flying?"

"Sure he is," Theo said. "Of course he can. I'm sure he watches you a lot."

"I wish we could have met him," Paul said. "He didn't even see us when he came here. He saw you and Mom, and Grandma and Grandpa, but he didn't see us."

"I never met Uncle Samson!" Eve said.

"I wish he could have too, Paul. I'm sure he wished he could see you kids. When he was here last year it wasn't a normal visit, and that's why he didn't see you then."

"He should have stayed long enough to meet the children," Maria said.

"Yes, he should have. He should have, but he didn't. Nobody's perfect, kids, not even Uncle Samson. Nobody is."

"Not even The Prophet?" Eve asked.

"Well, The Prophet is pretty close."

"Why don't you tell your father what you did today, Eve," Maria said.

"I rode a horse today, Daddy."

"You did?"

THAT NIGHT, WITH THE BEDROOM door locked, Theodore tore his wife's clothes off and they made ravenous love to each other. There had been a special passion between them since Samson had died. A new facet to their passion, something primal and instinctive. Maria had stopped using her birth control and they both craved another child. They made love all the time, constantly, as if it was the sustenance that maintained their lives. They made love more than they had when they were young. Theo pressed himself into his wife's body with a particular urgency. They were exhausted and exhilarated by it, so that sex became, even more than ever, the hazy punctuation of their nights and days.

Theo was always tense now. Maria tried her best to make home life peaceful for him and the kids. She wouldn't allow herself to be tense, so that she could help to carry his tension. She loved her husband more than anything, more than even their children if that was possible. It was a frightening, irrational, prideful love. He squeezed her breast and slid his hand down to rest on her sweaty ribs. She slid her hand along his thigh and hip bone, until it rested against his penis. They lay together, spent and wordless on their sweaty bed, until their hearts slowed down and the sweat began to dry, and they drifted back out of their naked half-sleep.

"They're determined to go to war," Theo said quietly.

"Why?"

"They may not have a choice, but they'll choose to go to

war even if they do."

"Are we in danger?"

"Only from ourselves right now. They're suicidal. They think God will protect us."

"Won't He?

"I hope so. But it would take the greatest miracle in history. They don't know who they want to fight, but they want to fight someone."

"Oh, honey."

"Maybe they're right, though. The genetic people might come for us. For some of them, the Solar System could never be big enough for us to exist. For some of them, it's like we're a part of them, like their own diseased limb, in their mind, that has to be destroyed for them to become well. Because we're a part of them they can't ignore us. They can't leave us alone."

"What will we do?"

"I don't know, love."

Theo fell silent. He pulled the covers up half over him, and squeezed his wife against his chest and wrapped his arms around her. He drifted back into half-sleep.

"We should have been pregnant already," Maria said.

He mumbled groggily and was silent again.

"We should have been pregnant already, Theo! It was always easy before."

"What? It's been– It hasn't been long. We're older now. Don't worry."

"If we don't get pregnant soon, I want us to go to the doctor and see if something's wrong," Maria said.

"Ok. Don't worry."

He pulled her back against him and kissed her neck, and went to sleep dreaming about war and death. Before morning he woke up and they made love again, then they faded back to sleep in a sticky, sweaty, haze of love and fear.

119

CHAPTER 18

LISA WAS IN THE VAN FOR a long time. It seemed like several hours. Maybe a whole day. It felt like they were flying fast and far. But it was hard to tell for sure. The headphones played classical music very loudly in her ears. Symphonies, operas, string quartets, piano, but all hashed up, and only loud parts, so that it was tortuous and impossible to enjoy. Sometimes the music became quieter and a loud voice came over it.

"Lisa Maui," the voice said, "your life and health are not in danger. You have been kidnapped because we need to talk to you in secret. Please do not resist and risk causing harm to yourself. Thank you." Then the volume of the music came up again.

The voice repeated over the music at regular intervals, perhaps every ten minutes or so. The hashed up classical music ran the gamut of the genre, sometimes it was Bach, or something near to Bach, and other times it was more like Brahms, or Tchaikovsky, or even atonal 20th Century music. Lisa's grandfather was a great classical music buff, and had insisted that she have instruction in classical piano playing. Sometimes it was music that she knew well, a few times it was pieces she had played and performed at recital.

She strained at her bindings and tried to pull her thoughts together. Her brain seemed to be arrested by her rapid breath and heart, so that it wouldn't work for her. The music was too loud to be calming, but it was an anchor. Someone wanted to talk to her. She couldn't talk like this. She couldn't even control her mouth if she wasn't gagged. Her body, seemingly of its own, let out occasional screams into the gag that were muffled and abrupt.

The first plan that came to Lisa, when she was finally able to start taking control of her fear, was to attack whoever was detaining her at the first opportunity while screaming and trying to get away. She had to fight. She wouldn't let them hurt her. She wouldn't be at their mercy. She would hurt them in any way possible, and call for help as loudly as possible, and run as fast and unexpectedly as possible. She would fight.

With a few more minutes to think, Lisa began to feel hopeless about the fighting plan. The music was so loud, it pounded into her brain. She shook her head and rubbed it against the walls of the van to try to get the headphones off, without success. They pressed around her ears tightly, as if they had been taped to her head. She thought of what had happened in the garage – the people who took her were prepared, fighting would have served no purpose. Screaming would have reached no one. She didn't have time to do anything, but – what could she have done? She would still fight, she would go down fighting, but maybe they did want to talk to her. This was the work of an organization. They could have killed her already. These were professionals, people with plans and resources, rational actors. They weren't psychopaths out for a thrill kill. Maybe she could work her way through this.

What would they want to know? What did they want from her? The music pounded into her head, symphonic arpeggios with clashing cymbals. Lisa banged the side of her head against the wall hoping to break the headphones. She was famous now, she was a spokesperson, but she wasn't a player. She assumed this must have to do with her work at the NBRA and the conflict over natural born rights. She was not an insider; major organizations like Bloodworth's and Rothschild's would know that. They must. A group that would kidnap her must be crazy, a group on the fringe. They could be a religious cult like Magdalena, with strange, religious gripes. Maybe they needed her to act as a liaison with the NBRA. Maybe they wanted her to be a spy. It could be some group that wanted to brainwash her. Maybe it could be Bloodworth's, though; maybe even a mega-corp could want to use her in some way, to undermine the natural born rights movement, or to spy on it. All of the things she knew were available to the public, basically, but someone might not realize that. They should, but they might not. Her grandfather was right. The men who kidnapped her were genetically engineered, but they could be hired by a natural born group. Maybe they would want to enlist or force her to harm some of the NBRA leaders, or to kill one of them. If it was something like that then she could get away. Some organization had made a big effort to kidnap her and bring her to them, they must want something from her. They must need something. Their need was something that could help her escape, help her get home.

The more she calmed down, the more Lisa began to feel the need to use the bathroom, until her urge to pee became even more distracting than the music pounding through the headphones. She wanted to kill the people who did this to her.

ALEXANDER GRUMIAUX OPENED THE DOOR of his little chambers adjoining the floor of the United Earth Congressional Assembly to discover a young page there endeavoring to relay him a message. Grumiaux was barefoot and wore a heavy, intricately embroidered, black silk robe that contrasted dramatically with his elegant gold and copper skin. The page boy was sandy haired and natural.

"Who's there?" Grumiaux said, looking directly past the boy. "I swear I heard a knock. Who's there?"

"Excuse me sir," the boy said.

"Who's there?" Grumiaux repeated, and glanced around curiously. The boy's face turned red.

Across the room behind Grumiaux, the delegate Rahima

Bernstein stood up out of her chair and gazed down at the young man as the door slowly closed.

"Get out of here, shit," she said. "Go back to where you belong."

"Doorbell ditching is what they used to call this," Grumiaux said to Rahima just before the door inched closed. "Doorbell ditching. Did you ever hear that expression?"

"You're a font of knowledge, Alexander," the woman said. "Don't bore me."

"I have to take care of this situation right away."

"You'll do what?"

"I'll call Siggi, just a moment."

"Siggi won't help you," Rahima said. "He's such a straight-laced idealist. Not even you."

"Hello, Siggi? Ah, Siggi, that's right, Alexander here. Listen, I'm having a problem today and I'm a little bit upset with you about it. It seems that no one is here to relay my messages. Nobody is relaying them to me. Surely you have somebody who can. Well am I right or am I wrong? I'm not asking for anybody special, but I insist that it be somebody. This is a matter I take very seriously. Well that's alright then. Yes. Yes. That's right. It's quite alright, I accept your apology. Thank you very much."

Grumiaux hung up the call on his card.

"Even Siggi?" Rahima said, her crisp green eyes reflecting envy and the tiniest shade of fear.

"Oh, Siggi's an old friend of mine," Alexander said, waving the issue away. "I'm sure it won't happen again. Please pardon me for the ungracious interruption of our meeting."

"I'll have to have a talk with Siggi myself."

"He won't be in a good mood," Grumiaux said, and allowed his face to betray the faintest hint of a smile.

"You're a disgusting excuse for a man, Grumiaux," Rahima

said. "Let's get back to the trade war, I want Rothschild's to be history."

"That's not what you said when you were in bed with me."

"That was a long time ago. Fuck you, Grumiaux."

"But it's not what you said."

Rahima stood up. She was such an extreme figure. Her black hair so severe. Her body so thin, yet strong. So tall. Her yellow skin so shocking and aggressively beautiful.

"I want them dead, Phillipe wants them dead, and we want to know what you are going to help us do about it."

"Well, Rothschild's can die. We could kill Rothschild's. But if Rothschild's died it would be very disruptive. You and Phillipe are too vehement, too idealistic, in your hatred of the natural born. Yes, they need to be quarantined. Yes, they need to be put out of our society. But these things take time. You're forcing the issue."

"Things have come to a head now," Rahima said. "This will all soon be decided whether you like it or not. And the path of history for at least the next century will be set. Phillipe and I will do whatever we have to do."

"What *you* are going to do," Grumiaux said, "is whatever I tell you to do."

Rahima stared at him, rage in her eyes becoming unconcealed.

"Don't you agree, Rahima?" he said.

She stood up and moved to walk to the door, but he blocked her path.

"I want to hear you say it."

While he watched them, the faintest tremble appeared in her eyes. She struggled to hold back tears. Alexander reached out and held her hand.

"You have to say it before you can go."

Rahima's voice was very soft when she spoke.

"I'll do whatever you tell me to do, Grumiaux," she said. "Just like I always have."

WHEN THE VAN FINALLY CAME to a stop, Lisa felt two people grab her heavily and lift her up. She squirmed and they gripped her more tightly and carried her somewhere. In the midst of this a little bit of pee leaked out of her and it took all of her will power to keep from emptying her bladder. She was terrified and humiliated, but the pee was probably only a few drops. She hoped it was less than anyone could notice. Somewhere far in the back of her mind it seemed curious to her that right at this moment she should even care.

The bag over her head and headphones were finally removed, then the gag, and Lisa was untied. A sharp looking man in a suit allowed her to use the bathroom. She could hardly hear him through the ringing in her ears, and bright lights dazzled her eyes. The bathroom was tiny, with concrete walls and no window. It also had no mirror. She washed her hands for a long time when she was done, waiting for her eyes to clear up against the light and for the ringing in her ears to calm down.

"I need you to come back out here now, Lisa," the man said very loudly. He understood that her ears were ringing and made it difficult to hear. He had done this before.

Lisa opened the door and came out again. The man's suit was black. His hair was sandy-brown and blue, and he had light, violet eyes. He had natural-hued skin, bronze skin, that was unnaturally perfect. He was perhaps 30 years old, and officious in his bearing. Behind him, near the door of the small room they were in, were two men who reminded Lisa of the men that had pulled her out of the taxi. It upset her that she could not remember clearly enough to say if they were the same men or not. She could feel herself breathing very fast, and tried to shift her shoulders into a pose of composure.

"Why am I here?" she demanded assertively.

The room, like the bathroom attached to it, had no windows and only one exit door. It was about 15' x 20', smelled sterile, and had a desk on the side opposite the door. There were expensive holo-cameras mounted in every corner.

"Please sit down at the desk, Lisa," the man said. "We are going to be here for a while."

"Why are you calling me 'Lisa'? I've never met you before."

"It seems too formal to call you 'Ms. Maui'," the man said. "You can call me 'Jim'."

"You can call me 'Ms. Maui', Jim," Lisa said.

"No, I will call you Lisa. Sorry."

FOR THE NEXT SEVEN HOURS, Jim interrogated Lisa. She was given no food or water and only allowed to use the restroom again after arguing with Jim about it for thirty minutes. In the bathroom she looked up and noticed for the first time that there was a holo-camera mounted high up on the ceiling. She drank some water out of the restroom tap, but it tasted slimy and bitter.

Jim asked her again and again about her relationships with Samson Ford and with Stephanie de Rothschild. No answer seemed to satisfy him, and Lisa could not understand what he wanted. He asked her about the NBRA and she told him what she could – none of it was secret, anyway – but he seemed only mildly interested.

"What do you want from me?" Lisa asked in an awkward, dry voice.

"I want you to tell me the truth," Jim said.

"I told you the truth!" It hurt Lisa's mouth to talk. "Can I please have some water?"

"You can have all the water you want, and food, and you can go home, as soon as you tell me the truth."

"I told you everything I know, and I can hardly talk."

"Tell me what you know about Stephanie de Rothschild!"

"I don't know anything."

"You were friends with her. And with Samson Ford. You dated Samson at the same time that he dated Stephanie. Do you expect me to believe that the three of you didn't even have sex?"

"Why are you obsessed with sex?" Lisa croaked. "Would it make you happy if I said we had? What do you want to hear?"

"The truth!"

"Ok, we had sex."

"Then why did you say before that you didn't?"

"What do you want from me? I don't understand this."

Lisa didn't cry, but her shoulders shook with heavy sobs.

"We've checked your card, how do you keep in touch with Stephanie de Rothschild?"

"I told you, I barely know her."

"You had sex with her and Samson Ford and you say you barely know her? You must know her better than that."

"We didn't have sex. Why do you care about that anyway? She was at the races, and I worked there. I talked to her sometimes. I didn't know who she was, nobody did. Don't you believe that nobody knew who she was? Even Samson didn't know."

"How do you know that Samson didn't know?"

"I don't think he knew."

"You said it like you were very close to him."

"I don't know, I don't think he knew."

"Stop lying to me!"

The interrogation continued until Lisa passed out.

"LISA, YOU HAVE A SPECIAL visitor," Jim said, brushing her arm roughly until the skin burned.

She pulled her arm away from him, and cocked her face slightly off of the desk towards the door without opening her eyes. She didn't know how long she had been asleep. Her face sunk back onto the desk again, groggily, and she looked up with just one eye. Then she gasped and leapt back in her chair.

Phillipe Bloodworth was there, by the door. He was watching her, and looked incredibly mean. He seemed shorter than he appeared on tv. Lisa couldn't believe he was really there. She couldn't recover from the shock and catch her breath.

"Hello, Lisa Maui," Bloodworth said in his most oily voice.

He walked forward and stood a few feet in front of her.

"I hope you're not too uncomfortable?"

Lisa sat up perfectly straight and tried to will the color back into her face. Jim was behind them, and the toughs. They all seemed almost as scared of Bloodworth as she was. They were too scared themselves to enjoy her terror.

"I don't understand why you have brought me here, Mr. Bloodworth," Lisa said in a slow, rough, but perfectly steady voice.

"It's nice to meet you, too. No, I can understand why you would be upset. Of course you would be! I'm sorry, these are difficult times. I didn't mean for this to be as uncomfortable for you as it has been. That's why I came down to talk to you myself when I heard it wasn't going well. I want to help you, Lisa. I want to work together with you, I don't want us to be enemies. As to why you have been brought here, that's because you are one of the few people in the Solar System who has, or had, personal connections to both Samson Ford and Stephanie de Rothschild."

"I already told him, I don't know anything. Are you going to let me go now? I want to leave."

Lisa stood up and stepped forward, but Bloodworth slammed her back down into the chair with surprising athleticism.

"Not yet, Lisa. I'm sorry. I need to talk to you first."

"I'm sure people are looking for me," Lisa said. "Everyone will be. This will be all over the news soon. Let me go now and I won't talk about it to anyone. This was just a bad dream."

"No, Lisa, it's not a dream. I have to talk to you first, can you listen to me?"

"Say what you want."

"No, you tell me what I need to know. How close were you to Samson Ford?"

"Not very close. We went out two or three times–"

"How many?"

"Two times. We decided not to keep seeing each other. Actually, we were just friends. We weren't even close friends. I already told Jim all of this."

"Even though you talk about him constantly on tv, you didn't know Samson well?"

"No, not well. Samson is dead, why does this matter?"

"What about Stephanie de Rothschild?"

"I saw her at races sometimes, she was nice. We were more acquaintances than friends. I already told Jim this over and over again, but he won't believe me."

"If we were, say, to send Stephanie de Rothschild a ransom note for you, she wouldn't be motivated by it?"

"Why do you need a ransom? You don't need money."

"Answer the question!"

"She might take an interest because she is a nice person, but it wouldn't be more to her than a ransom note for almost anyone else she knows. I'm not a special person to her or anything like that."

"You're certain of that?"

"Yes, I am certain."

New surges of adrenaline and hope had improved Lisa's color and helped her to stabilize her voice.

"Why do you talk about Samson so much in your interviews?"

"That's– When I'm done answering these questions, are you going to let me go?"

"Yes. If you're honest. Answer the question."

"I talk about him – look, it's not like I am some publicity whore doing all this because I love the attention. People have said that and say all kinds of horrible things about me, your kind of people, Mr. Bloodworth, the ones against the naturals. But I talk about Samson because that is what people want to hear about. And I didn't know him super well, but I knew him better than almost anyone else recently, that's what I've learned, or at least better than anyone else who will talk to the press about him, so that's the basis for me to talk about him. I'm not misrepresenting him or pretending that we were closer than we were. I've never done that. And I use the interview opportunities to talk about natural born rights and the NBRA, so it's for a reason. I talk on tv for a purpose. You probably don't agree with the purpose, or I know you don't agree with it, but it has a purpose."

"I understand. Then about the NBRA, how much do you know about their operations?"

Lisa sunk her elbows onto the table, unable to hold herself up straight.

"I already told Jim about this. Can you please get me some food and water? My throat is so dry it's hard to talk to you. Please."

"Just a little bit more, Lisa."

"You're torturing me."

"That hasn't happened to you yet. Bear it in mind."

"I'm telling you everything! Torture wouldn't get anything else, I'm already telling you everything."

"Ok, but tell me what you know about the NBRA."

"I'm not an insider, you must know that already!"

She started to cry, and the tears that rolled into her dry mouth felt peculiarly refreshing.

"How would I know that?"

"You're smart, you know how things work. You have intelligence agents. You must know all about the NBRA. You probably know more about them than I do. I'm just a spokesperson! Everything I say, everything I know, is in the public record."

"You don't sit in when they have executive meetings?"

"Not usually. The NBRA is a legitimate organization, they're transparent. Even when they do ask me to sit in on a meeting – it's only happened a few times – they talk about standard things, nothing secret. They want to generate as much media attention that is pro-naturals as possible, and as much negative media toward your company and the anti-naturals movement. That's not secret. I already told it all to Jim. They're good people acting in good faith, they're not trying to do any tricks."

"You're not an insider."

"I'm not! I'm just a spokesperson. I put a good face on the organization and the movement."

"How did you feel when Samson Ford died?"

"What?"

"How did it make you feel, Lisa?"

"I felt bad, how do you think I felt? Look, will you let me go home now or not?"

Lisa took a deep breath and stood up again, and Bloodworth slammed her back down into the chair harder than before. Her tailbone hurt. Jim giggled loudly for a moment in the background, but a sharp glance from Bloodworth stopped him in mid-laugh.

"The mistake you made, Lisa," Bloodworth said, "was choosing sides. You could feel however you want, you could vote however you want, in private, you could be friends with whoever you want, quietly, but you had to choose sides. You chose sides!"

Lisa watched Bloodworth's fat legs walk back and forth across the room. Like a toad. She could barely concentrate on what he was saying. He was irrational. She would have to choose her moment to fight, if he didn't let her go.

"I'll do whatever you want," Lisa said. "Tell me what you want."

"Shut up!!"

Bloodworth kicked the desk in front of her across the room.

"You chose sides!"

"Just let me go home," she said in a whisper.

"Do you know what natural born people are? They're human beings exactly like the rest of us, only worse. Only worse! Exactly the same, but worse, don't you understand? You're reasonably smart. You have fine genetic engineering. You're a beautiful young woman. You must be able to notice it. They're the same, but worse. Not as smart, not as beautiful, not as healthy, not as much energy, not as stable emotions, smaller dicks, weaker vaginas, sloppier vaginas, poorer eyesight, worse body odor. They're just like us, but worse. They're worse!

"But you chose their side. Samson Ford won a race, so now they're all wonderful. Samson Ford was a lucky piece of shit, that's why he won. He wasn't the best racer, he was the luckiest, anyone could see that. Natural born, a genetic freak, he wasn't representative of anything. And people like you cried

132

when he died. You chose the side of shit, instead of the side of the best that humanity can be.

"The side of 'natural born rights'. What about human rights? What about the right of humanity to move forward, what about that right? The willful natural born. They shouldn't exist anymore! One monkey stumbles backwards on a banana peel across a finish line and we all have to celebrate monkeys and scratch our bellies with our nails? You don't know anything, do you? People like you are afraid of what is good, afraid of quality in a way. You identify with the monkeys because you are afraid of being as excellent as possible. You don't want the responsibility! You want to go back, to be a primitive human, you don't respect the human right to progress and become exceptional!

"The monkeys have to be cleared out of the way. People like you should read history. They've been in the way for 150 years. Determined to be monkeys, determined to be nothing more than monkeys. Every path is opened to them for 150 years, but they want to make humanity worse not better. They want to make humanity worse! That's what people like you fight for, *who* you fight for. Monkey shit. Why do you love the kinderfucks so much, didn't you ever think about that? There are people exactly the same as them, but better, and you love the ones who are worse. You stand in the way of progress, the future! Animals will be animals, and harvested or kept in the zoo, but human beings have become more than animals. You want to remain an animal, you want humanity to. You side with beasts against civilization, that's what's wrong with you."

Bloodworth paced back and forth as he ranted, back and forth, back and forth, closer and closer to her until he was nearly screaming in her face.

"You're just like Stephanie de Rothschild, the animal loving whore who chose sides. She wouldn't even talk to me! Did you know that? She chatted with you all the time, but she wouldn't even talk to me. Not one meeting, not one call. She would only let me talk to her servants. She would have been happy to talk to an animal representative, she would have been happy to talk to the head of the NBRA! And fuck him too! She would be so happy. But Phillipe Bloodworth is beneath her. She has the most advanced genetics in the Solar System, the most! But she looks down on those like her and loves kinderfucks. She loves her monkeys, not the best of humanity! She tries to ensure that human beings remain animals, she is given the best, but chooses the worst for everyone else.

"Did you think about who your friends were when you were making them? Samson Ford and Stephanie de Rothschild, that was a stupid choice. That's what got you into all this trouble, Lisa. You should have been smart enough to know better. When you choose sides, you accept the consequences of your position. That's a proposition that is easy enough to understand."

Bloodworth held a finger up in front of her face as he finished his rant. Lisa tried to whisper something else, but the words wouldn't even come out of her mind for her to say them. She slumped back on the chair, the bones aching in her hips and knees from sitting so long. This couldn't be real, it must be a dream. She closed her eyes.

Bloodworth left the room, and a few minutes later the two men in the back bound Lisa up again, with the headphones, gag, and bag over her head. She felt a sharp pain in her buttock and faded out of consciousness as one of them lifted her body.

FAR AWAY, IN SCAMP'S APARTMENT in Neo Vega, a Rothschild's news wire was broadcasting breaking news of Lisa's disappearance. Her grandparents had reported her missing almost immediately and contacted the press. The broadcast contained surveillance footage of Lisa getting into the cab, and of the cab driving north through Manhattan, but it disappeared after that. What made this particularly disturbing was that the cab's plate number was not a registered plate number, and the cab's electronic key signature was forged. The cab driver could not be identified on any facial database. Therefore, in spite of the fact that she had been missing less than 24 hours, Lisa's disappearance was being treated as an abduction. At least, that was the case according to the Rothschild's wires. The Bloodworth's wires were telling a different story, but Scamp didn't watch the Bloodworth's wires.

"What is this all about, Trever?" a female news anchor asked her male counterpart. "This mysterious cab, forged license plates, forged key signature, a driver whose face appears on no facial database – this wasn't just some random abduction, was it."

"That's exactly right, Shereen," the male anchor said. "It seems to be the work of an organization with substantial resources. Lisa Maui has become one of the most recognizable players in the natural born rights movement, which makes her an enemy to any number of anti-naturals organizations right now. We don't like to talk about it, but there is also speculation that this could be some sort of collateral damage related to the trade war between Bloodworth's and Rothschild's. At this point, we just don't know who may have taken her or why, but we hope someone out there can help. Let's find this young woman and bring her back to safety. If you have any information, any information at all, please don't wait. Call or write in to the Earth authorities at..."

Scamp left the tv on, but didn't hear much more of it. He felt like he had been shocked out of a deep sleep. Lisa Maui was one of Samson Ford and Stephanie de Rothschild's friends. Professional agents had snatched her off the street.

She had seemed so innocent on tv. He remembered seeing her on the tarmac at one of Samson's races. When he had fought with Killian Gideon, probably. That was a time. Life had been good to him, he thought suddenly; he had gotten to fight people like Killian Gideon and Samson Ford. He had an amazing life. This bitter unhappiness that swallowed him up was unjustified, it was incorrect. But it was guilt that consumed him, that was at the root of it. He couldn't even understand what he was guilty about, not completely. Lisa Maui was a friend of Samson Ford. She was an enthusiastic campaigner for natural born rights. Natural born rights were almost like rights for people like him, it wasn't that different. She was a bright, pretty, good hearted, innocent young woman. She was Samson Ford's friend, and someone was trying to destroy her. She could be already dead, but he thought not. If operators like that simply wanted her dead they could arrange for her to die innocuously, it would be at least as easy as the abduction. She seemed so sweet on tv. She was Samson Ford's friend. Of course, she would be. He realized now that he was jealous of Samson Ford. He always had been jealous of him. But he hadn't disliked Samson. It wasn't the kind of jealousy you feel towards an enemy, or a stranger, it was that kind of jealousy you feel towards a friend. Or a child, even. You're happy for them; you're happy for them to have the great things they have, that you don't have – things that you will never have. You are happy for them and jealous of them at the same time. As if your heart and your stomach were clenching up against each other inside of you.

Scamp reached down, picked a bottle of vodka up off the floor, and gulped down half of it. He spent the next eight hours, well into the morning, researching Lisa Maui on the net.

The news said Lisa Maui was abducted off the street in New York. I can't get it out of my mind. She was a friend of Samson's, I saw her on the tarmac once when I was working that case. Now she's become famous as the spokesperson for the NBRA. I'm sure it's Bloodworth's Corporation. The story has had a strange effect on me. I wonder if other people know that? It's obvious, but people are so stupid. For Phillipe Bloodworth it's personal. Lisa is a friend of Samson Ford and Stephanie de Rothschild. He killed Ford, he wants to destroy Rothschild's and Stephanie is the physical representation of Rothschild's. Goddamnit I sound smart, don't I? People don't understand men like Bloodworth, even police and the people who should understand, they don't get it. He needs to make an example of someone, a natural born rights person. He needs to and he wants to, and he will enjoy it. He would like to hurt Stephanie and Samson and everyone who cares about them. Lisa Maui is automatic. It's almost amazing that it didn't happen until now.

I have this feeling I can get involved in this. Like, I want to, or I'm supposed to. It has power over me. I spent all night researching Lisa. She's a good person – clean. She's the kind of woman I wish I could have in my life. As if that matters, but maybe it's part of why. But it's not that. She was friends with Samson. This guilt has been strangling me. She's friends with Samson. She was friends with him. And this guilt has been killing me. What guilt(?) you ask yourself. I ask myself that. I don't understand why, it seems crazy, but I think I can make a difference here. In this thing, I think I can make a difference. If I could save Lisa Maui it would be – redemption. It would clear up this guilt, this suffocation that blankets me.

I thought about my life today. I thought something new about it. It's the only thing I can think of now. My life and Lisa Maui now, and saving her. I fought on the racing tarmac with Killian

Gideon. Killian Gideon, the legend! My life has been filled with amazing things like that. Other people can't even imagine the things I've done and seen. It was filmed and broadcast all over the Solar System, me fighting with Killian Gideon. This bitter unhappiness has become me, as if it was who I am inside. I don't have any reason to be bitterly unhappy! My life is amazing. Who knows how long I can live? I feel as young as ever. Nobody else has genetics like mine. I could have an amazing life, it might not even be half over.

I'm just so paralyzed by this guilt. Lisa Maui needs help and I have nothing to lose. There is this beautiful word: redemption. Redemption is something. I never used to think about it, and I didn't imagine it, but now I can see it in front of me. If I can help here, in this thing, I can become a new me.

The weird thing about it is I think I can do it. I can save her! I don't know why, but I have this — passion? My life had no meaning and this thing gives meaning to my life, that's how some wiseass smart guy could say it. It wasn't that my life had no meaning, though. Samson Ford was such an amazing man. He was everything the universe needs — he did it, he won! He was like a miracle from the god. I feel like I killed him. It doesn't make sense, but I feel I did it, that I'm responsible.

I have to do more research. I've already purchased express tickets to Earth.

- Scampadorous Maximus

C H A P T E R 19

"IT'S STRANGE THAT YOU ARE only able to connect with him occasionally."

Stephanie was sitting in the lab with Kenichi and Dr. Nguyen, where she spent nearly all of her free time now. Her excuse for free time. If it were not for Samson she would have none, and expect none. This was a time of crisis, a time of war. She made an excuse for herself, a need for free time, so that she could be with Samson. It made her a better leader to do it this way, than to not allow herself to go to the lab, and be tortured by that. She had only been able to make a mental connection to Samson a handful of times. Kenichi and Dr. Nguyen could not help beginning to doubt the reality of the mental connections she had made with him.

"What I mean is," Kenichi continued, "how can you be sure that you made a mental connection to him? No one else has been able to do so."

"Kenichi, it was him. He's in some weird – dimension, or alternate reality. He doesn't know who he is, or who I am, but he recognized me. He's searching for me. He's very confused, but he thinks there is some way that he can break through it."

"He's searching for you?" Dr. Nguyen asked, in a very level tone.

"I'm not crazy!"

Stephanie's personal guard, who stood by the door, stared at the two scientists stonily.

"Nobody thinks you're crazy, Mistress," Dr. Nguyen said, "but how can you be sure that it is not something else that you've experienced? As scientists, Kenichi and I have to consider every possibility. We don't understand the basis for your certainty."

SAMSON FASHIONED A MAKESHIFT PACK out of plant fiber and filled it with two dozen torches. Then he built a fire with dense wood, so that it would burn unattended for a long time. He left his fire burning, waiting for him, and climbed up to the top of his pyramid. He lay on his back on the top of the pyramid, as he often did now, but with renewed energy and resolve. Today he would make it night.

It seemed like he had spent a very long time thinking about night. He had a vague understanding of it, a shadowy concept in the back of his brain, but he could not remember it specifically. What was night? It was as if 'night' had come over his mind. Night was darkness and time. He had reasoned that much. Strange darkness and time had taken over his mind. He didn't know what would not be strange, but there must be something. Why was his mind filled with things that he could feel but not grasp? Things had happened to him that he could not remember, but he could still feel. Strange darkness and time.

Night had to do with light. It was an absence of light, like when his fire went out. The fire could make light in the shadows under the trees and bushes, but when the fire went out, the light disappeared, and the shadows were dark again. Night must be like this, like the fire going out. If there was a fire in the sky, it could burn down, it could dim. It could go out completely, and there would be darkness over the land. This would be like night, or would be night. Night meant darkness over the land. Then the light would come from his fire and his torches, without them he could not see.

A fire in the sky could burn down, could disappear, but the sky could not burn down. The sky was light. It was light everywhere, from every direction. There was no shadow in the sky, there could not be. You could take a bush up into the sky, and hold it over yourself, high in the sky, but there would

140

be no shadow. Even inside the bush, between the needles and leaves, if it was high up in the sky, there were no shadows. Light was everywhere and came from everything, high in the sky. The sky was nothing but light, if light was something. Light forever, endless and everywhere.

Heat came from the light. Perhaps? The desert was hot and the heat seemed to come from the sky, which was nothing but the light. It seemed to come from the light, but he couldn't say for certain that it did. The shadows cast by the sky, under the bushes and trees, were cool. So what was shielded from the light was cool. So the heat came from the light.

It was a working assumption. If the heat came from the light then darkness coming over the land would also mean cold coming over the land. He might need fire to keep warm, if it was dark. Birds would have no fire. Perhaps this was why it needed to be night.

The shepherd said that it would be night when he wanted it to be night. Yet, he had wanted it to be night for a long time and it had not become night. Night would come if the source of light in the sky was dimmed. Only, the light in the sky had no source. Did it? It must come from somewhere, after all. If what the shepherd said was true, and he felt that it was, then he could control the light. He, himself, was the source of the light. Is that what the shepherd meant?

If he was the source of the light, then the light came from inside of him. He could meditate on the light to change it. He only needed to imagine darkness coming over the land, to visualize and invoke darkness. He only needed to imagine the light receding, the sky dimming, like a fire's embers dying over time.

While Samson began to believe in the power that he held over the light, and to meditate on it, the sky gradually began to dim. The change was slow at first, almost imperceptible.

He maintained his focus and the change continued, and grew faster. The color of the sky changed as the light diminished, from blue to violet, then a darkening violet that shifted back to blue as it approached black.

Eventually, it was night, and when he looked around himself Samson could see little except for what was illuminated by his fire. He floated down to the fire and collected his bundle of torches. He stared into the fire and remembered something. Tiny sparkles of light across the sky. They weren't across this sky, but he had seen them before, in a sky. There had even been a sky where they were everywhere, in every direction around him, stretching off forever. They were beautiful. He wondered where that was, and where this was, and why he couldn't remember it. Had he known where this was, once? He had known stars? Stars. It was a beautiful word; he had forgotten it, but it was his again. Had he stood somewhere, once, surrounded by stars on every side, stretching off into the distance forever, and imagined this place, this sky? Would he forget this too?

He lit his first torch, flew up into the darkness, and rushed towards the distant temple which was only an outline of a shadow now on the dark horizon.

C H A P T E R 20

AMSON FLEW STRAIGHT FOR THE temple. He kept watching for a hummingbird, almost flinching in the anticipation of one, or for any bird, but no birds approached him. There was no sound of bird call in the distance. As he came closer to the tower, farther than where the birds had always stopped him before, he began to feel elated. The cool air of the night was exhilarating.

The pyramid temple was even larger than it had looked from a distance. A wide ramp running up the front face of the temple led to an open doorway in the squared-off top. The whole structure was made from smooth, carved stone that ranged in color from grey to pinkish tan. Samson flew around it with his torch and examined its outside before venturing towards the doorway. The ramp to the temple's top was less smooth than the rest, as if it was worn from many years of use, although the area of desert around the pyramid was dense with scrub and featureless. Who had been here, who could have been, was hard to imagine. If the unicorn men had come they would have flown to the top, there would have been no need for them to walk up the ramp. He had seen no hint of the unicorn men since his first encounter with them.

Samson walked up the ramp, imagining that he was a person or creature who needed it, imagining that he could not fly. It seemed strange not to be able to fly. He thought of the shepherd who came to the oasis, and the shepherd's sheep. They could not fly. Or it seemed that they could not. It had not occurred to him to think about it before. He felt that flying was intrinsic to his nature, and that it was natural for people, like the shepherd, to not be able to fly, and that, paradoxically, he was a normal person. The shepherd had to come from somewhere. He wondered about it now, and wondered that he had not done so before. It took a long time to walk up the ramp, to climb the side of the pyramid's face and reach the top of the temple. The wear in the ramp was reminiscent of footprints. Gentle ovals where feet had gradually polished away thin layers of the stone. He had to hold the torch close against it and bend down with his eyes to see anything clearly. The night seemed to suck away more than amplify the torch's light.

The torch in his hand was burning down, almost consumed, and Samson flew back into the air and up to the temple's peak. The empty stone doorway was an eight foot square. His torchlight jumped into it and illuminated paintings, and birds. He went inside. Birds lined the edges of a short corridor, whose walls and ceiling were painted with murals of mysterious scenes. The birds sat perched on the ground, or in cracks or alcove spaces on the wall, wherever they could squeeze in, with a clear path down the corridor between them. Samson felt a creeping sensation run down the skin over his spine. The birds stood motionless, eyes open, like stuffed corpses or waxworks, but were clearly alive. He walked down the corridor and the birds still did not move. There was every variety of bird, a hummingbird, a starling, an eagle – a vulture. Hundreds of birds. He tapped a sparrow with his foot and it fell over, quivering and sputtering, but unable to move. He gently picked it up and set it on its feet again. At the end of the short corridor was a stairway leading down. Samson gazed for a long time at a beautiful parrot that was perched on a short stump of structural beam sticking out from the wall. The parrot was white and red, with bright green highlights in its plumage. He held the torch up to it and examined it closely. It had a thick, hooked beak that could tear out great chunks of flesh. If the birds came awake and attacked him in a swarm the way that they did in the sky, they might destroy him instantly. He could be transformed into a cloud of bloody chunks of flesh and human dust. The parrot was so beautiful, and, like the humming bird that Samson had killed before, seemed unsuited to aggression. Not un-capable, only unsuited, like a large, strong, beautiful, and gentle man.

The paintings on the wall were difficult to fathom. They were dramatic, showing bright, cylindrical objects hurtling through a night-like plane. There were stars behind them, pricks of light, like he had imagined. There were people, too, in different scenes. Men and women, large and small, beautiful and ugly, people of every color and description. Some of the people repeated in the scenes, and a few of them were in most of the scenes. One particular man was in all of them. This man must be the hero of the people who built this pyramid, Samson thought. His torch flickered very low and he lit another one. The hero had brown hair and plain colored skin, he was tall but not overly tall, and strongly built but not to any extreme. The people around him seemed to love him, to admire him, and some of the crowds of people seemed to idolize him. Some of the crowds of people seemed to hate him. He was a great man, or a god. There were no birds in the paintings on the walls.

The stairs at the end of the corridor led downward to another corridor, which led to more corridors and more stairs. The length and complexity of the passageways increased as one went down. It had to be that way, Samson thought, because the pyramid offered more room for it the lower one went. At the very top there could only be one short corridor, just as there was. Each corridor was the same as the ones before, everywhere filled with birds and paintings. Samson examined the paintings closely, often transfixed by them, and gradually descended into the pyramid while trying not to become lost. He drew ashy marks along the floor to guide his way.

ON THE CEILING IN ONE corridor was a beautiful mural of a man and a woman loving each other. The man was the hero who appeared in all of the paintings, the woman was a dark haired beauty who appeared in many of them. Their love was intense, physical, and portrayed with unflinching explicitness. It did not make Samson feel aroused or titillated, or his senses voyeuristically engaged, but gave him rather – a feeling of familiarity. Like a memory of his own, it was less a discovery than a reminisce. After laying on the ground and gazing at it for a long time he realized that he was the man in the painting, that it actually was a memory of his own. These pictures, these images, were his life. Somewhere. The woman having sex with him in the painting, the dark haired beauty, was the woman he sought, the one who sometimes came into his mind. She was his love, somehow. Somewhere, not in this world. He was sure that it was not in this world. If this was a world. He didn't know what it was missing, but felt that it was not a world, that it was lacking too much. He couldn't bring to focus in his mind exactly what a world should be, what a world was, but he had an instinct, some ghost of a memory or buried one, that this was not it. This was something less than a world, and something more than it. The woman was not here, he could never love her here, she could come into his mind briefly but she could not stay.

He continued on, down other corridors and stairways, examining the paintings and trying not to step on the birds. The birds were fascinating in themselves and he regretted not having more time to examine them, but the paintings overwhelmed his attention. When each torch burned down until it was almost out he used it to light another one, and his bag grew lighter as he left the discarded ones behind, helping to mark the path.

146

Gazing closely at a painting with tiny details, he slipped and stepped on the foot of one of the birds. The bird did not move, but when Samson stooped to examine its foot one of its toes was crushed to a flat, gooey red. He could see it breathing, and felt guilty. He also felt afraid. The painting with tiny details was a segmented mural that told a story. It seemed to be an adventure story, with him fighting other men, and men with weapons chasing him, and flights through space, then him being caught, and escaping, and being chased again. Sometimes the dark haired woman was with him. In the end, an enormous ship flew up and saved him, and the dark haired woman acquired a halo around her head and left in the big ship. The last panel showed him crying and alone.

There were paintings of him as a child, in a distant land. Distant from what, he didn't know. These pictures often featured the figure of a cross, and in fact the paintings of him as an adult often showed a tiny cross in a pocket at his chest or hanging from his neck. He reached and touched the top of his chest and could almost feel the cross there, the impression in his hand if he squeezed it, but didn't know what it meant. The distant land was beautiful and restrained, he left it when he was still a boy. He seemed to be a very lonely boy. There was a taller, older boy who must have been his brother, who was sad when he left. His parents had been harsh. The distant land was too restrained for him, it choked him. The boy found freedom in space, which seemed to be a wonderful thing.

So many of the paintings were of him and space. He flew through space in some special way, that made him a special person. Often there was another man with him, a good friend, but often he was alone. When he was alone, he was in a special ship, a long, thin, white ship that he could somehow perch on the end of and control. Many, many people loved him because of what he did in space, in the long white ship, but they were not close to him. He was a hero to them, but it wasn't clear why.

There were paintings of other women and him loving each other, but none of them affected him the way the paintings of him loving the dark haired woman did. The other women were not important, they were passing moments in his life, but the dark haired woman was essential in it. He wondered why she had a halo when she left him to join the big ship. In some other paintings she had a halo, too. She was powerful somehow. Perhaps it was her power that could rescue him, that could bring him back to her world, wherever she was. He wondered if she was in the world that they had shared, the world of the paintings, or if she was somewhere else entirely now, like he was. He understood that he needed her. When she came into his mind, she needed him, but in a different way, in a way that was less essential. He needed her more than anything, literally. She was the destination of his journey.

There was one small painting that Samson could not get away from. It was a scene that kept repeating in different styles, portrayed in a myriad of ways. It was a painting of himself in the white ship, in space, flying very fast. It seemed to show him die.

He wondered then, if he was dead. Was this a life after life? He had not been able to grasp the past enough to wonder this before. Or were the paintings a prediction, a future? They felt like memories, even the painting of his death. He felt he had experienced that moment. In some of the paintings of it, thousands of points of light seemed to shine in on him at the very end, as if they would compress him to a point. It was like an atomic compression array he thought for a flicker of a moment and then forgot. Could he be dead, and could the woman be dead too? Did they need to join their dead worlds? Or did he seek to be reborn to a new world, together with the woman? Or was he even dead at all? Death was a vague concept, like the crushed hummingbird he had held in his hand, it seemed possible, but it was hard to understand what it would mean outside of a world. Death seemed a thing borne of a world, of a real life, a life like in the paintings. Where he was now was, in some way he could not grasp, not life. Or not that life, not his "life". The paintings were his life, although they were dead. He wondered if he had others, or if he could. Or perhaps he and the woman could simply repeat that one. That could be why he needed to find her. She should know.

SOONER THAN EXPECTED, SAMSON BEGAN to run low on torches. He estimated that he could probably still rush back to the temple entrance before all his torches burned out, if he started back now. When this torch burned out and his next torch was lit, that was the point he would have to turn back, or if he pressed on his torches would all burn out while he was still in the Temple. He wouldn't be able to get back fast enough.

There was a painting on the wall of himself and the dark haired woman smiling. They seemed so happy. It occurred to him that they never had a child. None of the paintings showed them with a child.

He glanced up at the ceiling, imagining the entrance to the temple. On the ceiling was another painting of his death. His death was somehow triumphant, somehow not sad. Perhaps it wasn't a death after all, but a transfiguration. Or something? A leaving of that world. It didn't have to be death. He looked at his torch, and thought about the hummingbird crushed in his hand, and looked at the woman and himself smiling until he felt jealous of them. She was somewhere, below. He could feel her getting closer. He lit another torch and pressed on.

C H A P T E R ²¹

A T THE BOTTOM OF THE TEMPLE, after proceeding through many more corridors and down several more stairways, the passageways all ended in a cavernous room with a spectacular mural on its wall. The mural was at least 20 feet high, and twice as wide. Samson caught his breath when he came upon it. He had only one extra torch left, so he resisted the urge to stop and jogged around the room looking for other exits or continuations of the path. There were none, and the outer walls of the room were all composed of large stone blocks. The blocks themselves had a sparkly, crystalline mineral in them that sent the torch light twinkling around the room, allowing it to be brighter than the corridors had been. Samson could sit in the middle of the room with his torch and still see the mural clearly.

The mural portrayed an epic contest that he seemed to be the central figure of. There were many ships, flying through strange spaces and racing around a yellow sun. There were countless people watching from a distance, from very far away. The dark haired woman watched from a little planet, curled up in a ball with a blanket clutched in her hands. Many important people were watching from another small planet that was close to the sun, or perhaps it was a beautiful ship that was as large as a planet; many of them were exchanging bets and had skin tones of exotic colors. Some of the ships killed each other, and some of the ships were destroyed when they crashed. The sun exploded and killed many of the ships. His ship survived. He seemed to battle with one other ship in particular, a ship piloted by a beautiful man with pale white skin and no hair. This man had appeared in other paintings that Samson passed; he was a dangerous man, and seemed to be a rival. Samson and the dangerous man battled with each other, but Samson came out ahead. Another ship came to challenge him and he escaped from it. In the end, he was the fastest one, the first. His body was compressed by a thousand fingers of light that seemed to emanate from the floating ghosts of souls, or even from every person in the mural. He couldn't understand what this compression was supposed to mean.

This painting, this mural, was not the thing he sought, but it seemed to be a reflection of lost memories, a path into the lost corridors of his mind. It was an end that must be passed to proceed to what he sought, that must be pushed through. He stared at the painting. This was not what would bring him to the woman, this was what separated him from her. He put his hand on the ground and scratched nervously at the cold, dry dirt. What did it all mean? What was he to do? If only he could push through the clouded reaches of his mind, and recover what was lost. That would make sense of it, if he could remember. If he could push through, it would make sense.

He glanced at a colorful bird with a great, long beak. It blinked at him and he shivered. The dark haired woman was not here, here was what separated him from her. This temple was a mausoleum, a hymn to his dead self. It was himself that he must overcome, somehow. It was himself that he must push through and overcome. Push through.

Night came when he wanted it to come. Not when he desired it, but when he understood it enough to want it, to know what he wanted and be the agent of it. Desiring something, of itself, was empty. He had to understand the implication of his desire. One could desire mercy, peace, fulfillment, retribution, but they were nothing without a comprehension of what they would mean, what they implicated and implied. You could desire to build a fire, but that was empty. You could desire to collect the wood, and find the rock, and shape it, to gather tinder and work to make a spark, to set the fire, build the fire, and keep it – you could desire this and have a fire. You must understand what it meant to have a fire. Just to desire a fire, was empty.

The space that he must push through was the space within himself that separated himself from her. It was even the space that separated himself from himself. He must push through it and become the man again, the man who was compressed by souls. He could push through it and become dead, or return to a world, or to some unexpected place, where she was. He could push through it and become the man in the paintings, the man that was himself, the compressed man. He must push through it, or– ? He was lighting his last torch. There was no way forward, or back, only through.

Samson walked forward to the wall. The painting began to grow and shift as he approached it. The expression on the dark haired woman's face changed. Other people changed, too. The lighting shifted like a kaleidoscope. He walked towards the wall with his free hand stretched out in front of him. His steps did not slow. His hand sank into the wall, then his body, and he was overcome for a moment, then he was through it.

ON THE OTHER SIDE WAS a room with crumbling ancient walls and a glowing, blue pool of water. Above the pool of water was a beautiful mosaic of the dark haired woman, whose name was Stephanie, with a magnanimous smile creeping over her face. At once, Samson's memories came back to him. He remembered himself, his name, his brother and parents. He remembered God. He remembered Stephanie de Rothschild, and his friend Ben Johnson who was dead, and the Solar Regatta. He remembered the end of the race, the fingers of the universe pressing in on him – he remembered everything.

And yet, the world he was in did not cease to make sense. His mind was multiplied. It was as if he were waking from a dream without exiting the dream world. The dream world became more vivid and concrete. It was terrifying.

CHAPTER 22

SAMSON REACHED TO GRASP THE cross he wore around his neck, but it was not there. His feet felt heavy on the ground, he could no longer fly. Where was he? The afterlife? Another dimension? Where was the God? He rubbed his chest where the cross should have been, where he wore it when he was racing, where he had pressed it into his chest so many times. He had won! He had won the Solar Regatta, and now he was dead. That must be it? He must be dead. This couldn't be a dream, not now, not when he was awake. He could find Ben here, if he was dead. The soul passed on, the next great adventure. Ben's soul must be the same. Who had imagined the afterlife like this? And where was God? The God was supposed to be here, in the afterlife. If this was the afterlife, what was after this? He felt that he could still die, again. He tried to float up into the air in thought, as he had become accustomed to, and fell painfully onto the ground on his back. He got up and rubbed his skin where it stung – a sharp rock had cut him. The cut bled, and did not heal quickly.

If Stephanie was here, then had she died too? She should not have died so soon. Was it soon? He tried to estimate the passage of time. He had been here for? It might have been weeks, or might easily have been decades. Time here had a strange quality. Time was relative, as the physicists say. Time was, more than relative, it was plastic and mutable, apparently. Time here only seemed to have begun when he regained his memory. Now the minutes and seconds ticked by so that he could feel them. Before, things happened, there was an order of events, but there was no time. No time.

This clock that had started would soon run out. His eyes shifted to the flickering of his last torch, then to the mural of Stephanie on the wall. The only way forward was here, in this room, there was no other way. He couldn't imagine what a way forward would be, but something would happen, inevitably. Inevitably? There were no birds in this room, mercifully. Mercifully? But could they come here? Could they cross the wall as he had done?

Death was supposed to answer the final questions, but it only brought him more of them. There was no answer here. This was not illumination, but clouding of the picture! What did it all mean, what was the point? He pounded the stone wall with his fist. Anger seemed fresh, bright – all his emotion seemed that way now. He should have been broadened, expanded, the events of his life, the events of the world, they should seem small now. The Solar Regatta? From this perspective of death it shouldn't matter. From this perspective it should be silly. It seemed more important to him than ever.

He had won! He had beaten Killian, he had beaten Chang, he had defeated all of them! He, Samson, was the victor, the greatest, with his plain skin and hair, with no enhancements, he himself, all from himself and of himself, with no boosts or crutches to stand on. He had been better than them, he had flown at the edge of death, he had flown into death, but he had won. He was sure he had crossed the finish line before he died. They could all live in a universe where Samson Ford, natural born man, a child of the Magdalena cult, a man who believed in the God, mostly – they could live in a universe where he was the champion, the legend. And all their self-engineering could rot. Stephanie would be proud of him. Ben would be vindicated, somewhere, in some plane overcoming strange puzzles and journeys of his own, he would be honored. There must be a way, being dead, to look at the Solar System, to see what was happening, to watch the people that you loved. There must be a way, mustn't there? But how could Stephanie talk to him if she was alive?

Why was there a mosaic here of Stephanie? Here, at the end. She was...redemption? Some literal redemption, some reified romantic notion of love? Love would be his salvation, love of this woman, his woman. They weren't even married, they hadn't even spent years together. She seemed to overwhelm his life, his afterlife. Stephanie – why? There should have been answers to things like that, in the afterlife. He hated to think that she was dead, although she might have lived her whole life and died of age already. They might both be dead, and could be together again now. She was trying to get to him too, maybe that was why they could reach each other. She was trying to get to him too, she had communicated that to him.

Samson?

Yes.

Samson!

I am me.

I am Stephanie.

I remember.

You are?

Yes. Here.

Here?

You dead too.

No.

There still?

Still.

I am here.

You remember.

Yes.

Here?

There still. I am here. Dead.

Not dead.

Dead.

Not!

She could not understand him. She wasn't dead! She insistently believed that he was not dead, either. If this was not death, then what? A dream or hallucination? It was not that. It confused and upset her, when he thought about this place. He was not dead – she didn't seem completely sure of it. She thought it and felt it, but not with conviction. He must be dead. She didn't want to believe that he was.

Yes. No!

Even in her mind she was confused. Where was she?

Here.

In a laboratory, with something, his body, a corpse, with doctors, Kenichi.

Not trustworthy, completely.

I know. But.

Yes, like me then.

Relied on him then.

Yes.

The shepherd walked into the room, and it seemed strange to Samson that he should suddenly appear.

What?

"You. What does it all mean?" Samson demanded from the shepherd. "Are you the God?"

The shepherd lowered his hood, revealing his face in the last flickers of torch light. He was Ben Johnson.

"Ben!"

Don't understand.

"Ben, you're here! Ben!" Samson ran to embrace him, but the shepherd remained impassive and did not return his embrace. "Talk, Ben, don't you know me?"

Who? Ben?

"How will you proceed?" the shepherd said.

The man looked exactly like Ben, every wrinkle, every

feature on his face was the same. His voice was the same. Samson couldn't believe he hadn't noticed it before.

"Aren't you Ben?"

"How will you proceed?" the shepherd asked again, impassively.

Samson shook him, and the man pushed him off, but it did not change the shepherd's bearing.

The last torch finally burned out. Samson caught his breath, then opened up his fingers and let it fall to the ground. The room was darker now, but still lit, by faint, glowing blue light that radiated from the pool. Samson walked closer to it. The mural of Stephanie was illuminated beautifully by the blue light, with consonant shadows of perfect contrast, as if it had been made to be seen this way.

Darkness? Blue?

She couldn't understand. He himself couldn't. How to proceed? How could he? Proceed to where, to what, how?

"How can I proceed?" Samson asked.

The shepherd said nothing. Birds began to hop into the room, as if they were passing through the wall, as if they were ghosts. He couldn't see any bird pass through the wall, but they came to be there, at the edges of the room, where he had crossed through the wall, and they slowly hopped forward. The birds chirped and squawked in a growing cacophony.

Fear.

Don't understand. Birds?

Don't understand.

How can I?

You can't.

Samson edged away from the birds and closer to the pool, his skin seemed a funny color in the blue light. How would he proceed? There was no way forward. He must die again here, death, a second death? There was no way forward.

No!

The white feathered, unicorn man suddenly sprinted into the room and attacked Samson. They rolled and thrashed in the blue pool. Samson's flesh was torn up again, and it was more painful than it had been before. He choked and swallowed great gulps of water. The unicorn man cut him badly as they struggled, then he twisted his horn into Samson's side, stabbing him deep. Samson worked his arms into a lock around the unicorn man's neck and held him down, gurgling, clawing at Samson's legs. It took several minutes for the unicorn man to drown. Samson's arms burned and ached from the effort, even through the pain of his wounds, but he held them fast until the body's twitching stopped.

Stephanie's thoughts grew muddled, hysterical.

Blood coursed from Samson's flesh. He dragged the unicorn man's body to the edge of the pool and lay it on the ground. The unicorn man looked familiar. He didn't have a unicorn anymore. He didn't have feathers. He was an ordinary man, with ordinary skin and hair. It seemed a pity to have killed him now; he seemed so fragile. Samson held the man's face in his hands and looked at it more closely. It was bruised and torn from his blows. The face was familiar, because it was his own face. It was him.

C H A P T E R 23

AMSON STUMBLED BACKWARD INTO THE pool and slumped to a sitting position in the shallow water near its edge. He watched his blood run into the pool and began to feel faint. The more faint he felt, the more he was afraid.

What? How can I?

You can't help.

Can't I?

Can you help?

She didn't understand. Her thoughts were distraught. She didn't know what to do. But it was comforting to have her with him then. It wasn't comforting enough to help anything, but it was comforting. She was more afraid than he was. He laughed, but she could not reflect any mirth. The mirth upset her more. Samson could be afraid and laugh about his terror, at least for a moment. She could not.

Come back now.

He was too weak to hold the blood in, to stop the bleed. He slumped further, until the water was up to his chest.

I am the man with the horn, Samson thought. I am the man with the horn. I killed myself, somehow. I am in a fight with myself here. He is me, but he is dead.

Come back now.

Samson's vision became cloudy, and he tried hard to focus.

I am the man with the horn. I am the shepherd. Everything here is me. I am this water and this blood. Everything is me. This world is me.

Come back now.

"I am the water and the blood!" Samson said aloud.

Come back.

"God, where are you? I am the water and the blood! I am the water!"

160

Come back, to me. Back now. You are here.

Samson began to scoop the water and the blood up weakly with his hands and drink it, his body consumed with a ravenous thirst so that it was impossible to drink enough. He slurped in gulp after gulp of the salty, ferrous water. Even as he did so, his vision clouded further and began to fade.

Come back now. Now.

"I don't want to die!"

The blue light of the pool blended gradually into a sparkling white haze that consumed everything. It was not something he could see, but a lack of seeing. Yet, it was bright. Soon he could see nothing at all, only the sparkle of the haze. He couldn't feel his breathing or his pain. He must be underwater, he thought. He must have sunk underwater. He couldn't feel anything except the brightness of the haze. And fear. He tried to fling his limbs, to shake his head. He could feel nothing. He wasn't even a body anymore, perceptibly. He was only the sparkle of the haze, which was nothing.

IN THE LAB, ON ROTHSCHILD, Samson's body let out a scream. It was a human voice, but did not sound like a human voice. It sounded more than human, more than natural, as if it came from another place, a different universe where physics and sound were traversable things, where a scream was as much generated by the radiation of your mind as by waves of compressed air. Everyone in the room felt their skin run cold at the sound of it. The word that Samson Ford screamed was 'Stephanie'.

Stephanie snapped her eyes open and tore the apparatus off of her head to get to him. His body had become normal, real. It *was* a body. He was coughing up strange fluid from his lungs.

CHAPTER 24

LISA MAUI WAS CHAINED TO a wall, in a stony dungeon somewhere deep in the bowels of Earth. Her memories of the days since her interrogation by Phillipe Bloodworth were a drug induced, empty haze. She could not have even guessed at how much time had passed. Whether it was days, or weeks, or even months. Now, chained to the wall, the haze was subsiding. There was a hood tied over her head. She could feel the pain of manacles clasping her wrists. She had not felt any pain, or any thing, since her interrogation. She could remember someone giving her injections, sometimes. She could remember laying in a bed and someone giving her injections.

Someone untied the hood and pulled it off her head. The light in the room was dazzling for a moment, but her eyes quickly adjusted. The room was not bright, it was lit by candles and torches. It was a dungeon, like one in a story book. The walls and floor were made of round, grey stones. The door was thick boards of wood and looked as if it were 1,000 years old. There were people looking at her, but not normal people. Lisa flinched.

There were little people watching her, but they were not entirely human. They reminded her of genetic experiments from the past that she had seen in a textbook. They looked like little monkey men. They grinned at her, but said nothing. This must be a dream. Their dress was absurd, tight black leather with buckles and studs. One of them had bright feathers sticking out around his belt. One of them was a girl. One had a black rubber strap wrapped tightly around his ears, and strings of off-white rubber strung under the top of it, to form a kind of wig. This must be a dream, a nightmare. They grinned devilishly at her, as if they were made of evil.

Then Lisa noticed the table. It was covered in objects and

devices. Some of them were dildos or other sexual objects that she recognized. Some of them had blades, and many more were hung on the wall. They were torture devices and sexual devices. Many of them were wooden or iron and bore an antique patina. Lisa squirmed against the wall and jerked painfully against the manacles that held her arms. This must be a nightmare, this could not be real.

It was only after noticing everything else that Lisa noticed Phillipe Bloodworth standing motionless in the corner. He was watching her too, but did not grin. He looked stern. Only after seeing Bloodworth did it seem strange to Lisa that none of them were saying anything.

"H-Hello," Lisa said, trying out her voice.

"Shut up!" Bloodworth said, and strode to the front of the room.

"What do you want from me?" Lisa said.

She realized already that she was going to die. She understood that they were planning to torture her. She understood these things as facts, but tried not to focus on them. She needed Bloodworth to come closer to her, or any of the monkey things. She would kick them as hard as she could, she would hurt them, somehow, she would inflict some kind of damage. There was no chance of escape and nothing at all to lose. She would do anything she possibly could to hurt them, if only Bloodworth would come a step closer. She would kick him so hard that he would remember this experience as pain, and never revel in it.

"I will speak and you will listen," Bloodworth said.

Lisa spat at him and it hit him in the face. Bloodworth brushed the spittle off with his hand.

"If you do that again, or if you interrupt me, I'll have them put a gag on you," he said. "Your situation is not hopeless yet. I have something to say, so listen quietly and think about these words."

Lisa decided to keep quiet and wait for him to step close to her. She would kick him in the throat, if possible. If it knocked him down and he hit his head on the stone floor, it might even kill him. She wanted to wake up from this nightmare, she jerked and writhed against the wall to wake herself up, but could not wake up. A part of her mind understood that this was real, and a part of her mind could not believe that it was.

"The reason you are here is because you are a piece of shit," Bloodworth said. "Do you understand what I said? I don't mean in some figurative way that you are a piece of shit, I mean that you are actually human excrement. Or the equivalent of that. You are pure shit, pure waste, completely objectionable and completely worthless. More than being worthless, you are a problem for humanity, an unfortunate aberration of the universe that has to be processed and disposed of. You explode out of the asshole of humanity regardless of what society wants, regardless of what we hope or wish, regardless of how perfect we try to be, you explode out of us in the disgusting and toxic essence of yourself, that is yourself. Did you think that you are some kind of interesting or important person because you were on tv? You are pure shit, that's why you are here. I hate shit.

"Do you see these things, these creatures? They are animal people that I have created to be my servants. I couldn't have a human being serve me, don't you understand why? A human being should never be a servant. But for these animal people it is their natural place in the universe to be servants. To be my servants, specifically, because I created them for that. I am their god."

The monkey people bowed reverently to Bloodworth when he said this.

"You see? They are exactly what I want them to be, because I created them. They are not humans, but they are like humans. They are animal people. You seem to be a person who loves animal people. Do you understand that loving animal people is a quality of shit? The affinity for what is disgusting, for what is toxic, that is a quality of human excrement like you. Your name is shit. Do you understand what I mean, shit? Your name is shit!! These servants of mine will call you by your true name. You love animal people, and they are animal people, so you will get to spend some precious time with them. They are my servants, and as such I do not love them. I use them, because I have made them for me to use. You who love them, you with the affinity for feces, will get to be comingled with them. Although they are not shit, they are only animal people, and you are shit, your natural affinity for whatever is disgusting in humanity will make you a natural friend to them.

"You see, shit, natural born humans are better and worse than these animals. I would kill a natural born human, in fact I am going to kill all of them, but I wouldn't make one be my servant. Natural born humans are humans, it is not their nature to be anything less than genetically engineered humans like me. Their nature is to be pinnacle creatures, the superior beings of the universe. The only problem with that, is that a superior version of themselves now exists. It is their nature to be superior beings, but it is impossible for them to be superior beings now that genetically modified humans have appeared. That creates an inherent conflict, and a diminishment that rubs off onto the genetically modified people. The natural born humans, who are in their nature pinnacle beings, have no place in a universe with genetically modified humans. It is an inherent conflict. One or the other has to be destroyed. Obviously, that is the inferior version."

Bloodworth's voice raised as he spoke, and his face turned more and more red. He was angry, but it was a weird kind of anger. It was anger mixed with deep pleasure, as if he were almost in ecstasy. Lisa threw up.

"You see what I mean, shit? You have a natural affinity for disgusting things, like vomit. When I look at you, and see your eyes, your body, I feel happy. I feel wonderful today.

"I always let my monkey people clean up my shit. Since I am their god, they enjoy cleaning it up. Sometimes they even enjoy eating it. That's why I'm going to give you to them, shit. Cleaning up shit gives them joy, when I give it to them. You may not be a direct product of my body, like much of the shit they are privileged to take care of, but you are given to them from me. That gives them joy.

"They like to play with shit. Even their own, we have to train that out of them, but especially mine. I thought you might be close to Stephanie de Rothschild, or somebody important. I thought you could possibly be useful, but it turns out you're not. These creatures like to play with shit, so I'm leaving you here for them to play with and dispose of."

Bloodworth walked toward the door. He had never come close enough for Lisa to kick him.

"No," Lisa said. "Wait! You said my situation wasn't hopeless."

"I was lying. I'll leave you with a parting thought, shit," Bloodworth said as he opened the door. "These creatures — it's *very* difficult for them to have an orgasm."

He stepped quickly out of the room and slammed the door.

"No, wait!!"

The monkey people grinned at her and inched closer. There were three of them, two males and a female. It was hard for Lisa to want to hurt them, they seemed pathetic. She remembered something her grandfather had told her about genetic engineering, that mixing human and animal DNA was one of the worst things genetic engineers had ever done. The people who were created, and her grandfather called

166

them people, had been damaged and pitiable. It was cruel to create people like that, her grandfather had said. It was a violation of nature. Everyone had agreed that human-animal hybrids should be banned, once they began to be created. These monkey people seemed like that, horrible and pathetic. They were creepy, they were intent on hurting her, but she couldn't make herself hate them.

"Hello pretty," the female said.

The two males echoed her and laughed nervously. They all spoke with a funny, salivary lisp.

"Hello," Lisa said. Then, as they inched closer, "My name is Lisa."

"We know your name, pretty name," the female said.

"Pretty name. We know it."

"We know it."

"What are you going to do? You're not going to hurt me, are you? Talk to me."

"We will pretty hurt you, pretty," the female said.

"We will."

"Pretty, pretty name. We know it."

"Why would you want to hurt me?" Lisa said.

"For fun!"

"For fun. For fun."

"Fun. Pretty fun, for fun."

The monkey people came close enough and Lisa tried to kick them, but they dodged her legs. They were remarkably agile. They grabbed her legs and chained them to the wall, one leg at a time. Then they stood very close as Lisa jerked against her chains.

"Get... the food," the female said.

The two males went over to the table and returned with a bowl of strawberries and grapes. While they were doing this, the female rubbed her hands and face up and down Lisa's body. Then the three of them took turns touching Lisa's face and pushing pieces of fruit into her mouth.

"Eat, pretty, eat," the female said, while rubbing her hands up and down Lisa's thighs.

"Ach, no!" Lisa screamed and spat out the food, but they only shoved more into her mouth and, in a perversely affectionate way, forced her jaws to chew.

"Leave me alone!"

After a few minutes more, the female walked over to the table and the two males followed her.

"Look, pretty, look," the female said, holding up a dildo.

One by one, she held up various sex objects and torture instruments. She and the two males waved their hands over the different objects as if they were showcasing fine watches or jewels, and made an elaborate show of "oohing" and "ahhing" for each one. Lisa felt nauseous and could barely focus on them. Her stomach clenched into a tiny ball. She began to breathe rapidly and could not make herself stop.

"You see what pretty we have," the female said. "Wonderful things, pretty, master, pretty, gave us and taught us to use. See, pretty, these beauty things? See? We have tools!"

The female finished her display and then motioned the other two with her towards the door. They all grinned.

"You sleep with that wall tonight," the female said. "Think about these pretty tools and what we will do with them and with you until tomorrow. In tomorrow, pretty, we play, pretty."

Then the monkey people left the room and Lisa was alone. She could not stop her rapid breathing. Her mind registered relief that they were gone, that they had stopped, but she could not feel it as an emotion. She tried to think about her grandparents, but couldn't focus. Her body was in pain from being chained to the wall. Time passed like this. She kept growing faint, and slumping against the chains, and waking from the

168

sharp pain of the manacles as she slumped. Someone must be looking for her. Something could happen, somehow. There was no hope, but she wanted to believe she could escape. She couldn't seem to summon the strength to hit her manacles against the wall. She couldn't stop breathing fast, and kept fainting and then waking up from the pain.

C H A P T E R ²⁵

I N AUCKLAND, ON EARTH, SCAMP was holding a man face down on a bed and tying up his arms and legs. Once he got the man tied, while still holding his face into the bed, he grabbed the man's pants and underwear by the waist band and tore them off of his body. Then he did the same thing with the man's shirt, leaving the man naked. Finally, he let go of the man, allowing him to roll over. The man's face was purple from having Scamp's weight on top of him and he gasped for air. Scamp went to the stereo system, which was already turned up very loud, and turned it up louder. The man was paying a price now for being such an asshole to his neighbors, Scamp thought. If he didn't have the music up so loud someone might have heard something. Although, a club next door was also playing music very loud.

When the man eventually caught his breath he started screaming for help.

"Stop," Scamp said.

The man continued to scream, so Scamp reached down and squeezed the hinge of his lower jaw with one hand until he stopped screaming and squealed from pain. Scamp held a finger up in front of the man's face to keep his attention.

"No one can hear you over the music. It doesn't help you to scream, and it forces me to hurt you. Stop screaming."

"W-who the fuck are you?" the man said.

Scamp squeezed his jaw again until tears came to the man's eyes.

"I'm asking the questions," he said. "I expect you to be helpful and polite. I don't want to hurt you, I don't enjoy it at all, in fact I find it unpleasant, but as you can see I am willing and able to hurt you as much as is necessary."

The man began to interrupt him and Scamp squeezed

170

his jaw again and then held up his index finger in front of the man's face.

"Helpful, and polite."

A large part of the resistance finally faded from the man's eyes, so that he looked withdrawn. He slumped back on the bed.

It had taken all of Scamp's resources and most of his considerable savings to find this man. Of course, he didn't start out knowing that this man was someone he needed to find. He had leveraged all of his connections in the underworld to find out what had happened to Lisa Maui. He had called in every favor, used every angle of personal intimidation, implemented every blackmail that had been vaulted in his files – he had done that incredibly rare thing: everything that he possibly could – in order to find out what happened to her. He had killed some men; he had known that would be necessary from the beginning. The search had led him quickly, although with great difficulty, to this man and this apartment. This man was the cab driver who had kidnapped Lisa. This was the man who had done it, and this was the man who could answer questions about it. The man himself didn't know yet, although he was beginning to guess, that he would answer the questions. He would tell Scamp anything Scamp wanted to know.

Scamp had been a lieutenant for Lucho Gonzalez, and Lucho's top enforcer. That fact had often left people who didn't know any better with a misapprehension. For people who knew, for savvy people in the underworld, Scamp was a much more frightening enemy than Lucho himself. Scamp wasn't ambitious, he wasn't a leader, and he didn't have a vision for a large enterprise, so he was Lucho's employee. But even Lucho, even with all of his psychological manipulations over the big man – even he was terrified of Scamp and knew to never cross him past a certain line. Scamp wasn't only huge and incredibly strong and fast, he was an expert in almost every kind of fighting imaginable. In a knife fight, he could catch the other man's knife between his fingers, take it from his hands as if the man were a baby, and then snap the blade in half between his forefingers and thumbs. He didn't need the knife to kill his adversary, he could literally grab hold of the man and tear his arms or head off, and the fact that he had done so before was not a legend. But those things were not the reason Scamp was feared; he was feared because he also happened to be highly intelligent, creative, resourceful, and extremely perceptive of human psychology. As far as a single, individual person, a single agent acting on their own, Scamp was the criminal underworld's worst nightmare of an enemy. In Lucho's more irresponsible moments, Scamp had almost single handedly held his criminal empire together.

"I know you were the cab driver who kidnapped Lisa Maui," Scamp said.

"I wasn't!"

The man looked at him with pitiful eyes. Scamp took one of the man's testicles between his thumb and forefinger and gave it a small squeeze, causing the man to gasp.

"Let's try again. I know you were the cab driver who kidnapped Lisa Maui."

"Don't! Ok, I was, but I didn't know anything. It was just a job."

"You still have the ability to have natural born children," Scamp said. "Maybe we should keep it that way."

"I have friends coming here, soon," the man said. "I'm telling you what I know, and I'm telling you that so you don't have to get caught here. I'm helping!"

Scamp looked at the man with a curious expression on his face.

"Surely you realize that I'll have to kill anyone who comes."

The man started to laugh, and then blanched. He had never seen eyes like Scamp's, and for the first time he realized that the man who was terrorizing him wasn't entirely human.

"A guy hired me to do a job," the man said. "I didn't know who the girl was, when I got her I thought that she was from tv, but I didn't know anything about her. I drove her to a warehouse, other guys put her in a van and took her away from there. I didn't know the other guys, I didn't know anyone except the guy who hired me. He didn't know anything about it, either. It was a simple pay job, I took my money, that was the end of it."

The man looked at Scamp with pleading, reproachful eyes.

"I feel certain you know more than that."

Scamp could tell that the man was lying to him. Or, rather, he could tell that the man was not trying to be helpful to him. He held the man's testicle again and crushed it between his thumb and forefinger. The man screamed a high pitched scream, like a woman, then passed out for a few seconds. As he came back to his senses, Scamp stood up and looked down at him, towering over the bed.

"You still have one left," he said. "You can still have natural born children and shop at a Rothschild's store if you choose. But, take a deep breath and think about this: I can tell when you're not genuinely trying to help me."

The man closed his eyes.

"Do you hear the words coming out of my mouth? Do you hear?"

"Y-yes. Yes, I hear. I hear!"

"I can tell, when you're not genuinely trying to help me. I can tell! You have to get on my side, and really try to help me as much as you can, or else I have to keep hurting you. This, with your testicles, having natural born children, this is still

173

just a joke. Repeat what I just said. Repeat that it's still just a joke, so I know you understand. Repeat it!"

"It's still, it's, it's still just a joke."

"It's still just a joke! I don't want to have to start hurting people you care about, to make you help me. But I hope you understand now that I will. Do you understand that?"

"I understand," the man said quietly.

"What do you understand? Repeat it."

"I understand, you don't want to hurt the people I care about...but, you will."

"I hope you don't make me do that," Scamp said. "I know you have a father, for instance, that you care a lot about. I need you to be helpful with me, genuinely do your best to help me. I hate to do these terrible things, but I am going to do them, until you genuinely do everything you can to help me with what I want. Help me with an open heart."

"I'll help you," the man said, holding eye contact with Scamp through his tears. "I'll help you. I want to help. Let me help you."

"Good. Let's start again. Tell me everything you know about what has happened to Lisa Maui."

IN A MEDICAL ROOM IN Magdalena City, Theo and Maria were waiting for their fertility doctor to come and talk to them. Doctors in Magdalena were the most advanced natural fertility specialists in the Solar System, and Theo and Maria had gone to the best fertility clinic in Magdalena. Fertility clinics in Magdalena were made up of teams of specialists working with individual fertility doctors who took one-to-one global responsibility for each patient's treatment. Theo and Maria had been subjected to a battery of tests and interrogations. None of the doctors had any answers for them, only, "Let's wait until the tests come back." Now the tests were back, and they sat waiting for their doctor to come explain to them what the tests had found.

They sat squeezed up next to each other, in two folding chairs, with the empty medical bed dominating the center of the room.

"It seems like something's wrong," Maria said quietly, glancing at the closed door.

"There's probably nothing," Theo said.

"The look that technician had on her face when they ran my scan – it seemed like something was wrong."

"Let's not jump to conclusions."

"You don't think the doctors have been acting weird?"

"I can't tell. How can we tell? If something is wrong, we'll cross that bridge together. We already have children."

"I just want one more baby!"

"I know. Well, let's see what the tests said."

"Yes. Oh heaven, that technician looked like something was wrong."

"The technician was just a technician."

"That's true. Oh, won't he hurry up and come? How long have we been here."

Theo rubbed his wife's hand.

"It's going to be alright."

"What do we need to wait for? We should just be able to view the tests online, we shouldn't have to come down here. Why do they make you wait?"

"I don't know. I wish they didn't make us wait so long."

"It's too long, Theo! It's cold in here. This is driving me crazy."

"Honey, relax. Breathe some deep breaths. No matter what happens, we have each other. We have our children. We have a wonderful life. We have a beautiful family."

"I love you, Theo."

"I love you, too."

Some minutes later, their doctor came in. He was a thin man, with grey hair and grey eyes. He shook each of their hands and attempted to smile, not quite accomplishing it. He went to sit down on the doctor's stool in the room, then thought better of it and paced back across the room. He flipped through their charts again, as if refreshing his memory, but they had already heard him reading their charts outside the door.

"Yes, well, I hope you two have been well."

"Thank you doctor," Theo said, "we have. What do the tests say?"

"Right, the tests. The tests."

He flipped through the charts some more, squinting his eyes as if he would spot something that had eluded him.

"Just tell us, please," Maria said.

"Yes, I'm sorry," the doctor said. "It's not good I'm afraid. Neither of you are going to be able to have more children. I'm sorry."

"Wh-whaattt?" Maria said.

Theo's face pinched, and the doctor avoided eye contact with them.

"What do you mean, 'neither' of us?" Theo asked.

"I'm sorry, Mr. Ford, I hate being the bearer of bad news, but you are both sterile."

"There's no treatments?" Maria asked.

"No, there don't seem to be any possible treatments."

"None at all?" Theo said, his voice rising. "What's wrong with us? With *both* of us?"

The doctor stepped back and sat down on the medical bed, with his legs dangling in the air, facing them. He set their charts down and knitted his fingers together.

"Try to take some deep breaths, Mr. Ford, and let me explain the test results. I know this news comes as a shock. Mr. Ford – Theo, may I call you by your first names?"

"Of course," Maria said.

"Theo, you will not be able to have another child because your body no longer produces viable sperm."

"Ok," Theo said. "That can't be fixed?"

"It doesn't appear that it can be, no. I'll explain more about that in a moment."

"Ok."

"Maria, you will not be able to have another child because the eggs in your ovaries are all dead."

"They're dead?"

"Yes, all of them are dead."

"Is that a–? Isn't that unusual? I've never heard of that before."

"It is unusual, it's extremely unusual. Actually, it is similar to Theo's situation, his body produces sperm cells but they are dead sperm cells. His body can no longer produce living sperm. This is also extremely unusual. Actually, I've never seen this before, for either of you, and neither have any of the doctors here. What has happened to your reproductive cells is not in any of the medical literature; at least twelve of us here have been searching for it for days.

"This is hard to understand, even for me. In a short period of time, with no other symptoms, you've both been stricken with a devastating reproductive disease that has never been seen before. We, the doctors here, are at a loss. We've also consulted with the best outside experts that we know. No one had seen anything like this before you came in."

"But, if it hasn't been seen before," Maria said, "how do you know there is no treatment?"

"Once the cells are dead, they can't be brought back. For you, Maria, there is no possibility of treatment."

"What about an egg donor?"

"That is forbidden!"

"I'm not saying I want one! I'm trying to understand this. The only problem is that the eggs are dead, right? So, in principle, if I had a healthy egg to use I could still bear a child."

"Yes. In a past time, in a darker time, you could still give birth to someone else's biological child. But you can't bear children of your own. I'm sorry."

Maria clenched her teeth together and watched the doctor with tears in her eyes.

"I'm sorry."

"Well what about him," she said hoarsely, "can't you fix him?"

"It doesn't appear that we can. I'm sorry, Theo. The only thing I can say is that, as your wife cannot have children anyway– It won't affect your overall health."

"You're saying it doesn't matter, because Maria can't have a baby anyway."

"Yes."

"Well can't you do anything?"

"The thing is, it won't affect your overall health. But for Maria, there is a large health risk. The dead eggs could cause an infection in her body. We need to do surgery to remove them. And we want to run more tests, to understand what has happened to both of you. Since your tests came in, we have had a few more couples come to us with charts similar to yours. There have also been rumors from a clinic in the northwest desert. They don't have the advanced diagnostic tools that we have, so their patients haven't been fully diagnosed yet. ...There is a concern that others may have the same disease."

"What does that mean, this is a virus?" Maria said.

"It means we don't know what it means. That's why we want to run more tests and try to understand."

178

Theo cursed under his breath and squeezed his wife's hand. The doctor got off of the bed and kneeled in front of them. He held his hands out to them, so that they could join hands in a circle and close their eyes together to pray. The doctor's hand were damp from sweat.

6/30

I had to kill another man today. I threw up three times after it. Maybe an hour later, I started throwing up. Hurting people bothers me more than it used to. This one was a bad one, though. It was the cab driver that kidnapped Lisa Maui, and I had to be hard with him. I finally caught up with him in his apartment, thankgod. Now when I tear off someone's humanity it seems like I'm tearing off my own. It could have been worse. He told me what he knew.

When I killed him, I didn't cause him any pain. I shouldn't feel bad about him, he was the piece of shit who actually kidnapped Lisa Maui, he doesn't deserve any sympathy. Even for that, I didn't want to hurt him. It gave me no satisfaction. I can remember killing men and getting satisfaction. Don't read that the wrong way, I'm not sick, I mean men who deserved it. I mean taking satisfaction from killing them because they deserved to be killed, or because they were trying to kill me. It isn't exactly the same thing is it? They were trying to kill me didn't mean that they deserved to be killed, it only means that we fought and I won. I can remember feeling satisfaction from killing men in times like that, but I never enjoyed the killing in itself. This piece of shit was fully deserving to be killed, but I didn't feel any satisfaction from it. I'm getting softer, or becoming a better person, that's what someone civilized would say. I lived my whole life with criminals, so I have not been civilized, and I probably can't be civilized. They could say I'm becoming a better person. For what it matters,

179

I killed him in a painless way. I put my hands around his neck and held it in a sleeper hold, so that he passed out quickly, and then I held it like that until he was dead. That's painless, to die like that, physically painless. I don't like to cause people pain, I've never liked it. I can remember taking satisfaction from it, but we just talked about that.

I had to kill him, it wasn't a choice. If I left him alive, Bloodworth's people would find out about me. They could stop me, if they knew I was coming. I'm coming at them from a complete blind side, they can't expect it. That's the only way I have any chance to succeed. So, I didn't have a choice but to kill him. He died for his sins, in a way. He kidnapped Lisa Maui, and I had to kill him to try to save her. It was all a chain of deservedness, if that's the word. It was a full circle, but I vomited three times. He was a bad criminal, no one will know why he was killed, but the chance that the connection will be drawn to Lisa Maui, by the tiny number of people who know there is a connection, is small. Even if they think it's connected, it will be at most a suspicion. They won't know I'm coming.

From what I learned there is a good chance she is still alive. She could be dead, maybe she's probably dead, but there is definitely a chance she is still alive.

When I killed that man today, I felt like I was killing him for Samson Ford. That seems strange, doesn't it? I didn't want to kill him, I didn't want to hurt him at all, but I could envision Samson Ford in my mind and I felt like I was killing this man for him. Bloodworth is targeting Lisa Maui because of her connection to Ford. I mean, that's obvious, but now I can basically confirm it as a fact. She's someone that both Samson and Stephanie de Rothschild cared about. They care about her at least a little bit, she was a friend of theirs. And she's just a girl, just a regular girl really. She seems really beautiful to me. And when I was killing the man, I felt like I was doing it for Samson. Not even for her,

180

but I want to save her. She seems like the kind of woman I wish I could have in my life. Someone like that.

Like I said, there's a good chance she's still alive. She could easily be dead already, but there's a good chance — say it is a <u>significant</u> chance, that she is alive. I have to act fast.

- Scampadorous Maximus

C H A P T E R ²⁶

Lisa Maui stood chained in her prison cell, body trembling against the cold wall. She had finally caught her breath, but was exhausted and in pain. The cell was only lit now by the light of a few candles, as most of the candles and all of the torches had burned out. Her eyes kept creeping back to the table of torture instruments. She wanted to put them out of her mind, but could not. She pulled hard against the shackles on her legs, until they cut into her skin, but it had no effect. Her wrists, as well, were now cut and raw from their braces. There seemed to be no possible way to escape.

Times like this were when people in the classic books would pray to the god. She had never understood exactly what it meant, to pray. They would close their eyes and fold their hands, or hold their hands up in funny positions, or kneel and put their heads against the ground, and pray. What did that even mean? It must have been nice, to have the god. Even though the god wasn't real. In the classic books they would always pray in moments like this. Her grandfather thought that the loss of the god was the greatest tragedy for humanity. She didn't know what her grandmother thought, but it was probably the same. He didn't even believe in the god, but he thought it was the greatest loss to humanity that had ever happened. It would be terrible for her grandparents to find out what happened to her. What was going to happen. She hoped that they would never find out. There wouldn't be closure for them, but it would still be better if she just disappeared. Than to imagine her going through – that.

There must be a way out of this! She tried to think of what she could do to make friends with or manipulate the monkey people. They were so inarticulate. It seemed hopeless. Someone must be looking for her, many people must be, her grandparents would make sure of that, but no one would ever find her here, wherever she was. She couldn't reach anything to break the chain or pry open the braces. She could only move her arms about six inches in any direction. The braces around her arms and legs didn't even have keys. Someone would have to cut them off, or cut her arms and legs off. She started to breathe more quickly again, and forced her body to slow down.

There must be something she could do. There must be something! She would rather commit suicide than let the monkey people torture her to death. She would rather commit suicide than give Bloodworth that satisfaction. There didn't seem to be any way. She was dehydrated, her throat was parched. She was almost thankful for that, as it meant that she did not have to soil herself. This was torture. Suddenly she realized that she was already being tortured, that it had already begun.

There was a creaking at the door and Lisa started.

"Who's there?" she croaked.

In the dim light of the room she could barely see the door inching open. The passageway outside was dark. The door inched open and then back closed again, before a monkey creature finally stepped out of the shadows and into view. He – it appeared to be a male – was dressed in patched up, blue denim overalls and dirty rags. He had tools on a belt, like a handyman, and the overalls he wore had big pockets that seemed to be full.

"What them's doing wrong. What them's doing wrong," he said to himself in a squeaky voice as he came further into the room.

Lisa watched the creature and held her breath as he approached her.

"Shhh," the creature held his finger up to his lips. "I help you."

"What?"

"Shhhh. I'm Melchit. My name Melchit. I help you. Shhh."

He produced a small torch and a strange, thick cloth and squeezed the cloth under the brace around her left leg.

"Insulating cloth," Melchit said, "from the master's space ship. Very special."

He began to cut the brace off of Lisa's leg with the torch, using the cloth to protect her from burns. When he finished with the first brace, he moved on to the next.

"What them's doing wrong," he continued to repeat as he worked.

"What are–"

"Shhh! You not talk. I help you."

"The master is wrong. The master is wrong!" he said and made glancing eye contact with Lisa as he began cutting off the braces on her hands.

This is what the people who believed in the god would call a 'miracle', Lisa thought. The word was hardly used anymore, you rarely heard a person say it, and when they did say it they meant that something was 'lucky', they meant it in a statistical way. Her grandfather used the word sometimes, and used it differently than other people. Although he did not believe in the god, he had explained to her that the ancient people who did believe in the god would use the word 'miracle' to describe an incredible intervention of the god in their lives. Such as if they fell off of a tall building and did not die. Her grandfather liked to use the word that way, although he did not believe in it that way. He liked the idea of it.

It felt of both great relief and pain to move her legs freely again and bring them together, with the shackles cut off. For her arms even more so. To lower her arms felt like needles were sticking into them, but it also felt like icy relief from the pain through her back and shoulders. It was too much feeling, as if her flesh would jump out of her skin. She sank down to her knees on the hard floor.

"Thank you. Thank you!" Lisa whispered in her dried out, cracked voice, with tears running almost unconsciously down her face.

"Shhh," Melchit said and held his hand up near her face, as if to cover her mouth. His hand smelled like motor grease. "You not talk. Follow Melchit. I help you."

He grasped Lisa's hand and pulled her towards the door.

AFTER SAMSON'S BODY BECAME CORPOREAL, after he cried out Stephanie's name, he was unconscious. She first embraced him, clutching his clammy and wet – but warm – skin, then remembered herself and jumped out of the way of the doctors. Samson was moved to a special intensive care ward that had been set up adjacent to the lab. He was monitored around the clock, as his heart slipped in and out of effective rhythm during the first two days. He began to have spells of consciousness and his condition quickly improved.

A week after Samson had woken up, while he was still in the intensive care ward, Stephanie and Simon Okunle sat in a small, sunny breakfast room in her quarters and sipped at cups of exotic coffee. Stephanie watched with executive scrutiny as Simon stirred his tea. It was hard to be the leader of your heroes, your mentors. Her father had done his best to prepare her for it, but she had found it painfully difficult at first. Simon looked at her and offered a benign expression. He was strained, and frustrated with her. The war was grinding him down. He was disappointed with the amount of time she had been devoting to Samson. He understood her feelings, but Samson was only one man, and he expected her to understand that her responsibilities held the weight of billions of men. It hurt him to think poorly of her. He would never say these things out loud.

"It's a miracle that he is alive, a true miracle," Simon said. "You know the history of the word?"

"I know it, Simon."

"I'm so happy for you. What is the latest news, how is he doing?"

"The doctors say that he is in good health, even perfectly healthy. He can't keep himself awake, he drifts in and out of consciousness, and he can't speak or move around much yet, but his body is healthy. The weakness is from a depletion in cellular energy, apparently. It's like what happened to me before, when I was in the protective stasis of the ring. They have him on IV blood nourishment and say it is a matter of time, weeks at the most, until he is completely recovered. He doesn't even have any muscle atrophy!"

"Amazing."

"I knew he was alive, Simon. Somehow I knew he was!"

Simon Okunle stirred at his coffee again with a little, gold spoon. He let the sun from the wrap-around windows sit pleasantly on his face.

"You wanted to believe he was alive," he said, "and you were incredibly lucky to be right."

"Maybe. But what are the odds of that? I could feel it so strongly that he was alive, as if he was in the room, looking at me. What are the odds that I would feel that way so strongly, and he would turn out to be alive?"

"I would say, Mistress, that the odds of Samson living again, after what his body was subjected to, were incalculably long. But also that they were completely independent of the odds of your having a strong feeling that he was still alive."

"Oh, you're right about that, of course, but mygod Simon, he's alive! It's so important to me."

Tears threatened to overflow into Stephanie's eyes and she swallowed hard and willed them away.

"What does Dr. Nguyen say about what happened?"

"He doesn't have any idea. Dr. Nguyen, Kenichi, all the doctors and everyone in the lab, they're completely mystified by it."

"They don't even have a theory?"

"Nothing specific, no. Well, the relativity effect has never been understood in the first place. And now this multiplies its mystery. It's – I'm actually worried that it has messed with Kenichi's head."

"In what way?"

"He can't get over it. It seems to have been almost a religious experience for him. He keeps talking about how the universe isn't what we thought it was."

"That seems to be true."

"Yes."

"Samson can't speak at all yet?"

"No, but he is starting to try. He will be able to speak soon."

"Good. We can use him in this war."

"I know."

"You have to think strategically, Mistress."

"I am."

A COUPLE OF DAYS LATER, Stephanie rubbed Samson's hands and tried to wake him up to drink a cup of tea. The doctors said he was well now, completely healthy, but he could do little more than lay in Stephanie's bed drifting in and out of sleep. They said his energy had not recovered yet, but it would be back soon. He could get up and go to the bathroom on his own, he could move around enough to avoid bed sores, but he usually fell right asleep again after any such expenditure of energy. Their conversations were short and had a dream-like quality.

"Oh," Samson said, waking up. "I love you, babe."

"I love you too. Try to sit up and drink this tea."

Samson's beard had grown out since he had come back. He looked wild and rugged.

"Thank you. Give me a minute, I'll try."

"What were you dreaming about?"

"I don't know. I never remember my dreams. It's not like– I don't think I dream about being in there, being where I was."

"Here, drink some tea. Be careful, it's hot."

He held the cup tenuously in his hand and peeked at her through half-closed eyes.

"I have that weird feeling now, whenever I'm awake. Do you feel it?"

"I don't."

"I told you about it before."

"Yes."

"It's something I've never felt before, I don't know how to describe it. There aren't words for it."

"You've felt it ever since you came back?"

"I think so. It's given a strange feeling to coming back. Like, instead of feeling natural, I feel like I've been thrust into water, or something. This should be a feeling of, going back to normal, but it's not. It's like there's something in the air that moves around and washes over me."

Stephanie watched Samson with a slightly nervous expression on her face. She sat down against his thigh, with her arm propped on the other side, and perched over him.

"The doctors haven't been able to find any reason why you are feeling that way," she said, "but they think it will pass soon. They think it may be a sense of disorientation caused by the transformation you have gone through."

"I don't think it's something they would know about," Samson said, focusing to open his eyes all the way. "I feel like it's connected to that world."

"What do you think that world was?"

"I don't know. It takes too much energy to think now. Here, take it."

Stephanie took the mostly full tea cup back out of Samson's hands and set it on a tray.

"Lay here next to me for a minute," Samson said, sliding back down onto the bed. "Lay here against me, so I can feel you. I'm going to fall back asleep again."

"Thank you for coming back," Stephanie whispered in his ear as she snuggled up against him. "I needed you here. Thank you for coming back to me, Samson."

He slipped into a deep sleep again, and Stephanie imagined laying with him and listening to his heartbeat for a long time. Then she jerked herself out of this fantasy and rushed back to work.

CHAPTER 27

LISA FOLLOWED MELCHIT INTO THE darkness of the corridor, and along it, in what seemed to be a maze of tunnels. Melchit held her hand and pulled her along. His little hands were hairy and had thick yellow nails that resembled short, trimmed claws. He glanced nervously up and down the corridors and avoided any that were lit. There were no windows to the outside anywhere. When they heard another person in the distance, or any unexpected sound, Melchit would stop and hold his breath. He used a screwdriver in his belt to disable a scanning device that spanned the hall at one point. At another point they dashed down a short, lit corridor and crawled under interior windows outside of a room with several people talking inside. It made Lisa dizzy to crawl and get up again. The people in the room sounded like regular humans, not like the monkey people.

Back in the unlit corridors, they rounded a corner to see a man dressed like a security guard standing about twenty yards down the passage in front of them. He had his back to them, and they leapt back into the corridor they had come from. Melchit held his breath, and the sound of the man's boot steps seemed to turn around and come toward them. Melchit backtracked several yards and pulled Lisa into a shadowy alcove. As the steps came closer, Lisa saw Melchit pull a dark metal object from one of his pockets. He cradled it in his hands like a treasure or talisman. The footsteps came closer, and Melchit glanced up and down at the object in his hands as if it held a magical power that he expected to protect them. Squinting her eyes, Lisa finally made out that the object was a gun. The guard came into view and glanced down the hall towards them, but continued past. After the footsteps disappeared into the distance, Melchit slipped the gun back into its hiding place in his pocket and tugged Lisa's hand again. They hurried along the path the guard had come from.

There was another short, lighted corridor, and Melchit grasped Lisa's hand tightly and sprinted down it, virtually dragging her along. He opened up a door half-way along the passage and pushed Lisa into pitch blackness inside, following after her and closing the door. She stumbled into a wall and braced her hands against it.

"Wait, wait," Melchit said quietly.

There was a clatter of objects being disturbed, a crash as something fell, then sudden stillness as if he had stopped and was holding his breath. Lisa listened intently, to what might be coming down the hall, what or who might have heard them, and to what might be in the room with them. The only thing she could hear was her own breath and heartbeat. After a few minutes, she heard Melchit move again and the lights in the room suddenly blinked on.

They were in a small utility closet that was filled with maintenance and cleaning supplies. Soap, mops, toilet paper, a drill, screws and bolts, a stack of ceiling panels, a ladder, a few buckets of paint. Melchit made the "shhh" motion at her again, with his finger in front of his lips.

"Drink this, drink," he said, and handed her a small bottle of water. "Drink all."

Lisa snatched at the water and drank it, becoming conscious again of how dehydrated she was.

"If it's our luck," Melchit said, "they don't find you amiss until in the morning. I believe it is. Them's be wrong. It's wrong. But we can escape. You will with me escape, you to join my escape. I made in six years this way escape. That of it is the plan. You can then join the plan with me to escape. And we can escape."

Lisa found it difficult to concentrate on what he was saying.

"Do you have a card?" she said, "Where we can call help? We need to call help!"

"Shhhh! No card. No card here, the card doesn't work here. Only Master can have the card here. No card can here, except for Master can his card. We can't call help, only can we escape. Who would help?"

"I can call for help," Lisa whispered, "if I can get a card."

"Not here, not help. Them here will help master. We must escape! Escape it's we need. It's we escape! They won't help, not them here. Them here will hurt us. Come."

He pulled the ladder into the middle of the room and climbed up it with a drill. He quickly removed the ceiling panel, revealing a sturdy crawl space above them. He slid the ceiling panel and the drill into the crawl space and climbed back down.

"You go up."

Lisa stepped forward to the ladder and glanced back to see Melchit nodding furiously at her. She climbed the ladder, which creaked and shook under her unsteady limbs, and glanced down at him when she was at the top. He nodded furiously at her again and motioned with his arms for her to climb into the crawl space. With some difficulty, she pulled herself up to her waist inside the ceiling and wriggled the rest of the way up. As soon as she was up, the sound of the ladder being moved away gave her a start. She glanced back down into the room and saw Melchit sliding the ladder away and stacking it carefully against the wall. He turned on a small, blue light attached to his shirt and switched off the lights in the room. The crawlspace became an inky blackness. In the dim light below, Lisa watched Melchit begin to climb up a set of heavy metal shelves near the wall. When he reached the shelf at the top, he stood on it and paused, crouched against the ceiling. Then he braced himself and leap out into the middle of the room, caught hold of the ledge of the crawl space like an acrobat, and pulled himself up into it. Once sitting at the top, he gave Lisa a big smile.

"HE WILL DEFINITELY MAKE A full recovery, then?" Albrecht Durer asked.

Stephanie looked into his bright, ancient eyes to understand why he was asking the question. He wanted certainty, it was important. When the stakes were so high it was essential to distinguish between what was definitely true and what was probably true.

"He's almost made a full recovery already," she said. "The doctors say he is healthy and the that the full return of his energy is a matter of time. Not very much time at this point, a week or two at the most. Even if he stopped recovering now, without progressing further, he could already lead a mostly normal life. He wouldn't be racing ships again, but he could travel, appear in public, speak."

Nominally, Albrecht was a Vice President at one of Rothschild's advertising subsidiaries. The particular subsidiary changed from year to year. In fact, he was the family's oldest living advisor. He ran a dry grey finger across a set of notes in front of him.

"He can stand up for thirty minutes," Albrecht said.

"That's right."

"He needs to sleep 14 hours a day."

"Right, exactly as in the report."

"Unexpected disaster can always happen," Simon Okunle interjected, "but Samson is back among the living now. We can rely on that fact as much as we can rely on it for any of us."

"Of course." Albrecht crooked his neck and stared up into the stars through the conference room's one-way, domed glass roof. The glass had a telescope-like property of magnifying the night sky. The stars appeared even brighter from inside it than they actually were. "I would love to see him," he said.

"You will soon," Stephanie said, "that will be our next step after this meeting. We'll bring him into the discussion with us then."

"I don't see any point in keeping him out of the discussion now," a young woman said, "if he is healthy enough to sit here and participate."

"The point in keeping him out of the discussion now," Stephanie said, her eyes shining anger-saturated photons, "is to allow us to speak freely and objectively about it, to understand each other and consider the situation strategically before he is here."

The young woman's name was Celes Vieira, and she was the youngest and newest member of Stephanie's personal executive team. She was unusually short for someone with advanced genetics and sat with exaggerated straightness in her chair. She had very dark blue eyes, hair that was vanishing shades of white-pink and yellow-white, and skin colored in smooth clouds of white and red. Stephanie had known her since they were girls.

Celes stared down at the table, then looked up in a stubborn attempt to meet Stephanie's gaze, which she could only hold for a moment before looking away again.

"I didn't mean to question what you were doing, Mistress—"

"Well what did you mean?"

"If you would let me finish—! Mistress— I only meant that you obviously trust Samson completely and therefore so can we."

Simon Okunle smiled.

"I'm sorry, Celes," Stephanie said quickly. "You are right about that, but this meeting will be more productive if we

194

have a chance to speak and think about the situation without Samson here."

"You haven't notified the family yet?" Albrecht asked.

"I have not, and it pains me. Samson and I have talked about it and he agrees that we should wait. But we will notify them before making a public announcement."

"The people in Magdalena won't believe you," Simon said.

"That may be, but Samson's brother will."

There was an awkward pause around the table and Stephanie noted her executives' tight, exhausted eyes.

"It goes without saying that we need to make as much use of him as possible in our PR efforts," Albrecht said.

"Samson returning to life will re-invigorate the pro-naturals movement more than ever," Simon said.

"I wonder if it will really help us any, though," Celes said quietly. Then louder, "The anti-naturals brigade have already gone too far to turn back. Samson miraculously turning to life and lionizing the naturals movement will only entrench the anti-naturals more."

"That's true," Simon said, "but does it matter? They are already entrenched and preparing for actual war. If nothing else, Samson's reappearance will be demoralizing for their less committed supporters. The fact that he won the Regatta undermines their entire world view. As long as he is dead, he is an enigma of history. As long as he is alive, he is a facet of reality."

"How should we announce it?" Stephanie said.

"Hold a news conference, with Samson and Kenichi and Dr. Nguyen, the same way we announced his death."

"We shouldn't orchestrate it too carefully," Celes said, "it should be authentic. But at the same time, everyone in the Solar System will watch that broadcast. We have to leverage it as much as possible. Samson will need to do a whirlwind media tour immediately after the announcement."

"I don't want him to do that," Stephanie said.

"What?"

"It's too dangerous. Bloodworth will try to kill him again."

"Everything is dangerous right now, Mistress! Nobody will believe it if Samson doesn't do a tour."

Stephanie's eyes shed anger again. Celes wasn't wrong, but she didn't understand. Stephanie needed Samson. If she lost him again, her ability to lead Rothschild's might be crippled. And the pro-naturals movement hinged on that. Whether Samson was alive or dead, whether or not he went on tour, wouldn't change the course of the war. Samson being alive was essential to her, but not to the movement. She wondered for an instant if Celes had ever really loved a man, and in the same instant cast the question from her mind. What an absurd and irrelevant thought.

"One thing that we shouldn't overlook," said a quiet, intellectual executive at the far end of the table, "are the existential questions that Samson's survival will raise. It is extremely difficult to predict what kind of effect it will have on people's conception of humanity and consciousness. How much are we prepared to share about Samson's experience of an alternate reality while he was in his altered state? What are Dr. Nguyen and Kenichi prepared to say about it? If people conclude that this is a giant Rothschild's hoax, as Bloodworth's allies will undoubtedly allege, it will hurt us severely. I'm not saying that we should disclose everything, but we have to consider very carefully what and how we choose to disclose."

"We won't lie about it," Stephanie said. "Rothschild's stands for honesty. But that doesn't mean we have to disclose everything."

"We have to show the video of Samson waking up," Simon Okunle said gently.

"We won't!"

"Mistress, it casts you and Samson in a beautiful light. It will be inspiring to the movement."

"It's a personal moment, Simon."

"I understand that, Mistress, and it contradicts our long held policies and procedure."

"The Mistress didn't even want you to see it, Simon," Albrecht Durer said.

"Thank you, Albrecht, I'll speak for myself," Stephanie snapped.

"I'm sorry, mum."

CHAPTER

OUTSIDE OF THEIR HOUSE IN Magdalena, Maria threw a semi-float ball into the air and the children raced to catch it. The little girls wore tasteful, flowered dresses and Paul had on brown pants and a white t-shirt under a buttoned brown vest. Their parents were both dressed practically and Maria wore the small, square, white, embroidered hat of devout Magdalena women. The ball floated up and down as if it were bouncing on wind. Eve giggled and raced along behind Paul and Judith, while Theo followed her, then lifted her into the air and raced her outstretched arms towards the ball. Judith was tall for her age and Paul was short, but he was quicker and leapt up to catch the ball first.

"Paul always gets it," Eve said, giggling.

"Alright Paul," Maria said, "what's your question of questions?"

"I want to ask a question!" Eve said.

"You'll get a turn, Eve."

"I'll get the next one!" Judith said.

"I have a great question," Paul said. "What's the best animal?"

"The best animal in what way?" Judith asked.

"Just what's the best one? Just that, that's the question."

"You're first, Eve," Maria said.

"Ok, I think squirrels are the best animal, because they're cute."

"Squirrels aren't the best animal!" Paul said with exasperation.

"They are!"

"What's your answer, Judith?"

"I think the best animal is homo sapiens."

"What's homo sapiens?" said Eve to the air around her.

"It means human beings," Theo said, leaning down and squeezing her shoulders.

"It's human beings, dummy," Judith said.

"I'm not a dummy!"

"Don't call people a dummy," Maria said.

"I'm sorry. Well I think the best animal is homo sapiens because that is the most advanced and most interesting animal."

"But when people say what is the best animal, do they mean to include people?" Theo asked.

"If they didn't want to include people they should ask what is the best animal other than people."

"Do you really believe that people are an animal?" Maria said. "If that is true then why are we so different from all the other animals in the world?"

"Maybe people are a special kind of animal," Judith said.

"Ok, ok, homo sapiens," said Paul. "Next!"

"I think the best animal is the dog," Theo said. "Because the dog is the animal that has the closest relationship with people. Dogs evolved alongside people for 100,000 years. They are work animals and companion animals, and probably the most important animals to the success of human civilization. Dogs helped to guard early humans, helped them to hunt, helped to keep them warm during the crushing weather of ice ages, helped to rescue lost humans and to track down fugitive criminal humans. Dogs are the closest animal to people."

"I want a dog!" Eve said.

"We can't have a dog," Maria said. "Even though they were wonderful animals, many people found the temptation to love an animal that would love them automatically so tempting that they chose that instead of loving other humans. This is why God forbade us from keeping dogs as pets. They are wonderful animals, but people have to open up their hearts to love each other, that's the most important thing."

"I want a dog!!" Eve said again, shouting.

Maria laughed.

"I do too, sweetheart. You'll understand it when you're older."

"Your turn, Mom," Paul said.

"Ok, I think the best animal is the unicorn."

"Unicorns aren't real!" Judith and Eve said at the same time.

"Jinx!" said Eve.

"You can't Jinx me, I'm older."

"Jinx, jinx! I jinxed you. You're jinxed."

"You can't jinx me. You can't jinx me."

"Jinx. Stop talking. Jinx! You're jinxed, Judith."

"It's not real," Paul said. "This is for real animals only."

"Well you didn't say that," Maria said. "You can't change the question now. And the reason why I think that unicorns are the best animal–"

"Are. Are! 'What *is* the best animal?' means it has to exist!"

"Don't interrupt like that, Paul. You let me finish first. What I was going to say is that I think it is possible that unicorns were a real animal once, on ancient Earth. Even today they find new fossils of new animals that they didn't know existed before. Ancient people all over the world believed in the unicorn, and maybe someday a unicorn fossil will be found on Earth and then everyone will know it was real. And it is the most beautiful and mystical creature, a legendary creature that human beings have always dreamed wonderful dreams of, so that is why it is the best animal."

"Ok, fine," Paul said. "Then Dad is the winner, but I don't want a dog."

"I want a dog!"

"Be quiet, Eve. Judith, mark another point for your father. Ok Paul, throw the ball."

"This game is boring!"

"Don't be rude, Eve. This is another chance to catch the ball, are you ready?"

Eve hunched down into a sprinter's pose, with her little fists clenched, and gritted her teeth.

"I'm ready."

"Go!" Paul said, and threw the ball high into the air.

Judith and Maria chased after the ball and Eve ran after them as fast as she could. Theo followed a pace behind Eve.

"It's too high, I can't get it!"

"I'm gonna get it," Judith said, preparing to outjump her mom.

Theo scooped Eve up with his long arms and held her high in the air.

"Hey, no fair!"

"Catch it in your hands, Eve. As soon as it comes down. Don't miss it."

"I'm gonna catch it!"

Judith started to protest again, but her mother frowned at her and she realized that they were letting Eve win.

"Fine," she said under her breath.

"I got it, I got it!" Eve said as the ball floated down, and she caught it between her two little hands before it could float back up. "I got it! My turn!"

"Good catch, sweetheart," Theo said, and set her down.

"Ok, my turn. I'm gonna ask the question now."

"We know that," Judith said.

"Good job, sweetheart," Maria said. "What's your question of questions going to be?"

"I know a question," Eve said coyly.

Judith looked sour, and Theo squeezed her shoulders and pulled her into a hug. She resisted a smile, but her mouth shifted into a pouty duck face.

"What's the question?" Paul said.

"I'm gonna ask it."

"We know that, dummy. What's the question?"

"No more calling people 'dummy'," Maria said. "If I hear that one more time today we can all do chores instead of playing the question game."

"Well ask it!"

Eve looked at the ground.

"Ok, Eve," Maria said, "what's your question?"

"I forgot it."

"You forgot it," Paul said and rolled his eyes while looking up to the sky.

"You shut up, Paul!"

"No telling people to shut-up."

"If you forgot the question then you don't get to ask a question," Judith said.

"That's not true, it's my turn! It's my turn, Mom!!"

"Calm down, Eve. Think of another question and ask it. It can be any question."

Eve stared at the ground and picked a daisy from their garden yard.

"I got a flower!"

"Ask the queessstiooonn," Paul grunted.

"Oh, I remember. My question is: will I ever have a little brother or sister?"

"What?" Paul said.

Judith's face changed, shifting from mild contempt to the faintest glimmer of respect.

"That's a good question. Why don't you answer it, Mom."

"You answer it, Judith. You have to answer it!" Eve said.

"Why– I can't answer that. Only Mom and Dad can answer it."

"You answer it first!"

"Everyone has to answer the question," Theo said, smiling,

202

and walked away from his daughter to put his arm around his wife.

"Fine. Well I don't know the answer, but I think you will have a little brother or sister. I think Mom and Dad *want* one."

"Your turn, Paul," Theo said.

"Yes, I think you will," Paul said. "It's obvious isn't it. *I* hope it's a boy."

Eve pointed the daisy at her parents accusingly.

"Your turn!"

Theo and Maria looked at each other.

"Well we never know about that," Maria said. "I think if you want a little brother or sister you will have to pray to God very hard."

"That's not an answer!"

"That's my answer too," Theo said, squeezing his wife tight in an embrace. He could feel her big heart beating against him through her chest, although her face was smiling. "Those things are always a surprise and a gift from God. You may always be the youngest one in the family, Eve, or you may have a little brother or sister some day. But if you want a little brother or sister you need to pray to God about it very hard."

"I don't want one!" Eve said.

"Well, don't pray for that," Maria said, laughing.

"You're not allowed to pray for that," Theo said, and they both laughed more enthusiastically than their children could understand.

LATE THAT NIGHT, LONG AFTER the children had gone to sleep, Theo and Maria lay in the dark in their bed and talked about that inevitable subject of their thoughts.

"Something's bothering me tonight," Maria said.

"I can tell, honey. I'm sorry."

"I can't believe Eve asked us that, about another child. Life is cruel."

"Poor baby," Theo said.

"She should have a little brother or sister."

"Life is never fair."

"How can it happen, Theo? We both became sterile? They can't tell me anything when I call them. It's not possible."

"It shouldn't be possible."

Theo wrapped his arms around his wife's chest and squeezed her into a bear hug.

"If we went to Mars or Earth could they help us?"

"No," Theo said, speaking slowly to keep from sounding shocked at his wife's suggestion. "Our fertility technology here is more advanced than anywhere else. They could give us a baby through gene weaving and an incubator, but they couldn't give us a natural baby."

"It's not fair."

"No."

Theo and Maria rolled and twisted against each other to find a comfortable position. Theo rested his hand on his wife's tummy, thinking of when he had rested his hand over his three children in their mother's womb. His heart beat fast and he was uncharacteristically tense.

"What's wrong?" Maria said.

He squeezed her tighter again, as if he would compress her body into himself.

"Ouch, Theo,"

"Oh, sorry."

"Tell me what's wrong."

"I haven't wanted to tell you. I was hoping it wasn't true."

"It's about us? Did the doctors learn something?"

"Yes, sort of. It's not about us completely."

"Just tell me."

"Our problem appears to have been caused by a virus."

"What? We haven't been sick."

"Just wait. Just wait and let me finish. It's a new kind of virus. But– But! It's not good. I'm sorry, it's hard to say, it seems like saying it will make it true. But it's not only us. It's lots of people, maybe it's everyone. The virus is sweeping through the whole population."

"What?" Maria pulled away to give herself room to breathe. "I don't understand, Theo."

"It's a manufactured virus, a weapon. Some of the scientists think it was designed to wipe out natural born people. They've decimated our population, all of us. That's what it looks like, all of us. Even the children, apparently. Paul, and Judith, and little Eve."

"They've decimated us – who? That's not possible. Everyone is sterile?"

"In a way, they've wiped us all out. We're all extinct already, even though we're still alive."

"Who Theo?"

"Nobody knows. The genetically engineered people, all the ones against the natural born. Bloodworth's Corporation maybe, the ones involved in the war. Nobody knows for sure."

"But, whatever the virus did, whatever the damage– There must be a way to fix it. I mean, we're still healthy!"

"The doctors don't think it is fixable. I don't understand it completely, it's all preliminary anyway, but it has to do with DNA being hijacked by the virus and the intricacies of DNA replication and repair. Maybe there is a way to fix it, but some of the best doctors are adamant that what the virus does is irreversible. I think they've already given up hope that it can be fixed. We could still have children, with gene weaving machines, but there wouldn't be any natural born children for that entire generation. And the ones later, will have the genetic changes coded into their genes already, there will never be natural people again. Not from Magdalena, anyway. That's what they are saying, or thinking."

"What will happen?"

"The Prophet won't allow gene weaving, of course. They're talking about total war. A suicide war. We're wiped out already. A total war driven by total madness. Oh Lord, Maria."

"Theo," Maria clutched her husband's head against her and cried into his hair. "Oh, oh, how can it be? Oh, Theo. Our children. Our children, too? Our children? Oh God."

No moon shone in the night as Lisa and Melchit splashed out of a large drainage tunnel and emerged outside. Even the stars were dimmed by the lights of the city around them. Lisa breathed the fresh night air in deeply, hardly perceiving the cold of freezing water running nearly to her knees. The water was nearly to Melchit's waist, but he splashed through it as if it were nothing.

"Outside. Outside is good! Hurry, hurry!"

They ducked, crawled, and scampered along various ditches and canals, through dense bushes, and along dark, empty alleyways behind buildings. There wasn't a hint of any person or vehicle that Lisa could see, but if there had been, thanks to Melchit's carefully planned course, no one ever would have seen them.

As they traversed a canal in an empty park, with maple trees, blackberry bushes, and ivy clumped along its banked walls, they came to a spot where there was a talking billboard that they could see and hear on the path above. Lisa was shocked to see her face flash onto the billboard's flat, projected plane.

"Be on the lookout for Magdali Reina, an escaped fugitive who has been attempting to pass herself off as missing celebrity Lisa Maui. Reina escaped a few hours ago while awaiting extradition to Venus. She is considered armed and extremely dangerous."

Lisa and Melchit stood still on the dark bank of the canal, staring up at the screen. The image of Lisa changed to an image of Melchit.

"And we actually have another fugitive to be on the lookout for tonight. This is an illegal animal-human hybrid that should be easy to spot. His name is 'Melchit' and he has an IQ in the 65-75 range. Melchit is an illegal experiment refugee with severe mental disturbances who has escaped from the secure ward where he was being housed and cared for.

"It is suspected that these two fugitives may be working together. Please contact authorities immediately if you see either one of them. Do not approach them, they are considered to be armed and extremely dangerous."

No one would help her, she suddenly realized. She didn't know where she was, but no one would help her here. She couldn't find a store, or a house, or a stranger on the street and ask them to call for help. That was her plan. She was still following Melchit out of habit, but that was what she had had in her mind to do. She was so tired. It was hard to think. She had thought she could find someone and ask them to call for help. Almost anyone would do. But she couldn't. They wouldn't help her. Everyone was looking for her to report her to the authorities. The authorities here wouldn't help her. She could hardly hold her body upright. It was hard to think.

Melchit pulled Lisa's hand hard.

"Come! Hurry. Them are fast. Them are very fast!"

Ten minutes later they shuffled through the darkness into an abandoned skyscraper in a rusting industrial scrapheap of blocks at the edge of the city. Deep in the basement of the abandoned monolith, behind two false walls, they walked into the last thing that Lisa expected to see: a bright and comfortable room that Melchit had prepared for his escape. The room had heat, electricity, and running water. They could talk freely, as loudly as they wanted. There was a small bed, and a couch. Lisa sat down on the couch immediately when they walked into the room. Melchit watched her with deep sympathy in his peculiar eyes.

"Thank you," she said.

He sat down on the bed and pulled off his shoes. Lisa started to say something else, but fell asleep.

CHAPTER 29

THE STREETS OF PHILLIPEVILLE, ON Earth, were beautiful and clean. No one who lived in Phillipeville ever littered, that would have been unthinkable to them. No one who lived in Phillipeville ever failed out of school. No one who lived in Phillipeville would bump into another person rudely in the street without offering a gracious and sincere apology. Everyone in Phillipeville wore expensive, fashionable clothes and had bright, perfect skin. There was no one short in Phillipeville. The people who lived in that city knew that they were special, and viewed outsiders with suspicion.

The cityscape was a marvel of granite, steel, and glass. Cement was frowned upon in Phillipeville. In the center of town was a massive, black granite monolith that soared 2,000 feet into the air, more than four times the height of the ancient pyramid in Egypt. The monolith was a single piece of rock that had been carved whole from the earth. What was even more amazing about the city's skyline was that the monolith did not look vulgar or out of place. It was complemented by dozens of thin, shining, metal spires, themselves accented with scattered planes of decorative glass, that blended gracefully into the surrounding city below. The effect was graceful and organic, without being any less epic than the monolith would have been by itself. It was conceived by the most legendary designer on Earth, given the monolith as a starting point to work with. The people who lived in Phillipeville were not friendly to outsiders, but that did not stop others from visiting to see it. Although, only those with high quality genetic engineering were allowed.

Buildings in Phillipeville were predominantly peach and blue – complex, earthy tones of those colors that blended organically into the surrounding landscape of hills and sea.

Canals and fountains channeled blue water throughout the city, so that all the air felt like a water front. Broad courtyards and green parks were within walking distance of everyone. Many of the citizens bicycled everywhere, eschewing powered vehicles to revel in the sensation of their beautiful bodies sweating in the clean air. They rode their bicycles in a relaxed, satisfied way, that was seductive in its wholesomeness. To be there, to watch the people there, was to wish to be one of them. That was the experience of many visitors, who were not particularly welcome.

All the property in Phillipeville was owned by the Bloodworth's Corporation, which strictly controlled who was allowed to live there. The city was not large, with a population of perhaps only 300,000. It wasn't where Bloodworth's Corporation was headquartered, and it wasn't even where Phillipe Bloodworth lived, although he often took holidays there. It was just a company town – a kind of corporate Potemkin which was the external representation of everything that Phillipe Bloodworth thought the world and humanity should be.

Phillipeville had an active, exciting nightlife and a dark underside. Citizens expressed their sexuality in an aggressive, unflinching way. Murders were slightly more common than in most cities on Earth, but the clean-up, prosecution, and punishment of such deeds was dealt with in an efficient, even beautiful way. Those who transgressed the line were swiftly executed and then burned. There was no waste. There were no dirty houses. There was never an unkempt person in the street. For the people who lived there it was an exhilarating and relaxing place to be. That, after all, is the rare, deeply craved emotion: exhilaration and relaxation, at once.

ANOTHER LARGE PUBLIC BILLBOARD BROADCAST its warning message about the escaped fugitive who looked like Lisa Maui as Scamp was walking past. Bloodworth was utilizing every resource to find her. City police and private security vehicles circled regularly wherever he went. "...Magdali Reina...attempting to pass herself off...", what a crock of shit. When he had first seen the message after he arrived in town it infuriated him. Now it made him laugh. He walked through the clean, brightly lit city streets in a drizzle of rain. Lisa Maui had been on the run for three days. Good for her, she had already done the hard part. Now if he could find her, he could help her. She was probably still in town. It would have been hard to get out of here without notice, and Bloodworth's people obviously thought that she was still here. He could help her with that, if he could find her before they did. He could protect her.

Scamp didn't even attempt to look inconspicuous in Phillipeville. He stuck out from these carefully engineered surroundings like a warped, half-hammered nail in a plank that had been neatly bolted down. There was no hope of inconspicuousness for him here, so he adopted a strategy of conspicuousness. It was elegant, in a way, that becoming as conspicuous as possible was how he could best blend in. He pretended to be an obnoxious tourist, he wore a bright yellow shirt and red shorts – the kind of vapid sightseer that nobody here wanted around. In fact, they didn't really want any kind of sightseers here, and by adopting that role he became a person that people didn't *want* to notice. They intentionally, or automatically, elided him from their sight and attention. A few went out of their way to give him a hard time. It wasn't inconspicuousness, but it was as close as he was going to get.

He walked through the streets of the city absent mindedly, stopping at random signs and curiosities and taking pictures. What he was really doing was listening to all of the people around him with a high tech, amplifying audio scanner that was concealed in his ear canal. He eavesdropped on every conversation in every building nearby, and listened to every unscrambled radio communications channel. He knew exactly what the police knew, which wasn't much. They were desperate to find the fugitive, though. They didn't understand who she was, or where she had come from, or why she was so important, but they understood the emotion of their commanders – she must be found no matter what, at almost any cost. Their voices were hard and cracked with adrenaline, even after searching for three days.

THE RAIN DIDN'T BOTHER HIM any. Scamp looked up and smiled into it. He was nearly impervious to cold. He listened to a conversation in a passing taxi. They were talking about Lisa. The cab driver had suggested that the identity of the fugitive was a lie, and the passenger was taking down his cab number to report him as a disruptive influence to the city authorities. The cab driver tried hard to apologize. The cab pulled over a block ahead of Scamp and the conversation continued as the passenger prepared to exit.

"If you don't believe our authorities here in Phillipeville, maybe you should move somewhere else where you will be more comfortable," the passenger said with gentle, almost good natured, hostility.

"No, man, this is my home," the cabbie protested. "I don't think the city authorities are lying. If I find the fugitive I will be the first person to report her. I'm on the lookout all the time, all day while I'm driving!"

"You said you had never heard of Magdali Reina before and that you tried to look her up on news and reference indexes outside of Phillipeville and couldn't find anything about her–"

"So, I was–"

"And you said that maybe Magdali Reina actually is the escaped fugitive Lisa Maui, and that the authorities are for some reason lying about it. That's disruptive."

"I said 'what if', 'what if'! That's my thing, to look around the world, around the world outside my cab, the whole world around me, and see 'what if'. It's imagination! That's all it is. You're taking it seriously, but it's not serious to me; it's like a game."

"I'm sure that can be very entertaining," the passenger said. "But it's also a convenient excuse. I'll be reporting you and the arbitrators can decide what they think about it. You wouldn't be kicked out if it's a first offense, anyway."

"Reporting other people for frivolous offences can also be a disruptive offense," the cabbie said.

"I'm well aware of that."

"I didn't do anything wrong, so you can report me if you want. I just try hard not to make my passengers uncomfortable or give them a bad ride, so that's why I have been trying to apologize to you. My brother-in-law is actually a police officer here, so I'm the last one to have a lack of respect for the city authorities."

"You have a good night," the passenger said as he stepped out of the cab.

"Yeah, whatever. Have a good night too."

Scamp watched the passenger proceed up the street and turn into a large apartment building. The people here didn't question anything. They worked strictly within the system of authority; it was their belief system. Scamp had been reading about the Magdalena cult and the philosophy of belief systems, during his long, drunken stupor, before he started searching for Lisa Maui. For the people here, authority was like the god. If the police said it, or if their supervisor at work said it, then it was true. What that truth was could change, because the authority was the truth, not what the authority said. The authority could say one thing this month, and a different thing next month, they could say that Lisa Maui was a fugitive named Magdali Reina this month, and next month they could say that Magdali Reina didn't actually exist and it was Lisa Maui all along, and both times for the people here it would be true, and for them it wouldn't be a contradiction. Because authority, the authority that they followed, *was* truth. Being good was following authority – dilligently, with alacrity – this was their belief system, a belief system that they were perfectly suited to and had greatly benefitted from. In their minds, it was the only belief system. Anything else was ignorance and disruptive irrationality.

The cab driver liked to think 'what if'. People like that didn't belong here, Scamp thought. The passenger was probably doing him a favor. Maybe the passenger himself even believed that. The cab driver must have known that what he said could be taken the wrong way. Maybe subconsciously he was trying to force himself to leave. On some deep, emotional level, he needed to be reported. This must be a horrible place for someone with an open mind.

It was a more horrible place for Lisa Maui. Scamp hated to think what Bloodworth and his people may have already done to her. He had a general idea, from persistent rumors in the criminal underground, of the kinds of things that Bloodworth liked to do. Lisa Maui had an open mind. She was young and had gotten mixed up in the business with Samson and Stephanie, that was bigger than them, like he had. But she was just young, and a girl, while he was very strong. He had never used his strength to protect someone before, not like this. Not in this way. In fights, in battles, he had protected his people, but that was doing a job. This was something different, more elevated. If he could find Lisa Maui and bring her to safety, that would be something. It would be like, planting clean, rich earth inside of him, planting good earth, and taking out some of the poison. If he could only do that. He could die doing this, doing that, and it would be ok, if he could help her first. That would be ok. He had never feared death before, but now he did. He needed to help her first, then it would be ok. He could die helping her, and that would be fine, but not before.

If Bloodworth or his people killed Lisa Maui he would assassinate Phillipe Bloodworth. Scamp had known this implicitly from the beginning. It wasn't even a decision, it was the automatic logic of his identity, obvious and unavoidable. He was certain he could do it, although he would die. He had to stay alive until then, until he could save Lisa Maui or kill Phillipe Bloodworth. Those were the new, hopeful, invigorating parameters of his life.

He wished he could call her Lisa, and sometimes thought about her and the fact that she was very pretty. She was beautiful, actually. Scamp didn't allow himself to call her – to even think of her – by her first name, because he didn't really know her. If he could find her, and help her, and know her then and call her Lisa – that would be good.

In a bar near the industrial outskirts of Phillipeville, Scamp sat down to a quadruple whiskey. He sipped it slowly, smiling, and listened to the conversations of the other patrons. They weren't friendly to him, and privately mocked then forgot about his presence. They were talking about the usual things: work, gossip, drugs, and fucking. Mostly about work, those were the kind of people who filled Phillipe Bloodworth's perfect city, but a lot about fucking and a little bit about drugs. Their gossip was mean spirited, but with little venom. They were all too narcissistic to get worked up very much about other people. One man kept talking about his children and irritating the group of friends around him, without understanding why. The pariah of the group.

215

Scamp made an intentionally sloppy effort to hit on a single woman who he knew was disgusted by him. After being visibly shot down, he feigned embarrassment and ordered another drink.

"I can't get any luck here," he said to the bartender.

"It's not your kind of town."

"What about whores? Aren't there any around here?"

"Not any for someone like you."

The bartender was a little bit fatter than your typical genetically engineered human. Not fat per se, but intimidatingly paunchy. He had smooth, white skin with red undertones, spiky pink-blonde hair, and bronze eyes.

"Everyone always says that Phillipeville is the best place on Earth to live, so I wanted to see it," Scamp said reflectively.

"You'd have better luck in New York. Try that."

"You don't like me very much. I'm tipping you enough aren't I? Twenty-five percent is usually a lot wherever I've been."

"You're tipping fine," the bartender said, "I'm just being honest with you. This is that kind of town, people are honest here."

"Oh."

The bartender looked around hopefully to see if anyone else needed his services, then set to polishing and organizing his glasses behind the counter and continued talking to Scamp.

"Nobody here is going to be mean to you or bother you, but nobody here is going to go out of their way to be nice to you, either. We only like locals here."

"Why is that?"

"We're all of a kind here, that's why we're here. It's that kind of town."

Scamp drank a long sip of his whiskey. The alcohol did not affect him, but he feigned a kind of looseness. It took bottles of whiskey to get him drunk. The bartender ran a sterile rag vigorously along the spotless surface of the bar.

"I can see why everybody wants to live here," Scamp said, "It's a beautiful town. Maybe even the most beautiful town I've ever seen."

"You've traveled a lot?"

"More than my share."

"Have you been to Rothschild Palace?"

"I haven't been there," Scamp said. "It's even harder to visit Rothschild Palace than to visit here!"

"It's harder to get to live here," the bartender said. "People compare us to Rothschild Palace, but there's no comparison. Phillipeville is a beautiful town, a piece of civilization in the great tradition of Earth. Rothschild's little moon is a crass, industrial pimple on the face of the Solar System."

"In the videos it looks beautiful," Scamp said.

"Video is video. Living there is living there. If you haven't been, you can't talk about it."

"Have you been there?" Scamp asked.

"No. And I wouldn't go, either. Rothschild's can fuck off. I hope we bury them."

Scamp ordered another quadruple whiskey. He turned and scanned the room with his eyes. There had been a few mentions of Lisa, or the supposed runaway fugitive, but none of the conversations were helpful to him.

"I'm surprised you guys have two fugitives running around here at one time," he said to the bartender. "That's not what I would have expected in Phillipeville."

"It's unusual," the bartender said gruffly. "I've been here twenty years and I've never seen that happen before. I've never seen a warning about a fugitive here in my life. It shows it can happen to anyone, no matter how great you are. There's always freak luck."

"They're strange fugitives, too," Scamp said.

"What does that mean? They're not that strange. Escaped freaks, that's what fugitives always are, isn't it? I'm sure it has something to do with all this war business. We're going to bury them, watch and see. The bodies will be piled to the sky, and I don't mean ours."

"You think there will be actual war?"

"I *hope* there will be."

"I don't want to see that," Scamp said. "It seems like they want this Magdali Reina fugitive really bad. Is she a known criminal around here? Should I be scared?"

"I just told you, they want any fugitive really bad. There has never been a fugitive here. I don't know anything about her, but I'm sure she belongs locked up if that's what they want to do to her. Or if that's what they did to her. Even if all she did is 'rob a gumball machine', whatever that means, our police here would be desperate to find her if she escaped. It's never happened before."

Scamp sipped his whiskey and looked around the room again. The single woman who had rejected him had gradually become amorous with a well dressed young businessman.

"You shouldn't be afraid of anybody," the bartender said. "Nobody I've ever met would go out of their way to bother you. Big, hulking, freak of a man like you are. This isn't your kind of town, but go to New York, they like people extreme there. They like freaks."

"Are you saying I'm a freak?" Scamp was emotionally un-affected, but attempted to sound irritated.

"I'm not trying to insult you, I'm being honest with you. You are what you are. Obviously you didn't get that way by accident. Here we like people a certain way. You wouldn't ever get in if you tried to apply to live here. But other places are different."

The people here are all Bloodworth type of people. None of them have ever had a struggle in life. If they did have a struggle, they probably wouldn't be allowed to live here, they would be too imperfect. That's what it seems like. The people in service jobs look down on me. The bartender tonight said I am a freak. It didn't affect me emotionally. 'That's the kind of town this is.' That's what he would say. That's what he said. That's the kind of town this is.

Lisa Maui is definitely here, or was. They are searching everywhere for her. She escaped three days ago and the people here believe she is a run-away fugitive. It's possible she got out of town already, but not likely. She must be somewhere here. I go up and down the streets looking for her, patrolling. Listening. I talk to people. None of them like me.

It cost me so much to get to here, it cost me everything I have. Almost everything, I still have a lot of money actually. A good chunk of money. But it cost me so much to get here. They must be tracing a trail that leads to here, where I came from, but they can't possibly expect me. I'm totally out of left field to them. From the left. The ancient people thought the left was weird. I'm from left field to them. There's no way for them to see me coming. I feel like I haven't lost anything. Even though it cost so much, I feel like I didn't lose anything at all. I feel alive again. I feel in a way that maybe I never felt before. Right now, in these days, as I walk the streets and hunt for Lisa Maui, to help her – my life means something. To save her.

There are these demons on my back that haunt me. Somehow these demons stopped haunting me and began haunting her. Although they haven't completely gone, but it is as if my demons shifted to her. And if I can kill them I can save us both. Or at least her. If I can save her then the demons will be thrown off my back. That's how I feel. She's always in my mind, but I don't know her. Somehow I feel responsible for Bloodworth's evil, for harm coming to Samson's friends. When I think about it, I'm not responsible. But I can see this demon claw, with talons sinking into my shoulders, and I can see it flapping its wings above Lisa Maui, and she is in trouble. Who else will save her? No one else would do what I've done. It leaves a trail, but they'll never connect it to me. Even these demons won't see me coming; that's what I think in the back of my mind when I walk down these streets. I come into this situation like a bolt of lightning from the sky. From left field, completely from the left.

- Scampadorous Maximus

C H A P T E R 30

"THERE WILL BE THE CARGO ship," Melchit said. "Automatic cargo ship. No one there to see us or detect. It comes at the eighty-sixty minute. At the eighty-eighty minute can we climb on board."

Lisa watched Melchit through the dim light of a little outbuilding that they had snuck into near the landing dock of a ship freight yard. It was amazing how carefully he had planned. She felt terrified, but strong. Everything leading up to this moment was like a dream. From the time she was abducted in the cab, the memories didn't seem real. This, finally, felt like life. It felt like reality. Her mind was focused for the first time she could remember since she was abducted. They were going to escape, and she was going to tell the world what Bloodworth was. From here, it didn't seem impossible. From here it could be done.

"Stay down," Melchit said. "Stand up, no. Look through windows, no. No one to see us, no one to stop us. At the eighty-eighty minute, then we go. We escape."

"Ok," Lisa said. "You tell me when it's time."

"Of course I tell you when it's time," Melchit said quietly. "Of course I say to you when it is the eighty-eighty minute. You and Melchit are friends. You and Melchit have to escape!"

"Yes," Lisa said.

"In the outside world, them won't sell Melchit? Them won't eat Melchit? Out there. I mean out there."

"They will not. I can protect you in the outside world. You will be safe."

"Safe," Melchit said. "Yes, safe. You will be safe and Melchit will be safe. It will be a safe world for you and Melchit. Because Master was wrong."

"He was wrong," Lisa said. "He is absolutely wrong."

"But Melchit is a monkey people," Melchit said.

"I know."

"Melchit cannot be a human, Melchit is a monkey people!"

"I know you are," Lisa said. "That will be ok. You will be safe, out there."

"Yes, out there I will be safe."

Melchit reached into his chest pocket and offered Lisa a small, foil wrapped candy bar.

"For you want it?"

"Thank you," Lisa said, taking and eating the treat.

"Li-Lisa and Melchit. Li-Lisa and Melchit is friends."

"We are friends."

"In the eighty-eighty minute, we will escape."

"Yes."

The outbuilding was sparsely outfitted with a long utility table, folding chairs, a tiny bathroom and a sink. There was a big utility cupboard in the corner, and a little door opening onto closet space. The building appeared not to have been used in a long time, and its intended use was unclear. It was in a dark corner of the grounds, but only about fifty meters from the outer edge of the landing zone. Automated vehicles rolled or glided around the compound like a hive of bees, but actual humans were nowhere to be seen.

A police siren sounded aggressively in the distance. Lisa and Melchit froze. For a moment it seemed to fade away, then it drew closer. The sirens of other vehicles joined in. They were near the compound. No, they must be inside. Alarms within the compound began to sound, blaring at the air in a chorus of obnoxious, tone deaf horns. Melchit pressed himself against the wall of the outbuilding, as if he could fade into it. Lisa clenched her fists. If there were police, they might listen to her. They might be able to save her. If nothing else, she could still fight. She could hide. She could run. Her stomach hurt intensely and her heart seemed to be beating against the roof of her mouth. They heard vehicles flying nearby, then boots, running, shouting, not very close but coming closer.

Melchit drew his gun out and cradled it in his hands.

"If they come in, let me talk to them," Lisa said.

Melchit stared at her, but said nothing.

"First let me talk to them," she said. "I will tell you if we need to fight. Don't show your gun yet."

All of Melchit's muscles were clenched and he did not respond to her. She pushed him back behind the table, and moved so that she would be the first thing anyone saw if they came through the door.

Suddenly there were footsteps outside their building and the doorknob turned. Lisa held her breath. What would she do? What could she say?

The door pushed quickly open and a man snuck inside, then dragged a woman in after him and closed the door. He didn't notice Lisa at first. He brushed nervously at the woman's hair and grasped her shoulders bracingly. He was an awkward looking man, with creamy, butter skin and old-style red hair. When he noticed Lisa he started.

"Who are you?" he said threateningly.

Melchit stepped out from behind the table into light that was coming in from the window.

"Jesuschrist!" the man exclaimed, half in surprise and half in disgust.

Lisa realized from the way they were standing that the woman was the man's wife.

Airbrakes screeched in the air outside and sirens surrounded the building. The noise was inflictive.

Melchit lifted his gun into the air.

"I'm Lisa Maui!" Lisa said loudly, above the sirens. "I was

abducted in a taxi. I'm not an escaped fugitive. You have to believe us!"

"Lisa Maui," the man said, as if it was difficult to compute. His wife looked faint. "I know you're Lisa Maui! I know that. I know you aren't a fugitive."

"David Ischewitz, we know you are in there," a voice above them echoed through a loudspeaker. "Come out of the building peacefully and give yourself up."

Lisa and Melchit looked up at the ceiling, as if they could see through the building to the vehicle above them.

"Come out and give yourself up, David. You and your wife will not be harmed."

"It's—" Lisa stammered. "They don't want us, they want you!"

"You have five seconds to come out peacefully, or else we're coming in."

David Ischewitz looked wildly at Lisa and Melchit. He glanced at the door, then back to Lisa and rushed forward to push something into her hands. It was a data card.

"Get this to Stephanie de Rothschild no matter what," he said, and simultaneously began pushing Lisa and Melchit into the large utility cupboard. "I know who you are. You have to survive and get this to Stephanie de Rothschild."

He slammed the cupboard door hard in their faces. Then there were explosions in the room outside and shouting. Ischewitz' wife screamed. It was hard for Lisa and Melchit to make sense of what they could hear. They held each other in terror and waited.

CHAPTER 31

"I CAN FEEL YOUR THOUGHTS," SAMSON said. "Not only your thoughts, but the thoughts of everyone here. They're subtle currents, but clear."

Stephanie looked at Samson sitting up in her bed. He was still mostly bed ridden, but becoming vital. She worried that he had lost his mind. What he had been through was...unique. It might be impossible for any human being to experience what he had experienced and remain completely sane.

She had made a conscious decision not to think too deeply about what Samson had experienced. At this moment in her life, to do so was a luxury she could not afford.

"You don't believe me," Samson said.

"I believe you. I believe that you feel that and think it is true. But I wonder if you're mistaken about this strange feeling that you have."

She sat down on the mattress next to him. Her long, silk negligee clung to her scientifically perfect body in the flattering and luxurious manner of bespoke designer goods. She had chosen a very soft, lemonade color that he had once said was beautiful on her. Samson didn't look at her body.

"It's taken me a while to figure out what it was," he said. "It's the strangest feeling. There are these patterns that I can sense, like sound or smell, but a different sense. And they gradually began to come into focus for me. I started to realize that they are other people's thoughts – I mean, that's what they are. And I can understand them."

"It must feel very strange," Stephanie said.

"It should feel strange, but it doesn't. It feels natural. I'm sorry that it upsets you, but you'll realize soon that it's really the truth. I can feel what people are thinking. It seems like it's becoming more and more clear. It will be obvious soon.

If I want it to be. You won't be able to deny it."

"Ok," Stephanie said. "Let's wait until then and cross that bridge when we come to it. What's happened to you is completely unique and unexplained."

She watched Samson rub his hands together. His recuperating energy had been strange. He could leap out of bed one moment and fall into it barely able to stand the next. He was too weak for sex. He didn't seem to have any libido, either. It was hard to have him back and not have that. Her body was parched for it, but while he was gone she had been able to block it out of her mind. Now that he was back it seemed impossible to do.

"I'm sorry," Samson said, wrapping his arm around her hips and squeezing her.

"What are you sorry for?"

"That I'm so weak. That I haven't been able to get into the mood. I feel weak in this strange way. But I'm sure it will change. It'll come back. You're my woman and you're beautiful and attractive to me."

"It's ok, Samson."

"You're beautiful and attractive to any man, but especially so to me. It will be ok, don't worry. I'm sure this won't go on forever. My mind just doesn't – go there."

He squeezed her breast through her clothes and started rubbing her body with his other hand. It felt good to her, tempting, but also wrong. In a way, it made her skin crawl.

"Stop."

"Why does this feel bad? It is what you want isn't it?"

"Yes. But no."

"Kiss me," Samson said.

He pulled Stephanie's head down to his face and they kissed, in what was a loving, and resembled a passionate, embrace. It felt so good to her, so warm, but it was not sex. The absence of that seemed to echo through her body and drain away the pleasure.

"Ok, stop," she said.

"I'm sorry."

"It's not fun if you aren't enjoying it too. If it's mechanical."

"I understand."

"I want that, but not–"

"I understand," Samson said, squeezing his body against her. His body felt cold against her skin.

"How soon do you have to leave?" he asked.

"Soon. I should have left already."

"Your life is hard," he said.

Stephanie sat with her head tilted back, staring up at the ancient painting of the maid pouring milk that was installed into the ceiling of her bed frame.

"It's hard now, but I've had it very easy in the past. Now it's my turn to do heavy lifting."

"You have the graciousness to say things like that," Samson said, "and even to half-way believe them. But your life was never easy. You have always carried a heavy burden of responsibility. It's something most people couldn't even imagine."

"Lots of people would wish to have my life," Stephanie said.

"They would wish for the fantasy of your life," Samson said, breathing against her shoulder. "They wouldn't be able to lift your shoes a step if they put them on."

"It would be self-flattering for me to believe that."

"No, I'm serious, Stephanie. I'm so glad that you are the person that you are. You're the perfect person to be who you are. You matter so much, and you're the perfect person to be – you."

Stephanie lay her hand on his head and rubbed his temples.

"Thank you for saving me," Samson said.

"I don't think I really saved you. You need to stop saying that. You would have come back no matter what. It was like a nightmare that you were in. You would have woken up."

"It wasn't a nightmare. You can't understand what it was like. Something was going to happen to me there, I don't know what. Something was going to happen to my soul. Like, it seemed like it would flicker out, or be smudged out, or something. I don't know if that is even possible. What I experienced, that place, made it seem like it's not possible, but it felt like something bad was going to happen. It was like wanting not to die, except more definite, or deeper in some way. It's not something I can wrap my mind around, but you definitely saved me. You saved me."

"You're the perfect person too, Samson," Stephanie said. "You're the perfect person to be you. I'm so glad you're back. You don't understand how important you are."

She kissed him on the forehead and got up. Samson curled into a fetal position and seemed as if he was drifting back to sleep.

"I know you have to use me," he said without opening his eyes.

"What?"

"I know you have to use me to win the war. I understand. Don't feel bad about it, you're doing the right thing."

Stephanie's reflection in the dressing mirror froze in front of her as she stood rapidly putting herself back together.

"That's— I would never do anything that's bad for you."

"Mistress!" Cylla's voice came from the other room. "Mistress! You're late! Everyone's going crazy. Please hurry, Mistress! You're late!"

Stephanie finished perfecting her mascara and rushed out.

"I love you," she said softly as she left.

228

"I understand," Samson said as her footsteps trailed away. "You have to do what you have to do to win the war."

CHAPTER 32

T HE SOUNDS OF VIOLENCE QUICKLY passed as Lisa and Melchit crouched holding each other in the cupboard. The sounds of anything amiss passed too, more slowly, and the vehicles nearby could eventually be heard flying away. It was well past the eighty-eighty minute, now. Lisa didn't completely understand what eighty-eighty meant to Melchit, but it was well past the appointed time.

They waited longer, both still shaking with fear. Finally, they came out of the closet. The building was empty. There were black burned marks on the ground, and a strange, empty canister in the corner, about the size of a man's fist. Only the space dock robots appeared to be outside. But the eighty-eighty minute was gone.

"Eighty-eighty," Melchit said despondently. "Eighty-eighty minute. There is no eighty-eighty minute, it was past. It was past!"

"I know," Lisa said, squeezing his shoulder. "I know it passed. We have to go back to your room. We have to hide."

"It was past! Go back to there. But it was past. There is not another eighty-eighty minute. There is not another of that. It was past! There is not another again. It was past! It was missed!"

Lisa grasped the little being by both shoulders and looked into his eyes.

"We have to go back to your room. We have to make a new plan."

"A new plan. We have to make that new plan. But it past! But there will be a plan, but it past. It past."

"I know," Lisa said. "They'll be back. Melchit, they'll come back here. We have to leave, now."

She pulled Melchit to the door and opened it. Then Melchit recovered himself and led the way outside.

"Back to the room," he whispered. "It past, but back to the room."

"Hurry," Lisa said. "They're going to come back."

"Back to the room. Back to the room."

LISA AND MELCHIT SNUCK THROUGH the shadows of the ship cargo port. The security patrols that they saw seemed to be more wary than before. There were also more of them, on the perimeter of the facility, manned patrols as well as robots. It felt like being in a movie – James Bond: Escape From Mars. Except this was Earth, and she had no special gadgets or technology, not even a card. Lisa cried tears of fear without losing any determination.

"Don't cry pretty lady," Melchit said and lightly gripped her arm. "We'll back to the room and hide. We'll be back to the secret room. Melchit will protect you."

"I'm ok. Thanks, Melchit."

"Don't cry. It past, but we will hide. And think! We will think it again, even though it past. We will think it again and find how."

"Thank you, Melchit. I'm ok."

"Shhh!"

A human guard on foot patrol walked out from around the corner and passed 10 meters in front of them. Lisa and Melchit were ducked down in the shadows of a trench. Lisa couldn't believe that they couldn't hear the guard coming. The way sound travelled was unreliable.

The guard didn't notice them and passed on.

Melchit and Lisa proceeded forward as well. Melchit was incredibly adept at sneaking through the shadows. Watching him, Lisa realized that he must have years of practice doing this. Maybe decades. Under the threat of Phillipe Bloodworth's personal heel. He was a remarkable creature, or person.

After what seemed like hours, but was really only 30 minutes, they emerged from the threshold of the transport facility and sprinted across a wide, shadowy street towards a canal. Lisa's heart nearly jumped out of her chest as she ran, but it felt good to run. It felt like freedom, physically. She had been so cooped up, trapped, for – weeks? It had almost been a month. Melchit leapt into the inky blackness of the bank of the canal like it was water in a swimming pool.

"Lisa Maui, wait!" the voice of a stranger said.

Lisa, half in the light of the street and half in the shadow of the bank, spun. The light exposed her face unevenly. An enormous man emerged out of an outdoor stairwell in which he had been invisible, but which, now that he could be seen, seemed a perfectly natural place for someone to be.

"I'm a friend, let me help you," the man said rapidly. "Both of you."

Melchit made a hostile squealing sound from the shadows and Lisa could imagine him holding his gun.

"I don't know you," she said. "Stay back!"

The man had red eyes and was one of the largest men Lisa had ever seen.

"I'm a friend of Stephanie de Rothschild," he said. "We can't stay here. Let's follow your friend and talk somewhere safe."

An hour later, Scamp walked into his hotel lobby wearing a large backpack. The pack didn't look abnormal against Scamp's frame, but would have been comically large if placed on the back of a regular man. He lifted the bag casually off of his shoulders and set it down against a large potted tree. The lobby was empty, except for a young female concierge manning the front desk.

"I've been hiking around town and shopping all day,"

Scamp said, and smiled at the young woman.

"I can see that."

"My name's Scamp."

The woman had pale, slightly cloudy blue skin and conversed with Scamp contemptuously across the tip of her nose.

"I know your name, it's on the books. Do you need any room service tonight?"

"Well, I don't need anything," Scamp said, "but I wanted to ask you–"

He stopped and smiled, half awkwardly, half overconfidently.

"Yes?"

"Well it's not as fun to go shopping by yourself. I was wondering if tomorrow you want to go with me, to let me take you out and buy you something. I need a pretty woman to shop for."

"I'm afraid I can't do that."

"Why not?"

"Because I don't want to."

"Oh, right."

Scamp picked his bag back up and headed towards the elevator.

"Uh, well, thanks," he said as he walked away, half turning his head.

"Don't mention it."

In the elevator, Scamp could hear the woman talking to herself through his earpiece.

"Disgusting, cocky shit," she said. "I can't believe they let people like that come here."

CHAPTER 33

"How are you going to get us out of here?"

"I don't know," Scamp said. "I don't have a plan for that yet."

Lisa rubbed her ribs, which were bruised from being squished up, motionless, with Melchit in the backpack.

"You don't have a plan? Aren't you Stephanie de Rothschild's agent?"

"Him no plan, him no plan," Melchit said regretfully.

The hotel room was dominated by two queen size beds. Lisa was sitting on the bed closest to the door. In the corner at the far end of the room, by the shuttered up window, Melchit was curled up in a ball on a chair. Scamp stood in front of them awkwardly, trying to explain himself.

"I don't actually work for Stephanie de Rothschild."

"You said you were a friend of hers."

"I had to say something to get you to trust me."

"But–"

"Listen, I don't know Stephanie de Rothschild at all, but I'm sure she would want me to help you. I was a friend of Samson Ford's."

"You– I don't understand."

"I saw on the news how you disappeared. I knew the story they were telling was a lie, what happened to you was part of the war, so I started my own investigation to see if I could save you."

"You're a friend of Samson's?"

"Yes."

"You look sort of familiar to me, have we met somewhere?"

"No."

Scamp double checked that all the locks on the door were thrown and sat down on the second bed, opposite Lisa.

"How him find us?" Melchit said. "Him tell us how."

"How did you find us?" Lisa echoed the question.

"That's— a long story. When I got here I saw the billboards, so I knew that you had escaped. I guessed that you were probably with him, too. Well, the billboards even practically said that. So then I started walking around, talking to people, scanning the streets. I heard on the police channels that there were fugitives at the cargo facility, so I went there to find out if it was you."

"And then?"

"Then I used my scanning audio pinpointer to find you and him. Bloodworth's people would have found you that way too, except they were looking for someone else. They didn't know you were there."

"We saw who they were looking for. David Ischewitz."

"Yeah? I haven't heard of him. So, well lucky for you they were so worked up looking for those guys and just assumed the two of you wouldn't be there at the same time. I didn't. I wasn't looking for them, I didn't even know about them, so after they captured them I didn't stop looking, and I found you."

"That seems convenient."

"How him scan it on us?" Melchit said, pulling a hand crafted electronic object out of his pocket and holding it up. "I'm have this disruption of the scan."

"That won't work against my scanner," Scamp said. "Maybe that's why you guys didn't get found until now. Keep it on."

Melchit's expression didn't change.

"My scanner uses a multi-parallel probabilistic-cloud computation to isolate and pinpoint sounds. It was invented by a guy who was then killed by my old boss. It's not an available technology."

"Me see it."

"No, sorry."

"So you're a mobster," Lisa said.

"I used to be one. I'm a friend of Samson's. I'm doing everything I can to help you because I owe a debt to him."

"Now that he's dead, you can't pay him back."

"That's right. But maybe by helping you I sort of can."

"But you don't have a way to get us out of here."

"Not yet. But I will!"

Scamp looked into Lisa's eyes. They trembled, but stared back defiantly. She was strong.

"I promise you I will get you out of here," he said.

"But you don't even have a plan. What about Melchit?"

"Him too. We're all in this together now. I don't have a plan yet, because I had no way of knowing when and under what circumstances I was going to find you. I had a plan to get you temporarily to safety – and that worked. Now we have to get you out of this city, and I have to figure out a way to do that. We have at least a few days. Don't worry, I will."

"I need to take a shower," Lisa said. "Is that allowed?"

"You're not my prisoners! There's towels in the bathroom and you can both do what you want."

Lisa stood up and walked to the bathroom door.

"I'm gonna take a long shower, so go now if you have to go. Melchit?"

"No," Melchit said.

"I'm fine," Scamp said.

Lisa walked into the bathroom and started to close the door.

"Wait!" she exclaimed, and jumped back into the main room. "You have a card! Don't you? Just call for help. Just message the EICB, or even message Rothschild's! Or you can message my friends at the NBRA, they'll get everyone in line to help me."

She was grinning tentatively, as if certain that her problem was solved, but suspicious of the solution for appearing so easily.

"It's not possible," Scamp said. "Bloodworth's has all the communications in this city locked down. Anything going out gets screened. And that's one of the main things they're looking for from you. If we sent a message for help, not only would it get blocked and never reach anyone outside of this town, it would very likely lead back to you."

Lisa stood in thought, and it occurred to Scamp how pretty she was. Even with her clothes dirty and her hair all tangled up. She was special. That was why he was here, that was what Samson had seen, too.

"Well, that's," Lisa said, "that's... shit."

"Take a shower. It will help you think."

Scamp pulled some of his clean clothes out of the dresser.

"You can put these on for now. They'll be like a tent on you – very modest. Tomorrow we can wash your clothes in the tub and hang dry them."

"Ok," Lisa said, taking the clothes reluctantly. "Melchit, protect me while I am in the shower, ok?"

"Yes," Melchit hissed from his chair.

7/08

I found them! Lisa Maui and the monkey creature. He's some kind of monkey genius. His language skills aren't good, but he has all kinds of devices that he invented or built. He's a strange being. So now I have to rescue Lisa and him too.

But the point is, I actually found them! I'm sheltering them in my hotel room now. They're both asleep and I'm writing this *from the bathroom. This journaling thing has grown on me, it's like I <u>have</u> to do it now. It makes me relaxed.*

Lisa Maui is ok. She's traumatized, but she doesn't seem to have suffered any permanent harm. She's suspicious of me, and the monkey man is even more, but they're starting to trust that I'm on their side. Right now they don't have any other option but to let me help them.

Lisa Maui still doesn't know my name. I wonder if she realizes that. It's been crazy. I found them outside a cargo transport facility where two other fugitives were captured. There were fugitives there, so I went. I have no idea who those other fugitives are, poor bastards. Bloodworth and his people are cruel. It was luck that I found them. But I put myself in the way of luck. That's how the universe works.

The other fugitives saved them. And are — well, fuck them anyway. There's nothing I can do for them. Lisa Maui didn't seem to know who they are.

When I watch this girl, Lisa Maui, I can tell that she's special. Samson must have seen it, too. That must be why I'm here, why I sacrificed everything to save her. It must be — a reason. As if there was a reason for anything. It feels good that there is a reason for something. I don't believe there is, with my brain, but I feel that there is. This is how I can find my justification for living, my redemption.

I don't know how I will get her out. Obviously we have to take a transport. I haven't figured it out yet. Renting a car won't work, they'll be right on top of me. Bloodworth's people aren't dumb. It was beautiful how I got them in here, I put them in this giant backpack and carried it in. Everyone here thinks I'm this shit eating tourist. They want to believe that, so it's easy. It's what they expect to see.

I remember when Lucho told me to play into it. Don't fight what people want to see, play into it. It's like judo.

I've never understood how Lucho could be so smart and so stupid at the same time. Did I write that before? I often think of it. I think of Luch more than he deserves. Samson Ford kicked the shit out of him in a bar, lol. It's good that Lucho's dead.

- Scampadorous Maximus

CHAPTER 34

L ISA ROSE EARLY THE NEXT morning. The huge man stirred enough to notice her moving around the room, but then pulled the covers of his bed up past his head, so that his feet stuck out the bottom. His feet were enormous. Melchit was curled up, sleeping on the chair, and continued to snore.

It was hard to trust the man, but he seemed to be genuinely protective. She didn't feel safe, but she felt safer than she had since she was abducted. He didn't seem like any of Bloodworth's people. She squeezed the data card in her pocket that David Ischewitz had given her. She hadn't told the big man about that. She wondered what was on the card. She thought that the big man had told the front desk clerk his name was Scamp, when she was in the backpack, but she couldn't remember for sure. Scamp wasn't a normal name. She would have to find out his name for sure as soon as he was awake. The sun wasn't up yet. They had all been exhausted, so the man and Melchit might not be up for hours. That was ok.

The big man's clothes did hang on her like a bag, as he had said, and felt very modest once she had them belted and cinched up securely to prevent them falling off. She went into the bathroom and ran a pool of lukewarm water into the tub. The hotel had supplied them with liquid body soap that was colored like honey and had almost the same texture. It was scented with lemon and cinnamon. She poured a little bottle of it onto her hands and rubbed it in and around her fingers and palms. It felt luxurious in a way that evoked the scents and feelings of her life before she was abducted. That was only weeks ago, not much more than a month, and yet, it was hard right now to imagine. She ran her hands through the water vigorously, stirring the soap into it. The big man's clothes were better than nothing, but she wanted her own clothes again. After taking a proper shower she was able to smell her clothes' stink. Thank goodness it hadn't given them away when they were hiding in the backpack. She started washing her clothes in the tub, alternately agitating them in the water and ringing them out.

What the big man said about the cards was probably true. She hadn't thought of it before, but it was plausible. This was Phillipe Bloodworth's personal city, he would have it completely secured. She again wondered what was on the data card that had been thrust into her possession. She was supposed to get it to Stephanie de Rothschild no matter what. It must be something damaging to Bloodworth's, something that would make a difference to the war. Or was that too easy, too wishful? The man who gave it to her could be a criminal – maybe it was something to prove his innocence. Maybe Stephanie for him was like a mystical figure – the only person he could completely trust. He was so desperate when he gave her the card. And the woman who was with him – she must be his wife. They were terrified. They were more frightened than Lisa and Melchit had been, at that moment. Lisa stopped her mind from thinking about what might be happening to the man and his wife now.

The big man could probably read the data card with his card. Then they could find out what was on it, but she didn't want to trust him that much. Although, there was a chance that the information on the card could help them somehow. She might have to take the risk. Melchit, it seemed like, was not in danger of giving anything away. He was even more suspicious of the big man than she was, and seemed content at this point to follow her lead. Melchit was such a strange little person. He was brilliant and simple, and cunning. He had a cunning that seemed like it came from being around dangerous, untrustworthy people all the time. But he himself was good. It was something he needed. He was a tiny person who had risked and sacrificed everything to save her. She trusted him completely.

Of course, being completely trustworthy did not mean he was completely reliable. Melchit was unpredictable and seemed potentially unstable. He didn't understand the way normal people thought and interacted, or the way the world worked outside of Bloodworth's terrifying dungeons. She had to keep in mind that, intentions aside, when it came to his actions he was a wild card. And she had to get him out. Melchit was in just as much danger now, if he was caught, as she was.

She drained the tub, ran a pool of clean water, and began rinsing her clothes out. She tried to imagine, if the big man was lying, what his true story and intentions might be.

If he was one of Bloodworth's men then he would have gone ahead and captured her and Melchit already – right? There didn't seem to be any reason why one of Bloodworth's people would be stringing them along with the story that this man was telling. And she remembered him, too! He had fought with Killian Gideon at one of Samson's races the year before. She hadn't been able to pinpoint it at first, but eventually she realized that this had been the same man. She was nearly certain. In spite of the media around the race, the story of the fight had gotten relatively little attention and the man involved was never publicly identified. But she had seen it. The man and Killian had been fighting near Samson's racer bay. It was plausible that he really was Samson's friend. Or had some connection to Samson. Nothing about him seemed consistent with the kind of people that Bloodworth employed.

But Bloodworth's people had been trying to sabotage Samson at that time. This man could have been a saboteur. For all of his nastiness, Killian was a fair racer. At least, according to his own idea of fair. He may have wanted to kill Samson in a race, but he wouldn't have wanted any help doing it. He would have been offended if someone was sabotaging a racer, no matter whose racer it was. He might easily have stepped in if he saw something happen, and that could be the reason they were fighting.

It could be, but it didn't seem to fit with what had happened. Her gut didn't approve. But, if he was Bloodworth's man, what could explain his current lies and behavior? Could it be he knew that they received the data card? Maybe he was trying to get them to reveal some information to him, by pretending to be a friend. Maybe what was on the data card was so sensitive that Bloodworth's had to go to every length to find out where the information had gone. What the man with the data card might have told her and Melchit, for instance. About other hidden cards or information, for instance. Maybe the big man befriending them was a case of better safe than sorry. First find out what they will reveal to a friendly party, then find out what they will reveal under torture. It was possible, but didn't seem to fit.

It was also possible that the big man was one of Bloodworth's agents who was, for whatever reason, going rogue. Maybe he sympathized with her and Melchit for some unknown reason. Maybe he was supposed to track them down and capture them, but decided to track them down and help them. He could be lying about who he was and still be helping them. If that was the case, he could also change his mind. He might be deciding whether or not he wanted to help them.

It was also possible that he was insane. He might just be a crazy guy who happened to find them and was living out some sort of imagined adventure. Although, he seemed too professional and intelligent for that explanation.

If he wasn't one of Bloodworth's men, did that necessarily mean that she could trust him? If he wasn't one of

Bloodworth's men then he was putting himself in danger for her sake, too. Although, it might only be because he wanted something from her. It could be something to do with the data card. It could be anything.

There was something about the big man, though. His genetics didn't seem quite kosher. It wasn't something you could put your finger on. He was big, and weird looking – ok, he was giant – but some people made their kids that way. Something about him seemed different from that. When you added him all together there was a hint of something animal. As if he weren't entirely human.

That would be a strike in his favor. She had met people who were part animal since becoming involved with the natural born rights movement. They were, invariably, sympathetic to the movement even though they were, in a way, the opposite of the natural born. Their lives and the discrimination that they faced, or that they had the potential to face, were almost exactly the same as the plight of the natural born. They were genetically inferior, or, if not actually inferior, genetically taboo. They were judged harshly because of their genetic background, if people knew it, not as individuals. If the big man was part animal, if he even suspected that he was, then he would be sympathetic to the naturals movement, and most likely an ally.

It wasn't even that they were part animal. That was something philosophers could debate, but the ones she had met were as much people as anyone else. They were just people with some animal derived genes. They just had the genes they were born with and made the best of them, like everyone else.

She kept remembering something her grandfather had told her when she was a child – that if you aren't sure what decision to make, and you have to make one immediately, go with your gut instinct. Her grandfather had been adamant about this. Trust your gut, let your instincts work for you, that's what they're there for. Her instinct was unambiguous that the big man was genuinely trying to help them.

She wrung her clothes out a final time and hung them carefully on some of the hotel hangers to dry.

A knock at the bathroom door startled her. She could tell from the sound of it that it was the big man.

"Yes?"

"Are you done in there yet? I have to use the head."

Lisa cracked the door open defensively, peeping out before opening it wider. The big man stepped back against the wall to be out of her way. His eyes were half closed.

"What's your name?" Lisa asked, as she walked past him into the hall.

"What? Move! I have to go," he said, and groggily pushed past her and closed the door.

Melchit was still snoring on his chair. Lisa looked at the clock on the desk in the room – it was almost 9 AM. The ventilation from the hotel's climate control system hummed. Lisa lay down on her bed again and immediately sat back up. She had not slept long during the night, but she had slept deeply. She felt restless now and knew that she would be cooped up in this room all day.

The big man came back in, rubbing his eyes.

"You don't sleep much," he said.

"I didn't sleep much," Lisa said, "but I slept well. thank you for helping us."

She spoke softly, because of Melchit, although the big man made no effort to.

"These rooms are well insulated," he said. "This is a nice hotel. Our neighbors can't hear us."

"Ok."

"My name is Scamp."

"Oh, right. Ok, Scamp? Actually you said that in the hotel

lobby when we were in the backpack, I remember it now. It's nice to meet you properly. It feels more comfortable now, in the day."

He watched her with a funny expression in his eyes. It seemed as if she mattered to him in some personal way that she didn't understand. Well, he had told her the thing about owing a debt to Samson. But it was unsettling. His eyes were a startling shade of red.

"Is it ok if I call you Lisa?"

"Well, that's my name."

"Ok, thanks, I just wanted to— You know, to find you, I had to do a ton of research. I had to find out about you, like who you are. Who your friends are, where you go, what you like to do. I always called you Lisa Maui to keep it from messing with my head. I mean, to keep it impersonal, you know? Like, not to start pretending that I know you."

He rubbed his face with the palms of his hands.

"That probably doesn't make any sense to you. But if you're ever, like, a private investigator or something, you'll understand. It feels like you know this person even though you don't know them. But now we are meeting each other, so I can call you Lisa. Shit, I'm probably scaring you."

"No," Lisa said, "that's ok. I understand what you mean. It must have been super hard to find me, since you're apparently the only one who has."

"You have no idea about that," Scamp said, suddenly very distant.

Lisa noticed that Melchit had woken up and was watching them.

"And what now?"

"I'm open to ideas about that. We're in a pretty tight spot. It would be nice if no more people have to die over this."

"What does that mean?"

Scamp glanced around, embarrassed, as if he was remembering himself.

"It doesn't mean anything, just that this is really dangerous."

"No, you said something. Who died?"

"Just, I had a partner who didn't make it this far, that's all," Scamp said woodenly. "It doesn't matter right now, what matters is getting you to safety."

Lisa's eyes darted to Melchit.

"And him!" Scamp sputtered.

"You – what, well what are we gonna do?"

"I don't know, that's what I will figure out today."

"How did your partner die?"

"I'm not talking about that until you're safe."

"That's–"

Scamp stood up and peered out the window blinds.

"It's going to be a beautiful day," he said.

Lisa couldn't fathom what was going through his mind. She turned on the news on the holo-tv and started talking to Melchit instead. Melchit was talking even less than normal.

"Don't tune it to Rothschild's!" Scamp said imperatively.

"I know," Lisa said, and flashed a resentful glare in his direction.

THE NEWS ON THE TV TOLD them that Samson was still alive. Lisa and Scamp couldn't believe it. Melchit didn't know who Samson was. The news anchors had few details to offer, but Google Media had gotten a scoop and Rothschild's had been prompted to make a preliminary announcement. There was little other detail, but rampant speculation.

"Do you think it's really true?" Lisa asked Scamp.

"I have no idea," he said.

"They wouldn't have faked his death," she said.

"It wouldn't be like them, but who knows."

Lisa felt her chest clench as she watched the news updates. She had become more attached to Samson as a dead man than she had been when he was alive. Dead Samson was a towering figure in her new life and public identity. News that he was alive left her with strange emotions including happiness and anger. If Samson had been alive all along, or if this new story was a lie, she would be so angry. It was horrible to play with people's emotions this way. A tear rolled down her cheek and she couldn't bring her mind to focus on the things that were being said on the holo-tv. Samson had won the Solar Regatta, he really had! Of course she knew that, she knew it as something abstract, as a fact, but in this moment it touched her. She had liked the racers, and Samson in particular. She had liked the races, but had never really cared about the outcomes of the races. Samson had done impossible things, he had won against all odds! Then he had died before he even felt the satisfaction of winning. Yet, if he was alive… She slumped to the floor, weak. Scamp knelt and gripped her shoulder, Melchit leapt out of his chair.

"Are you ok?" Scamp asked.

His enormous hand felt strong and gentle – comforting.

"Yes, I just feel like I have too many emotions right now. Too much emotion, that I don't understand."

She slid across the carpet to sit with her back against the side of the bed.

"How did you know Samson?" she asked. "How were you friends with him?"

"I – well, when I used to work with the Martian mafia, I knew him and Ben on Mars."

"Is that all?"

"It would be amazing if he were alive still, wouldn't it."

Melchit stood tensely at the foot of the bed, watching Scamp.

"Why were you friends?" Lisa pressed.

"I don't know. Why? Actually, we weren't friends, except I was supposed to intimidate Samson, and he somehow made me a better person than I was."

"You weren't friends?"

"Well, we were later."

"Melchit, sit down," Lisa said. "It's ok. I'm ok."

"I tried to save Samson's life, when there was a hit on him. It ended up Ben being the one who got killed. I tried to warn them, but – it was Bloodworth's. It was Bloodworth's, you know. Like with you, it was Bloodworth's."

"Is that why you owe him? Because of Ben?"

"No. Maybe that's a part of it. I'm not sure."

"What?"

"It must be a part of it. I didn't think about that before."

Lisa stood up and grabbed a tissue to blow her nose. Scamp's clothes seemed to hang on her body uncomfortably now, as if she shouldn't be wearing them.

"Are you crazy?" she said.

"What? No."

"Is everything you say some kind of lie?"

"It's not a lie," Scamp said.

"Well why do you owe Samson a debt then? You don't know?"

"No. I know. I mean, it's hard to explain. I feel like I was responsible for Samson's death."

"Were you?"

"No."

"Were you working with Bloodworth's?!"

"No! Why are you say–"

"Then how could you be responsible??"

"I don't know. It's hard to explain."

"Lisa not shout," Melchit said nervously, sitting again in his chair.

"What do you want from us?" Lisa said, crumbling emotionally but staring hard at Scamp's eyes. "Samson might still be alive. You don't owe him anything. Why are you here? How are you fucking here? It's – you can't be real. I'm having a dream, or I'm dead, or something. You and Melchit can't be real, this can't be real. Ohmygod. You– I'm having a dream, or I'm being tortured, this isn't real, I'm imagining things. You don't know, you don't know anything, you don't, you just say things that–"

Scamp grabbed Lisa and hugged her to him. She didn't want him to touch her, but it felt ok. Her mind was spinning. She could feel kindness in his embrace.

"It's alright, Lisa," he said. "Take deep breaths. This is going to be alright. I promise you I will get you out of here. I will get you back home, ok? This is going to be alright. This is going to be alright. I promise I will get you back home. Ok? I know I don't make sense, but I'm not an imagination. I can't explain about me and Samson, not in a way that makes sense, but if he's alive you'll get to see him again. Ok? And I probably will, too. Right now, if Samson is alive or dead, it doesn't change anything for us. We still have to get out of here. Him being alive won't help us any. So I'm not even thinking about it until we escape."

"Ok," Lisa said quietly.

Scamp stepped back politely, but kept one hand on her shoulder.

"You and Melchit have to stay strong, because this is going to be hard."

"Ok."

"I'm going out today and I'm going to find a way for us all to escape."

"It's ok, I'm ok."

"Melchit, do you believe me?" Scamp asked.

"Melchit believe Lisa," Melchit said.

Scamp stuttered for something else to say and Lisa cracked a tiny smile. He was an awkward man when he was trying to be nice. His feelings seemed too raw and genuine to be fake. He seemed like a man who wasn't a bad man, although he was dangerous. He seemed like a man who no one had ever loved.

A LITTLE WHILE LATER, SCAMP left to reconnoiter and get supplies. His plan was to feign illness at the front desk and ask for directions to a drug store. A button and small display on the hotel room door controlled its 'do not disturb'. Scamp pressed the button and set the do not disturb time to 'ALL DAY'. To double check, he pressed it again and it flashed 'ALL DAY' back at him and blinked off. He did not realize that pressing the button a second time had actually turned the do not disturb flag back off in the hotel's computer system. It worked like an on/off switch. He proceeded out of the room and on down the hall. Lisa and Melchit stayed behind and quietly talked.

Melchit did not know what to do. A situation that he had been in complete control of, that he had ever so carefully planned, had now spun completely out of his control. He did not know how to adjust or adapt. When he talked to Lisa, he seemed to find it difficult to focus on the situation at hand.

Lisa had been tense and scared with Scamp there, but without him there she found herself terrified. He was formidable, and his confidence, whether or not it was justified, made her feel safer. Now that he was gone, she kept looking at the door and trembling. She had seen him press the 'do not disturb' button, but someone could still come through the door at any time. There weren't any extra locks to be thrown, the door was all electronic. She didn't know what she would do if they came to capture her again. Melchit would fire his gun, but it wouldn't save them. If they were found, disaster seemed inevitable. She didn't know what Scamp could do if they were found, but he seemed to believe he could do something.

Just the fact that the door was there scared her. She wished that she was in a room that had no door, that had only a window. She tried to push irrational thoughts from her mind.

There was nothing they could do but wait. She tried to push everything from her mind and focus on talking to Melchit. She couldn't stop looking at the door. What if someone knocked on it?

"Those monkey people," Melchit said, "like Melchit. Those monkey people have – nil. Have no thing – nothing. Thems have nothing. Nil inside for thems. Nil to be taught or nil to believe."

"They have nothing to believe in," Lisa said.

"Yes, it's nothings inside for them. For Melchit, it's the same from the past."

He touched his hands to the center of his chest.

"It's nothing, from the past," he repeated. "It's Melchit with a dream, it's Melchit with the something then. Always was the something, then, always inside. But Melchit didn't know. Those monkey people didn't know. About something."

"What didn't they know?"

"Melchit had the dream! But thems didn't believe. Melchit said, Master, hims only the man. Hims only the man! Thems said it was not. Hims was what was. But hims only the man!"

"I don't understand you," Lisa said.

"Melchit had the dream of hims, up there! Hims over it all, hims created it. Hims up there is God! Master only the man. Hims, was, only the man. Thems monkey people bited and scratched Melchit. Thems have nothing. Thems of this bottle with no water."

"I see."

She found it hard to concentrate on what Melchit was saying, but tried. His speech was so convoluted. She kept glancing at the door and her heart pounded.

"Thems monkey people hurt for fun. Thems have no thought inside. Thems die – and laugh! Thems die and laugh! And Melchit was thems, but Melchit had the dream!"

"What was the dream, Melchit?"

"The dream of God! Hims over all. And all people with hims on inside. All people with hims! Thems monkey people even with hims inside. Thems is wrong. All have hims inside. Thems is wrong to hurt people with hims inside."

"It's bad to hurt people."

"And – and master is wrong! Master is wrong! Master is only the man. Master is only the man. Master would hurt Lisa, and thems would hurt Lisa, and Lisa is people with hims inside. And Lisa is good!"

"Thank you."

Melchit started to say something more when the lock on the door suddenly clicked open. Blood rushed to Lisa's head.

"Housekeeping!" a woman called loudly, and the door began to open up.

Lisa grabbed Melchit's arm and yanked him towards the closet. It was near the door to their room. They dove into it as the hotel door swung all the way open, but didn't have enough time to close the closet door behind them. It was still a half inch open, and Lisa watched through the crack as a housekeeping lady walked into the room. She had to exercise every fiber of willpower in her body to resist jerking the closet door shut. Melchit trembled against her. Quietly, and very slowly, tiny bit by tiny bit, she narrowed the crack in the door and finally squeezed it closed.

C H A P T E R 35

LISA AND MELCHIT SAT HUNKERING in the closet while the maid cleaned the rooms. All they could do was wait and fear and hope. They hardly breathed. It sounded like the woman was doing a very thorough job. The minutes seemed endless. It sounded like a second maid may have come in too. Lisa wondered what Melchit was thinking, and had no idea. He drew his gun, but seemed disoriented. The maid ran a vacuum cleaner around the room. Then they could hear the vacuum approaching the closet door. It came closer and closer. Lisa realized that with the roar of the vacuum she wouldn't be able to hear if the maid started to open the door. She put her hand on the door handle. Melchit, startled, put his hand on hers and tried to pull it away. She took her hand off the handle for fear that they would accidentally cause it to move. The maid was right outside the closet door. Lisa could very faintly hear her singing pop songs while she worked.

A bead of sweat ran down Lisa's forehead and dripped off her nose. The vacuum moved on past the door and then shut off. Lisa held her breath.

"Thanks for the tip, troglodyte," she heard the maid say.

Then the hotel door seemed to open and it sounded like the maid was pushing her things outside. The door slammed closed and there was silence. Lisa and Melchit still did not move. More sweat dripped off the tip of Lisa's nose.

"I think she's—" Lisa started to say.

"Shhh!" Melchit hissed, pushing a hand over her mouth.

He was right, Lisa thought. What if there had been two maids, and one of them was still in the room. She might be finishing dusting or something. She might be standing outside the closet door playing with her card. They couldn't afford to take a chance. Lisa remembered her clothes, hanging in the bathroom. The maid must have seen them! What must she have thought? She must be telling somebody about them right now, she must be calling the police.

"Shh," Melchit said.

No, she wouldn't call the police. This was a large hotel. She would ask someone in the staff about it, who would look up the occupants of the room, and then call the police. They might need to start running again. They might need to find a new place to hide right now. Immediately.

She started to open the door, but Melchit stopped her. Melchit was good at this. She needed to take a deep breath. Acting rashly would get them caught right away. There might still be a maid in the other room. They were trapped. She felt the walls of the little closet closing in around her, compressing the air. They were trapped. They were cornered in a little box. Trapped.

The handle of the hotel door outside clicked. Someone was there! Lisa heard the locking bolt shift. The door squeaked slowly open. They were trapped in a little box, with nowhere to run. They were done for.

"Hello?" Scamp said, slamming the hotel door behind him.

Lisa burst out of the closet and threw her arms around Scamp's big waist. She cried into his shirt. In that instant she gave up her efforts to distrust him.

"Ohmygod, ohmygod, ohmygod," she said, shivering. "Ohmygod, ohmygod."

"Woah, calm down. What happened? It's ok. What happened?"

"We have to leave," Lisa said. "We have to leave now. Maids were in the room. We hid in the closet. They saw my clothes drying. They must have seen my clothes. They must be coming back. We have to leave."

"Calm down. Did they say anything about it? Did they see you?"

"They didn't say anything about it. They didn't see us. But they saw my clothes! We have to leave!"

"Ok, calm down," Scamp said. "Take a deep breath. Take a deep breath. Ok, how long ago did they leave?"

"Five minutes ago, fifteen minutes ago – I don't know, not long."

"Did they see Melchit?"

"They didn't see us!"

"Thems not see me," Melchit said from across the room, where he had reseated himself on his chair.

Scamp squeezed Lisa around the shoulders and pulled her over to sit down on the bed. He paced back and forth while he talked to her.

"Ok, they saw your clothes drying. That's probably not as bad as it seems. Think about it from their perspective – this is a big hotel, they see all kinds of crazy things, and they don't have a lot of time to think about it. As long as we aren't damaging the room, they don't care. They saw your clothes drying, that seems like a dead give away from your perspective, but from their perspective it doesn't mean anything. People do all kinds of things in hotel rooms, they have sex with strangers, they rent whores. Use of whores is really big in this town. And they spill things on themselves, or get hungover and take a cold shower in their clothes. So they saw a woman's clothes hanging to dry. Ok. But they probably didn't even think about it at all. Did it sound like they were doing anything unusual, or did they just move on to the next room?"

"It sounded like they were moving on to the next room."

"Ok, breathe deep breaths. I think we're ok. Thankgod. Thank fuck they didn't look in the closet. Jesuschrist. I definitely put the 'do not disturb' sign on."

"I know, I saw you push it."

"Jesuschrist. Thank fuck they didn't look in the closet."

"Don't leave again," Lisa said.

"Ok. Ok. It's going to be ok. Jesuschrist. No, I won't leave again. I think I have a plan to get us all out of here. I think we can leave the day after tomorrow.

THAT NIGHT, SCAMP FEIGNED ILLNESS and ordered room service to their room. He had Lisa and Melchit hide in the closet again and made sure the bellboy came all the way into the middle of the main room. Scamp could order a large quantity of food without it seeming suspicious. When the food finally arrived, although Scamp ate a little bit less than he was accustomed to, Lisa and Melchit ate well.

The next day was long. They went over their plans for escape again and again. Scamp had made arrangements for them to take a public bus. He thought it was the safest way to get out of town. They roleplayed and brainstormed what problems could arise. They tested and rehearsed.

When they weren't rehearsing they watched the news, where a man certainly appearing to be Samson spoke briefly at a press conference. Samson looked weak and Scamp and Lisa both watched him with tears welling up in their eyes, neither noticing the other's because each was trying to conceal their own. When Samson smiled at the camera, Lisa remembered him smiling at her when they had gone to the ancient-style soda fountain together. She remembered how little she had known him, and was glad that he was with Stephanie.

If it really was Samson. The thought wouldn't dislodge.

Melchit didn't understand any of the excitement over Samson. For that matter, he didn't understand much of what was on the news. He was fascinated by the most random things, television commercials especially. It confused him immensely

257

when Bloodworth appeared in the news segments.

The three of them slept early, or tried to sleep. Lisa and Melchit ate nothing for dinner. The next day would be grueling. After they were all tucked into their beds, Lisa couldn't sleep and talked quietly with Scamp for a long time. He was a frightening man, but he was remarkably kind to her. She didn't think that he would be kind to everybody. The thought kept coming back to her that he had never been loved. She tried to be kind to him in return. He seemed to be incapable of expecting kindness.

When she fell asleep, Lisa dreamed of being back in Manhattan with her grandparents, living a life where she had never become involved with racing.

CHAPTER 36

THE HANGAR SMELLED LIKE GREASE, and hydrogen cells, and electricity. It smelled like home. Samson strapped into one of the Rothschild's racers and was surprised to realize how much he had missed this. The smell of ships, of racing; the pressed leather smell of a pilot's suit. The air inside a hangar was rich. This was the atmosphere of his youth, of his maturity, of all the triumphs and adventures of his life, of his death– He felt like he had died and risen again. His life before and his life now seemed indelibly demarcated. This was the smell of what that life had been. He squeezed the cross that hung again against his chest. The cross had been so meaningful in that life. In this life, it seemed merely sentimental. Or maybe that was because he wasn't about to face death, like before a race. But it seemed like he had now experienced death.

He twisted the control wands of the ship and brought it rising out of the hangar. Space beckoned. He hadn't been out in space since the end of the Solar Regatta. He missed the enormous emptiness of it, and the freedom. This is what the ancient sailors must have felt, who sailed Earth's oceans. Men like Christopher Columbus. The feeling of space, of endless openness, the feeling, profoundly, of being unbound. It was a strange, simultaneous feeling of vulnerability and mastery. It was exhilarating, as if yourself, whatever was you, was exploded by the endless expanse around you, the vacuum waiting to be filled. It meant more to him than other people, or it had, in his first life.

He piloted the ship up through the atmosphere and toward gradually appearing stars. Rothschild Palace was beautiful from above, like an intricate painting of vines and flowers in some old style, some 1800s or 1900s style – 'art nouveau' he thought it might have been called. On the ground it more closely resembled a child's fairy palace. What human beings could create was amazing.

The vista of the stars infected Samson's soul. It was a pain erasing salve and soothing stimulant that seemed to function as proof of where he belonged. He turned the ship in an easy barrel roll. He had resisted the temptation to do any maneuvers so far. It had seemed appropriate to fly steady, orthodoxly, until he was in space. The barrel roll felt good. He was the best pilot in the Solar System, he had won the Solar Regatta.

The little planet, Rothschild, spun imperceptibly below him. Samson accelerated into a loop around the planet, effortlessly adjusting the ship's attitude to keep the cockpit out of the sun. The ship pressing into his back felt good, the rush of speed felt natural. He turned another barrel roll, faster.

The sun flashed across him as the ship rolled. Bright, blinding. He did another half-roll, closed his eyes, and basked in the brightness of it. The sun seemed to smile on him, as it always had. To have a planet or an atmosphere separating him from it, from the essence of life– The sun had been dim in Magdalena. The light there was reasonably bright, thanks to Magdalena's enormous solar reflectors that fanned out through space, but the sun itself there had been dim. He could remember the first time he had flown by himself in a bright sun – above Mars. He had just begun working with Ben then.

The man in the afterlife – in the other life, in that phase – had not been Ben. Ben had not been there. Everything there was Samson himself, and sometimes Stephanie. If Ben was dead, where was he? If Samson had not died, where had he been? He had, in some sense, ceased to exist. To the doctors and scientists on Rothschild, at least, he had ceased to exist. Yet he had existed. If Stephanie had not saved him, what would have happened? Would he have met Ben? Would he have met God? Would he have become nothing?

Kenichi said that what happened to Samson raised existential questions that had been forgotten for centuries. Kenichi was shaken up by what had happened. He seemed to be more upset in the aftermath of it than Samson himself, or Stephanie. Dr. Nguyen was merely excited. It seemed like to Kenichi the whole universe had changed.

Existential. Samson hadn't ever heard the word spoken outside of Magdalena before. In Magdalena it was a word sometimes used by theologians and intellectuals. Few people in the Solar System would understand it. Stephanie, of course, had.

He spun another quick barrel roll and pulled up into a long, arcing, loop.

Everything felt good, but it didn't feel fast. He didn't feel fast. He began to put the ship through a series of tight maneuvers. Obstacles and other ships appeared before him in space, projections of his mind. He twisted and braked and hopped the ship around them. He sunk into a gravity loop around Rothschild and instructed the computer to calculate a theoretical trajectory. He pushed the ship close, hard. He pulled up late. It was a half-second, but in a race it would have meant death. He accelerated again and pushed farther out into space, practicing maneuvers as he went. His timing was off, his reflexes. It didn't feel like being rusty, it felt like being numb.

Space beckoned, and Samson accelerated for an hour, far out into it. He practiced maneuvers for a long time before cruising back to Rothschild. By the time he landed again in the ship hangar he was certain that he was no longer the best pilot in the Solar System.

STEPHANIE WAS WAITING TO GREET Samson when he climbed down out of the racer. She gave him a quick kiss and embraced him in a big hug. He held her tightly. She was dressed

261

for business, but didn't seem out of place in the hangar. The other people there were more accustomed to being around her than most inhabitants of Rothschild, and proportionately less star-struck.

"This is a nice surprise," Samson said. "I thought your day was filled with important meetings."

"I cut–"

"one of the meetings short," he said, finishing her sentence.

"Yes, that's right," Stephanie said, disengaging and standing back from him as if remembering the dignity of her position. "I didn't want to miss your first time flying in space again."

Samson looked at her sympathetically. None of the other people in the hangar would say anything to him because she was there, but some of them wanted to.

"I'm sorry, it upsets you when I fill in your sentences."

"No, it's ok. It's just amazing how good you are at it."

"I'll try not to do it anymore," Samson said. "It's so automatic, it's really hard not to do it."

"It's ok." She hugged him again. "So how was flying? You looked great up there!"

"You could tell I was a little off," he said. "That's amazing."

"I didn't say that. You looked good. Did you feel off?"

Samson squeezed her hand.

"You guys thought I looked off, too?" he said loudly towards a couple of race jockeys who were surreptitiously watching them from several yards away.

"You looked good, sir–"

"Don't call me sir, Juan. It's Samson."

"Please sir, the Mistress," the man gestured, reproachfully. "You flew well, without doubt, but it wasn't as crisp as your race flying. But you weren't in a race!"

"I don't expect you to fly like you're in a race," the second man said.

262

"Yes, thank you gentlemen," Stephanie said, and sent them away with a slight motion of her hand.

She walked toward the exit of the hangar and Samson followed her. He felt at ease. He would never race ships again, but he didn't feel bad. Was it because he had already won the Solar Regatta? He didn't think that was it. They were separate things. For some other reason, it didn't bother him.

"It's true that I was off," he said. "My reflexes, my timing. I'm still a good pilot, but I won't be able to race again."

"Do you want to race again?"

"I would if I could race like I did before."

"This is your first time out," Stephanie said. "It will come back. Although, I would be happy if you didn't race again, Samson."

"I'm not afraid of it," he said defensively.

"I don't think you are."

"No, I'm really not afraid of it. I'm not afraid of it at all. But my timing, the way my brain is clicking, it's not the same as before. It feels like this is just how I am now, it doesn't feel like something that will get better."

"Well, I don't think you're afraid," Stephanie repeated, "and I'm glad if you don't race, but I want you to be able to do what you want to do. I want you to be able to live your life."

Samson pressed his lips into a smile, looking away from her.

"I love you," Stephanie said.

"I love you, too."

"I have to go now, I have meetings–" she waved her hand to end the sentence. "I'm glad you're flying again."

"That's right, how has it been going today?"

"I'm late, Samson," she said, walking quickly out of the hangar and being immediately joined by three men, one of whom was her head of personal security, Boris. "I'll tell you about it tonight."

Samson nodded recognition at Boris and the man stared back at him impassively.

"You probably won't have time tonight," Samson said after her, echoing Stephanie's thoughts.

She smiled a small, tight smile and gave him a half-wave before turning completely away.

SCAMP WOKE LISA AND MELCHIT up at 4 AM. In fact, neither of them was actually asleep, but they were gamely trying to. They were dehydrated and their stomachs were growly. The stomach growling worried him. There was nothing he could do about it now. Neither of them talked, they were trying to steel themselves for the journey.

He gave them their diapers and they each went into the bathroom and put them on. Hopefully, because they hadn't had anything to eat for more than 12 hours, the diapers would be unnecessary. He gave each of them a narcotic pill. The narcotics would slow them down, way down, but wouldn't put them to sleep. Melchit was given a half dose. The narcotics would keep them calm, and comfortable, no matter what was happening to them, and would last about three hours. He fitted capsules into each of their mouths with a semi-permanent dental adhesive, in such a way that, with some effort, they could break the capsules open and consume a second dose of narcotics later if the first one was wearing off. The second dose of narcotics was doubled, because its potency diminished quickly when used successively over time. He couldn't put them completely to sleep, because there was too great a risk that they might suffocate or snore.

With the first narcotic dose kicking in, Lisa and Melchit sat on the side of the hotel bed nodding passively. Melchit, in particular, seemed to be almost falling over, and Scamp worried that he had dosed the little creature too high. He hoped that

Melchit would not throw up. If he did throw up, he would probably aspirate it and die. Which wouldn't be the worst possible thing – dead people lay still and were quiet – but it would upset Lisa. And he would rather that the little fellow didn't die, if that were possible.

He took Lisa by the arm and led her over to the backpack. Her arm was thin and soft, yet sturdy – feminine. He wished he could hold her arm like this when she was awake. He squeezed her shoulder reassuringly, while feeling pleasure from touching her, and felt a slight twinge of guilt.

The bottom of the backpack was padded with a thin, dense foam pad. Scamp helped Lisa climb into the backpack and curl up tightly into a ball. Just as they had practiced, he twisted her in the bag and turned her, curled up, onto her side. Then he took a mesh nylon band and wrapped it around her along the inside walls of the backpack, pulling it tight and locking her into position, fastening it with contractor's tape.

It was amazing how small of a space a human being could curl up into. Luckily, Lisa was not tall, only average in height. Lucho used to think it was fun to carry his girlfriends around in a suitcase. Of course, Lucho wasn't nice. And he couldn't carry a suitcase like that for very long. If anyone ever treated Lisa that way, Scamp would kill them. Of course, how would he know? Did those girls' parents know that they were dating a Martian crime lord? That he liked to tie them up and treat them roughly? That he laughed when they cried? Some of their parents did know, must. Sometimes the parents were friends of Lucho. Most people were such shit. Scamp thought about Lucho seeing him now. He was doing something that Lucho had never done – something. Something genuine and legitimate. Lucho would have laughed at him. He was surprised, when he thought about it now, that he hadn't killed Lucho back then. Lucho was trash. He had felt such loyalty to

Lucho, and desired Lucho's approval. Lucho was like a father to him, in a way.

Scamp carefully checked that Lisa was breathing well and put the pad into the backpack that would go between her and Melchit. He had changed so much. He had thought he was too old to change, although he wasn't old, but now he could hardly identify with the person he had been a year before.

Melchit was nearly falling off the bed. Scamp picked him up and lifted him feet first into the backpack, then curled his limbs up into the same position that Lisa was in, shifted him onto his side, and secured him with a nylon strap in the same way. On top of Melchit he put a pillow case, then a thin layer of dirty underwear, then an electronics tablet box that stretched out all four walls of the backpack, then a second electronics box of the same type. On top of the second box he pressed and squeezed the rest of his dirty clothes haphazardly, with smelly socks clustered near the top, until the bag was over-flowing. He closed the top of the bag up and cinched it down tight. He listened closely to Lisa and Melchit and confirmed that they were breathing fine. The fabric of the big backpack wasn't waterproof, it was porous enough to slowly circulate oxygen, and with their metabolisms slowed they didn't need very much. Their breaths were slow and shallow, but steady and relaxed. He stuffed the rest of his belongings into a smaller, normal sized shoulder bag.

The hotel room looked completely empty and well-used. Scamp set a ten minute timer on his card and meticulously scrutinized every corner, every drawer, and every square inch of the floor, to ensure that they were not leaving anything revealing behind.

He lifted the backpack and the smaller bag onto his shoulders and walked with an appearance of carelessness through the door and out into the hallway. Once in the hall, he stopped and felt at his pockets, and counted distractedly into space on his fingers, as if to be certain that he was not forgetting anything. Then he left the building through the hotel's side exit door.

C H A P T E R 37

ᔕCAMP WALKED INTO A CROWDED bus station and monop-
olized two of the remaining empty seats. He lifted the big
backpack off of his shoulders with one arm, as if it weighed
little, and set it on the ground against the front of the seat next
to him. He set his other bag on the seat itself. Scamp's own
chair protested under his weight, and the man sitting beside
him got up and moved away to stand. The bus was going to
be full. Scamp had purchased two tickets for himself, so as not
to infringe on the seat space of anyone next to him.

An old woman sitting on the opposite side of the aisle
looked him up and down.

"You're a big fellow, aren't you," she said with a gravelly,
condescending tone.

"I certainly am," Scamp said, and smiled.

He was perfectly relaxed and gave off the appearance of
not realizing that someone was trying to insult him.

"I don't think I've ever seen a person as big as you, and
with a big backpack like that."

"I've got about five hours ahead of me," Scamp said. "Are
you traveling far today?"

"What do you care where I'm traveling?"

"I ordered two seats," Scamp said, "so you don't need to
worry about sitting next to me."

"Oh, that is a relief."

Other people in the station were watching them. Scamp
didn't care very much, but it was less than ideal.

"You're trying to give me a hard time, aren't you?" he said
in a still friendly tone.

The woman was very old, her skin was no longer taught.
Her hair was dyed and she wore a woven violet dress highlighted with intricately patterned thin white lines. She looked

up at the ceiling. They still had twenty minutes until the bus boarded.

"I'll have to tell my daughter in Manhattan about you when I get there," she said without looking back at him. "It's quite a story to see a man like you. Your eyes are so red and scary looking. I'll give my grandkids a thrill telling about them."

"They don't like old people in Manhattan," Scamp said. "Have you been there recently?"

"Wh–? Not for a few years."

"Try to look young when you are there, with all the make-up and stuff. They've been being mean to old people in the streets there lately. You heard all the young people who are saying the old ones should just hurry up and die?"

"Well-" the woman tried to cut back in.

"It's because of the new exo-xygote gene, they're going to have double lifespans and won't ever deteriorate in their faculties. They say people under 35 may be able to get modified for it, so there's still hope for me. But there's been a lot of incidents with old people in Manhattan. When I was up there a month ago I saw some teenagers spit on an old man in the street."

"I don't have to–"

"They called him 'crustkin', that's the new slang they have. I don't think old people should be killed, but a lot of people in Manhattan do now. If you try to look your youngest that will help some."

"Shutup you f-faggot!" the woman snapped in a stuttering, snarling hiss.

Scamp put a pair of large headphones over his ears, leaned back, and half-closed his eyes, pretending to tune the woman out. She tried to appeal to people around her for support, but they were all laughing at her.

Two armed Bloodworth's security agents arrived out front and walked through the station waiting room. They gave a cursory glance around and proceeded through to the curb on the other side where the bus was parked and waiting.

Scamp watched the two men out of the window through his half-closed eyes. They had given him a longer look-over than anyone else, although it wasn't much. Other passengers went outside to board, but Scamp sat in his chair and waited patiently. Boarding would take at least ten minutes.

The security agents were manually inspecting each person's large bags before allowing them to board. This was, apparently, the reason why the agents were there. They were going through the contents of every large bag as it was loaded into the luggage belly of the bus, without skipping any of them.

Scamp checked the time on his card, grunted, and stood up and went to the bathroom, looking at the employee behind the desk meaningfully as he passed, pointing at his bags, pointing at his eyes, and pointing at the bathroom.

In the bathroom there was one other man. Scamp went into a stall against the wall and waited for the man to leave. When the man left, Scamp ripped the ventilation cover off of the wall about 8 ft above the floor, then pulled from his pocket a can of flammable aerosol. No one else had entered the bathroom yet, so he then stood up gingerly on the toilet and thrust his arm deep into the vent, spraying the aerosol down towards the end. He threw the can into the vent, too, and then produced a small ignition torch. He lit the torch and threw it deep into the vent as well, which immediately lit up and exhaled hot fumes. To finish, Scamp put the ventilation cover back up to the hole and pressed it in concavely with his palm, so that it was again stuck into place. He brushed his sleeve off, rinsed his hands in the sink, and walked back out of the bathroom.

Everything in the station waiting room was normal, although it was much less crowded than before. The employee at the station desk made an exaggerated display of pointing at Scamp's bags, pointing at his eye, and pointing at Scamp. Scamp picked up his bags and walked out to the bus.

Several people were milling around and about three quarters of the passengers had already boarded. Scamp walked forward, set his bags down nearly on top of the security agents' feet, and opened the tops of the bags while rolling his eyes.

An alarm in the station went off and startled everyone. Scamp flinched noticeably at the alarm. The security agents looked toward the station windows, then down at Scamp's bags, then back to the station again. People started rushing from the station doors.

"What's that alarm?" Scamp demanded from the agents.

"Keep quiet."

He backed around to the agents' other side, putting them between himself and the station.

"What kind of alarm is that?"

"Shut-up! We don't know."

The agent who seemed to be in charge, or who had more initiative, kicked Scamp's smaller bag testingly and then slid it aside with his foot. He pulled open the top of the big backpack and dug a little bit through Scamp's smelly socks and underwear, down to the first electronics box.

A man rushed out of the station and said, "There's a big fire on the roof inside!" More alarms began to sound.

"Jesus," Scamp said, "look at that smoke."

The agent quickly peeked under the first electronics box down to the second one, then slapped the top of it and said, "Fine, you can go."

Scamp snatched up his bags and swung them himself into the very back corner of the luggage belly under the bus, where it would be inconvenient for anyone to try to rearrange them. He jogged to the front of the bus and jumped on board. Emergency vehicles began arriving at the station, which was becoming completely engulfed in flame.

"Everyone here ready?" the bus driver said on the intercom. "We're taking off, we have to get away from the fire and out of the way."

Scamp sat in his two seats and stared at the fire as the bus rose into the air.

"Jesuschrist!" he said. "Where did that come from?"

"They said there was a fire on the roof."

Everyone on the bus was spinning. Scamp exchanged breathless, disbelieving remarks with the people around him. Down below, he noticed the old woman that had bothered him being ushered by firemen away from the station. She was one of the ones who hadn't made it on board, and was awkwardly dragging along only one of her bags.

8/2

I'm writing this from on board a bus. I can't write completely freely because it's not totally private here. I'm ok. Lisa and the little guy are ok, too. It looks like we are all going to be ok.

There was trouble at the bus station, a big fire. The station lit up like a match box, I'm sure it burned to the ground. People were screaming. I barely made it on board. Imagine if I didn't make it!

This bus is flying to Rio de Janeiro, with several stops along the way. Rio is the closest city that is really neutral. It is good to get out of Phillipeville. The air feels freer. But Bloodworth's territory extends for a long way. I've had enough of it.

I didn't have to kill anyone this week. That's something positive. Things are starting to look good, but I can't relax until — this is all over, and the people I care about are all safe and happy.

Apparently Samson Ford is really alive. Reality doesn't seem real. It's like I went into Phillipeville in one universe and came out in another one. My life seems like a series of transitions between alternate universes. I step from one reality into the next. Where I was before, Samson Ford was dead. Where I am now, Samson Ford is alive. Mygod, I hope I get to meet him again.

  - Scampadorous Maximus

CHAPTER 38

THE MAGDALENA WAR COUNCIL'S REGULAR weekly meeting had become a crisis meeting. Several men were there who had never been there before. Everyone was tense. The Prophet himself was overseeing the meeting, and his eyes were red from exhaustion, or stress, or – crying? Theo, as usual, sat in the back. He wasn't even really at the table, he was merely near it. The talk was of war, but no longer in the abstract. The agenda for the meeting was to formulate a plan of action for Magdalena's attack. If not a detailed plan, at least a general strategy and targets for the initial assault.

Theo had not known, going into the meeting, that its intent was to begin the war. He did know the other news: the virus that had swept through Magdalena and infected him and his wife was a deliberately engineered weapon. It had stricken their children, their friends – literally every human being in Magdalena. It had made them all sterile; it had made their children sterile. Even their babies. Half the men in the room had come to the meeting without yet being aware of how bad the virus really was. Some of them had been brought to tears. One, a fat man, was still crying. One, a small thin man, kept drifting off into his own mind and gesticulating arguments with his hands above the table space in front of him, apparently unable to convince himself that it was really true.

Magdalena virologists had determined that the virus was designed to render all natural born people sterile, and that it was 100% effective. With an indefinite incubation and subtle symptoms, the virus had already spread through the entire population before it was identified. There was no possibility of quarantine and no foreseeable possibility of treatment. That was the apparent point behind the virus, the doctors said: something that once done could never be undone. Magdalena contacts in other natural born communities in the Solar System confirmed that the virus had already spread there, too. It had spread to every there, everywhere it was possible for them to check – quite conceivably, no one in the Solar System had escaped it.

Theo and others had doubted the doctors' conclusion that the virus was 100% effective. Some of the men – they were all men – shouted angrily at the doctors, and even threatened to attack them, to the extent that two of the senior researchers had begun to tremble and stutter in their speech. The fact remained, as the researchers could only repeat, not a single individual, out of more than 400,000 that had already been tested, had been able to avoid the virus's harmful effects.

It was difficult to argue with reality. People could easily deny reality, they constantly did, but they did that by ignoring it, by pretending it wasn't there. It was hard to dispute with the hammer swinging towards your face.

Theo had known the worst of it already, then, but he had not known that they were actually going to war. Actually taking action, now. This came as a shock to him. Going to war he had expected, but now, right now, planning the attack, sending the warships, launching the bombs – he wasn't ready.

Who were they going to war with? With everyone?

"This is where we need your input, Theodore," The Prophet was saying. "You understand their society, their values. Where are their nerve centers? Where can we strike that will damage them the most? We're familiar with your report, but that was based on tactical considerations. Those are, sadly, largely irrelevant now. The question we must ask is: where can we attack that will cause them the most pain?"

Theo hoped that this was a question open to the floor, but everyone including The Prophet sat silently and waited for his response. He felt a bead of sweat drip down the back of his neck and cleared his throat.

"I'm sorry, Holiness," Theo said, "I don't understand who specifically we are trying to hurt."

"Are you thick?" Magdalena's senior general snapped from the head of the table. "We're trying to hurt THEM!"

"We can't win a war against the whole Solar System," Theo said.

"We've already lost the war! You are thick. Don't you see what's going on? We're already dead!"

Theo didn't completely understand.

"We have been destroyed by the genetically engineered people," The Prophet said. "These are the end times. We are like a dying man, a mortally wounded man, a brave and noble and good man, who has been mortally struck down by a vicious demon. We have our sword out, with the demon standing in front of us as we fall, and as we fall we will thrust our sword into it as best we can."

"They'll kill all of us," Theodore said. "Not just on Magdalena, they'll kill all the natural born, everywhere."

"We're already dead!" the general shouted. "Daft fool."

"Well don't attack all of them! Attack Bloodworth's. Attack Google. They're not all the same. They're not all our enemies. Rothschild's has been fighting to protect the natural born."

"They are all our enemies now, Theodore," The Prophet said in a dry croak, almost wistfully. "All of them have destroyed all of us. The only thing we can do is the righteous thing, the act of justice – to thrust our sword into them as hard as we can."

Several men in the room spontaneously voiced, "our Father, hallowed by thy name," under their breaths and The Prophet caught up their words and repeated the utterance with his eyes closed. Then all of the men in the room followed suit.

"The only logical option we have left is Option Omega," said a white haired old man sitting directly to The Prophet's

276

right. He was The Prophet's oldest friend and closest minister.

Several of the other most senior men in the room quietly bowed their heads, or knit their jaws, and the senior general nodded assent stonily. Many of the younger men in the room stared blankly ahead.

"I fear you are right, Jacob," The Prophet said quietly.

Option Omega? Theo wanted someone else in the room to ask about it, he didn't want to be the only outlier, the outsider, the pariah. But when another man began to raise a different subject, his hand was forced.

"Wait! Wait. I'm sorry, Holiness, forgive me for slowing the meeting, but what is Option Omega? I'm sure I've never heard of this before."

"Let your mouth close and be silent, child," The Prophet said with tempering gentleness in his tone. "Many of the men here do not know about Option Omega. It has not been given to you to know. When the time comes that it is necessary you will be enlightened with it. For right now, content yourself with the already inhumanly difficult task of figuring out where we should aim our thrust, or thrusts."

As the meeting continued, Theo felt his soul become a piece of tissue paper torn into shreds. He tried to think about the sword thrust; he wanted to help The Prophet. He found that he could not. All he could do was visualize a sword thrusting into a man and think of his family. And it seemed like the man was him.

AFTER THE COUNCIL MEETING, AS Theo walked home, he passed through the enormous city courtyard where work had just been completed on a giant statue of Samson. He felt in a daze, and yet, peculiarly focused. As if his mind were a glass of liquor that was clouded only at the bottom, and above that crystal clear. Although it was after dusk, there were people in the courtyard who had come out to see the statue. Some of them were laughing. Most of the citizens of Magdalena still did not know about the virus and the devastation their society was facing; they didn't know about the war.

He walked across the middle of the broad, bricked courtyard where it was empty, as if he were a boat drifting over a placid brick sea. The statue of Samson was realistic, if dramatic, and a good likeness. It had Samson standing with his head flung back triumphantly, and crossing himself at the same time. Theo crossed himself too, automatically, as he looked at it. Large white walls that ran along the courtyard behind the statue told Samson's story in giant letters. It was a story about Samson, and the Solar Regatta, but it wasn't the story that Theo knew. In this story, Samson was a crusader sent out into the world by The Prophet, who triumphed in the Solar Regatta and proved for a fact natural mankind's quality and grace. He was a Magdalena Saint.

Theo wondered if the rumors could be true, that Samson had miraculously come back to life, but stopped himself from hoping that they were. Official Magdalena news sources said that Samson was dead, but that a false Samson had been presented to the public on Earth as resurrected, for propaganda purposes. Surely, if Samson was alive, he would have contacted Theo or their parents. Or Stephanie would have written to them. Surely. Although the Magdalena authorities could intercept those communications if they wanted to. If they believed that Samson was really dead they might not let such communications through. In his position as a shepherd, and now as an advisor to the military council, Theo's communications were usually left alone.

Samson would have enjoyed the statue. He would have thought it was hilarious. Maybe he was somewhere laughing about it now. It was a beautiful statue.

STEPHANIE DE ROTHSCHILD HAD A large office located in the executive suites of Rothschild Palace. The office had been her father's and had sat empty in the years after his death, when she refused to use it. She had nearly refused to ever be on Rothschild at all. Now she occupied the office constantly.

It was still decorated as her father had decorated it. She had not had any reason to change anything before, when it sat unused, and when she had finally begun to use it she didn't have any time. She liked how the office was, though; her father's spirit was there, present in its shelves and on its walls. An old photograph of her mother still sat on the desk that her father had taken with an ancient camera. It wasn't a beautiful picture, but it must have been special to them when they were young.

The office felt like home to Stephanie, although she had hardly had time to be conscious of that. She used it because she needed it, and it became a part of her through the use. It was a large and beautiful office, and very masculine. Her father had been the greatest man in the world. The masculinity here suited her position, and seeped into her, or at least had the appearance of doing so, so that it complemented her natural feminine personality.

There was an intimidating mechanical eagle mounted on one wall, brass and leather and titanium arrayed in exotic feathers, that watched people in the room and occasionally flexed its wings. The eagle had haunted her nightmares as a child, although she had only rarely been inside the office before her father died. She remembered the first time she had ever ventured into the office after it happened, after he was gone and everything became hers, and feeling like an interloper and wondering what secrets of his she would find there. Simon Okunle had refused to enter the office until she had gone through it herself. She was waiting for Simon now.

C H A P T E R ³⁹

IMON OKUNLE CAME THROUGH THE door of the office and walked along its entrance chamber toward Stephanie, who was sitting at her desk. He looked old and tired. He smiled, but did not seem able to translate the emotion into his steps, which were quietly labored.

"I want you to rest more, Simon," Stephanie said.

"That's impossible, Mistress. The only thing possible now is to work more."

He sat down in one of the large, saddle-inspired leather chairs in front of Stephanie's desk.

"I want you to delegate more, and look after your health. I need you there to the end of this, and I need an organization that can still function well without you if you're not."

"Yes, Mistress."

"That's an order, Simon. Delegate more, rest more."

"I understand, Mistress."

"Tell me the bad news."

Simon did not hesitate to collect his words, although his face was pained as he spoke them.

"A new virus is spreading rapidly through the naturals population. The virus causes sterility in both male and female victims. Analysis is still preliminary, but it is a near certainty that the virus is an engineered weapon. As far as we can tell, it has already spread throughout the Solar System."

His eyes were extraordinarily grim. Too grim. Nothing could possibly be that grim.

"How many of the victims suffer sterilization?"

"All of them, mum."

"What?"

"It appears to be all of them. I am being told the virus is a marvel of virological technology, far more advanced than anything that has been known before."

"Well how many people has the virus infected, are we talking about millions?"

"It infects everyone, mum. On three planets and five moons, our scientists haven't yet been able to locate a natural born person who was not infected."

Stephanie felt her stomach rising into her throat and made a conscious effort to block out her emotional consciousness.

"So all natural born people in the Solar System have been sterilized?"

"Yes."

"What prospect is there for treatment."

"None."

Simon cleared his throat and blinked uncomfortably without looking away.

"Don't tell me that, Simon! It's not even possible to make a conclusion like that yet!"

"I'm sorry, Mistress. Of course it's preliminary, but without exception our top infectious disease specialists are telling me that there is no hope for treatment with current or foreseeable medical technology."

"So they're all just dead then? That's incredibly hopeless, Simon. Give me something better than that!"

"I'm sorry, mum. It is entirely bad news."

"What about everyone else, what about the rest of us?"

"That's not yet clear. The virus seems to be designed so that anyone who has had the basic immunological booster panel will be protected from it. That would be anyone born from a gene weaving machine in the last 100 years. So, hopefully, as horrible as it is, it will only affect the natural born. But one of our senior virologists thinks he has discovered the virus incubating in some patients with advanced genetics. It isn't certain yet, and other doctors think he is mistaken. But even if it infects the rest of us, for anyone with the immunological booster panel the virus' effects should be benign. We will know about it with more certainty soon."

"Where did the virus come from?"

"We don't know."

"It spread through the whole Solar System already, there are only a few organizations that could be behind it."

"That's true, mum."

"It must be Bloodworth."

Stephanie enunciated the name with a disconcerting raw hatred in her voice. She didn't notice that she did it.

"I suspect so, too, mum, but the manufacture and distribution of the virus has been carefully concealed. It may turn out to be impossible to conclusively determine where the virus came from."

"Surely you don't suspect Google?"

"No. I don't believe Google would, or probably even could, do this. I agree with your suspicion of Bloodworth's."

"Godamnit!" Stephanie threw a glass ball against the wall and it shattered, sending crystal shrapnel throughout the room. Simon flinched and touched his hand.

"Are you ok?"

"Of course, mum."

A small trickle of blood began to run down the back of his hand.

"Ohlord, you're cut Simon. Forgive me."

Simon pressed his other hand over the cut to staunch it.

"It's only a shallow cut, mum. Think nothing of it."

Stephanie's office secretary came into the room, saw the glass on the floor, and walked quickly back outside. Stephanie started to sit back down again, but could not. Her eyes burned.

"Simon, if Bloodworth's did this we'll have to kill them all."

"I know, mum. But we can't go kill them all if we can't be certain it was them."

"We have to notify Magdalena! We have to talk to them before they go straight to war."

"Samson is the only person who could stop them, mum."

"I know."

Simon put his strong old hands on the arms of the chair and squeezed deep impressions into it. Blood began to run again down the back of his hand. He snatched it back into his lap before it dripped on the chair.

"I'm sorry that I have nothing to give you but terrible news. No hope to offer. No silver lining."

"What about Samson?"

"We should isolate him and test him immediately, just in case. But the virus is here. It is almost certain that he is infected too."

"Jesus, Simon."

"I'm sorry, mum."

"I wanted to become pregnant. To have a child with him in the old way. I was going to do that."

"I know."

"Samson claims he has acquired this strange ability since he came back. He says that he can perceive the electromagnetic radiation around him, like it's a sixth sense, and he says somehow it allows him to read people's minds."

"Is any of that true?"

"I don't know; I mean, it can't possibly be. I'm afraid his mind has been damaged. But sometimes it seems to be true. It's starting to unnerve me."

"No matter what, you can still have children with him through gene weaving, Mistress."

"Yes."

"That may be the answer to the devastation facing the natural born, too."

"It may be, but that will be hard. We have to get them

to talk to us. We have to get people to be reasonable when their fate is unreasonable. And Bloodworth's will undermine it. It feels like we are in a spaceship at the edge of an event horizon – everything we perceive is rushing to destruction, and we have such little time."

"You have to meet with our friend in the Assembly who can help get people to talk. He may be the only one who can."

"Yes, it's back to planet Earth for me. I'm already planning the conversation. But he's not our friend."

"No, he's not."

ON THE BUS RIDE TO RIO de Janeiro, Scamp had little to do but worry and watch the news. He ran the bulletins from all the major planets on his card. Minutes passed excruciatingly. The bus was stuffy and his seat was uncomfortable. He suppressed the urge to tear off the bus window and get fresh air, and imagined smashing in the heads of the people on the bus around him with his fist. Although he had no real desire to do that to them, for some reason it made him feel better. The luggage compartment under the bus must be extremely cold by now. It wouldn't be cold enough to hurt Lisa and the creature, not quite enough to give them hypothermia or frostbite, but it would be miserable. Rio was still two hours away. If the narcotic wasn't zoning them out like it was supposed to, they would be experiencing hell.

On the Earth wires, a breaking news bulletin about Lisa Maui appeared at the top of the list. Scamp clicked on it in shock. "Missing Activist, Lisa Maui, Wanted For Murder!"

A clip of surveillance video showed a taxi dropping Lisa off by the sidewalk in Manhattan. She walked down the street and a man walking the other way bumped into her quite hard. The two of them shouted at each other. Then, when the man began to scream into her face, Lisa punched him, causing him to fall awkwardly and strike his head on a stone bench. After falling, the man went into convulsions. Lisa knelt next to him and seemed unsure of what to do. She glanced around the street, which was otherwise empty, then stood up and sprinted away.

Scamp stopped the video and replayed the surveillance clip again and again. The woman in the video looked exactly like Lisa. It had to be a fake, but it might as well have been real.

He finally let the video play on, and as it ended the newscaster said:

"And in other breaking news, a mysterious new virus is sweeping through Mars with a shocking fatality rate. One top researcher believes this virus has been purposely engineered and that some health authorities are trying to cover it up."

CHAPTER 40

STEPHANIE CAME HOME EARLY IN the evening and found Samson in her living room working out. In their living room – was it 'their'? She didn't know. He was wearing nothing but a pair of shorts and she resisted the temptation to touch his sweaty muscles.

"Samson, something terrible has happened."

"Ohmygod, it's something horrible. I'm sorry."

He embraced her supportively, responding to a devastation that she had not expressed. She tensed at his embrace and pushed him away.

"We don't have much time. An engineered virus has been released throughout the Solar System; it causes natural people to become sterile."

"Jesuschrist, no one is spared."

"It seems to be that way. You have to go to my medical lab and be tested as soon as we get done talking. Unfortunately, you are almost certainly infected, too."

"Ok."

"Assuming that's true, you have to leave immediately on a deep-space transport to Magdalena, to act as an envoy and try to prevent them from going to war. The transport will leave in an hour."

"Why do you feel so cold toward me?" Samson asked.

"There's not time. I'll get you a shirt. I have to go to another fucking meeting."

"I understand, but your feelings toward me are cold."

"It's not what I want! Don't think that you can feel what my feelings are."

She stood looking at him with tension around her eyes and forehead, as if he were standing on a distant plateau.

"We'll talk more when you're underway," she said. "I'm sorry. Kiss me goodbye."

They kissed and she rushed away again. Light rain sprinkled on her floating platform as it crossed through the courtyards outside. Deep within herself she felt nauseous, and like some part of her was dying, perhaps the best part of her. But she didn't cry.

In Rio de Janeiro, Scamp got off the bus and retrieved his bags. The security presence at the station was minimal, which gave him a sense of relief. Nevertheless, he couldn't let Lisa and Melchit out, under the new circumstances, and couldn't even contact authorities. If they were taken into custody by police anywhere on Earth, Bloodworth's agents would probably be able to kill them. He pulled out his card and began searching for hotels. Something expensive, busy, and close to the station would be perfect. But not too close.

Lisa and Melchit would have to wait. He felt squirming in the backpack against his back.

"I wish I was home already," he said to a man exiting the station alongside him, slightly loudly. "I wish I could put this huge thing down, but now I have to walk to my hotel first."

"What have you got in there?" the man asked.

"All my possessions, mate. All my possessions in the world."

Scamp turned off, and walked as quickly as he reasonably could toward a hotel that he had found on his card and where he had immediately booked a room. The hotel was a mile away. The squirming against his back had stopped, but whenever he had to pause his walking now he felt a second heart beating hard against him.

A ragged, natural looking man with dirty, grey hair ran out from an alcove and walked half-way in front of Scamp, forcing him to slow.

"Give me some money, man," the bum said.

287

"Fuck off, get out of my way."

"A credit, man, just one credit."

"No."

"Look at you," the bum shouted, waving in all directions as if he had an audience, "big, scary monkey, with all engineering. I got nothing, man. I was born poor. You owe me."

Without slowing, Scamp reached out to cave the man's face in with his fist, then resisted the temptation at the last second. Several people on the street were watching them already.

"Just a few credits, man. Just one credit. Just one. What do you want me to suck your dick for one credit? Is that the stingy kind of fuck you are? You want a lot of service for one credit? You stingy fuck. Give me a credit, just give it to me!"

Scamp quickened his pace, so that the man had to jog to keep up. He looked down and memorized the man's face with eyes that would have terrified any lucid human being.

"Fine, be that way, big, fat backpack, fat fuck, fat prick!" the bum shouted as he stopped jogging and Scamp trailed away. "You think even a bum like me will suck your dick for 10 credits? Fuck you!"

I should have just given him a few coins, Scamp thought. Now everybody's looking at me, planting this moment in their brains, remembering it. Shit. He heard a faint, miserable whine from inside the backpack.

"Almost there," he said while inhaling, as if to himself.

The big hotel finally loomed in front of him. Scamp walked into the voluptuous cement and maple burl lobby and made his way to the front desk as quickly as he could.

THEO AND MARIA LAY IN their bed late at night, exhausted, unable to sleep, trembling against each other. Their bed quilt, which Maria had made while she was pregnant with Paul, was insufficient to insulate them from the world. They prayed, and held each other, and prayed, and tried to sleep, and prayed. Of course, they talked too. About everything. About anything. When they could summon a moment of strength, out of their fear and exhaustion, they talked about specific things.

"I think we should take the children and flee Magdalena," Maria whispered. "We can go to Neo Vega, we can go—anywhere."

"It's blasphemy," Theo said. "It's going against God."

"The Prophet isn't God. He's a holy man, but not perfect. I've never believed he's perfect."

"Maria!"

"It's also a sin to commit suicide. It's also a sin to kill your children. But that's what he wants us to do."

"Even if we wanted to, it might be impossible. I've thought about it, too."

"We're all dead if we stay here. You said so yourself. It's true, isn't it?"

"It's true. But we're all dead now, anyway. It's only a question of lifespan."

"Maybe our children aren't actually sterile. Maybe there are doctors out there who can help them."

"That's possible," Theo said, "but I don't think it's very likely. For natural procreation we have the most advanced science in the Solar System. I don't think they're lying about the virus, or hiding anything about it. But technological breakthroughs are unpredictable. They can't know that in twenty or thirty years it will still be impossible to cure. Eve is only six!"

"The Prophet must believe this is the end of the world," Maria said.

"He said that. He said it is."

"But is it really? Maybe Samson was right, Theo."

"Don't say that."

"I don't mean in everything. Lord forgive me. But maybe he was right to want to leave Magdalena."

Theo and Maria both instinctively drew the ancient cross across themselves with their thumbs; from forehead to heart, from left shoulder to right.

"Father have mercy on us."

"Maybe he was, Theo!"

"Maybe he was."

"Is it really the end of the world, or only the end of our world?"

"We won't be able to kill all the genetically engineered people," Theo said. "Or even most of them."

"We shouldn't even want to! What about that Stephanie, that woman Samson brought, she was a good person."

"No, we shouldn't. A lot of them are good people."

"I had a nightmare last night that The Prophet is a devil."

"Don't say that."

"Maybe he's a devil, Theo. Maybe he is! Maybe this war is a great evil. A virus wasn't made by billions of people, or even millions of people. A virus is made by thousands or hundreds of people. Maybe only a few engineers. The Prophet wants us to commit suicide and kill innocent people at the same time. It's murder. It is murder!"

"Shush! Shush. Shush. Stop. Stop."

Theo squeezed his wife's shaking body tightly against his own and brushed her hair back gently from her forehead again and again.

"Even if they can't be healed, our children deserve the chance to live their life!"

"I know, love. I know they do. I know."

CHAPTER 41

ARLY IN THE MORNING, AN urgent call came through for Theo on quantum-loop relay chat. It was from an unlisted number.

"Who is it?" Theo asked roughly, pulling on a robe and switching on the channel projection.

A crackling image of Samson appeared in the air.

"Theo? Thank God. Theo, can you hear me?"

"Who are you?"

"Is your projection working? This is Samson. Jesus, it's hard to get a connection through to you out there."

"Samson is dead."

"I didn't really die. Well, maybe I did, but that's complicated. Anyway, I'm alive. Is your projection working? This is me."

"I can see you. Stephanie de Rothschild informed us that Samson is dead. We haven't heard from her again saying that he is alive. We haven't heard from him. I think you're a fake."

"Who is it?" Maria said groggily, coming into the room. Then she saw the projection and jumped. "Jesuschrist!"

Theo raised an eyebrow at his wife, and she turned red in the face as she crossed herself.

"She sent you a letter," Samson said. "I've written you a couple of times since then, too. Shit, Theo, we don't have time. Magdalena security pricks probably cut the letters off. Who knows how long this connection will last."

"That's easy to say."

"Theo, it's me! Listen, I'm losing the connection. Remember when you were here and Kenichi beat you at chess? And you thought he hated to be beaten by a natural, but I told you he wasn't prejudiced."

"Maybe."

"I'm coming there, Theo. I'm already en-route on one of Stephanie's fastest transports. I'm coming to talk to The

Prophet, to stop Magdalena from going to war."

The connection flickered.

"Can you hear me? Rothschild's is trying to connect with you, but Magdalena isn't talking to anyone."

"It's the non-communi–"

"I know it's the non-communication policy – I know. I'm coming in person. Don't let them go to war. We can fix this."

"Samson, everyone here still believes you're dead."

"They'll believe I'm alive when I'm there!"

"Samson!" Maria shouted, dashing up to the table and putting her head next to Theo's.

"I'm losing you. Tell The Prophet. I love you guys. Tell our parents I'm not dead."

"Samson? Samson?"

The image of Samson flickered a final time and was gone. Theo and Maria stared at the space where the image had been. Suddenly, the projection blinked on again.

"I'm sorry to bother you, sir," a man in the garb of Magdalena security officers said. "That transmission you just received was unapproved and believed to come from an enemy channel. I just want to warn you and apologize for any inconvenience. One of our trainees let it through."

"I see," Theo said.

"We want to send an officer out to talk to you about the contents of the communication. Right away, if possible."

"I'm going to speak with The Prophet about it first thing this morning," Theo said. "Perhaps your officer would like to debrief him."

"Uh, n-no sir that wouldn't be – Uh, that won't be necessary. We'll let you go back to bed. Please accept my apology and let us know if we can be of any assistance."

"Thank you," Theo said, and terminated the connection.

STEAM IN THE HOTEL SHOWER clouded the air around Lisa's body, insulating her from the world. It felt protective, but didn't warm her. It took a conscious effort to stop breathing too fast. Or to even slow her breaths, which came shallowly. She picked up a bar of soap and put it down again. It seemed overwhelming to hold. She needed to wash. She picked up the bar of soap, and breathed rapid, shallow breaths, and put it down again. The shower was beautiful, large, luxurious. Scamp seemed to think that they were safer in expensive hotels. He'd gone out to find transportation for them. She couldn't believe that she was still trapped. They were in Rio de Janeiro, an open city, a free city, not a Bloodworth town. And she was trapped. They would kill her if she was arrested – someone would. She knew that Scamp was right about that. Bloodworth's tentacles stretched to every end of the Solar System. She still hadn't told Scamp about the data card. Trapped. She picked up the soap again and put it down again.

The shower was large, but seeing its close granite walls made her pulse race. Only the fog of the steam allowed her to stay inside it. Trapped. Confined. She kept flashing back to the hours in the backpack. The narcotic hadn't worked, she could remember every minute of it. Or it seemed like every minute. So many minutes. Hours of torture. She picked up the bar of soap again and put it down again. The narcotic seemed to have worked well for Melchit, he was mostly unfazed by the experience. She couldn't stop shaking. It had hurt so bad. And the pain was amplified terror. Wrapped up in a ball, in the cold, unable to move, barely drawing breath, slowly suffocating, with her chin pressed into her chest. Completely trapped. It had felt like an ice pick was jammed into her spine below her neck. Her neck still hurt. She picked up the soap again and put it down again, almost dropping it, hands trembling. What would she do?

When she did finally emerge from the shower, Lisa tried to put herself together in front of the huge bathroom mirror. She glanced down at the adult diaper sitting in the bathroom trashcan and wretched.

Pulling on a thick hotel robe, Lisa came out of the bathroom and lay down on top of one of the beds. Scamp had left to buy supplies and Melchit was curled up in a chair in the corner of the room. She switched on the tv news. Most of what they were talking about was a strange new virus spreading around the Solar System. It sounded bad, but seemed distant from her circumstance. She couldn't focus enough to wrap her head around it and understand the details. The virus was pushing most other stories out of the news cycle, including the stories about her.

"How are you doing, Melchit?"

"Melchit ok."

"Are you sure?"

"Lisa and Melchit need the new plan."

"What about Scamp?"

"Him can't be trusted."

"He can't? I think I'm starting to trust him? Maybe I trust him a lot. I think he's on our side."

"Him is dangerous."

"Yeah."

"The new plan. The new plan can be, if there is a place outside. A wilderness of far. No people there. In that place we can go, and live. Melchit can build things. In a wilderness, Lisa and Melchit can live and be safe. It can be a good live."

"I don't know if we can do that," Lisa said.

"Why no?"

"I don't think we can find a place like that."

"We find that. Far away."

"People are everywhere. And I need to see my family. And I have friends."

"Thems will kill Melchit and sell him at Hong Kong."

"Nobody will do that. Melchit, what Phillipe Bloodworth told you is not true. Monkey people aren't killed or sold in Hong Kong."

"Master is not true."

"He's not true. He's just a disgusting, old, lying, sack of shit. We can find a safe place for you, if I can get safe, and I'm your friend. I'll visit you and you can visit me."

"Lisa is Melchit friend."

"That's right. I'm your friend, aren't I?"

"Melchit love Lisa. Lisa and Melchit is a friend."

"Thank you, Melchit. So that's right, we're friends, and we'll do our best to take care of each other. I won't let anyone hurt you. And you can probably live with my grandparents in New York, once we get safe. They're great people. And you'll make other friends, too. Don't be afraid, be strong."

"Melchit will be strong for the Melchit friend."

"Ok."

"And that Scamp is the dangerous man."

"He's dangerous, but we need him. And I think he needs us."

CHAPTER 42

"WHEN THE STAFF CHANGES DURING the night we'll leave," Scamp said. He had returned with bags full of supplies, a plan, and an imperative attitude. "I have a rental car with tinted windows parked in the garage. I've got disguises for both of you. In most hotels the staff changes at 12 AM, but we'll wait until 2 AM to be safe. 2 AM, we'll leave then."

"Nobody's looking for you?" Lisa said.

"Not that I know of. Bloodworth's agents probably are, but this isn't Phillipeville anymore. He doesn't have eyes everywhere here. No one was tailing me."

"Well that's good."

"This is going to work. We'll take the car to meet with a contact of mine. He'll arrange a ship for us that we can take to Mars."

"Why Mars?"

"I have connections there, I can hide us underground, in comfort. From there we can open up a dialogue with Rothschild's and work on clearing your name."

Scamp paced the room heavily and a small part of Lisa's mind imagined the people below them, hearing the heavy footsteps.

"But Mars is where that virus thing is killing people," Lisa said.

"The virus is here, too. I heard people talking about it. They're trying to keep it covered up – that's probably true. Anyway, we can take steps to avoid the virus, and it only affects a small percentage of people."

"It kills most of the people it affects!"

"Right, maybe all of them, but we don't have a better option. If the police on Earth find you, and they're looking, you're as good as dead. And what do you think they'll do to *him*?

That's probably true anywhere. Think about it! You're famous, and everyone in the Solar System has their eyes out for you. The police will be monitoring for communications with any of your friends and family. I can protect us on Mars, it's the only decent option we have."

Lisa wanted to argue with him, but she couldn't think. She was exhausted and scared, and – shattered. Her hands had been trembling since Scamp came through the door, and it was slowly spreading into her limbs. Her stomach felt sick.

"Anyway," Scamp continued, "the virus works in our favor. Did you know there's another virus out there that only affects the natural born? My contact who is getting a ship for us told me about it. It's been hushed up so far in the media, but it's devastating them. Apparently. It's a weaponized virus and it's all over the Solar System already. This might be a new virus wars. Remember in history, someone developed a virus to wipe out the Chinese? It didn't work, and mutated, and killed 5% of humanity. In the 22nd Century, or the 21st. Anyway, the mood on the streets is really bad. There's this tension in the air, unstable energy, like a frightened bear trying to protect an exposed, raw nerve. People are scared of so many things right now, and trying to decide which side to join, who to fight with or fight against, where to hide. They think, when is it a line too far? When do I have to fight? Who do I have to align myself with? They think, is it already too late? They don't have enough attention or energy to notice us. To notice much. My contact is in racketeering and he says business is the best it's ever been. Chaos feeds the dragon. But he also said it's more dangerous. People are desperate, and unpredictable."

"I don't care about that!" Lisa said.

"I'm sorry. But this is exciting, isn't it? There's life in the air. We have a way out now, we're going to make it. We're going to be the winners."

For a moment Lisa flashed back to when she was tied up in Phillipe Bloodworth's dungeon.

"Thank you, Scamp."

"Don't mind me. I've got my adrenaline up. What else did you learn while I was gone?"

"My grandparents have been fighting for me since I disappeared. The NBRA has too. They joined up with the NBRA and have been working together."

"That's good."

"They don't believe the video at all; most people do, but my grandfather's getting on the news saying it's a fake. I need to write to them or something, to tell them that I'm ok. Sort of ok. They look bad."

"We can do that safely when we get to Mars."

"Couldn't we take the car, or the ship, to Manhattan? They can help us there."

"That's what the police and Bloodworth's agents are watching for."

"I just want to see them."

"I'm sorry."

"The NBRA can protect me."

"They can't even protect themselves."

"What?"

"Sorry, it doesn't matter, the point is it's not safe."

"What about the NBRA, what do you mean?"

"A lot of them have been dying."

"I didn't see that on the news."

"You wouldn't, it's being suppressed. They're all dying from natural causes, but they're being wiped out."

"That's not—"

"The war is boiling over, it's a real war now, see? People are killing each other already. The NBRA is a soft target, see? They were trying to be peaceful, and the war's on."

Lisa started shivering uncontrollably and breathing again in short, shallow breaths. She couldn't concentrate on anything. Who was this strange man, these strange men in the room with her? Her life had become a nightmare. A nightmare. Bizarre. This was a nightmare, but she couldn't wake up.

"Hey, are you ok? Hey, calm down."

This wasn't reality. She wasn't in reality. She couldn't stop shaking. Her body felt pain, or something. Felt wrong. Like she could crawl out of her skin. Who were these people? This freakish man, this perverse little creature. These ghouls. They were haunting her nightmare. She couldn't wake up! She couldn't breathe. She was in pain. Or not pain, wrong. She felt physically wrong. This wasn't her world, she wasn't meant to be here. It was horrible.

She felt a huge, strong arm around her, warming her, physically supporting her. Her vision was bleary, she couldn't see. She felt a kind arm holding her, a man's arm. She felt kind skin touching the skin on her arm, warmly, kindly protecting her from the nightmare. She couldn't wake up. She felt wrong. She tried to concentrate on the warmth of the arm.

SCAMP SAT AND HELD LISA for a long time. She cried and cried. She seemed to hardly know that he was there, but clutched his arm tightly. He wanted to cry with her, to cry for her, but his eyes had long found it almost impossible to cry.

Melchit stood out of his chair, a few feet away. He watched them intently, unmoving, with something like compassion. And without any inkling or conception of what he should do.

CHAPTER 43

THROUGH THE TINTED WINDOWS OF the rental car, from the passenger seat, Lisa watched the lights of the streets of Rio passing around and underneath them. Stitching inside the wig she was wearing scratched at the top of her forehead. Large sunglasses which Scamp had procured as part of her disguise sat on her lap. They passed over burning vehicles, and a riotous mob. They saw what looked like a man being assaulted by several other men. Emergency vehicles ran everywhere, continuously, with sirens blaring. In the relatively quieter areas of the city, the people below walked quickly, and sometimes ran. A few stores were still open, but they seemed different, cold. The storefronts seemed dry and dangerous, like an explosives cache.

"It seems like everyone's afraid," said Lisa.

"And the ones who aren't afraid are angry," Scamp said. "And a lot of them are afraid and angry."

In the back seat, Melchit slid back and forth, from one side window to the other, pressing his face hard against the glass.

"I wish we were in Manhattan."

"It's not necessarily better anywhere else," Scamp said, "but at least we'll be getting out of Rio soon."

"We're not staying here, Melchit," Lisa said.

"Thems not safe down there."

"I know; we're not staying here. We're going to leave this city."

"Thems isn't safe for Melchit."

"I know. Try not to worry about it. It's not safe for me down there, either. Not even for Scamp."

"We're probably infected with the virus," Scamp said. "It seems like it's almost impossible to protect yourself from it.

One of us could be dead soon. I don't know if there's anything we can do, but we have to keep an eye on ourselves, and each other."

"We can't be infected," Lisa said. "We haven't gone anywhere."

"We probably are."

THEY PASSED OVER A LARGE, industrial area of town that was mostly deserted. Scamp glanced at Lisa and Melchit, both of whom were completely absorbed in watching out of the windows. He slowed the car and glided down toward a grey and blue warehouse that was shedding rust. The warehouse was yellow the last time he had seen it. That was ten years ago. When he worked on Earth he had come here often. The big warehouse door was open, anticipating him; he could see the bright, clean concrete floor inside and a car with tinted windows parked on it. He swooped in through the door and set down near the car, in the center of the warehouse floor. He had his listening earpiece in and was listening for any chatter or sounds amiss. Chains rattled as the warehouse door closed slowly behind them.

"He doesn't know you're with me," Scamp said, glancing between Lisa and Melchit. "Keep quiet and stay in the car."

He could see the man he was here to meet coming out of the warehouse office on Lisa's side of the car. Nobody else appeared to be there. Scamp got out quickly and closed his door.

"Grimby!" Scamp said.

The man approached the car. He was a large, stocky man, with a shaggy, midnight blue beard and olive skin. He was a scary looking person, although he seemed less physically imposing than normal when compared to Scamp. Scamp knew for a fact that Grimby was a scary person.

"Scamp. Long time. Where's the girl? And the it?"

"She's somewhere safe," Scamp said. "That's not your concern."

"Touchy."

"You would be too."

"I know," Grimby said softly. Then he broke into a huge grin and lurched forward to embrace Scamp in an affectionate bear hug. "Where have you been, you big bastard?! I haven't heard fuck from you since Lucho died."

Scamp returned the embrace enough for Grimby to remember how strong he was. Grimby was used to being stronger than most people. Scamp clapped the man's shoulders with brutish affection and pushed him away.

"I downed some time in Neo Vega."

"Working?"

"No, just downing time."

"Not in prison I hope."

"Just downing time. Thinking."

"Must be nice."

"You could retire if you wanted to," Scamp said.

"I've been to Neo Vega, it's a shithole town. I'm sure it was hell."

"It was the right place at the time. It gave me a chance to clear my head."

"Thinking, huh? Did you hitch on over and sneak into Magdalena while you were there?"

"People who try to do that aren't alive anymore."

"Haha, that's what everyone told me when I was there. I'd sure love to do it. Fucking weird, godfucker freaks."

Scamp thought about Samson, and his weird scarecrow brother. The word 'godfucker' was a strange old word. It wasn't a word people used, and it made him mad to hear it. Grimby said words like that because people didn't expect it of him. Unusual words. Grimby said it with real hate, but was also watching Scamp's reaction as a kind of test.

"You're just as bright and positive as I remember you, Grim," Scamp said. "Every bit."

He sat down on the trunk of the car, which sagged under his weight, and motioned for Grimby to follow suit.

"You don't want to come inside, Scamp?"

"Let's talk here."

"Ok. Let's talk."

"I need to rent a transport, immediately. I'll pay with a non-revocable transfer; take the car you brought me; take care of a few errands. I need to leave for Mars tonight."

"Ok."

"You have a ship for me?"

"I have a ship. Can you fly it?"

"Fuck yes, I can fly it."

"Normally I have a few days to set this kind of thing up, Scamp. You're making it hard on me. Normally I have a week."

Weasel words.

"I'll pay double."

"Double? You made a lot of money working with Lucho."

Scamp took a breath.

"It's good to see you, Grimby. I wish I could take some time to have a drink with you. But don't fuck with me."

"I'm fucking?"

Scamp shifted his mind to unscreen the cold, violent place behind his eyes and let Grimby see it. For a moment, Grimby believed he was about to die.

"I've done a lot of horrible things to people on this mission already. And you know I don't like to do that."

"I know, but you're so good at it. What are you talking about missions for, Scamp? You're no soldier, you're a gangster like me. And what are you giving me that hate look for? We're friends aren't we?"

"I'm already to the point where I'm killing anyone who gets in my way. Friend, enemy, or family. I was just letting you know."

"You don't have family, Scamp."

"People like you are my family, Grim."

"I'm your family? You should show some fucking respect for what I'm doing here, then. Shit, Bloodworth's? You're putting my neck on the chopping block, too. And that girl is worth more money than you, and Lucho, and me ever dreamed of cribbaging. I'm only helping you as a friend, you couldn't buy this with money. I've never met another man who wouldn't sell you out to Bloodworth right now. Do you know what the price on you is?"

"We're friends, Grim. But these are bad times. You owe me a favor, and after this I will owe you. And I don't care what someone else would do. If I thought someone was going to double cross me–"

"I brought you the car, didn't I?"

"Thank you, Grim."

"The transport's in Mexico City. I can hot transfer the keys and location onto your card. I'll do the keys for this car, too. All you have to do is get to the transport and take it."

"Ok."

Scamp pulled his card out of his pocket and handed it to Grimby for the transfers.

"You're an asshole, Scamp."

"I was born this way. Just like you were."

"What are you in love with this girl or something?"

"Maybe."

"You joined the war for the kinderfucks?"

"I didn't. But I probably will. Are you going to join the war, Grim?"

Grimby snorted.

304

"Not if I can help it. I'll make what money I can out of it. I've started a business to transport refugee naturals off Earth, and then on Mars we transfer them to Bloodworth's people for 10,000 credits a head. I love war."

Scamp got up and walked over to the car that Grimby had brought for them; he opened it up and carefully inspected the inside.

"Just remember, whatever happens in the war," Grimby said, "you can't kill me after I helped you today."

"I'll remember."

Scamp opened the doors to both cars and told Lisa and Melchit to get into the new car as quickly as possible.

"Holy shit," Grimby said, "you've got them here?"

"Open the big door, Grim. Thanks for your help, I'm in your debt now."

"Holy shit, Scamp. Don't ever tell anyone this happened. Not anyone."

"Goodbye, Grim."

Scamp revved the vehicle's engines and accelerated out of the warehouse door as it opened, escaping back into the night.

C H A P T E R 44

WHEN THEY SWITCHED CARS, LISA jumped into the back seat with Melchit. He seemed to be terrified. She squeezed his shoulder reassuringly while Scamp said goodbye to his friend. Melchit's shoulder was wet. Looking more closely at him now she realized that he was soaked with sweat.

"That man bad man," Melchit said as soon as they got out of the warehouse and into the air.

"You're damn right he's a bad man, but he also has a weird sense of honor. And he's afraid of me. He'll do what he said."

"Melchit, are you ok?" Lisa felt Melchit's head for fever.

"Hungry," Melchit mumbled. He looked pale.

"Are you afraid? We're safe again now."

"Stomach. Hungry."

"Are you sick?"

Melchit slid over to the window and gazed out of it distantly.

"Scamp, he's all pale and sweaty. I think he's sick."

"Melchit. Hey, Melchit!" Scamp snapped his fingers. "What's wrong? Hey, Melchit, what's wrong?"

Melchit put his hand against the glass of the window and whimpered.

"He said he's hungry. We need more food."

"The transport will have food on it. I'm hungry too. But we shouldn't stop."

Lisa glanced out her window. They were rising fast and gaining speed. It was 3 AM, with the sky to themselves. She could see the bright edge of the city gradually approaching, and the darker countryside beyond it. She could start to see the stars. Her stomach hurt. She was hungry too.

"Maybe we could run through a convenience store on our way out of town. You could grab us a few snacks. It would only take five minutes."

"It's not a good idea. Melchit, what's wrong?"

"Food!" Melchit hissed.

"Goddamnit, don't you hear us talking? There's food in the transport. You have to wait."

"Don't yell at him."

Melchit started tearing frantically at the seat upholstery with his claw-like fingernails.

"Something's wrong with him. Melchit, stop it. Stop."

"Eeeeeeeeeee! Hungry. Hungry. Now."

"We're not fucking stopping! Melchit, stop that right now. Stop now! If you don't stop, I'm going to–"

Scamp glanced in his mirror at Lisa and didn't finish the sentence.

"He's sick or something," Lisa said. "Yelling at him isn't going to help."

"Well fucking tie him up then."

"Are you crazy? He's sick!"

"I can't control that!"

"Eeeeeeeeeeeeeeeee!"

"Melchit, stop it, you're scaring me," Lisa said, patting his back.

Melchit looked her direction, but his eyes didn't seem to see her. He clapped his hands to his ears and whimpered.

"What kind of food do you need?"

"We can't stop!"

"Melchit, what kind of food do you need?"

Scamp pounded the car's steering wheel with the bottom of his fist and left a dent in it.

"Food, food, food. Hurts, hurts," Melchit said quietly and very fast.

"We'll stop and get you food, stop tearing at the upholstery."

"We can't fucking stop," Scamp said. "Do you want to die?"

"Do you want him to fucking die? Something's wrong."

They were still picking up speed.

"You think we can go to a fucking hospital or something? There's first aid equipment on board the transport ship. That's the best we can do."

"Scamp, you have to fucking stop before we get out of town. While you can. We'll stay in the car, you run in and get us some chips and soda and burritos or something."

"Didn't you hear what I said? Not stopping!"

"Goddamnyou!" Lisa said, and punched the back of Scamp's seat.

Near the bright outer edge of the city a flashing convenience store sign loomed ahead of them.

"There's a store right there," Lisa said. "If you don't stop I'll never forgive you."

"You won't forgive me anyway," Scamp said. "I accepted a duty to keep you alive and that's what I have to do. No matter what happens."

He didn't slow or change course. Lisa sucked in her breath to shout, but then spoke softly.

"If you don't stop, I'll take Melchit to a hospital instead of getting on your fucking transport."

"Bullshit!"

Scamp decelerated, but still didn't turn.

"You're not-in-fucking-charge-of-me, Scamp. I'm not your prisoner and neither is Melchit. You don't give us orders. You don't tell us what to do."

"You're the one ordering me!"

"JUST TAKE US TO THE GODDAMN STORE!!!!"

"Fuck!"

Melchit was clawing into his own face, and Lisa tried to pull his hands away.

IN THE CONVENIENCE STORE, SCAMP grabbed chips and soda and some packs of instahot burritos, like Lisa had suggested. He felt sick. He should be scared – scared for himself, scared for Lisa, scared for Melchit. All three of them were still running a very high risk of being caught on Earth and dying horribly. But all he could seem to care about was the fact that Lisa was upset with him. Goddamn, why did he care so much? When she had yelled, she sounded like she hated him. Goddamn, what if she hated him?

He threw the food on the counter of the register and the young man operating the store began checking it out. These 24 hour stores always had a human checker on the premises, to keep hooligans from coming and destroying them. They also did better business than the robo stores; people liked people. The young man was slow.

"You going on a trip?" the checker asked.

"No. Please hurry."

Scamp heard a car door open, and glanced out of the store's big windows. Melchit scrambled out of the car and rushed inside. Scamp distracted the checker's gaze and heard small feet patter over to the candy aisle.

Now Melchit was where the clerk could not easily see him, but Scamp could. He sniffed desperately along the aisle, then grabbed a packet of M&Ms and began devouring them. Lisa walked into the store too, wearing her wig and sunglasses.

"Honey, I told you to watch him!" she said, and walked across the store toward Melchit.

"Oh shit! What are you doing that for, John Dee?" Scamp shouted, turning around.

The clerk was scrutinizing them closely.

"You have to pay for that."

"We'll pay for it."

"He's making a mess."

"I'm so sorry."

Lisa grabbed Melchit's arm and tried to drag him back down the aisle toward the door. He squealed and struggled with her.

"Ok, so include two packs of M&Ms," Scamp said. "How much is that?"

"Wait," the clerk said, holding a finger up to his head like he was thinking. He had bright pink skin, and black hair with white-blonde streaks in it.

Just as Scamp reached back to grab Melchit's arm and help him and Lisa along, Melchit's other arm knocked Lisa's wig and sunglasses off. Recognition lit up instantly in the checker's eyes.

"Wait, you're–"

Scamp had the young man by the throat before he even realized that Scamp was moving towards him.

"Don't hurt him!!" Lisa yelled desperately.

"I won't hurt him. Get in the car."

Scamp dragged the checker into the store's back room and tied him up rapidly with power extension cables. The young man struggled and Scamp had to bruise him up, although he tried to do it gently.

"I'm sorry," he said. "We weren't here to cause trouble."

He cut the store's main power breaker and switched the sign on the door from open to closed. He also grabbed all of his food and several packets of M&Ms as he walked to the door. Then he was outside in the parking lot again, which was now dark. Lisa had the car door open, but was still struggling with Melchit. Scamp grabbed him and threw him through the car door, then pushed Lisa herself inside.

Another car pulled into the parking lot and the people looked at Scamp with quizzical expressions.

"They're fucking closed!" he said loudly, as if he were ir-ritated about it.

Then he got back into the front seat of the car and they sped away.

CHAPTER 45

"So," Pavel Williams said, sitting under the amplified stars of Stephanie's executive meeting room, "we have strong reasons to believe that this virus is a product of Bloodworth's Corporation. Strong reasons mean the likelihood is more than 80%."

The head of Rothschild's intelligence knitted and unknitted his fingers in front of him.

"Forgive me for being emotional."

"These are emotional days for all of us, Pavel," Stephanie said. "Go on."

"Yes, mum. Well, it is also most likely that the virus is Phillipe Bloodworth's 'Plan B' project that we heard rumors of. It sterilizes all natural born, but it *kills* about 15% of human beings with an upgraded genetic package. Our friend Albrecht," he choked on the name, but quickly continued. "It seems likely that the impact on genetically engineered people is an unexpected side-effect of the virus. It doesn't discriminate. Bloodworth's people are being devastated, too. As you can see in the report from Dr. Smith, the virus is tailor made to cause sterility among naturals, and the deadly effect of it on those with upgraded immune systems is a consequence of several bizarre and probably unforeseen coincidences."

"Thank you, Pavel. All of us are devastated by Albrecht's death. Based on the 15% figure, we are lucky that he is the only one of us in this room that has been lost. One or two more of us could still go, although our doctors think it unlikely based on our tests. They tell me that I, myself, am almost certainly safe, because I have certain prototype immune sequences that have never been in production. But others of us could possibly succumb at any time in the coming months. Barring an unexpected medical breakthrough, there is no treatment for the virus, only palliative care."

"Now what are we going to do about it?" Simon Okunle asked.

"One moment, Simon. You'll all be receiving scheduling about notices, but to let you know, Albrecht's memorial service is going to be on Thursday morning. I know that everyone in this room would like to be there, and I am going to do everything I possibly can to make sure I can be there myself. But what killed Albrecht can still kill many others too. Bear in mind your responsibilities and that if you cannot make it, Albrecht would be so proud of you for the sacrifices that you are making."

"I am, unfortunately, going to be on Earth," Simon Okunle said, with a quiet mist over his eyes.

"The virus hibernates over random intervals," Pavel Williams said. "Already it has killed 3-5%, but the damage will continue for at least a few months. Possibly longer. It will burn itself out, but about 15% is the expected final figure in human losses."

"We also understand that you may have other funerals you need to attend," Stephanie said. "Unfortunately we have to press on to business. We have to act."

"I don't believe in total war," Pavel said quickly.

"We may not have a choice, Pavel," Simon Okunle said.

"We may not, but right now we still do."

"I don't disagree with you, Pavel," Stephanie said. "I don't think anyone here does."

"What has happened is terrible, but total war will make it much worse."

"Pavel—"

Pavel Williams stood up. He ran his hand through his hair and clenched it into a fist.

"I don't believe in total war," he said again, looking at Stephanie desperately. "I'm not prepared to kill as many of them as possible. They've lost as many people as us. We have to find a peace through this."

"Pavel–"

"No! You're young. You don't understand what total war is going to be. We have to avoid it."

"Pavel sit down," Stephanie said.

"You're young. You can't lead a total war. You're not ready for that yet. You don't know what it will mean."

Stephanie stood up.

"SIT DOWN."

Pavel Williams glanced around the room and sat back down in his chair. His pale blue skin was flushed.

"It's just– It's just–" he stammered.

"Close your mouth."

Simon Okunle cleared his throat.

"Pavel, look me in the eyes," Stephanie said. "Look at my eyes right now."

Pavel did it with difficulty now, although only just before he had been staring wildly at her.

"Do you see my eyes? My eyes don't shake."

As Stephanie watched him, he began to try to recover some of his dignity and looked aghast.

"Don't look away from my eyes. I have no intention of fighting a total war. But if it becomes necessary for us to do so, you *will* support the Rothschild's effort with every breath of air you breathe and every drop of your sweat."

"I'm sorry, Mistress."

Stephanie's head of personal security and chief bodyguard, Boris, stepped into the room. He was average sized, of older middle age, and wore a thin, creased, grey hat. His physical presence was not overtly intimidating, but vaguely formidable. He had a face that was hard and unforgiving.

"How can you question my leadership, Pavel? What would

you recommend that I should do with an executive who challenges my leadership?"

He cleared his throat.

"Well?"

"I have advised you in the past that an executive who does that has to be killed, Mistress."

"That's what you've advised me, although we have never yet had to cross that bridge. Why would they have to be killed?"

"If they're an executive, they know too much to be allowed to be disloyal. They could do irreparable damage to Rothschild's. They could do irreparable damage to you."

"That's true, isn't it," Stephanie said.

She quickly met the eyes of every executive in the room.

"Boris, take Pavel Williams outside and secure him."

"Yes, Mistress," the man said and advanced toward Pavel, who rose from his seat and followed without resistance, holding his head in his hands.

Stephanie held a finger in the air to prevent anyone else from speaking. She wanted to cry, or to scream. Or to do both. More than anything she wanted to run away. In some part of the back of her brain, she did those things. But it was very far back in her brain. She had been trained to be able to control those emotions since she was a little girl, when the time came. Trained since she was born, by the greatest leader in the Solar System, the Baron de Rothschild. His daughter's mind was not built like his own, but it was also formidable, and he had understood it and shaped it. Stephanie's thought process was barely affected by her emotions when she closed them off. Her face betrayed nothing to her executives except sternness.

"I've lost Albrecht Durer, one of my chief pillars, today" she said to the executives remaining in the room. "And now I must lead Rothschild's through a battle with the most wicked and formidable enemy we have ever known. Quite possibly, against the greatest force of evil humanity has ever produced. They have just sterilized half the human population, and killed at least three billion of the other half. My capacity for mercy under these circumstances is limited. As is my tolerance for weakness. Everyone in this room is here because they are strong. I want you to remember that about yourselves. Humanity requires your strength at this time. And I personally expect it."

Stephanie looked from eye to eye in the room again. Simon Okunle began to say something.

"Nobody speak."

She stepped out of the room and the assembled executives were left to exchange glances with each other in silence. Several of them simply looked down. When Stephanie returned, Pavel Williams was with her, unbound. With an arm braced around his shoulder, she led him back to his seat. He had tears in his eyes, but quickly brushed them away.

"I've forgotten what you said before, Pavel," Stephanie said. "I'm sure it was nothing. This is a hard day for all of us, a day of grief. The days to come will be even harder. None of us have the strength for what lies ahead, but we must find it. We have no choice."

"Forgive me, Mistress," Pavel said. "Thank you, Mistress. I won't let you down."

"I have no way of predicting the course of the future, but I guarantee you all this: at the end of this war I will still be standing. Rothschild's will be stronger than ever. And Phillipe Bloodworth will be dead."

"Hear, hear," Simon Okunle said.

"Hear, hear," the room echoed.

Stephanie sat back down in her chair.

"But I have no intention of going to war," she continued. "I've been holding meetings with Alexander Grumiaux for months in an attempt to find a solution to the escalating natural born rights problem. With his help, we will try to avoid real war even now, and hopefully put an end to the trade war, too."

The executives in the room, with the exception of Simon, gasped in surprise at Grumiaux's name.

SAMSON KILLED TIME ON BOARD Stephanie's deep-space transport ship, which was making its way with all possible speed to Magdalena. 'All possible speed' meant within a completely safe range – they did not push the envelope of relativity at all. But it was a fast ship, and the speed was fast. A communique from Rothschild's had been sent that morning to inform them that contacts with Magdalena had not gone well. No progress had been made. It seemed likely that none would be, at least until Samson got there. By then it might be too late.

The ship's interior lights, as was common, were synced to Earth's day/night cycle, as was the rotation of the little planet of Rothschild. Stephanie was able to call through and talk to Samson for about ten minutes each evening. It wasn't much, and sometimes it wasn't even that. The quantum-loop relays were sometimes unstable. The networks weren't in great shape. It seemed like nothing in the Solar System was. Stephanie hadn't told Samson the worst details of the virus, that it had killed Albrecht Durer, for instance, but the basics of what was happening on that front trickled through to him and the ship's crew. No one on the crew was affected by the virus, or at least not yet. Samson himself was now sterile, of course, but not at risk of death.

He sat at a big, blue, soft benched table in the dining room that adjoined the ship galley, and stared out the window at the stars. He missed Stephanie. He didn't miss anyone else. He picked up a tall, thin glass of heavy pink liquor and put it to his lips. The glass was like a very elegant test tube. The liquor was thick and viscous on his tongue. The warmth of it in his throat was soothing.

Space wasn't good for him now. That was strange. Space had always been good for him. It had been his place. He had spent so many months cruising through the emptiness of space with Ben. Years, when you added it all together. He had spent months in space alone. In his racer. Space was his peace. Even days before it had been like that. But it wasn't now. The stars seemed cold, and in a bad way. Not the calming, soothing cold he used to know.

He wondered why he didn't miss anyone else. Only Stephanie. Of course, Ben was dead now. Ben. Samson had never had many friends. Not real friends. And he was too intense and honest of a person to have very many casual friends. People liked him, but they didn't think they were his friend. So was it bad not to miss them? He didn't miss Theodore. He didn't miss their parents. He had never missed their parents. They weren't like him. He missed Theo sometimes, but not right now. Although he wished he could see him. He hadn't been able to get through to Theo again since that first time. Only Stephanie he missed. Ten minutes a night, or a whenever it was, was nothing. They couldn't even get past the awkward moments in ten minutes. She was living the most intense days of her life, and he wasn't there. He was rediscovering his life and she wasn't there. It would pull them both apart. He knew that was true.

He didn't want any other woman.

The stars were beautiful, even for their cold. He did still feel that they belonged to him. Space wasn't good for him in this moment, but it was still his. He wanted to fly the ship, but the pilot wouldn't let him. That was ok. The pilot was a good pilot. There wasn't really any flying they could do anyway, it was a straight course. No one needed to fly the ship, the computer did it. Flying, like Samson wanted to fly, would slow them down. Sometimes he disabled the anti-gravity in his luxurious cabin, which was possible to do on this beautiful ship, and flew in the privacy of the walls and the door and the window. He would spin and twist and dance in the air, spring from wall to ceiling to wall, and be free. Sometimes with music. It was almost like being in that world again, the one he had gone to when he died. Or when he whatever it was.

The stars. They were his in a way that was different now, in a multiplied way. He could feel them with his new feeling, with his sixth sense. The doctor and Kenichi hadn't gotten to study him much, to try to figure out what it was. Kenichi had desperately wanted to. The doctor was a little bit skeptical that the sixth sense was real. It had become stronger now. It kept getting stronger and he kept being able to control it more. He could feel the stars. Alone in their vast distance, piled on top of each other in the space that was him, the vast distance aloneness piled on top of itself – they felt cold.

The sun was warmer. He smiled through the back of his head at where it was behind him, screened by a window that was set to be completely opaque. The crew on the ship were warm, too. He could feel their thoughts all the time now, dimly but strongly, as if their thoughts were shadows of thoughts in his own mind. They were warm men, every one of them; they were men who were intelligent and dedicated and good. They were men who had been hand picked, who were Stephanie's best. He wondered if she had requested for the crew on board to be only men. He doubted it. It was a common practice to avoid mixing genders, if possible, when small ships went on voyages. Mixing genders was a safety issue – it caused problems. On a small ship if a love triangle formed, an unwanted infatuation, or an obsession, the parties couldn't get away from each other. They were stuck at each other's throats. On a big ship, it was just like a small community, and the community could work its troubles out. Of course, gay people were a thing too. No practice is ever perfect. But this ship wasn't even that small. But it also wasn't big. As likely as not, it was only a coincidence that all of the crew on board the ship were men. Or, they were all military men from combat divisions. Yes, that was it.

When he was alone with his thoughts, Samson often practiced reading theirs. Then when he talked to them he would try to see if he had been right. Of course he was never wrong about the outlines of their thoughts or the subjects, he perceived them after all, it was only the details, the interpretation of the nuance, that he had trouble figuring out. He was getting better at it. The sixth sense was growing stronger and more sensitive. Sixth sense. What should he call it? Telepathy? Mind reading? It wasn't exactly that, and it was also more. He could feel the ship, the wiring, the processors, the batteries, the engine, each impression different, each uniquely formed in its own way. He could feel the cosmic rays as they passed the ship outside. Fewer and fewer of them as they got farther away. It was as if he could feel the universe's radiation. As if sight were touch, and as if it included everything. It was a sixth sense. Maybe he could call it his relativity sense.

THE AIR IN THE STREETS was troubled. People in Magdalena
didn't riot, but this had that sort of quality. Tension. Theo
had seen riots in his travels. He had seen a riot on Venus that
killed ten people. He had seen a riot on Mars. The texture of
human unease was a palpable thing. When it manifested in
large groups it became a monster. Magdalena was becoming
like that.

His car zipped across the Magdalena skyline.

The people in Magdalena wouldn't ever riot, so their collective angst would have to find a different outlet. Some of
them would beat their children. Some of them would beat
their wives, or husbands. Some of them would fast, and pray
extra hard. All of them would pray extra hard, whatever else
they did. More than anything, though, they would go to war.
They needed war.

Most people in Magdalena understood about the virus
now. Several carefully composed announcements about it had
been made on the news. They didn't realize how bad it was,
how universal it was, how permanent. But they understood
that it was profoundly bad. They understood that there was
nothing they could do. There was nothing any of them could
do, nothing Theo or his wife could do. The only option left
to them was to strike back, to kill. To simply whimper and
die was not an option.

Do not go gentle into that good night.
Rage, rage against the dying of the light.

The ancient poet didn't know of what he spoke. Why
rage, why kill? Rage how, kill who? The war would only kill
more innocent people like themselves. It wouldn't kill the
unknown people who made the virus. That wasn't a collective
act. It was a very small number of people who did it. Not billions. The hate of the billions who resented the natural born,

the billions who hated God, was not what created the virus. Thinking so, assigning blame based on that, was fallacy. The Magdalena martyrs wouldn't be killing their enemy as they died, they would simply be forcing luckier innocents to suffer their equivalent fate.

He and Maria were going to escape from Magdalena with their children. They had decided to flee to Neo Vega and then try to make their way to Rothschild Palace. They had almost finalized plans.

The Temple loomed ahead of him, and Theo's car began to descend. He slowed it and took over manual controls. The Prophet had called an unexpected meeting of his War Council, calling Theo away from his family. Interrupting his and Maria's planning. The unexpected meeting didn't necessarily mean there was anything new; the same thing had happened a few times before. Some things were just The Prophet's whim. Theo crossed himself against the blasphemous thought.

The children didn't understand what was happening, but they were scared. They had a vague sense that their parents were doing something that was secret, something that was possibly bad. Theo and Maria couldn't tell their parents, of course. Their parents wouldn't understand anyway, their parents would try to stop them if they knew. But it hurt not to tell them. It would hurt not to say goodbye. Theo's parents were worried terribly about him, and proud of the importance of his role. Now they always wanted to hear stories about The Prophet. Theo couldn't share much of that with them, either. He told them what he could. They would be devastated when they found out that he and Maria had gone.

It might make them go to hell, he and Maria. It almost certainly would. He liked to think of God as merciful, God was merciful, but mercy also had bounds. Leaving The Prophet and the sheep of Magdalena in the blackest night of their darkest hour meant they would go to hell. But he and Maria didn't doubt their decision at all. They had to do what they could for their children, that was the end of it. Their children would not be held guilty for their parents' sins.

Theo retched a little bit.

His wife was strong; he thought about how lucky he was to have her. He had lived a blessed life, he had been blessed. Perhaps God could understand what they were going to do and forgive them. Perhaps God would. He liked to think that might be true, but he knew that it wasn't.

SAMSON SAT ON THE NAVIGATION deck of the Rothschild's transport ship, which was large and comfortable. It was like a small lounge. The captain, a man named Tomas Batista, sat at the control panel, even though he didn't need to do anything there. He was watching a spaceship race from the week before on the instrumentation screen, occasionally glancing away to gaze out of the ship's big cockpit window at the stars. Samson felt no curiosity about the race. It didn't even occur to him to wonder what race it was. Two junior crew members were playing Overchess at a table in the back of the room. Samson mixed himself a drink at a small bar near the table.

"We were supposed to have a case of Chianti on board for you," said one of the Overchess players, a young man named Jacob. "Direct order from the Mistress. But in the rush we didn't have time to pick it up."

Jacob was thin, with a sharp face and blue skin. It was hard for him to concentrate on the Overchess board.

"That's ok," Samson said. "That was sweet of her to think of, but I'm not picky."

"What are you drinking?"

"Just whiskey."

"Venutian whiskey?"

"Of course."

"That's the good stuff."

"It is good. Although, they have better whiskey in Magdalena."

"They do?"

The young man was uncomfortable, holding back but trying not to. He wanted to please Samson, but also resented him. He wanted to be friends, but felt inferior and beholden.

"I'll make sure to bring some back to the ship when we're there," Samson said. "So that you and everyone can try it. Hardly anyone who isn't from Magdalena has ever had Magdalena whiskey. You can't even buy it in Neo Vega."

"I can't wait," Jacob said.

"You should pay more attention to the board," said Jacob's opponent, a man with yellow, almond shaped eyes who was named Matthias.

"I'm watchin', I'm watchin'."

"Watching and thinking, it's not the same."

Mathias was deeply absorbed in the game. Their conversation barely registered with him. Everything in his mind was moves and positions and counter-moves. He didn't need to work this hard to beat Jacob, but how he won was as important to him as winning. Samson could almost feel the exact moves that were running through Matthias' mind. He was bringing his bishops into line and hanging out the queen, trying to set up a perfect sacrifice trap. In Magdalena they called those 'gambits'.

"I almost never beat him," Jacob said to Samson.

"You only beat him once before?"

"I don't know exactly. Once – I think so."

"Only once," Matthias said with finality.

"Because you were drunk?" Samson said, turning to Matthias.

"It's like you're reading my thoughts," Matthias said. "That's right, because I was drunk."

Samson didn't tell anyone about his relativity sense. Not anyone aside from Stephanie and the doctors and scientists who already knew about it on Rothschild. The men on the ship did not know about it. Whatever the relativity sense was, its existence was considered classified information by Stephanie and her people, and it was Samson's instinct that it would be better if most other people didn't know. He didn't understand it himself well enough to talk about yet, anyway.

"It's not because you were drunk that I won. It's because I was good that day. I was on fire that day, my mind was clear."

"Let's see how you do today."

"I'm good at reading people," Samson said.

"You play Overchess? Why don't you give me a game after the kid here. We're about to be done."

"Not quite," Jacob said, "I'm taking your queen."

"We'll see how well you can read me during the game."

Samson sipped his drink. The ship's captain was thinking about him, about spaceship racing, the Solar Regatta, and the natural born. He wasn't even registering their conversation about Overchess.

"Well, how about it?"

Matthias felt slighted by him for some reason. He couldn't tell why. Probably Matthias himself didn't know.

"Do you play?" Jacob asked Samson. "It won't bother me any if you take the next game."

"I'm not real great, but I play a little," Samson said. "I do a thing where I try to say what move the other player will make right before he makes it. I don't know why I'm good at it. I think it's funny, but some people get mad. I'll play if you don't mind me doing that."

Jacob and Matthias both thought this was a very strange thing to say. Samson smiled.

"I'm a strange guy," he said.

"I don't care what you say," Matthias said. "Kibitz all you want."

"Ok then. I'll take the next game."

"Great. Three moves to mate, Jakey."

"Fuckoff. And don't call me Jakey."

Matthias captured Jacob's last knight with one of his bishops.

"This is one."

"Fuuuccckkk."

Samson chuckled and gulped the rest of his drink. The kid really hadn't realized that he was in the middle of a trap.

CHAPTER 47

THEO AND MARIA KEPT THEIR children home from school.

"I don't understand why we're staying home from school today," Paul said, lounging on a simple green couch in the family living room and looking very adolescent.

"We're having a family holiday today," Maria said, "like your father told you. Try to have a good attitude."

"But we're not doing anything!"

"We're going to play some games and have fun."

"I want to play games!" little Eve said.

"But just playing games, that's not a holiday. This is just playing hooky."

"It's not hooky, because your father and I approved of it. Here, shuffle these cards. In a minute, let's play a card game."

"I want to play a card game!" Eve said.

"I know you do, Eve. You're going to play too."

"Yay!"

"You and dad are acting funny," Judith said, glancing at Paul attempting to shuffle the cards on a big latticed wood and glass coffee table in front of the couch. "Paul, you're doing it wrong. I can shuffle cards better than you."

"You can't."

Paul's brow knit in concentration and he made another unsuccessful attempt to riffle the cards.

"We've been on edge lately, because of all the news from the rest of the Solar System," Theo said, walking into the room.

"The news you can't tell us about?"

"That's right. And we don't want you to talk about it with your friends. But because of all this tension and stress your mom and I felt like the whole family needed a day off to just be together and relax. A day to have fun!"

"You're not having fun, though," Eve said precociously.

"I'm trying to, love."

"We all have to try to have a good attitude and have some fun, because your father has been the unhappiest of all," Maria said.

Judith snatched the cards away from Paul.

"Hey, give those back!"

"I'm just cutting the deck."

"Well cut the deck and give them back. Hurry."

Judith squared the jumble of cards up into a neat deck and set them back on the table. The cards were coated with a slick, thin plastic film. The back of the cards was patterned with an intricate, old fashioned illustration of stars and crescent moons, in hues of white and blue and yellow.

Theo looked at Maria meaningfully as the children distracted themselves with shuffling the cards.

"I can't play yet," he said. "It will be a little while, and then I can play games, too. It's only half of a holiday for me. I have to do some work first."

"Awww," the three children said in unison, although little Eve's voice was the most sincerely disappointed.

WHILE MARIA DISTRACTED THE CHILDREN with games in the other room, Theo packed bags for the family. A backpack for each of the children, and one suitcase each for himself and Maria was all they would be able to bring with them. They had to be able to leave quickly when the call came. It might come today. He checked his card for any calls or messages.

Theo had made arrangements with a friend who had connections in Neo Vega. The man had been one of the first lost sheep Theo had tracked down and returned to the fold, back at the beginning of his career. Long ago, this man had been a smuggler, and it turned out he still had connections in that trade. He could get Theo and his family to Neo Vega, but that was all he could promise. Once there they would be on their own. Theo had friends in Neo Vega. Not good friends, but they might be willing to help.

He also had three pounds of solid gold that he had squirreled away for a rainy day. Gold was hard to hide, because it was so heavy. He had flattened half of the gold into sheets with the vice in the family tool shed and used it to line the bottom of his boots, underneath the insoles. The rest he had glued into the cylinder of a trophy that Judith had won for memorizing scripture. He slid the trophy into her backpack. He checked the card again.

One change of clothes for each of the children. Two changes of socks and underwear. A water bottle. A toothbrush. They wouldn't carry much. They would have to leave almost everything behind.

'This place will be wiped out anyway,' Theo thought to himself, and made the motion of the cross over his chest. 'If we didn't leave it would all be destroyed anyway, along with us. We can't possibly take it with us. This house, this land, these things – these are only memories, or may as well be.'

"Dad, come play a game with us!" he heard Paul shout from the other room.

Theo checked his card again. He put the three backpacks and two suitcases into the closet in his and Maria's bedroom. He might be contacted at any time now. It would be sometime in the next few days. Maybe today, maybe any minute. When the message came, the family would have to act immediately. He had memorized where he needed to drive, what he needed to say.

"Dad!"

When he was contacted, he and his family would leave their home forever. They would find a new home, in a world that was cold and hostile to them. A world where they had no place. In that world they would have to find a new home, to make one. Maybe on Rothschild Palace, maybe Stephanie would take them in. Then they would just keep living until they died. Maybe they would find some happiness or maybe they would just get by. There would never be any grandchildren.

"Dad!!"

Maria still hoped that there would be a way to fix them, to cure them. Maybe not only the children, maybe her and Theo too. It was possible. Wasn't it?

"Dad!"

"I'm almost done. I'll be in there in a minute!"

The Prophet and all the leaders of Magdalena were not committing suicide because of something that might be fixed. Although it might be possible in some mathematical sense, there would never be any cure.

When he was about to go back into the family room to play games with Maria and the children, he received a call to attend an emergency meeting of the war council that was convening in less than an hour. They had emergency meetings almost every day now. It would be suspicious for him not to appear at one of these meetings, and he could only hope that the expected contact signaling the beginning of their flight from Magdalena did not coincide with one of them. Theo put on his sport coat and hat and left the house in a rush, apologizing to Maria and the children.

THE STREETS OF MAGDALENA CITY were eerily empty as Theo flew over them. The few people that could occasionally be seen went about their business quickly. Walking fast, staring straight ahead, tense – like in an active military camp. They weren't soldiers, though, and they didn't know who they were expected to fight. For all they knew, maybe each other. He watched a man and a woman pass on the sidewalk below without any flicker of friendliness or recognition. They were worried about their children, their families. They didn't know what threatened them, only that something did.

The bright white buildings and pink stone roads of Magdalena fanned out underneath him. Although Theo had spent more of his adult life away from it than almost anyone here, this was his home. It seemed unreal that he and his family would be leaving it. It seemed unreal that it would be destroyed. This was the place, these were the people, that he always thirsted to return to when he was in the field working. It was a beautiful city. An atmosphere like this, streets empty and tense, didn't suit it.

In front of the Temple, in stark contrast to the rest of the city, many people had quietly gathered. More people and more quietly than normal, a huge crowd. They spoke softly among themselves, or stood and prayed, or stared up at the Temple with eyes wide and confused. Some of them were dressed in their nicest clothes and some of them were disheveled, still in their pajamas. Theo wondered what they were all doing there, but realized as soon as he wondered it that even they themselves didn't know. The society was coming unmoored. How many others, like himself, were planning to flee? They wouldn't know how to. Most of them were trapped now in an uncomfortable storm of imperative agency and impotence. War would give them a direction for their energies and pull the community back together again, even a suicidal war. War would be their answer, their call from God.

ON EARTH, A MAN NAMED Thomas threw a brick through a storefront window.

"Fuck you!!!"

People screamed and sirens blared. There was smoke and

331

blood in the air. Occasionally there were the sounds of explosions, not close, not far away.

Thomas ran forward with a dense crowd of people. There were hundreds of them, or thousands. They were thick around him as far as he could see. An egg sized stone came flying through the air and cracked the head of a woman running next to him. She stumbled, bleeding, and he propped her up and helped her continue forward with the crowd, who would trample her if she fell.

"Aaahhooooo!" the woman wailed.

"Are you ok? You'll be ok."

"Where are they?" an angry voice shouted.

"You need to get to the hospital," Thomas said, as the woman stumbled forward with him, blinking blood from her eyes.

He helped her maneuver through the crowd to a side alley where she could sit down on the ground. As soon as the woman had sat down she slumped over, unconscious.

"Hey, wake up!" he shook her.

He tried to feel her wrist for a pulse. She was a blonde woman. A natural woman, but pretty underneath the blood. She had long, curly hair and was wearing a green leather jacket.

"Wake up!"

A canister of riot gas flipped with a "ding!" into the alley and bounced past them, spraying toxic incense everywhere. Thomas's eyes filled up with tears and he could barely breathe. Another man approached them.

"She ... hit ...wi-...a rock." Thomas said, coughing and hacking.

He couldn't understand what the other man was saying, but the man kept pointing to his card and shaking his head. It was a young man, and he jogged away to join the crowd rushing past on the street.

Thomas couldn't find the woman's pulse. Streams of tears and snot ran off of his face and fell onto her shirt. She didn't seem to be breathing. He tried to do CPR on her, although he didn't know how to do CPR. He knelt over her and pumped her chest up and down, 1 – 2, 1 – 2, falling over in coughing fits between some of the pumps. His eyes and nose streamed. After several minutes with no response he decided that the woman was dead. He folded her arms over her chest and got up to rejoin the crowd. Another riot gas canister pinged into the alley and Thomas grabbed it and hurled it down to the end of the block, away from the crowd.

On his way back out into the rushing people on the street he picked up another brick.

SAMSON WORKED OUT IN THE small gym on board Stephanie's transport. He finished doing a set of push-ups and began running through some martial arts katas. Since re-emerging from the relativity effect his body had felt fresh, even new. The time in bed recovering his energy had been like an incubation. His muscles and joints were crisp. It felt good to move, to flex. He was strong again now, as strong as he had ever been. His movements were smooth and easy. The reflexes, the nerves, didn't snap quite as tautly as they used to, but he felt great.

A young man named Dorian, who was one of the two security agents on board, came in and was startled to find himself alone with Samson in the gym. Samson watched him. Dorian was nervous and wished that Samson wasn't there. He didn't dislike Samson, but he was uncomfortable because Samson was so famous. They made eye contact and the young man looked away awkwardly, so Samson stopped staring at him. Without seeing it, he could sense that Dorian was wrapping his hands quietly and intended to work out on the heavy bag that hung in the corner. After a few minutes, Dorian began punching the bag.

Samson finished his katas and did some jumping and tumbling exercises. The pounding of the heavy bag echoed through the gym with stony blows. Dorian was genetically engineered and extremely fit. He was a little bit taller than Samson and had pale blue skin. He had stopped thinking about Samson and now had his mind focused completely upon punching the bag.

"Excuse me," Samson said. "Would you like to do some sparring with me before you tire yourself out?"

"This won't tire me out," Dorian said. "I'm afraid if we spar I might hurt you, and it would get me into trouble."

"We'll use the soft gloves."

The young man looked skeptical.

"What's your name, by the way?" Samson asked, although he knew the man's name. "We haven't properly met yet."

"My name's Dorian," the young man said, pulling off one of his bag gloves and shaking Samson's outstretched hand. "It's a pleasure to meet you, Mr. Ford. I'm really a fan of yours."

"Oh, well don't go easy on me because of that."

"I don't like to lose at sparring," Dorian said. "It's hard for me to go easy."

"That's good. I don't often lose, myself."

Samson pulled on some of the soft sparring gloves and moved to the padded area of the floor. Dorian was apprehensive about fighting him, but also determined not to lose. That was good.

"You've studied Wu-shin techniques," Dorian said.

"That's right."

"I used to do Wu-shin, too."

"And I've studied other things."

"Kickboxing is what I do mostly. When I'm not working I do competitive kickboxing on Rothschild. And sometimes I travel to competitions on Earth. I'm a ranked fighter on Earth."

"Kickboxing is good," Samson said. "Let's do that."

The two men circled each other and neither made an aggressive move.

"Try a jab," Samson said.

Dorian feinted and threw out a soft jab. Samson could sense the moves in the man's mind before they occurred. He stepped past the jab and hit Dorian hard in the ribs, drawing a grunt of pain. The young man began to worry less about hurting him.

Samson changed to a southpaw stance and Dorian felt insulted. He feinted again and swung forward with a hard leg kick, but Samson stepped away from it before it even began. In frustration, Dorian threw two hard punches at Samson's head, then followed with a spear-like front kick that was remarkably fast, but Samson stepped away from and around each attack easily. He didn't bother to hit Dorian again this time, it seemed cruel.

The sparring continued in the same pattern for several minutes, until Dorian's frustration turned to rage and he began to feel that Samson was mocking him. Samson stepped past another one of Dorian's kicks and crushed a hard fist into his solar plexus while sweeping his leg and throwing him to the ground. Dorian tried to jump back immediately to his feet, but couldn't suck air into his lungs and rose only to his knees. After a few more seconds he was standing again.

This wasn't what Samson had expected from sparring, it was too easy. His body felt amazing, but he felt bad for his opponent. This fight wasn't fair.

"That's enough," he said. "That's all the sparring I wanted, I'm getting tired."

Dorian stared at him with bewildered and somewhat awestruck eyes.

"I can do better," Dorian said.

"I'm sure you can," Samson said, "but I'm done. Thank you for sparring with me."

He pulled off his gloves and walked over to sit on a wooden bench. Dorian still stood staring at him.

"To be a world class racer," Samson said, "you have to be born with such incredible reflexes. It really isn't fair. I'm sure you could outmuscle me eventually, but I just wanted to see how I'm doing. I haven't sparred with anyone since the Solar Regatta. I wanted to find out what I've lost, or how strong I still am. My body went through so much. But I think I haven't really lost anything. I feel stronger than ever."

"Well, that's good," Dorian said. "That's great, then. I have to say I'm impressed. I've never sparred with anyone who has reflexes like yours. And I've sparred with some of the best fighters on Earth. Thanks for the match, or the sparring. No wonder you won the Regatta."

"No, thank you."

"I'm glad I couldn't hit you, actually," Dorian said. "I don't know what I was thinking. If I hit you, the Mistress probably would have killed me. I mean, my boss would have just from thinking about it. But I was trying hard. You got under my skin there."

It was difficult to be nice to people, Samson realized, when you could feel their thoughts. People didn't want to have their thoughts felt. They couldn't realize it was happening, but the experience of it alienated them.

CHAPTER 48

"BLOODWORTH IS MOVING," ALEXANDER GRUMIAUX said in his chambers adjoining the floor of the United Earth Congressional Assembly. "He wants total war and thinks he can win."

Stephanie sat across from him in a brown leather chair and sipped expensive coffee from a thin china cup. She was wearing an intimidating black suit and blood red, patent leather heels. She raised an eybrow.

"We won't lose, Alexander."

"You're such a beautiful woman, why is it you only visit me on business?"

"Business takes up all my time these days. Who knows what the world might be like when this is all over."

"Now you're teasing me."

"Of course."

Stephanie shifted in the chair coyly, changing her legs from left crossed over right to right crossed over left.

"I don't mind, though," Alexander said.

"I know you don't."

"You won't be able to come here again, anyway. Not until the Solar System is very different."

"That's true."

"I appreciate you taking the risk to come here today."

"It was necessary."

Alexander sipped from his own tea cup. A holo-screen behind him silently broadcast the latest news.

"This business doesn't help anything, either," he said.

"No."

"I'm surprised your people aren't making you stay back on Rothschild, near your medical facilities, just in case."

"My people do what I tell them to do," Stephanie said.

"But our doctors have given me the all clear, I'm not susceptible to the virus."

"That must be nice," Alexander said. "The doctors I have access to aren't able to give out such assurances yet."

"But it's assumed you are safe."

"Yes."

"Thank goodness for that. I'm sure that, like myself, you have lost people close to you who were susceptible."

"Everyone has."

"Yes. I'm sorry. For us it only entrenches our determination. And since the virus almost certainly came from Bloodworth's, and since it surely affects their people as devastatingly as everyone else, it can only hurt them."

"That fucking idiot has given half the population of the Solar System no alternative than to fight to the death."

"And half of the other half support that half," Stephanie said.

"I know you won't lose. That's why I'm working with you and not Phillipe. Of course, he still thinks I'm working with him. But he's beginning to suspect. I'm not fully in the loop with him anymore."

Stephanie sipped her coffee again. It was special coffee, grown from soil in Antarctica. She had never tasted anything quite like it.

"The thing is, I'm not really on your side," Alexander continued. "I think Bloodworth is right, I only disagree with his timing. The Solar System isn't ready for quarantine yet, or a purging of the natural born. Maybe in 100 years, maybe then. Eventually it will happen. But not now. It's a losing proposition now, and will only bring harm to everyone, as it is already doing. But fundamentally I disagree with you."

"That's enough agreement for us to work together," Stephanie said.

"Precisely. As we've talked about. So the question is what

exactly we are going to do."

"Precisely. As we've talked about."

A news bulletin on the screen in the background distracted Stephanie's attention.

"Alexander, turn that on."

He glanced behind him to see what she was referring to.

"The holo-screen, turn on the sound."

Scientists at Pfizer Laboratories in New York were holding a press conference.

"...working closely with prominent virologists from the Bloodworth's Corporation," the man leading the press conference was saying, "we have been able to trace the genetic composition of the virus to direct antecedents that were smuggled out of the Magdalena cult a few years ago. It is well known that they have had an active viral weapons program. Every genetic compositing lab has equipment that leaves traces on the genetic material that it produces, forming a kind of fingerprint. The virus devastating the Solar System today bears the distinct fingerprint of labs in Magdalena. Furthermore, regressive analysis of the vectorization of the virus and its geographic distribution leads in all cases directly back to Magdalena, at the edge of the Solar System. There can be no question that this virus was created by the Magdalena cult."

"This is bullshit!" Stephanie said angrily, losing her cool.

Alexander Grumiaux looked shaken.

"We will have to act fast," he said.

THREE HOURS AND MANY HOLO-CONFERENCES later, Stephanie emerged from Alexander Grumiaux's office with assurances and a plan. She felt ragged and empty, and resented having to spend so much precious time with a man she despised. She was also grateful to him for his help. She didn't like being grateful to such a man.

Her security detail greeted her with guarded relief. It made them uneasy to have her on any territory they did not control. They wouldn't be able to relax at all until she was back safe and secure on Rothschild.

The sooner the better. She led the way down the hall at a rapid pace.

A man stepped out from a side corridor and fired a gun at Stephanie's head. She ducked under it instinctively, with reflexes that would rival any athlete. Her team drew their weapons and gunfire erupted everywhere.

For Stephanie, time slowed down. She could see the attackers, there were five of them. She could see her security detail moving to rush her away. She sprinted fast at their direction, but it felt slow. One of her security men was shot in the neck, and blood sprayed from the wound. Another one of her men shot the front attacker in the head and the man's head exploded. Local security forces began sprinting to help them, but for some reason were stationed far down the hall. She held the wound of the man whose neck was shot as they ran, then he collapsed and she dragged him. Her agents were shielding her with their bodies. Three of the attackers still stood, two more of her men went down. An explosion knocked her sideways and for a moment she couldn't see.

Her personal bodyguard, Boris, who had watched over her since she was a child, picked her up with one arm and gunned down another one of the attackers at the same time. More men from her transport shuttle stormed towards them down the hall. The men passed them and Boris sprinted with her out of the hall and across the transport bay floor. Sirens flashed and wailed throughout the Assembly compound. From the other end of the big transport bay a large rocket came flying at them. Without thinking, Stephanie snatched Boris' second gun from out of the holster on his lower back and fired a shot at the rocket, detonating it in mid-air. The backdraft from the explosion, still 200 meters away, knocked them to the floor. The transport shuttle's guns began to open fire on something and two of the ship's crew members sprinted down the ship's small gangplank.

"Go!" Boris screamed and pushed her towards them, turning with his gun to cover their back.

"I need you with me, Boris!"

She grabbed his arm and dragged him along with her at a sprint, waving the two crew members back to the shuttle. As she and Boris crossed the ship's threshold, its doors slammed shut and it lurched into the air.

Her doctor on board the ship was already standing at the door waiting to attend her, and, while they rose, Stephanie allowed the woman to quickly confirm that she was not seriously injured.

Boris, in his black uniform and creased grey hat, looked like a demon – a warrior exploding with bloodlust and no one left to kill.

CHAPTER 49

SCAMP, LISA, AND MELCHIT WERE cruising over the dark, deep interior of Brazil, where only an occasional light on the ground blinked up at them, when news on the wires hit that 'Lisa Maui' had been spotted robbing a convenience store in Rio, along with a male accomplice and small child. Scamp was described in detail and would surely be identified soon. The news stories said that they were armed and should be considered extremely dangerous. Well, that was true. There weren't any videos shown, so either they had gotten lucky and cutting the power had caused the store's surveillance files to become corrupted, or the authorities were choosing not to release it for some other reason. Perhaps Bloodworth's people did not want the video released because it would show Melchit.

Melchit was doing badly. Food had accomplished nothing for him other than stopping him from continuing to beg for it. He lay on his back on the bench seat of the car, sweating and wheezing, holding Lisa's hand, whimpering. He seemed to be getting worse. Lisa was in a state of panic, but controlling it, turning it into fuel and building strength from it. She was becoming adjusted to crisis and calamity. Scamp had occasionally seen that happen to people before, people who could gain strength from things that broke most others. There was something steel inside of her.

"It's amazing that any place on Earth is still this dark," she said, watching the lonely lights that passed below them while gently patting Melchit's hand.

"The whole Solar System is becoming dark," Scamp said.

Lisa was silent.

"Do you think I'm a dark person?" Scamp asked, with a break in his voice.

"What do you mean?"

"Dark, bad – do you think I'm a bad person?"

"You're a scary person," Lisa said.

"I'll try not to be."

"My grandfather is a philosopher," Lisa said.

"I didn't know that."

"His work isn't very well known. But he says that the difference between good people and bad people is that good people admire those who sacrifice themselves for others, while bad people admire those who sacrifice others for themselves."

"That's interesting."

"By that standard I think you are a good person."

Scamp stared straight ahead and didn't look back at her.

"Oh. I'm– trying to be a better person than I was."

He didn't speak again for a long time.

WHEN THEY GOT TO MEXICO City everything went smoothly. The transport was waiting for them in a gravel lot in one of the city's remote industrial areas. It was a small, boxy ship, dirty on the outside and inconspicuous. There were no other people in the vicinity. Melchit had improved enough on the second half of their journey to sit up and walk from the car to the ship. Scamp covered their car up with a tarp after Lisa and Melchit got on board the transport. The entire process from parking the car to taking off again in the ship took only a few minutes.

They rose and rose into the sky. Lisa watched out the window, then glanced around to find Melchit passed out in his seat. She couldn't wake him up. As she carried him back to lay him on one of the bunks in the ship's small sleeping area, she heard Scamp plotting them a course to Mars.

"No, you can't go to Mars!" Lisa yelled down the short metal hall to the cockpit.

"Of course we can. That's where we have to go!"

"We have to go to Rothschild Palace!"

The ship shook violently as it ascended through the atmosphere and Lisa strapped Melchit into the bunk for safety. He was breathing and his heart was beating in what seemed like it might be a normal way. But his whole body was limp and sweaty. He wouldn't wake up.

"Ohgod."

The ship shook more and Lisa ran back to the cockpit.

"We have to go to Rothschild Palace."

"We can't go to Rothschild Palace," Scamp said, "there's no way they would let us into their space! Plus they would probably give us back to Earth authorities. Plus, we barely even have enough fuel to get there. We'll be interdicted long before we get there and if we don't want to go back to Earth we'll end up adrift in space."

"No, you're wrong."

"And this ship only has enough resources to sustain us for a few weeks in an emergency. That's assuming it's fully stocked, which I haven't had a chance to check yet."

"No, we have to go to Rothschild Palace," Lisa said. "Change the course."

"I can protect us on Mars," Scamp said. "It's our only option."

"No, Scamp, it's not! Listen to me. I was friends with Samson and know Stephanie de Rothschild. Stephanie will help us. If we go to Rothschild Palace they won't turn us away. It's the safest place we can go and it's where I need to go. And they can help Melchit! Mars won't be safe, Rothschild Palace will be safe."

She put one hand on Scamp's huge knee, beseechingly.

"I'm taking us to Mars," Scamp said, gripping the steering wands even though the ship was on auto-pilot. "What you said is just speculation, but it won't happen that way. You're never going to get to talk to Stephanie de Rothschild, we'll be stopped by some ship with low level security agents long before we get there and we'll be either captured or forcibly turned back. And if we're captured we'll be put on a security transport back to Earth. You won't ever get to talk to Stephanie."

Lisa took a step back away from him.

"Scamp, I'm not going to Mars."

"Well that's where we're going, I'm sorry."

He fiddled with the instrument panel and looked straight ahead out the cockpit window, but didn't look at her.

"Scamp, I said no! Look, Melchit is back there dying!" Lisa waved her arms in the direction of the bunks.

"Didn't you hear what I said about it?" Scamp's face was turning red. "Going to Rothschild Palace is suicide!"

Lisa lunged for the controls and tried to wrestle them away from him.

"Stop it, I'm afraid of hurting you."

In a frenzy, she started slapping him in the face.

"Stop it. Stop!"

Scamp wrestled her into a bear hug, then let her slither out of his grasp and she half leapt, half stumbled into the co-pilot's chair next to him.

"Why do you make everything so hard?" Lisa said, with tears in her eyes.

"What? I'm—"

"I have to give Stephanie David Ischewitz's data card."

"His what?"

"This," Lisa said, pulling the card out of her pocket.

"What in the world is that?"

7/15
So we're heading to Rothschild Palace now. Possible suicide mission. Lisa and I had a big fight about it. She might be right.

345

She didn't cry much this time, I don't know if she cried, but she yelled at me and hit me in the face. She thinks she can talk to Stephanie. Maybe she can. She knows Stephanie and knew Samson. Maybe Samson is even still alive like they say.

She has this data card that she got from David Ischewitz, one of Bloodworth's scientists, when she was escaping. It's encrypted, so we can't tell what's on it, but Stephanie's people will probably be able to. Whatever is on it, he and his wife died trying to get that information out. Lisa says he insisted that the card be brought directly to Stephanie. So that's the biggest reason Lisa insisted that we go to Rothschild Palace. It's about 18 hours cruise away from us now.

I looked David Ischewitz up, and there wasn't much information I could find. But at some point he was an undergraduate honors student at Harvard and wrote a prize winning thesis on weaponized viruses. This could really be related to the terrible viruses that have suddenly appeared all over the Solar System. Or maybe they are both one virus, that is what some of the news outlets say now.

The monkey man, Melchit, is doing bad. He was doing better, but took another turn for the worse. Lisa is frantic and blames me for it, or it seems like she does. There's not much we can do until we get to Rothschild Palace. Luckily we got well underway before it stopped seeming like he was doing better, otherwise she might have insisted on stopping at a hospital on Earth. I can't control her.

It would be weird to meet Samson Ford again, if he is really alive. I feel like I have paid off my debt, or I will have, if we can get to Rothschild Palace safely. He has been such a giant figure in my thoughts, my sense of guilt, and now I hardly think of him most of the time. I think about Lisa now, constantly. Is this love? I have never felt this way about another person. Maybe fate brought us together for a reason. Of course I don't believe in fate.

It's amazing that we made it off of Earth. Like we were being looked after by some higher power, like the god. Samson Ford believed in the god. And they say he is alive again. And I went from Neo Vega to Earth to find Lisa Maui, and she is safe again, at least for the next 18 hours. It is all coincidence, but it feels like more than that. It feels deep. That doesn't make sense.

- Scampadorous Maximus

CHAPTER 50

"You're not authorized to enter our space," the security officer on the com said. "Turn around and go somewhere else."

It was true that Scamp and Lisa were running low on fuel by the time they approached Rothschild. Melchit was also doing much worse, he was practically comatose. The attack on Stephanie that had happened at the Congressional Assembly building was reported while they were en-route. The Solar System was entering a nightmare. Rothschild security interdicted them on their com much farther away from the planet than was normal.

"Do you know who Lisa Maui is?" Scamp said. "She's a personal friend of Stephanie de Rothschild. We've escaped from Bloodworth's Corporation prisons and have–"

"I don't care about your story, sir. Turn around!"

"We won't turn around!" Lisa yelled from behind Scamp's seat, standing on her tip-toes to make herself more visible. "We're having a medical emergency, do you understand that? One of our crew members is dying. And we are carrying crucial information smuggled from Bloodworth's Corporation, do you understand that? Just relay the message to Stephanie!"

Lisa and the security officer spent several seconds trying to shout over each other.

"JUST RELAY IT TO STEPHANIE!"

Scamp pushed Lisa back out of the way.

"We're not leaving," he said.

The security man exhaled audibly.

"I'll try to talk to my boss one more time to see if there is anything we can do for you."

"Thank you."

"But do not proceed forward or take any unusual action.

If you do, we will shoot you down immediately."

"Thank you. We won't."

The com link disconnected.

"I can't believe this," Lisa said.

Scamp rotated in his chair to face her.

"We have to be careful, they aren't joking about shooting us down."

"That's ridiculous."

"Stephanie was nearly assassinated on Earth. This is shifting into open war. They are deadly serious."

"What could we possibly do to them?"

"Exactly. They have no way to know. Bloodworth's people wouldn't open up hostilities if they didn't have something up their sleeves."

"I'm going to go check on Melchit."

PHILLIPE BLOODWORTH SAT ALONE IN his home and shed tears of some emotion that resembled sadness. At his feet, on the polished marble floor that stretched off at least 50 meters in every direction, lay the monkey-like corpse of one of his servants. He kicked the corpse occasionally, not hard, as if it would wake up.

"I don't have them anymore," he said softly to himself, and rubbed his bulbous hands back and forth along the quilted snow leopard skin bench he was sitting on. "They're all gone. Dead. And I'll never be able to have them again. Not them. From now on, forever, I won't have them."

A huge holo-monitor floating nearby silently broadcast the news. Bloodworth got down slowly onto his knees and kissed the dead servant on the mouth. He licked its cheek. Then he rested his head and shoulders near the ground, like a bull, and flung the dead body away. As it flipped and slid across the marble it left a tiny trail of smears and droplets of blood that had been pooled up in its mouth and ears.

"Rothschild's did this to me," he said in a cracking hiss. "Rothschild's and the shit-eating kinderfucks! They did this. Because of them I won't have my people anymore. My monkeys. My monkeys."

He shed more tears, of some unusual emotion, that resembled sadness.

THE COM TO ROTHSCHILD'S POPPED back open before Lisa had returned to the cockpit.

"I'm sorry, sir," the same security agent told Scamp without sounding very sorry, "we cannot make any exceptions to our current security protocol. I will, of course, forward your messages to Stephanie de Rothschild, but you must understand that she receives millions of messages a day and even if she is able to review yours it will not be for at least two to three months. Now I must insist that you turn around and proceed to a different destination until such time as you receive a response."

"We won't leave," Scamp said.

"If you don't leave within the next ten minutes, or if you proceed forward at all, our fighters are on orders to shoot you down."

"We can't!"

"I'm sorry sir, but there's nothing else I can do for you. Please turn around."

The com disconnected.

"Shit!"

STEPHANIE STOOD ON THE COMMAND platform of her cloaked battleship as it approached Rothschild. Rothschild sparkled as beautifully as ever, a shining little marble of green and blue, even as the Solar System turned dark around them. If the assassination had been successful – if. Thinking about

350

it made her nauseous, as if her mind had the power to recoil from her will of its own accord. If the assassination had been successful – Simon Okunle would lead her people onto a war path that could only end with the annihilation of Bloodworth's. And billions of corpses. If. Thank the god that it didn't happen.

They wanted to start down that war path anyway.

It wasn't certain yet that the attack actually came from Bloodworth's. It probably did, but it wasn't certain. Some third party might be trying to instigate or interfere. Many things were possible. And they would probably have to have an open war with Bloodworth's anyway. Bloodworth's was likely responsible, among other things, for the virus that was devastating the Solar System. But nothing with certainty. They couldn't kill billions over uncertainty. Not yet. It would be worth a lot of sacrifice to avoid killing billions at all.

The stars shone brilliantly behind her planet. The Milky Way poured across the blinky void like a magic smorgasbord of endless resources and possibility – real, but never reachable. Mercury rested bright red in the distance of the black horizon. These were the stars that Samson watched and loved, that he had spent so many hours with. She wondered how he was. She hadn't been able to speak to him in days.

One of the ship navigators had zoomed his screen in to show a tiny transport ship that had every appearance of being adrift.

"What's that?" Stephanie said to the navigator.

"An uncleared ship that won't leave, Mistress," the navigator said, cocking his head as he listened more closely to his headphones. "They're the reason we're taking a wider loop instead of proceeding directly to Rothschild. It looks like they're going to be shot down."

"What?"

She ran to the nearest console and immediately pulled up a holo-link with the captain of the fighter squadron that was circling, cloaked, in the vicinity of the little transport. It surprised everyone in the room that she was able to do this.

"Wha– hello?" the man on the screen said.

"Captain, this is Stephanie de Rothschild. Temporarily belay any orders to shoot down that transport ship."

"What – yes, Mistress," the man said, visibly confused. "This is highly irregular, Mistress. Please speak to my commanding officer right away, mum."

"I will right now. Hold tight."

Stephanie cut off the com link and stepped away from the console. The fighter squadron on the screen moved into a defensive formation.

"Admiral, link me immediately with the acting officer in charge of planetary space security."

"Yes, Mistress. Right away," the commanding officer of her ship said. He was a tall, square-faced man whose copper hair was highlighted with distinguished streaks of aging grey, an unplanned genetic aberration that had worked out visually to his advantage. "It's General Elman, Mistress. Do you want him on the main screen?"

"Yes."

General Cyril Elman materialized into view above them on the bridge's big holo-projector. He had stern black eyes set with determination

"Cyril, what's happening with that transport? I was told you are about to shoot it down."

"It has no authorization and refuses to leave our space, Mistress. We *are* about to shoot it down. We've given them several warnings already."

"Why won't they leave?"

"As I understand, Mistress, they claim to be low on fuel

352

and experiencing a medical emergency. A woman on board says that she is Lisa Maui and claims to be a friend of yours."

"Lisa Maui *is* a friend of mine!"

"I'm sorry, Mistress. We have been unable to confirm her identity, but also on board with her is a notorious criminal gangster named Scampadorous Maximus."

"That makes sense, they are reported to have been together."

"I didn't know that, Mistress."

"Jesuschrist, Cyril," Stephanie said, and the man's face drained. "Don't shoot them down."

The general muted audio on his com briefly and could be seen to be barking orders.

"Yes, Mistress," he said. "And – I should tell you that they claim to have information about the war that has been stolen from Bloodworth's corporation."

"Jesuschrist, Cyril."

"We were ordered to exercise extreme caution and act with maximum prejudice against any threat, Mistress."

"Well I am going to be talking to your bosses about that, too," Stephanie said, using the business term intentionally. "Extreme caution is right, but we have to remember that we are the good guys."

"Of course, Mistress. Please forgive my overzealousness. How would you like us to proceed in this case?"

"You don't need forgiveness, Cyril, you're a good officer and I appreciate your professionalism. Board the ship with all caution, scan it thoroughly, and confirm the identity of its occupants."

As she spoke, Stephanie walked over to stand near the console of the ship's communications officer.

"Of course, Mistress. We will do that immediately."

"And keep me personally updated about this situation. If

that ship does have Lisa Maui on board I want to know about it right away."

"Yes, Mistress."

She reached out quickly over the communications officer's shoulder and switched the com link to the general off.

"Everyone in the Solar System is going crazy, Admiral."

"It seems so, Mistress."

"I return the bridge to you."

"Thank you, Mistress."

She walked back off of the bridge without saying another word, and every single member of the bridge crew watched after her in awe.

C H A P T E R ⁵¹

{ECURITY SHIPS AND AGENTS SCANNED the little transport
for several hours, as well as its occupants, inspecting every
panel and compartment on the ship and virtually every hair on
Scamp's body (they treated Lisa with more deference, after con-
firming her identity with a quick DNA scan, and she argued
with them constantly). Melchit was carried off the transport
unconscious and rushed to a hospital. Lisa and Scamp, once
fully cleared, were towed to Rothschild and escorted into a
secure housing unit that was something like a comfortable
jail. A few hours passed.

"They're keeping us here too long," Lisa said, pacing. "I
need to know what is happening to Melchit. They need to let
me talk to Stephanie."

"I'm sure they're taking care of him as well as they possibly
can," Scamp said.

"How can you be sure about that? I'm not sure about it."

"Well, it's the Rothschild's culture. That's how they're
trained to treat people. And they wouldn't discriminate against
him."

"They would."

"Let's wait and see what they report to us about him. I'm
sure they'll let us out of this holding area soon, or at least you."

"You're optimistic."

Scamp stretched out over a big leather sofa, breathed a
long, slow breath, and smiled.

"Lisa, look how far we've come. We did it. We're safe now!"

"We're not safe," Lisa said. "Melchit's somewhere dying
for all we know. He's a person, even though you don't seem
to realize that. He's one of us, too."

Scamp reeled in his smile and watched Lisa for a moment.

"I'm sorry," he said. "You're right. But we did everything

we can for him. We got him to a hospital in a safe place. We'll find out more about him soon."

"You don't know any of that."

"But we did. And – don't you feel it? After standing in the center of the jaws of death for so long? And we escaped. We got out, we won. It's a feeling like, elation. It's the best feeling in the world. It's hard for me not to jump for joy. We should be dead, but we fought and we won. It's the best feeling in the world."

"You're a scary person, Scamp."

"I'm sorry."

"It's ok."

"WE'RE GOING ON A TRIP," Theo and Maria told the children.

"What?"

"Hurry up, put your backpacks on."

"But we haven't even packed our backpacks."

"Your Dad and I packed them for you."

Eve unzipped her backpack to look inside, and Paul started to unzip his.

"Paul!" Maria scolded, "Just put it on."

Judith held her backpack in her hands looking shocked.

"Where are we going, Dad?"

"It's a surprise."

"But just where?"

"It's a surprise trip to somewhere special. We're going to be gone for at least a few days."

"What do you mean 'at least'?"

"Don't ask so many questions, this is a surprise."

"Yay, we're going on a trip!" little Eve said.

"It's also a secret, so don't say anything about it."

"Ok."

The cab driver was kind and the children began to get

excited once they were in the car. They also wondered why their parents were acting strange.

"You know where we're going," Theo said to the cabbie.

"I do, sir. I hope you're all comfortable, because it's a long ride."

"Mommy, what if I have to use the bathroom?"

"Do you have to use the bathroom?"

"No."

"Well, if you have to later then we will stop somewhere and go."

"Ok."

They cruised along the pink streets between the beautiful white buildings of Magdalena City, not fast. To help pass time, and especially for little Eve's sake, Maria told the children a story.

"Listen close, I'm going to tell you a special story, a story that no one has ever heard before."

"Is it a happy story?"

"Does it have dragons in it?"

"Is it a true story?"

"Just listen and see.

"Once upon a time there was a family of mice that lived in a church. It was a big, old church with beautiful stained glass windows and dust and cobwebs in the corners. There was a papa mouse, and a mama mouse, and three baby mice. And the papa mouse was a good mouse who loved his family very much, so he went out all day and sometimes all night, out into the church and even to the big world outside the church, to find food for his family and to protect them."

"Did they live in a hole in the wall?"

"That's right, they had a little home inside one of the walls of the church. Their home was just the right size for them, it was warm and comfortable and safe, and they loved their home very much.

"And the papa mouse had to brave many dangers going outside to find the family the food and other things that they needed."

"What else did they need?"

"Oh, bits of thread and string for the children to play with. Shiny things for the mom that she liked to look at. And bits of paper newspapers and books, because the mice were very smart mice and they loved to read."

"I love to read too," said Eve, and Judith rolled her eyes.

"The papa mouse braved many dangers to take care of the mama mouse and the baby mice. He had to brave giant cats with sharp claws that wanted to eat him. When the cats smelled him they would drool and lick their lips, because they thought he would taste so good. And he had to brave special traps that were covered with the delicious food that he was looking for, that would kill him if he tried to take the food. And always he had to be so careful to avoid the big, giant humans who hated the mice and wanted to kill them, even though they didn't know anything about the mice.

"And the reason the papa mouse did all this and faced so many dangers was to take care of the mama mouse and the babies, so that they could have a good life and be safe."

"He's a lot like Daddy."

"He is a lot like your father. Your father is very special."

"But Mice aren't people," Paul said.

"Just listen to the story," Maria said.

"The mama mouse often sat at home and worried about the papa mouse when he went out, but she smiled at the children and pretended that she wasn't worried, because she didn't want for them to worry too."

"And then what happened?" Paul said impatiently.

"Well, one day when the papa mouse went out he found a huge piece of the mouse family's favorite food – cheese! And he looked carefully to the left, and he looked carefully to the right, and he looked up and down, trying to see if there was any danger. And when everything looked safe he sniffed the cheese from far away. He didn't go too close to the cheese, but he sniffed the cheesy air in the room very carefully, because sometimes the giant humans put poison in cheese. When he sniffed carefully he could smell it well, even from the other side of the room, and the cheese definitely smelled like pure, delicious, 100% cheese. He wanted to grab the cheese and rush home to eat it, but something made him suspicious. Where did this big chunk of delicious cheese come from? He wasn't in the kitchen, he was in the basement of the church, so why would there be a big piece of delicious cheese down there? And why was it dangling in the air, at exactly the height where a mouse could reach it?

"He walked up to the cheese very slowly, very carefully.

"That was when he saw it: there was a tiny wire attached to the cheese. It was a trap! He ran away from the cheese as fast as he could, back to the safety of the shadows along the wall. This was a kind of trap that he had never seen before. The giant humans were getting more and more dangerous to the mouse family.

"So the papa mouse stood in the shadows along the edge of the basement wall, shaking with fear and with his heart beating very fast. He had almost been caught! He had almost been caught, and there was no one to take care of the mama mouse and the little baby mice if he was gone.

"But then his heart started beating even faster, because do you know what happened?"

"What happened?"

"A huge cat walked into the room, a cat bigger and scarier than any one he had seen before. The cat had grey and black fur that was patchy and tufted from scars."

"Oooh."

"What's 'tufted'?"

"It means that some bits of his fur were long and that others were short."

"Oh."

"And the big cat walked into the room and he said, 'I know you're in here, mouse. I can smell you.'

"And the papa mouse's heart beat so hard, but he was very brave and stood very still and tried to think of what to do.

" 'You won't get away from me,' the cat said. 'No mouse ever gets away from me. You're going to be my dinner tonight.'

"And the big cat stalked across the floor slowly, sniffing the air, peering this way and that, trying to see into the shadows. He came closer and closer to the papa mouse. He came closer and closer until the papa mouse could see the shiny saliva running down the big cat's sharp fangs, and even smell the cat's disgusting breath, which smelled like fish and dead birds and rotten eggs and garbage."

"Eww, Mom!"

"Well that's what the cat's breath smelled like. And the papa mouse stood very still as the cat came closer and closer, and tried to think of what to do.

" 'I know where you are, mouse,' the big cat said, and crouched down about to pounce.

"The papa mouse sprang into action, kicking an old screw that was on the ground with his foot, so that it bounced along the edge of the wall.

"And the big cat pounced on the screw, and the papa mouse sprinted in the other direction, running as fast as he could run. But the big cat turned right away and leapt after the papa mouse, so close that the papa mouse could almost feel cat claws on his back.

"And do you know what the papa mouse did?"

"What did he do?"

"He turned and ran towards the cheese as fast as he could. He ran faster than he ever ran before. And the big cat ran after him just as fast, until he could feel its stinky breath against his fur, which smelled like fish and dead birds and rotten eggs and garbage."

"Gross, Mom. Stop it!"

"Well that's what it smelled like.

"And right before the cat got him, the papa mouse ran past the big chunk of cheese that was hanging above the ground. He ran so close to the cheese that his whiskers touched it. And the big cat leapt into the cheese, which was really a trap. As soon as the cat touched the cheese the trap was sprung, a wire loop snapped tight around the cat's foot and yanked him up into the air. He was yanked high into the air, twisting and turning, and he thrashed and howled, clawing at the air with his big, sharp claws, but he couldn't get away. The humans would have to find him there in the morning. And the papa mouse ran away, back towards his house, and he felt so relieved. He laughed at the big cat getting caught in the trap, and laughed and laughed, because it was very funny, and because he was so happy to be alive and free.

"On his way back home the papa mouse found a big scrap of paper that had fallen off of a desk, so he brought that with him for the family to read.

"And when he got back home he hugged the mama mouse and the children tight. And then he told them all about his adventures. The children were so shocked and excited about the adventures their father had, and the mama mouse was so scared.

" 'Oh honey,' the mama mouse said, 'I'm so scared when you go out. I'm terrified that something will happen to you.'

" 'Nothing will ever happen to me,' the papa mouse said

bravely. 'I'm smart and fast and strong, and I know how to beat all the tricks.'

"But the mama mouse worried anyway, because her husband's life was very dangerous. And that night, something else happened that would change their lives forever. After the children were asleep, as the papa mouse and the mama mouse were getting ready for bed, the mama mouse looked at the scrap of paper that the papa mouse had brought back from his adventure.

" 'Oh my goodness!' she said. 'Honey, did you read the words on this paper? Oh dear, oh dear.'

" 'I didn't look at it yet,' the papa mouse said. 'What does it say?'

" 'Come over here and read it with me,' the mama mouse said. 'I think I know what it says, but I can't believe it's true.'

"So the papa mouse came over and read the scrap of paper with the mama mouse. It was a square yellow paper with sticky goo along the top of the back side of it. They sounded the words out slowly and carefully, because even though they were very smart animals, they were still only mice, and reading for mice is very hard.

"And the note said: 'Ex-ter-min-ators Mon-day take care of mice'.

The papa mouse and the mama mouse looked at each other.

" 'They're going to kill us,' the mama mouse said, aghast!
"What's 'aghast' mama?"
"It means that she was very surprised, in a very bad way."
"Oh."
" 'But we won't let them kill us!' the papa mouse said.
" 'Of course we won't.'
" 'We have to protect our children.'
" 'Of course we do.'

362

"They hugged each other tightly and thought for a minute."

" 'It won't be safe here,' said the mama mouse.

" 'No, it won't.'

" 'We'll have to leave our home. We'll have to leave the whole church!'

" 'I'll find a new home for us tomorrow,' the papa mouse said. 'A safe home, where I can go out and get food and you don't have to be scared anymore.'

" 'It's so dangerous out there.'

" 'I'll find a safe place,' the papa mouse said. 'I'll protect you.'

"So the very next morning the papa mouse went out to find a new home for the little mouse family. And he was so scared, but he didn't let the children and the mama mouse know that he was scared. Although, the mama mouse knew anyway. And the mama mouse hid the paper about the exterminators away so that the children would not see it, and pretended that everything was fine, even though she was so worried and afraid.

"And do you know that the papa mouse went out into the city and had many new adventures and found a brand new home for the mouse family, a home that was safe and wonderful. And the whole family had a giant adventure when they moved to the new home. But those are stories for another day."

Maria felt the cab accelerate a little bit as she finished her story.

"What kind of adventures did they have?" Paul asked.

"Big, exciting adventures, but you'll have to wait to hear about them, because I only tell one chapter at a time."

The cab swerved and accelerated again, and Maria instinctively grabbed hold of Eve. She looked out the window and was surprised to see how fast they were going.

"Easy," Theo said to the driver.

"But mama," little Eve said, "why did the people want to kill the mouse family?"

"Because they didn't understand the mice, honey. And so they thought that the mice were bad."

"Just because they didn't understand them they thought the mice were bad?"

"That's right."

The cab moved faster and Maria noticed that Paul was staring behind them out the back window.

"Stop looking out the back window and look ahead," Theo said quietly to his son, in a gentle but very serious voice.

"But this story is just pretend, Eve," Judith said. "Real mice don't talk or read, and they have to be trapped and killed if they get inside your house, because they carry germs and diseases that make people sick."

"Like with a mouse trap? Like Dad used?"

A siren suddenly sounded behind them, making Maria jump. The cab accelerated and swerved again, and kept accelerating.

CHAPTER 52

"HELLO LISA, I'M SO GLAD you are safe," Stephanie said.

"Hello, Mr. Maximus. I'm sorry for all the trouble we have put you through since you came to Rothschild yesterday."

She floated life-size in front of them, almost perfectly recreated by the holo-projector.

"Thank you for helping us," Scamp said.

"Stephanie, I'm glad you're safe too," Lisa said. "We couldn't believe it when we heard you were attacked. But why are you keeping us here?"

"I'm sorry, that has been an unfortunate security precaution. We are in a state of extreme alert. Later today I want to meet with you in person, Lisa, and after that you will be free to come and go on Rothschild as you please. Mr. Maximus will still be restricted, though."

"That's fine. You can call me Scamp, ma'am."

"Thank you, Scamp. But you will both be able to visit your friend in the hospital later today."

"How is Melchit?"

"He's not good. He has not regained consciousness since you got here."

"Ohmygod."

"I'm sorry, I don't have much time. Lisa, I will meet with you in person later today. In the meantime, I understand that you have an important data card smuggled out of Bloodworth's that you have been unwilling to give to our security agents."

"The man who gave it to me, David Ischewitz, said I should only give it to you," Lisa said. "He was a Bloodworth's scientist and died trying to smuggle it out. I don't know what it is."

"I understand. Would you be comfortable giving it to the head of my personal security team? He is one of my absolutely most trusted people."

"I guess that would be ok."

"Thank you." She motioned Boris forward into the camera's view. "This is Boris. He will visit you shortly to collect the card. We want to analyze it right away."

"Ok–" Lisa started to respond.

"Now I must go. Please forgive me for being so impersonal. I will see you later today."

"Wait!" Scamp said.

"We need to be with our friend Melchit," Lisa said. "We want to go to the hospital right away!"

"Forgive me, that isn't possible. But he is receiving our best care. Yes, Scamp?"

"Is Samson really alive?"

Stephanie smiled a quick, thin, cryptic smile.

"Please tell us the truth," Lisa said.

"He absolutely is alive, and well. Right now he is on an urgent trip across the Solar System, otherwise I'm sure he would want to talk to you. I must go. Goodbye."

The hologram blinked out and Lisa and Scamp were again alone in the room.

"He's alive," Scamp said. "He's really alive."

MARIA HUGGED THE CHILDREN TO her as the sirens blared behind them and the cab continued to accelerate and rise into the sky. Magdalena security vehicles were chasing them.

"You must stop," Theo said to the cabbie. "We can't outrun them and we aren't guilty of anything."

"Speak for yourself, man," the cabbie said. "I've been smuggling hundreds of people. They'll kill me."

"It's not safe!" Maria said. "Take us back down to the ground and stop the cab."

"I won't crash," the cabbie said. "You wanted to go to Neo Vega, I'm taking you to Neo Vega. It's just a more direct route than I expected."

The security vehicles, which were faster than the cab, began to catch up and surround them, trying to box them in. The sound of the sirens was deafening.

"They don't know that you've smuggled hundreds of people! You're making it worse! Slow down! Stop!"

One of the security cars started firing at them, grazing the sides of the cab, targeting the engine.

"Oh shit. Oh shit."

"Everybody get your heads down," Theo said, pushing his wife and children down against the seat.

"What's happening, Dad?"

"I don't know. This is scary. I need all of you kids to pray very hard for God to protect us. Pray now."

The children prayed and the cab began to slow and descend to the ground. The security cars didn't seem to be trying in earnest to shoot them, only to scare them. It was working.

The cab came to a rest on the desert floor, far away from any ranches or farms. Theo didn't even know if they were still in Magdalena territory. The security cars set down at a safe distance in a circle around them. The 'cabbie' was gripping the car's steering wheel tightly and seemed to be in shock. Theo got out of the car with his hands held unthreateningly open. The desert stretched off to the horizon around them in all directions – faded green, rocky pink, and smudgy grey. The air was dry and dusty in Theo's throat.

Security agents with guns drawn approached Theo and led him away. Others got Maria and the children, and the driver, out of the cab.

"He didn't do anything," Paul said to them, "it was the cabbie!"

"It will be ok, Paul," Maria said.

The dust of the desert blew over them causing everyone to cough, and Maria instructed the children to breathe through their shirtsleeves.

"We'll take you and the children back to your home, Mrs. Ford," one of the more senior security agents told them.

"What's going on? Where are you taking Theo?"

"Your husband has sinned against the Church and is being detained."

A FEW HOURS AFTER BORIS collected the data card from Lisa, three more Rothschild security agents knocked on the door to the apartment. Two of them escorted Scamp to the hospital to visit Melchit, and the third led Lisa to a meeting with Stephanie.

To Lisa, Stephanie's office seemed huge, antiquated, and intimidating. The office's peculiar mechanical eagle stared down at her from the wall. Stephanie ran forward and embraced her in a big hug as soon as Lisa stepped through the door and crossed the threshold.

"I'm so glad you're ok, Lisa," Stephanie said.

Lisa was surprised at the amount of warmth in the greeting and returned Stephanie's embrace uncertainly.

"Thank you for taking the time to meet me," Lisa said. "You must be incredibly busy."

Stephanie let go of her and stepped back.

"I'm sorry it's taken so long. And I'm sorry you can't go immediately to the hospital to be with your friend, Melchit. This was the only time that I could schedule for us to meet. After we talk you can go straight to the hospital if you want and your card will be unblocked on our system so that you can communicate with the outside world again and come and go as you please."

"Ok," Lisa said.

"Come sit down."

Stephanie led Lisa over to the sitting area near her desk,

where an elaborate spread of snacks and coffee had been laid out. They sat down on big leather chairs near each other.

"I'm so glad you're ok too, Stephanie. Everything is so crazy, I just can't believe it." Tears came to Lisa's eyes and she looked through them at Stephanie defiantly. "I've been through a lot."

"I know you have, dear," Stephanie said. "You're safe now and Rothschild's will protect you, I want you to know that. As soon as we confirmed your identity and health we also let your grandparents know that you are ok. They're anxious to talk to you, and I'm sure that you are anxious to talk to them."

"Oh. Thank you."

"But I don't have very much time and I need you to tell me everything that you know about this data card that you brought to us and how you acquired it. The card turned out to have details of weaponized virus research undertaken by the Bloodworth's corporation – how they engineered and released this virus that is devastating the Solar System."

"Bloodworth's made it?"

"It turns out to have been a project that they were working on for decades, as an option to annihilate the population of natural born human beings."

"Ohmygod," Lisa said, "things have been so crazy I never thought about it until now – are my grandparents ok, from the virus?"

"They are."

Lisa cleared her throat hoarsely.

"Things have been so crazy. It's like life isn't even real."

"Tell me how you got the data card."

SAMSON SAT CROSS-LEGGED ON the bed in his cabin, looking at the stars through the window. His brow was furrowed. Something was out there, he could sense it. Something that

369

wasn't only space. He tried to concentrate on it, to bring it into focus.

A few minutes before, he had been relaxed. He had been worried about the outside Solar System, which they had lost contact with for days, but he had been relaxed. Rothschild was large and powerful, and the quantum relays that allowed easy communication throughout the Solar System were sometimes unreliable in deep space. This had been especially true since the trade war between Bloodworth's and Rothschild's began.

But now there was something near them, near their ship – in deep space. It was something that felt wrong. Nothing that could be seen, nothing to appear on the ship's sensors. He could tell that the crew members on the ship's navigation deck didn't notice anything. He tried to wrap his mind around what it was that was out there, to fathom it with his new sense. It had emotion, but its emotion was unclear. It was still too far away, although so close to them in the relative terms of space. He tried to squint at it with his mind. It was vague emotions and a vague shape.

Suddenly he realized that it was people. There were other people near them, somewhere. Close. He leapt out of his bed and rushed to the bridge.

"There's something out there," Samson said to Captain Batista, who was groggily contemplating the stars.

"What do you mean?"

"There's nothing out there, mate," the navigator at the console, Jacob, pointed at the ship's various sensors. "Look."

Samson frowned.

"I know it doesn't show on the sensors," he said, "but I can feel it. There are people out there. Other people nearby."

"We've seen that you can feel a lot of things, Mr. Ford," Captain Batista said, reigning in an impulse of disrespect, "but there's nothing there."

Samson focused his mind on the thing again, the cloudy presence of people. Their emotions were becoming more intense and distinct.

"Is it possible a cloaked ship is out there?"

"Not possible, mate," Captain Batista said. "We'd see interference in the solar radiation patterns. And nobody knows we're doing anything important. And cloaking technology is incredibly expensive and rare. Rothschild's are the only ones I know for certain that have it. Space pirates couldn't possibly. Even if they were cloaked, no one would have any reason to approach us. If they even could, at the rate we're moving. And also we would see aberrations on the gravity sensors."

The people's emotions became clearer. Samson could focus on them now. They were behind the transport ship, following it. He could sense distinct individuals. He could sense the outlines of their ship, which was slightly larger than the transport. Their thoughts were tense, violent thoughts, anticipation and fear. Samson stared at the back of his own ship's bridge as if he could see through it. They were about to do something.

He shoved the pilot roughly out of his seat and shifted them into a hard brake. Everyone in the room was thrown into the air. A coal black warship blasted past them as it materialized in space, firing a barrage of plasma shells from a battery of heavy war cannons into the emptiness where they would have been.

CHAPTER 53

"WHAT IS *that*?"

Shockwaves from the plasma cannon bursts rocked the deep-space transport cruiser. As its crew members picked themselves up, Samson strapped fully into the pilot seat and began evasive maneuvers. A brake at these velocities wasn't anything like a stop, just a deceleration. The enemy ship had shot past them, but still wasn't far away. The ship's pilot, a man named Oda, climbed into the co-pilot's seat and sent out a quantum-relay distress signal.

The enemy warship disappeared into space again, but Samson could sense it, where it was and what the people on board it were feeling – they were surprised.

"They're not gone yet," he said. "Everybody strap in! They're setting up to attack again."

The men on the bridge all looked perplexed, but did what he said. Some of them were injured. Samson's own head ached where it had smashed against the pilot's console.

"Get the guns ready," Captain Batista said. "Everyone prepare for battle." He got onto the ship's com and ordered tactical members immediately to the bridge and for everyone else on board to strap into their nearest safety harnesses.

The Rothschild's transport was equipped with two laser cannons, which now emerged from the sides of the ship's body. Each cannon had dual barrels resting on rotating platforms that extended far out from opposite sides of the ship, allowing both cannons to concentrate fire together into large areas of space, and at least one cannon to fire any direction relative to the ship at any time.

"Cannon one ready."

"Cannon two ready."

"They're still in front of us," Samson said. "They're waiting for us to catch back up and pass."

"How do you know that?" Captain Batista said.

"Be ready with the guns, when they attack it will be sudden."

Everyone in the room looked at Samson apprehensively, but the captain with irritation.

"How did you know when they were going to attack?"

"I don't know how. Everyone be ready. They're trying to track with us, but I'm making it difficult for them."

"You know where they are?"

"Be ready."

Samson stared through the big bridge windows without blinking, as if he could see something there. He piloted the ship this way and that, in gentle curves, accelerating and decelerating. Maneuvering potential was limited at the high velocity they were traveling and the transport was unwieldy compared to a racer. He tried to pilot in a way that would make it seem to the enemy like he was maneuvering blind. As minutes passed, the other men on the bridge began to wonder if what they had seen had really happened – if there really had been a battleship that suddenly materialized outside and tried to shoot them down.

"Stay with me," Samson said, "they're going to attack soon. You'll only have a second or two to fire back."

The thoughts of the people on board the enemy ship had been confused, but slowly grew more confident again and more resolved. Samson could feel bloodlust and anticipation in them well up. There weren't a lot of people on board, only a handful. Their ship was like a bird of prey, equipped for sudden, devastating attack but not pitched battle. It was an exotic ship. Its defense was to escape.

And they were Bloodworth's men. He couldn't read their

individual thoughts, but that came through.

"Now!" he shouted and dropped the transport into another abrupt brake.

The enemy ship appeared again as the men on the transport were thrown violently into their restraints, and it fired out into empty space as it flashed past them. Immediately again, it disappeared. The Rothschild gunners opened fire on it before they had even fallen back into their seats, even as their ship shook from the wash of the plasma bursts, and their lasers seemed to impact something in the void. Then the lasers blinked out to the horizon as if nothing was there.

The enemy ship pulled far away from them, so far that Samson could only vaguely sense it, but it didn't leave.

"We hit them, didn't we?" one of the gunners asked.

"We got both our cannons right on them, they should have been shot down."

"If they were shot down then they wouldn't still be cloaked, would they? But I'm sure we hit them."

"How strong are those cannons?" Samson asked.

"Strong enough to cut right through a ship like that," Captain Batista said. "I don't understand this. Are they dead? Are they an illusion?"

"They're still out there," Samson said. "We must have hurt them, they've moved away to keep a distance from us. But they're still out there."

"How do you know?"

"I don't know how, but I do. It's not something I can explain. You can think of it as if I have psychic powers or something, it's like that."

The captain scowled at Samson.

"Under the circumstances, I think we should listen to him, sir," said Dorian from the back of the room, followed by the nods of everyone on deck.

374

"Of course we'll bloody listen to him!" Captain Batista said, but his voice quavered.

"At the distance they are now, I won't be able to sense when they're about to attack," Samson said, staring again unblinking into empty space, "but hopefully we are out of range of their weapons. What is the effective range of your laser cannons?"

"Two miles. But the cannons can focus down any projectiles they fire at us from range."

"Ok. Good. We must have done some damage to them if the cannons are as powerful as you say."

"How far away are they now?"

"Five, ten miles, maybe more. I can't tell exactly, but they are out there still, and still shadowing us."

Captain Batista twisted his neck back and forth, with a faintly audible pop, and pinched his nose between his eyes.

"So what do we do?" he said.

"We'll keep our course, and I'll continue making evasive adjustments as we fly, to make their pursuit difficult. Send out whatever calls for help we can, and keep sending them out. Gunners stay ready in case something changes. If you can think of anything else I'm open to ideas."

"I'll try to think of what I can," Captain Batista said, "but it seems we're at your mercy. And theirs."

"My mercy is benevolent, captain," Samson said drily.

The enemy ship continued following them for hours, and Samson continued flying gentle evasive maneuvers. As the time passed, the other men on board began to doubt more and more that the enemy ship was still there.

"Let my pilot take over flying the ship again," Captain Batista said more than once.

"He can't sense where they are."

All of their efforts to communicate with the rest of the Solar System were unsuccessful.

CHAPTER 54

ECURITY AGENTS, AND THEN PRIESTS, brought Theo to The Prophet's plush personal chambers in Magdalena Temple. Two of the priests brought Theo into a room punctuated with polished silver, pillowy red velvet, and dark carved wood. They knelt and prayed silently in opposite corners of the entranceway when The Prophet walked in. The Prophet was wearing his white and brocade robes, woven with spider silk and pearls, and a tall, shining hat, as if he had just returned from a public ceremony. Beneath the vestments he was a pasty and ordinary looking man, except for a pair of huge grey eyes.

"Theodore, my child, you have sinned."

"Forgive me, Father," Theo said with his head bowed, unable to make eye contact with the older man.

"I've had a long morning, Theodore. I'm tired and must sit down. Please kneel at the stool and talk to me."

Theo knelt as directed and The Prophet sat down in front of him on a plump, yet somehow austere, couch. With his long frame, Theo's eyes even when kneeling were almost on a level with The Prophet's own, although he continued to look down.

"Why do you want to run away, child?"

"I don't know, Father."

"Speak truthfully here, Theodore, and freely. Tell me why you wanted to run away."

"I was afraid, Father."

"And your wife, daughter Maria, she was afraid too?"

"Yes, Father."

"Was she more afraid than you were, child? Did she want for you to flee?"

"No, Father. No. We were both afraid, but..."

Theo's voice trembled. The two priests that had escorted him into the room continued to pray silently in the corners of the entranceway.

"Yes?"

"Running away was my idea."

"I feel so betrayed, Theodore, so hurt," The Prophet said after a pause. "You are one of my most trusted disciples. I feel so wounded by what you have done, child."

"Forgive me, Father."

"What were you afraid of?"

Theo clenched his fists. The overload of emotions that were working on him was unbearable. He felt as if his mind would pop out of his brain. The Prophet waited patiently for him to answer.

"Of the war, Father."

"Only of that? You were afraid to fight? To die?"

"No, Father. We were– I was afraid for our children. The little ones. We wanted them to have a life."

"A life away from God?"

"Forgive me, Father."

"And Maria wanted that, too."

"No, Father! It was me. It was all me."

"God loves mercy, Theodore, not vengeance. We would never hurt Maria, our dear daughter. It is you who have hurt her."

"Forgive me, Father."

"You wanted to take your family to Neo Vega, your babies. Theodore, you of all men know what kind of place that is. A place so hateful to God. Which He will soon obliterate."

"We hoped– I hoped, Father, that somewhere in the Solar System, outside of Magdalena, we could find a cure to the virus for our children. We– I told Maria that we could. So that they could live and have children of their own."

"You do not trust in God, Theodore?"

"Forgive me, Father."

"You want to steal your wife and children away from the

377

heaven of God, to give them a so-called life in this earthen hell?"

"Forgive me, Lord!"

Theo bowed his head to the floor. He felt faint.

"Ye children of little faith," The Prophet said, casting his eyes up and raising his hands passionately. "This earthen hell, the insignificant molehill of this so-called life, this is the true death. This is what you want to give to your children?"

"Yes, Father. Yes. Forgive me."

"Do you remember when you told me that you had a passion to live for God, Theodore? Do you remember the mornings when you brought your babies to me, to bless them into the life of heaven? Paul, and Judith, and sweet little Eve?"

"Forgive me, Father."

The Prophet leaned forward and put his hand on Theo's head.

"Pray with me, child. Pray very hard. Lord God almighty, creator of the heavens and the Earth, protector of the just, annihilator of the wicked, oh purest love and truest truth, oh one and only One – forgive us of our sins, which we know are grave. Lord, we are weak! Have mercy on us. Have mercy on your stumbling, spoiled children who pierce your heart. We are afraid, Lord! We can see so little, Lord, and you so much. Yet we thirst to greet your heaven and to leave this hell of death.

"We are weak, Lord! Have mercy on your child, Theodore, who is afraid. Who in his fear would try to snatch his children out of heaven and hurl them into death. Forgive him, Lord. Have mercy on us who are small and weak. Whose timid minds are clouded by fear in the haze of our nearsighted, earthen hate.

"Have mercy on Theodore, Lord! Have mercy on your son Theodore, who loves you in his heart. Have mercy on your son, Lord. And give to us your strength."

The Prophet's hand rested heavily and hot on top of Theo's head, as if it was a molten leaden weight. And Theo wept.

CHAPTER 55

"ARE YOU SURE THEY'RE STILL out there?" Captain Batista asked, not for the first time.

Samson was tired. Focusing on the enemy ship was exhausting, and he had been piloting for hours. They had gradually slowed down to give themselves more maneuverability if and when the enemy ship reappeared. Almost everyone on the ship was skeptical that the enemy was even still out there. And many of them doubted that the enemy ship had ever been there at all. Samson could feel the thoughts of the captain and crew, vaguely, as with peripheral vision, although he could not take his focus off of the enemy ship to concentrate on the men around him.

"They're there. They're a little bit closer now. I don't know if we're in their range, since they came in so close the other times, but if they attack again the same breaking maneuver to dodge them isn't going to work."

"I'm surprised they fell for it twice already," Captain Batista said.

"Yeah."

"How are you on guns?"

"Eh? I'm probably ok. I've manned guns on ships before, although not in real combat. I'm a much better pilot than a gunner, obviously."

"Our cannon systems are simple," Captain Batista said. "We can easily show you how to man one. And the lasers are visual, you can see where they go and adjust it."

"So I should let Oda take back over and man one of the guns?"

"If you can sense where they are, then you can target them and shoot them, even when they are cloaked. It makes more sense."

"That's true."

"Like you said yourself, if they attack again a simple dodge or brake maneuver isn't going to stop them. You can man one of the guns and tell our pilot what to do. You might even be able to snipe them now, from far away, if they are drifting closer than they were."

"They are drifting closer," Samson said. "They might even be only a couple of miles away."

"Then you might be able to shoot them already. Especially if they are even closer than your estimate."

Samson relinquished the ship controls and took over the seat of one of the gunners, who showed him how to operate the laser cannons. Both cannon batteries were set to fire on the same point at the control of the lead gunner. It didn't take Samson long to learn the controls, but during these minutes the enemy warship continued to gradually close the distance between them. Once he understood the controls, he began to fire out into space where he sensed the enemy ship. From a distance of more than a mile, the aim needed to hit even a whole ship was very precise, and even with his relativity sense Samson could not tell if he hit them or was having any effect. At least the warship stopped coming any closer. Every five minutes, Samson fired toward the space where the enemy ship seemed to be. He couldn't fire more often than that, because the laser cannons were a heavy drain on the transport ship's power core, and they had to maintain some reserve in case the enemy ship fired on them from a distance or came in for another close attack.

After what seemed like an hour of this, firing their lasers into empty space, Samson faintly sensed a change in the enemy ship. He couldn't tell what it meant, it was vague at this distance, but something changed in the emotions of the enemy crew.

"Get ready," he called to the pilot, Oda, and the other gunner, "they're about to do something."

"What are they about to do?"

"I don't know, but something just changed."

"Are they still there?"

"Yes, they're still there!"

The warship suddenly de-cloaked about two and a half miles behind them and fired two rockets. The rockets accelerated forward at a relative speed of about a half a mile per second and both laser turrets automatically locked onto them and began to fire.

"Oh shit."

"Our cannons will shoot them down," Captain Batista said.

The rockets coursed towards them and the lasers beamed out steadily. In the last second of the rockets' approach, the other gunner switched to manual control and locked onto the rockets with admirable skill, but Samson could tell that missing was not the problem. He could sense the lasers scattering off the rockets' fronts. They were shielded by something, perhaps something as simple as small mirrors. Everything seemed to slow down. Samson felt peace and could see the rockets in his mind's eye more clearly than on the screen as they inched through the last quarter mile of distance separating them from the ship.

"Brraaacee!" yelled the captain.

Suddenly, Samson's peace was broken and everything sped up. He clutched at the cross around his neck as both rockets exploded into the ship. The next instant was flashing, heat, horrible shattering wrenching sounds, being violently thrown into the seat restraints, and a long, vibrating, all encompassing roar.

As the world stopped spinning, or the ship did, or his mind did, Samson rubbed blood off of his face and noticed that the ship's internal lights were dim. They were in an emergency power state. He heard moaning and the sound of someone vomiting. He tried to operate the laser cannon console in front of him, but it was offline. One of the laser cannon batteries outside was completely gone.

The enemy warship approached without cloaking now, very slowly. Samson could focus on them more and more clearly. He could sense the thoughts of individual crew members on the enemy ship. Violent thoughts, no longer scared. And the enemy ship was damaged too.

"Do you have any other weapons? They're going to kill us!"

"None," Captain Batista said, and hacked and spit out blood. "We have guns to fight with if they try to board us. If we want to do that. But short of that there's nothing we can do."

The enemy ship was very close to them now. Samson could sense the thoughts of the enemy crew clearly.

"They're going to fire again, we have to ram them."

"Hold steady," Captain Batista said to his men.

Samson unbuckled his harness and lunged towards the pilot's console. The captain and several other crew members held him back.

"Steady, Oda," the captain said to his pilot. "No ramming."

Heavy plasma cannons at the front of the enemy ship began to glow as Samson struggled with the men who were blocking him from the pilot's seat.

"Ram them! Ram them!"

The enemy's thoughts were violent and absolutely confident. And merciless. They had no interest in capturing the transport. Their orders were to destroy.

Plasma energy arced across space. It seemed to blink slowly into existence as time slowed down again: a huge, wet, silvery arc of energy. But it didn't come from the enemy ship, rather it appeared out of empty space and arced towards it, before the warship's plasma cannons had a chance to fire. When the plasma touched the warship it exploded. What had been life and incredible machine rushed through space as a cloud of dust and debris. Some of it peppered the windows of the Rothschild's transport as it passed.

AMSON AND ALL OF THE crew on the bridge gazed out from the ship's windows and held their breaths in shock. A space fighter materialized in the emptiness from which the plasma barrage had come. It was a Rothschild's ship.

"You folks alright in there?" a voice crackled at them through the damaged com console. "Life support ok?"

Captain Batista and the other men released their grips on Samson and everyone began to return to their senses.

"This is Captain Batista," the captain replied. "Life support seems to be ok. We still have to assess our damage and injuries. Whom do I have the pleasure of addressing?"

"Captain Jack Lemieux, fighter squadron Baron 12, at your service captain."

"Well thank the god for you, captain."

"Is Samson Ford alright?"

"He's right here on the bridge with me. He's fine. It seems like he saved all of our lives. Along with you."

"I'm not sure I can detect it if there is another Bloodworth's ship around us, if it's cloaked," Jack Lemieux said. "I should probably re-cloak myself for the time being."

"Do you sense any more of them around?" Captain Batista asked Samson.

"There are none, none close enough for me to tell, which is probably out to five or ten miles."

"I think we'll be alright for the moment, captain. We have a sort of way to sense them here."

"More than one probably couldn't follow you for long without creating enough disturbance for your sensors to notice it," Jack Lemieux said.

"That makes sense, captain."

Samson eased himself into a seat at the back of the bridge.

His heart was still beating very fast. The man in the space fighter, Jack Lemieux, was a good man. He couldn't believe that Jack had arrived in the exact moment of impending catastrophe. The thought that Stephanie might have been killed bubbled out of Jack's thoughts and overwhelmed Samson for a moment. Jack had been sent here for an urgent reason... to protect them... because something had happened to Stephanie. Samson's stomach rolled. But no, she was ok. Or she had been. Samson squeezed the cross he wore around his neck through his shirt. Thank God.

By THE TIME LISA MADE it to the Rothschild's hospital, Melchit had died. They were keeping his body in a small aluminum coffin, a child's coffin, that was simple and elegant. Lisa held the hand of Melchit's little corpse and cried.

"Thank you, Melchit, for saving me," she said. "I hope that what the people used to believe, that now you're in a better place, is true."

Scamp wrapped an enormous arm around her shoulder and she was surprised to discover that it felt good to be comforted by him.

"He didn't suffer in the end," Scamp said. "I was there, this morning, and he passed peacefully. The virus is fatal for people like him the doctors say. Probably all of the Bloodworth's hybrids are dead. Poor guy. They couldn't even save the Rothschild's executives who were vulnerable to the virus, did you know that? As far as any news or any Rothschild's people know, it has been 100% fatal in people who are vulnerable to it. Genetically engineered people, I mean. Not one person in the Solar System has been saved, of the ones who are susceptible. All of the rest of us are completely unaffected at all. Although, we're carriers."

Lisa sobbed.

"Melchit was a hero," Scamp said.

"He deserved a better place," Lisa said. "Not this hell."

Scamp squeezed her shoulder tighter and Lisa felt like she was sinking into a hole in the ground, something inside of her was sinking, into someplace black and cold.

"Hold me, Scamp."

Scamp embraced her little body, looking down into her bleary, color shifting eyes, and felt anguish at her pain.

"Why Melchit? Why you and me and Melchit? Why did we have to go through it all? Melchit and I. What I went through. And he saved me. And you saved me. And me. And me. And me."

Her voice trembled and choked. Scamp held her tightly and brushed the hair back out of her face.

"It's ok," he said. "You'll get through it. We will. I'll help you. I don't know why life is hard. It's so hard. There isn't any reason why."

"His life... was harder... than ours, Scamp."

"I know it was. I know it was. Here, let's go outside and get some sun. We need some sun, and some fresh air. Let's go outside and get some air. The funeral will be another day, and we can't do anything else here."

They wandered the grounds outside of the hospital and finally ended up sitting on a bench in an elaborate garden courtyard. The sun shone brightly and happily on them, as if it were impertinent, and they were surrounded by blooming flowers and tropical plants. The air smelled something like heaven.

Two security agents stood inconspicuously at the edges of the courtyard, observing them.

"Those guys," Scamp said, gesturing in their direction. "I'm sure they'd leave you alone, but they'll go everywhere that I am. I'm sorry."

"I don't care about them," Lisa said without looking up.

She blinked more tears onto the ground, and Scamp wanted to put his arm around her again but felt that the moment wasn't right. She seemed now not to want to be touched.

"The air smells so good," she said, sniffing.

"Yeah."

"Melchit never got to experience a place like this."

"No."

"Because of Phillipe Bloodworth and all those pieces of shit. And they killed him. That's what was on the data card. They made the virus, Bloodworth's did. They made it and released it on purpose."

"I know they did."

"You know it. How do you know things like that? Maybe you think it, but you couldn't know."

"I knew it," Scamp said, and squeezed Lisa's little knee. "I knew it right away. I don't think I'm an evil person, Lisa. Maybe I'm a bad person, but I don't even think I'm really bad. But I understand evil things. I know how evil thinks. I guess I've been around evil all my life."

He breathed a hoarse breath of air and Lisa did not look up from the ground.

"I didn't used to think that there was good and evil, I didn't believe in those things. Or maybe I did believe in evil. You can feel evil. Maybe I just didn't believe in good. I've done so many bad things, and now I discover this thing called good. And evil I understand, but good not so much. I don't know if it's possible anymore, I think it's too late for me, but I want to be a good man. Like Samson, and Melchit. It seems impossible for me, but I wish I could become better than I am. I wish I could be a man who understands good. But I understand evil, and I can usually see what evil does."

"You're not hopeless, Scamp," Lisa said, and finally looked

up at him with her pretty, sunlit eyes and an expression that was impossible for him to interpret. "I believe you can do it."

Scamp stood and walked out into the garden, moving between the bushes and rows that were near the bench.

"There's going to be a war over this," Lisa said. "A real war. I don't know how to fight in a war, but I want to fight."

He came back with a ruffled, nectar scented, yellow rose in his hand.

"I want to fight too," he said. "And I'm good at fighting. Maybe we can fight in this war together."

"Yeah."

"I think this rose is what Melchit would have picked and given to you, if he was here. So I'll do it for him."

Lisa held the rose up in front of her, turning it slowly and admiring its perfect organic form.

"I think you're right," she said, and cried tears that were ever so slightly less sad.

THE ROTHSCHILD'S TRANSPORT HAD BEEN heavily damaged and it was quickly determined that even a basic repair job, to get the ship underway, would take weeks. Their progress to Magdalena had already been dramatically slowed. Several crew members had suffered significant cuts and bruises, but with luck they had avoided any deaths or major injuries. Samson had superficial cuts on his head and a minor concussion.

"Can you take another passenger on board your fighter?" Captain Batista asked Jack Lemieux over the com while he and Samson sat eating a quick meal in the transport's dining room.

Samson could tell that both men had already made up their minds.

"There's room here for one other person," Jack Lemieux said, "in case of emergencies, and even that's uncomfortable."

"With the delay for the repair and how much we've already

been thrown off course, our arrival at Magdalena will take weeks. And getting Samson to Magdalena as quickly as possible is the highest priority of our mission."

"I understand how important it is, that's why they sent me to escort you."

Samson stirred the protein-enriched porridge in front of him with a silver spoon. They always gave him polished silver utensils to eat with, although he had asked them not to. Crew members all ate with stainless steel. The silver did make the food taste better, he had to admit.

"We can't just leave you here defenseless and practically adrift," Samson said to the captain.

"Our quantum communications channels are jammed and I'm sure theirs are too," Captain Batista said. "They somehow knew where we were before, or what our course was, but they won't know where we are now. And they won't know our status, or the status of the destroyer. Thankgod the Mistress was unharmed in the attack, as Jack has told us, but who knows what else has been happening in the Solar System since he left his base."

"Exactly," Samson said.

"Well, exactly, so we need to get you to Magdalena as quickly as possible. We'll be fine here, we have life support for months, not the weeks that we will need, and you can also send help our way when you have a chance to communicate."

"I want us all to finish this trip safely and together," Samson said. "I don't believe in leaving people behind."

"You're not seeing the bigger picture, Samson," Jack Lemieux said on the crackly com, a dim image of his face moving in stutter bursts on a little holo-projector.

"Mr. Ford," Captain Batista said, rubbing his eyes, "even if we knew that another destroyer was tracking us, and was on its way here, the most important thing that we could do would still be getting you to Magdalena as quickly as possible. I don't know if you know this, or realize it, but I assume you do: every man on the crew of this transport is a Rothschild soldier. We aren't part of the civilian service, we're all military. We all understand our duty, and are proud of it. Even if we have to die to complete our mission, we're going to complete it."

"Nobody has to die," Samson said, "that's the point."

"Nobody's going to die."

"Your mission was already critical, Samson," Jack said, "but it's even more important now. What's happening with the quantum relays being jammed, it's not just Bloodworth's and Rothschild's. Open war is starting and everyone is choosing sides. There's chaos and uncertainty all through the Solar System. So many people have died from the virus, and the natural borns have been devastated. Many people blame Magdalena for that, and Magdalena apparently blames everyone else. You know more of the Magdalena details than I do, but if they explode into the rest of the Solar System like a bomb going off, it will turn a conflagration into an inferno."

"I can only help the people in front of me," Samson said. "Everything else is fantasy."

"Don't be stubborn, man! Jack, you can take him to Magdalena, right? And you can get there fast, right?"

"Absolutely."

"I can't control the Magdalenas like Stephanie thinks I will be able to," Samson said. "I might not be able to do anything at all."

"You're the only one who has any chance."

Their conversation went on. In the end, Samson transferred onto the space fighter with Jack Lemieux and they proceeded to Magdalena. But he insisted before he did so that they bring the transport's remaining laser cannon back on line, which took a full day. Samson worked without rest throughout that day, helping with ship repairs, while Jack Lemieux sat cloaked in his space fighter nearby, ready for any trouble. There was none, but they continued to be unable to establish any contact with the outside world. As Samson crossed the airlock to board the fighter he felt a sense of nostalgia. This was like many of the journeys and adventures he had had with Ben. Small ships, deep in space, entirely dependent upon their own wits and resources. The stars still looked as beautiful and unbounded as then, although a little bit closer. The sun still glowed over them in its distant magnificence. It was all even more a part of him now than before. They were even more a part of him now than before. The new sense that he had grew all the time, the relativity sense, it seemed stronger every hour. He could see the other men's thoughts more and more clearly. And even more than that, the flow of energy through the ships, the flow of the sun's energy through space around them, the shape of gravity. He could sense more than he could understand, and he was understanding more than ever.

CHAPTER 57

STEPHANIE SAT IN HER OFFICE, that had been her father's office, with Simon Okunle, who had been her father's closest friend, and they sipped at luxurious coffee in thin bone china cups that her father had prized. The coffee perked up Stephanie's mind, which was often worn down to a ragged edge. She had taken over her father's work and duties under more difficult circumstances than he had ever faced. But his office had been made for days like this.

"How is young Lisa Maui?" Simon asked.

"Not good. Her friend died, the monkey person who was a servant of Phillipe. At least she's safe, and we can protect her. But it makes me feel terrible not to be able to treat her with more attention, and as a friend."

"I know."

"She doesn't completely understand the significance of the data about Bloodworth's virus weapons program, but she has a good idea. I'm not sure whether we should publicly disclose that she is the source of the information or not, or tell her story to the public. But we probably should."

Simon furrowed his brow, and for the first time in her life Stephanie had the impression that he looked old.

"I don't think we should publish the Ischewitz data," Simon said.

"We should keep it a secret?"

"Mistress, publishing that information could hurt our cause more than help it. Many people who were neutral will be forced to take sides. Bloodworth's will say that the data is fabricated and that we are trying to cover up the fact that the virus was created by Magdalena – because of our political agenda with regard to natural born rights. And regardless of Samson's efforts, Magdalena is likely to launch an indiscriminate and irresponsible war against most of the rest of the Solar System, justifying Bloodworth's vilification of them and earning them many new enemies."

"That's all true."

"Have you had any new communications with Samson's transport?"

Stephanie rubbed a bead of sweat off of her forehead and pushed her hair back away from her face.

"The deep space communications channels are still jammed. We can link intermittently with major stations, but not so far at all with lone ships. So we haven't had any successful communications with them, but under the circumstances that's normal. I dispatched two more escort fighters to find and join them as a precautionary measure."

"That's good."

"I want the Ischewitz data published and announced at a live press conference, and I need you to do that, Simon," Stephanie said.

"You understand my reservations, mum."

"I absolutely do understand them, but I don't agree. You're our best voice to the public and I need you to do this enthusiastically, as something you believe in."

Simon smiled a tired smile.

"You're right, of course, Mistress. Of course I will do my duty, and with enthusiasm. You're right, but I'm an old man to be going to war, mum."

Stephanie gulped down the coffee that was in her cup and it burned her throat.

"I still hope we don't have to go to war, Simon."

"We are already at war, mum."

Simon's wise old eyes peered into her with pain and love, and something like an X-ray vision into her soul, but Stephanie met his gaze without effort.

"We have to let the truth be heard," she said, "by those who are able to hear it. If we cannot stop the war now we never could have."

"That's true, but it will be a bitter symphony."

"You're my best soldier, Simon. Old or not, I depend on you now more than ever."

ALTHOUGH THE SPACE WAS CRAMPED, Jack was excited to have Samson on board with him. Right away he told Samson that he was a personal fan. This normally would have made Samson uncomfortable, but being able to perceive thoughts and emotions in the other man's mind somehow normalized their interactions for him and allowed him to be relaxed.

"I model a lot of my flying after you," Jack said. "My high performance stuff. The way you fly is unique, very creative and unpredictable, with every move specific to the situation at hand. I use that for inspiration."

"Thank you," Samson said.

"I mean, like in combat simulations. I've never done any real combat flying, like dog fights and that, although the way things are going that will probably change soon. But that kind of flying is a lot like some of the flying in your races."

"That's true, it's very similar," Samson said.

"Did you ever fly any space fighters?"

"Not specifically, but I've been chased by them a few times."

"Wow."

"So we're not under cloak anymore?"

"Right. We can only stay cloaked for a little while if we are using the engines. I'm also routing us onto a slightly non-direct path to Triton, so that if anyone did want to intercept us they won't be able to."

"Ok, but you can fire while under cloak?"

"Right. Well this is actually a prototype ship. I mean, production on them has started now, but it was accelerated because of everything that's happening. Lab level, state of the art."

"That's amazing."

"Oh, it's unbelievable. This is all super secret stuff, by the way. Please don't tell anyone else, or tell anyone that I told you."

"No, I won't."

"As far as we know, Rothschild's are the only ones with the technology to fire under cloak, and nobody on the outside knows that we have that capability. It will be a huge tactical surprise when the war gets under way."

"That's good," Samson said. "That's scary technology."

"Yeah."

The space fighter had an extra half-bunk in its cargo bay for Samson to sleep on, a bedroom sized lounge, the cockpit, a small kitchen and dining room, and the pilot's bunk, which was the size of a large closet. Jack tried hard to insist that Samson take over the pilot's bunk, but Samson adamantly refused. They both slept little, anyway, anxious as they were to find an open communications relay and get back into touch with the outside world.

SAMSON SPENT HOURS SITTING IN the fighter's little lounge, staring out of its thick blast-shield windows into the stars. Jack sat in the cockpit, obsessively watching every panel readout and sensor, although all of them were equipped with automated warnings and could be monitored from anywhere on board. Samson found it difficult to be conversational when he could read the other man's mind. Or all but read it.

Bloodworth had tried to kill Stephanie. Samson was certain that it was Bloodworth. Bloodworth had tried to kill his woman, his wife. He had found himself starting to think of her as his wife, although she was not. He decided that he would propose to her, as soon as he possibly could. As soon as he could touch her again. He would get a ring for her on Magdalena. They would get married when he went back to Rothschild, after he proposed. She would say yes, and it would make them both happy. Unless something had changed. The Solar System was changing fast, and becoming more and more dangerous. Stephanie was the most protected person in the Solar System, so she would be safe. Now that the assassination had failed, she would be more careful. And her people would be. Samson pressed the cross that hung around his neck so that it marked his chest. He might be dead before they saw each other again. Even when they talked again, over relay, he wouldn't be able to feel or see her thoughts. He hadn't appreciated before how sweet it was to feel her thoughts. Those new sensations had been so new. Now they were stronger, he could 'see' more clearly, and he wanted to see the mind of the woman he loved.

She might not like it, she hadn't. He had to use the time he had now to control it, to learn to talk to people in a way that let them be comfortable, even when he could see their mind. He had to learn how to make it ok for her when they were together again. He missed Stephanie's body, and often enjoyed thinking about her and about how beautiful and sexy she was. But he didn't feel pent-up. This new sense he had, or whatever had changed in him when he came back physically from the Regatta, it raised his consciousness, or some vital aspect of him, his soul, to a higher level. His physical drives and pleasures, and sensations, good as well as bad, were still the same, but had less power over him now. Less than they ever had.

Samson had never feared death. Had he? Almost not, or his fear of death was different from other people's. Stephanie had survived the assassination, she would be ok. He might easily be dead before they saw each other again. He thought he could even feel it in the stars, death coming for him. He had cheated death, more than once. He had really cheated death, more than anyone probably ever had. Except the Christ? Perhaps. Had the Christ come back from being even more dead than what he had been?

Samson felt the outline of the cross with the tips of his fingers. The man on the cross, who had come back from death, so many centuries ago. If the Christ was even real. If the Christ was more real than The Prophet, who was a fraud.

He didn't mind dying. But he wanted to be with Stephanie again before he died. He wanted to marry her, more than anything. That was suddenly so clear to him. He thought that he could feel her through the stars. Stephanie would marry him and it would make her happy. He had to get a ring for her. She would also send him to his death, if she needed to. If it would save millions, or save Rothschild's, or stop Bloodworth. That might be how he would die – before he could even feel her mind again, before he could ever see it clearly. She would kill him if she had to, although it would crush her. It wouldn't destroy her. Stephanie was strong, stronger than anyone knew. He had felt her strength. Thank God the universe had her. His woman, Stephanie. He didn't mind dying, but he wanted to touch her again, to feel her again, to see her mind.

What was she thinking now? Was she looking at these stars? Did she feel their power and feel close to them? Did she think of him when she saw them, when she saw these stars that they could share?

Samson caught his breath and a single tear rolled down his cheek, he didn't know why. It seemed like the universe was sad.

CHAPTER 58

WHEN THE SPACE FIGHTER FINALLY did pass through a working quantum-relay channel they were already getting close to Triton. Samson and Jack began uploading all of their data and attempting to contact Stephanie's office immediately. The fighter was carrying not only its own logs, but also those from the transport, which had all been transferred before Samson changed ships. The people in Stephanie's office were overjoyed to hear from Samson, and Stephanie's personal attendant and closest friend, Cylla, came on to talk to him, although the live connection was filled with static. Stephanie herself was unable to interrupt an important meeting she was in with a prominent Venutian political leader.

"She wants to talk to you so bad, Samson," Cylla said. "I'm sure this is killing her to be missing you right now."

"It's ok," Samson said. "It's killing me too, but I understand. Maybe this link will stay available for a while and we can talk when she is done."

"Oh, I hope so Samson."

"I'm just glad that I can check in. I'm downloading Stephanie's messages and will be uploading mine after we finish with our ship data logs."

"I can't believe you were attacked! Thankgod Stephanie sent that fighter and you are all ok. I don't know if she could cope with it if something happened to you again, Samson."

"She could cope with it."

"I'm not sure she could. You take care of yourself out there. The Solar System needs you."

"I will."

Jack tried to contact his fighter squadron, but was unable to establish a link. The transport ship they had left behind had not been heard from by anyone since they had left it, but

Cylla and others told them that this was not unusual with all the deep space communications blackouts that had been plaguing the Solar System.

While they were waiting in hope to hear from Stephanie, or from Jack's squadron, they caught up on news from around the Solar System. None of it was good. Samson was able to watch security videos of the assassination attempt on Stephanie, which were horrifying. He also tried to contact Theo in Magdalena again, or anyone in Magdalena, but was unable to do so.

As Samson and Jack watched yet another news roundup, it was interrupted by a live news conference being held by Simon Okunle. Simon's faintly amber eyes were bright and deep, but he looked older and wearier than Samson remembered. He was flanked by diagrams describing the virus, its development, and its connection to the Bloodworth's Corporation.

"These facts are now known:" he said, "this virus, delta-tau, that has caused so many untimely deaths among genetically engineered human beings is the same virus, gametomegavirus, that has swept through the natural born population and caused universal sterility among them. There is one virus, not two, that is a fact. And thanks to this data heroically smuggled out of Bloodworth's corporation by David Ischewitz, the virus's inventor, we also know that it was intentionally engineered to cause mass sterility among our natural born population and thereby bring a historical end to the existence of natural born humans. That is a fact. Phillipe Bloodworth and other senior Bloodworth's executives were active participants in the funding and development of this virus weapons program – fact. Phillipe Bloodworth personally approved the actual disbursement of this virus into human populations throughout the Solar System – fact. The virus was not intended to affect genetically engineered people, but its inventor feared that it could have unforeseen effects when released into the wild and tried desperately to stop that release – fact.

"All of these facts and much more, including incriminating audio and video recordings, can be found in the many terabytes of data that were smuggled to us by David Ischewitz at the cost of his own life and that of his wife. We are making the entirety of that data available, unfiltered, online – you can find it linked in a banner at the top of any Rothschild's web page. The data is available not only online in an organized and indexed form, but also as a raw image of the data card exactly as it came to us from Mr. Ischewitz.

"We are also transporting the original data card, unaltered, to the iner-planetary historical archive on Venus, where it will be appropriately analyzed, conserved, and made available to investigators, historians, and academic researchers now and in the future."

Simon cleared his throat and folded his hands gravely.

"All of this information has also been relayed to prosecutors and law enforcement throughout the Solar System. More than a billion of our people, which is human beings, have been killed by this virus. 50% of the human population has been permanently sterilized against their will. Under these circumstances, and in light of the overwhelming evidence, Rothschild's calls for the immediate arrest of Phillipe Bloodworth, Abujani Chan, Gregory Epitokales, and anyone else found to have been willfully involved in the development, manufacture, and disbursement of this virus, the creation of which violated several inter-planetary laws and treaties, and which has caused, in a matter of weeks, human tragedy to sweep through the Solar System on an unprecedented scale. These men and women, who have killed billions, must be stopped. Action must be immediate.

"And most importantly – people of Earth, people of Mars

and Venus, all human beings throughout the Solar System, from the harsh ice mines of Haumea to the pleasure gardens of the Solarium – the wheels of war must be brought to a stop! More than a billion of us have already been killed by the virus or are dying. The price is already far too high! We must stop this. We must come together, work together, to put a stop to this tragic insanity and look to the future.

"Peace is possible. Reconciliation is not a daydream. Bloodworth's agents tried to assassinate our owner, Stephanie de Rothschild, in the chambers of the United Earth Congressional Assembly, but we at Rothschild's are determined to reconcile. We're determined to have peace. Please help us. On the same banner above all of our websites where you can find the David Ischewitz data, you can also find lists and suggestions of things that you personally can do to help bring a halt to these grinding wheels of war. We must bring a halt to it before war becomes an engine with power of its own.

"Lastly, before I take any questions, I want to speak directly to the natural born people throughout the Solar System. Please hear the words I have for you, believe in them, and stay your hand. Rothschild's is working actively with the authorities on Earth to reverse the damage that has been done to you and to make you whole again. I can't reveal the details yet, but we believe it is possible and that it will happen. We will make a detailed announcement about this in the next week or two, but until then please believe in us, believe in hope, and have patience. All is not lost, and you may live to have children yet. Please have faith in us and hold on for just a little bit longer."

After concluding his presentation, Simon took questions from the assembled journalists, who shouted over each other aggressively.

"Why should we believe you when other experts have traced the source of the virus to the Magdalena cult?" asked a sweaty reporter with an opened collar and loosened tie whose intensely scarlet-orange goatee had become unkempt.

"The link to the Magdalena cult was erroneous," Simon replied calmly. "The Ischewitz data is incontrovertible and includes video and audio recordings from inside Bloodworth's during the release of the virus, including video of Phillipe Bloodworth himself."

"Under whose authority do you think Phillipe Bloodworth should be, or can be, arrested?" asked a tall woman with lightly metallic-pink skin.

"I think that virtually every law enforcement entity in the Solar System has a legitimate claim against him in light of this evidence, but the most obvious candidate to take immediate action would be the United Earth Congressional Assembly itself."

Growing impatient, the mob of reporters in the room began shouting and bickering even more for attention, to the extent that order was lost and Simon appeared increasingly unsettled. After a few minutes of this, Jack's ship lost the relay signal they had been communicating on and the footage of the press conference abruptly cut off.

CHAPTER 59

"I STILL DON'T UNDERSTAND WHAT HAPPENED to Samson," Lisa said.

It was a week after Melchit's funeral and Stephanie had invited Lisa to breakfast unexpectedly early that morning. Lisa had been surprised by the invitation and cancelled an interview with some Martian journalists in order to attend.

"It's hard to explain because no one does understand it," Stephanie said. "The relativity effect somehow shifted his matter into an altered phase, and eventually he shifted back to normal. Our scientists are mystified by it."

"That's crazy. Well, I'm glad he's ok."

Lisa picked up a crumbly little raisin and brown sugar cookie from the tray on the table and set it on her plate. She found it difficult to talk to Stephanie now, although she was trying hard to think of things to say. Before, Stephanie had just been a nice woman who was often at the races. Now that Lisa had a sense of Stephanie's power it made her tense. Stephanie was like Phillipe Bloodworth in a way. It seemed impossible for someone to exercise that much power and still be a nice person. She didn't know why. And she still thought Stephanie was a nice person. She swallowed a bite of the cookie while hardly tasting it.

"I read the whole story of your abduction in *The New Yorker*," Stephanie said. "You've been very heroic."

"It's not heroic. It just happened to me. Melchit was heroic. It was all him. And Scamp too. God, I can't think about it."

"I'm sorry."

"I can't believe you find time to read *The New Yorker*."

"I read very fast."

"My grandfather is like that. Sometimes he reads three or four books a day. Thank you so much for helping my grandparents to come here. They left today on one of the big Rothschild transports."

"Well, you can't go there," Stephanie said. "Will your grandparents return to Earth?"

"I don't know. We'll have to find out how long they can stay. We might try to apply for permanent residency."

"They can stay as long as they want."

"Thank you."

Stephanie lifted a cup of tea delicately to her lips and Lisa couldn't help thinking that she looked regal. She was surprised she hadn't noticed it before.

"Will there be a war?"

"I hope not. We have a plan to try to prevent it. But war is very hard to stop now."

Lisa tried to pick up another one of the cookies, but it crumbled in her fingers and fell back onto the tray.

"You can help us," Stephanie said. "By advocating for peace and for people to be patient. You have a voice, that's one of the reasons that you were targeted by Bloodworth. And if you advocate for our proposal, for this plan we have – we'll be announcing it soon – if you advocate for that when we announce it, that will help a lot."

"You can't tell me about it?"

"No. I'm sorry."

"But you can't stop Bloodworth's without a war. If you join with them that isn't something I can support."

"We think we can stop them. We hope we can. If there are enough rational actors left in the Solar System, and especially on Earth. They've killed 10% of the human population, indiscriminately. Everyone has someone that they lost."

"Including them."

"Exactly."

KENICHI SAT ON THE BANKS of a large body of water on Roth-schild called the Sea of Harmony. The sound of the waves on the pebbles of the beach below him had a rich harmonic quality, something that wasn't quite white noise and wasn't quite music. It was wonderful.

The sun was warm on the backs of his hands and his face and he wished he had worn a lighter shirt. He rolled his sleeves up. A perfect breeze was blowing off the water, and it too echoed resonantly as it passed. But not unnaturally. He often came here to think.

People on bicycles rode by occasionally on the path behind him and sailboats and yachts drifted in the distance on the water. A family with children walked past him and down to the beach. They found a sandy spot and laid out a big picnic blanket. The children splashed in the waves.

He thought for a moment of his own childhood. It had been nothing but work. There was no play. If he hadn't mastered advanced mathematics by age 12 his father would have killed him. Study, study, study, invent, invent, invent. His sister had killed herself at age 11, but their father had left the pills by her bedside and let her know that she was a failure and what a deep disappointment she was to the family. They would be better off without her, he told her, and the pills would cause no pain. Invent, invent, invent. Not everyone could create new things, in fact very few people could. His sister couldn't. She had won many childhood awards, but wasn't a genius. And that was that. He was glad that some children got to play at the beach.

Where was his sister now, or his father? He was sure that his father and mother were together. He hoped they were in hell, but of course he didn't believe in hell. They were all just dead was what he used to think. And he would enjoy life as much as he could before he became dead too. Although he

405

was always getting in the way of his own enjoyment of life. But that's just how it was.

And it turned out that dead wasn't really dead. Or that's what he came here to think about.

What had happened to Samson? Dr. Nguyen could only process it on a technical level. He was only technical! He didn't see the deep questions. Yes, it was amazing that Samson had been preserved, that he had been re-animated, that his body had in some sense 'changed phase'. That was all fascinating, but also beside the point. His consciousness had gone – somewhere else. It had a pattern like brain waves, they had been able to interact with it, but it had not been a function of the brain! The brain, like all of Samson's corporeal self, had been – celestial goo? Or ether? Something. It wasn't synapses and neuro-transmitters, it wasn't bio-chemical processes, it wasn't brain. It wasn't even cells. It wasn't even matter. It wasn't even reality.

What was it? It had to be reality, didn't it? By definition it couldn't be anything else. Right?

Where had Samson been? He was somewhere. What had he been? He was something. He had occupied a space between this reality and some other reality. He had been a small tear in the fabric of the universe. Or so it seemed. That wasn't the fabric that they thought the universe was made of. Now everything was up for grabs.

Was his sister also, somewhere? Was the woman he had loved somewhere, the one Phillipe Bloodworth had killed? Could he meet them again, somehow? Had Samson been dead? And if he hadn't been dead, what had he been?

Kenichi didn't like to think about death. It wasn't worth thinking about. But now it was. Hadn't it been the most important thing all along? It had been the most horrible thing, so he had thought. Everything was different now. The universe, the strange aspects of fundamental physics, the strange qualities of life. It was all different in this light. The universe was bigger and more open than he had thought. And he realized that he knew so little, and that a lot of his questions had been wrong. What was it to build a cutting edge racer, to harness quantum phenomena to useful work, to invent new technologies and processes? He could see himself now as an ant, piling up bits of dirt and digging out others, rolling tiny pebbles around, believing its work was important and profound. Piling up bits of dirt and tiny pebbles. And missing everything. Not having any idea what the dirt and the pebbles were.

He wondered if his sister was out there somewhere. Somewhere past the little bits of dirt and pebbles. She had protected him from their father more than once. And she was gone, dead. Nothing. Was it like that, or had he simply been blind? Seeing nothing beyond the specks of dirt and pebbles. Being proud of himself. He was one of the most productive ants. He was one of the best at building the tunnel walls and rolling the little pebbles out of the ant farm.

He could build a racer and take it out past the sun, accelerating until he was crushed by the relativity effect, and maybe he could go where Samson had gone. But he didn't think so. What had happened to Samson hadn't happened to anyone else who experienced the relativity effect. Almost all of them had died. The ones who hadn't died had described mainly physical symptoms. Headaches, vertigo, nausea, DNA mutation, cancers, mitochondrial aberrations. What happened to Samson had only happened to Samson. Everything had lined up perfectly for him. Everything always did line up perfectly for him. Didn't that also beg a question?

Synchronicity was what early psychologist Carl Jung had called it. And Samson himself believed in the god.

Well in an expanded universe, who knows?

He could take a racer, give it some custom upgrades, blaze

it out past the sun, and maybe he would die and maybe he wouldn't go where Samson went, but he might go somewhere. Or, he could just gulp down a bottle of pills. And maybe that would take him where his sister was. Or where the woman he had loved was. Samson's alternate reality had been profoundly affected by love. Which must be something more than bio-chemical reactions.

But he might go to where his father was. 'Yakuza Ken' they used to call him. They didn't call his father that, they celebrated his father, but his father was worse. He might go where his father was, if his father was somewhere. His sister had been a good person, but he himself wasn't a good man.

Kenichi watched the children playing and was glad that some children got to play at the beach. Most children did, on this world, and in this Solar System. Bicyclists rode by behind him. The wind and the waves washed across his body in their gently inorganic resonance. And he found, as he expected, that he could visualize equations, and that theorems ran through his head, and although some of them were quickly discarded others stayed for a while as he mused. Was it all just pebbles and sand?

He was a better person now than he had been. And his sister had loved him. She said so. Was that anything? Was she somewhere? Did she still know him? Where Samson had been he didn't know Stephanie. Or even himself. Was it all just pebbles and sand?

Kenichi smiled. The children on the beach were laughing and their parents were laughing. They were happy. The warm sun felt good on his skin. Equations and theorems percolated through his head. Some of them were quickly discarded, as always, and some of them stayed a while to play.

LISA WALKED DOWN A HALLWAY near Stephanie's office thinking

about Stephanie and their meeting. Stephanie wanted her help. Lisa didn't think of herself as a person important enough to help Stephanie. She wondered what the Rothschild's plan was, and still feared that it was some sort of unacceptable compromise with Bloodworth's. She wouldn't compromise, not now.

She opened the door to an empty conference room that Stephanie had directed her to and stepped inside.

"Well if the ships aren't in place then this attack will fail!" hissed a man in the corner of the room into his card.

The man started and dropped the card onto the table when he noticed Lisa. His face turned red and Lisa realized that he was one of the aides she had seen leaving Stephanie's office earlier. Even as this realization struck her the man regained his composure and smiled.

"I'm sorry," Lisa said, turning back towards the door. "Stephanie thought this room would be empty."

"Don't leave," the man said as he picked back up his card. "It's no problem, I'm just finishing up. One second. Gosh you startled me!"

"Abdul?" the man said into the card while holding up an index finger to Lisa. "Yes, I'm sorry, I dropped my card. But I have a meeting I'm already late for, so we'll have to talk more about this tomorrow. Yes. Yes. That's right. That's perfect, thank you. Ok. Yes, then. Goodbye."

He stood up and walked toward the doorway where Lisa was standing uncertainly.

"Crazy days," he said. "These are crazy, crazy days."

"I'm sorry," Lisa said again. "I didn't mean to interrupt."

"Not at all. Not at all. This is a nice quiet room to have a conversation in, but normally nobody ever comes in here. I'm sure that's why the Mistress suggested it to you. Well it's very unlikely that there will be anyone else, so I will leave it to you."

"Ok."

The man left and Lisa closed the door behind him. Then she stood watching the door for a minute or two before remembering that she had come here to conference call an interview with a journalist on Mercury. She took her card out of her pocket to make the call. But she couldn't stop thinking about what Stephanie's aide had been saying when she burst in. Was Rothschild's launching an attack somewhere? After a few minutes' hesitation, Lisa put her card back in her pocket and left the room. Somehow, she didn't feel safe there. The interview would wait.

"WE'RE TRYING TO CONTACT MAGDALENA to warn them," Simon Okunle said, while standing tensely in front of Stephanie's huge desk. He was too upset to sit down. Beside him sat Stephanie's war minister, General Kucic.

"Shit! And no one has been able to get through to Samson?"

"No, mum."

"Shit. And he'll be getting there soon."

"This could completely wipe them out, Mistress. It might even damage the atmosphere enough to destroy all of Triton."

"The Magdalenas only have second generation counter-reaction devices," General Kucic said, leaning forward to rest a hand on the edge of Stephanie's desk. His grey eyes had gold flecks in them that seemed to glint with his emotions. "As you know, Bloodworth's developed technology to defeat those devices ten years ago. The rest of us have quietly communicated that information and developed third generation devices to maintain the security of the Solar System. But because the Magdalenas are so isolated, it is believed that they have never been aware of the new threat and the need for stronger protections."

"I want you to tell them everything we know about the threat, and also send them the necessary technical information to manufacture third generation devices. Have people working on every possible communications channel to get through to them, around the clock."

"Of course, mum. But the attack could come at any time. Our intelligence indicates that the Bloodworth's warheads are already placed in Magdalena, or are being moved into place as we speak."

"I understand that," Stephanie said, "but all we can do is all we can do. Unless you can think of something else?"

"No, mum."

"Then we do what we can and hope for the best. I want Samson's ship warned away from the planet the instant we establish any communication with him."

"Of course, mum."

"The war has begun," said Simon. "We can't keep holding our hand."

"We won't take military action until Alexander Grumiaux gives his speech and the UECA votes."

"But Mistress," General Kucic said, "Bloodworth's are moving now. We don't know everything that they will do, but we know it won't only be an assault on Magdalena. They will also strike at us and our allies in concert, across the Solar System. Of course it's better to avoid a fight, but when a fight is inevitable it is a huge advantage to strike the first blow. Especially in a fight to the death."

"Alexander Grumiaux's speech is only eight hours away," Stephanie said. "Then they will have the vote immediately. It could stave off the war and save billions of lives. So we have to give it a chance to succeed."

"Yes, mum."

"Maintain our defensive posture and prepare our pre-emptive strike to begin in 12 hours if things at the Assembly do not proceed as planned."

411

"Yes, mum."

Stephanie stood up from her desk.

"Thank you, gentlemen. Update me immediately about anything that changes."

"Yes, mum."

As the two men left her office, Stephanie flexed her hands to keep them from shaking. Samson could be landing any time now on a planet that was about to be wiped out by nuclear weapons. Everyone in Magdalena City would die, which was exactly where he would be. She reached out and tripped a mechanism that sealed the office door. He would die. Her head spun and she felt sweat running down her neck and arm. She consciously slowed her breaths.

Every decision was so heavy now. Every choice affected so much, so directly. The responsibility was crushing. But she could show no weakness. And she would not. Even if Samson died.

She had to seal Samson away in her mind. To stop this. If she thought of him, with any emotion at all, it overwhelmed her. She had to put all of her emotions about him away. And not only Samson. To seal away everything, all of it. She had been in denial, resisting fate, she had allowed herself to be weak.

It was herself that she must seal away, it was Stephanie, her personal self. Everything that was personally her didn't matter. Which was hard. The only thing in front of her, the only thing affecting her, her only vision and goal, must be the war and the individual decisions that would each affect the lives of millions or billions of people. She must become that responsibility. She owed humanity that. Or not even owed. It was her role in life. It was the inevitable benevolence of power.

Stephanie sat back down and unsealed the door to her office. Her eyes saw everything clearly. Her body was relaxed. She took a sip of coffee from the china cup in front of her.

"Send the Nike Vice President in."

CHAPTER 60

LISA WAS STILL STAYING AT the security compound where she and Scamp had been housed when they first came to Rothschild Palace, or just 'Rothschild' as the people here called the little planet. She had been offered other accommodations, luxurious ones, but found it comforting to stay with Scamp. He was required to live here until Rothschild's decided what they wanted to do with him, or until he left the planet. It was only Lisa's status as a friend of Stephanie that protected him from immediate expulsion and afforded him a small degree of free movement and liberty. Scamp didn't mind. He seemed like a new person, or at least a remade one. He was happy, and grateful. He wanted to wait on Rothschild at least until Samson returned, so that he could talk to Samson one more time, and bury that ghost.

"He said, 'we can't attack unless the ships are in place!'," Lisa told Scamp, after returning from her breakfast with Stephanie. "Or something like that. And when I came in he freaked out and dropped his card. Like he was shocked or something. It was really weird. I don't want to say he seemed guilty, but – he seemed guilty. Then he was really nice to me, but it gave me the creeps."

Scamp frowned at her. She sat down on a couch in their main room.

"He was one of Stephanie's aides?"

"I think so. I saw him leaving her office when I went in. He works with her in one way or another."

"Then we need to pack our things," Scamp said decisively, and immediately went to the closet to get his backpack. It was a regular backpack, not like the giant one he had used for their escape.

"What?"

"There's going to be a battle. We're going to have to fight."

413

"No, here? No, it's not that big of a deal. I might have even misunderstood what he said."

"You didn't misunderstand. Is there any way you can contact Stephanie about this?"

"I don't think so. I mean, I can send her a message, but it will probably be one of her aides that reads it and she might never see it personally. She gets way more messages than she would ever have time to read, and that's from people that she actually knows."

Scamp was stuffing what few possessions he had into the backpack.

"Maybe we can relay a message through her security," he said. "We have to at least try."

"I don't think it's that big of a deal," Lisa said. "You're overreacting."

But her stomach had been clenched into a knot since she encountered the man in the conference room. She thought about getting her own bag.

"I've been thinking about this," Scamp said. "Bloodworth's tried to assassinate Stephanie. Everyone knows it was them. I'm sure that Stephanie's people know it. And what is it when an organization tries to assassinate your leader? That's more than a declaration of war, it's an act of war. They wouldn't do something like that unless they were committed to finishing the job. And they wouldn't make a commitment like that unless they believed they had a way to accomplish it. Why is Rothschild's security so high? Yes, Stephanie was attacked, but even considering that, the security around this planet is insanely tight. They are expecting more from Bloodworth's too, they've taken a wartime posture. But apparently they have no idea what Bloodworth's has up its sleeve."

"This is the safest place in the Solar System," Lisa said.

"Not anymore. Bloodworth's must be planning an attack

on this planet. Even Rothschild's themselves suspect it. Your aide that you saw, he's their man on the inside. They probably have a lot of agents that have infiltrated here. But if he works with Stephanie directly, and even now, that means he is in a position of high security clearance here. That means he's in a position to do a lot of harm."

"You think they're going to attack Stephanie again? You're leaping to conclusions, Scamp."

"Maybe I am, but we need to be ready to leave. If they attack the planet it will be hell unleashed. And you need to do whatever you can to warn Stephanie about what you saw. Shit, we might not even be safe here now. If that's a Bloodworth's agent he might decide that they need to eliminate you."

"Scamp, stop."

"I'll protect you. Whatever's going to happen will happen very soon. You said you wanted to fight. It looks like we're going to have to."

Scamp pulled Lisa's backpack out of the closet and held it out towards her, but she didn't get up and waved it away with her hand. He set it down against the wall. She thought that he must be unbalanced or crazy. He was jumping to conclusions, exaggerating things. Maybe he was someone who needed to have constant excitement in his life. Rothschild being attacked directly, the planet – that couldn't possibly happen. They would literally see any attack coming from 100,000 miles away.

She didn't get up. But her stomach would not unknot.

AT THE SAME TIME LISA was talking to Scamp on Rothschild, Theo Ford was being released back to his family. And at the same time as that, elsewhere in Magdalena City, the manager of a cargo hangar, a man named Tom, stood staring at a huge tanker that had arrived the day before from Neo Vega. He had a funny feeling about it, but couldn't say exactly why. He rubbed his chin. The pilot who had brought the ship in was not the usual tanker pilot. There was something different about him, like he didn't belong in Magdalena at all. It was hard for Tom say exactly why. He scratched his head. The man's eyes were too bright. That's what it was. He wasn't a natural born.

Tom went back to his office to double check all of the information he had about the tanker and its pilot, and to review its arrival and departure logs. There wasn't anything unusual there. The tanker traveled between Neo Vega and Magdalena City once a month, supplying the Magdalenas with fuel oil that was needed on their farms and that they had difficulty producing on their own. It had arrived on schedule, as normal, and would be drained of its cargo the next day, then it would fly back to Neo Vega again. Nothing unusual. Tom was a short, round man with with grey hair and blue eyes, whose face turned bright red whenever he felt a strong emotion. He rubbed his chin again.

"Did you notice anything weird about that oil tanker when they came in yesterday?" he asked his assistant manager, Kevin, who handled much of the hangar's day-to-day work. "The big one, over in slot 36."

"I didn't notice anything in particular."

Kevin, a thin, middle-aged man with a receding hairline, sat at a desk with a big computer monitor on top of it, checking and reconciling the morning's records.

"There's something funny," Tom said. "The tanker pilot, did you notice him? I saw him yesterday before he left."

"I talked to him."

"And?"

"He didn't do anything weird, if that's what you mean."

"But he's not the same pilot that we usually get, is he?" asked Tom, turning red.

"No, I guess he's not. I didn't think about it."

416

"Dial up the hangar company in Neo Vega, see if they got a new pilot recently. Ask what happened to the old pilot. Just tell them it's a security check, or you are a friend of the old pilot or something."

"Ok boss."

Tom scratched his head again. It was probably nothing. It wasn't even that strange to have a different pilot. But something was off. The man's eyes had definitely been too bright.

C H A P T E R 61

ALEXANDER GRUMIAUX SLAPPED THE NAKED young woman beside him on the butt and got out of bed. She groaned sleepily, but barely shifted. He pulled on some underwear and took a handful of pills with Seltzer water while staring into one of the bedroom's big mirrors.

"I want some more drugs," the girl croaked thickly as he began to walk out of the room.

"Well, take more. Take more. Do what you want."

He took a warm steam shower, infused with the scent of musk and roses, in a big granite room with J.S. Bach playing in the background. He cleaned his body slowly, immaculately. Today was a historic day and he would be the one making history. He loved making history.

He stood in front of the bathroom mirror and admired himself as he dried. His body was sleek and muscular, a perfect body. And he was a perfect man. A historic man. And today he would be a hero. He inspected his charming smile in the mirror out of habit, double checking that it was just so, and then shifted to the deeper, more serious face that he would need during his speech. It was good.

He spent the next two hours alone in front of the mirror, practicing his speech again and again. It had to be perfect. It had to be historic – a speech that would sway hearts and minds both today and in the future.

Of course, the speech didn't really matter. He already had secured the votes he needed – cajoling, bullying, bribing, twisting arms. Even Rahima would vote with him and against Bloodworth. Although she knew it might mean her death. Phillipe Bloodworth would take that betrayal as personal. But Phillipe would be either dead or in prison himself soon, or hunted, and his organization dismantled. There would be a fire sale and everyone with enough capital to purchase the major assets would prosper greatly. He estimated that he himself would double his net worth, which was already very large.

"The Ischewitz data is a fact," he said to the mirror. "It has been validated and confirmed by every independent source. The Bloodworth's Corporation story has been validated by no independent source and contradicted by all of them.

"Bloodworth's have good reason to lie. They have created an illegal weaponized virus and intentionally seeded it throughout the Solar System, killing billions. We have had friends die, sons and daughters, mothers and fathers – all of us have lost someone dear. What tragedy!

"I am introducing special legislation now, as authorized by the Emergency Means and Measures Amendment of 2151, to mobilize our armed services to effectuate the immediate arrest of Phillipe Bloodworth and the other Bloodworth's executives known to have been involved in the Bloodworth's virus plot. This legislation will also instruct our justice department to create a special tribunal to further investigate the creation and production of the virus, to identify everyone who was knowingly involved in that creation and production, and to prosecute them fully under Earth and inter-planetary law. These people must pay for their crime!

"The legislation will also order the immediate dissolution of Bloodworth's Corporation and organize a special independent board to oversee that dissolution. The tragedy that has happened to humanity in this year must never be allowed to happen again.

"Now, since our session is broadcasting and so many people throughout the Solar System are listening, I want to speak directly to employees of Bloodworth's Corporation. You, decent hard working people of Bloodworth's, I know that you are victims of Phillipe Bloodworth's horrible crimes as much as any of us are. All of you have lost friends and loved ones too. Rest assured, we are not going to victimize you again. Ladies and gentlemen, do not be afraid. Bloodworth's Corporation will go away, but your companies and your jobs will not disappear. The dissolution will be like a corporate bankruptcy – your businesses will continue, only the ownership and organization of your companies will change. We will bring the men and women who harmed you to justice, and open up the road before you to a better and brighter future.

"There is one final section of this legislation that I have saved talking about for last, because it is a ray of sunshine, a blessed rainbow in the storm of tragedy and conflict that necessitates these emergency measures. With regard to the natural born human beings throughout the Solar System who have been grievously wounded, who suffer and despair – this legislation removes, for a period of ten years, the requirement of basic genetic enhancements in all gene woven embryos produced on Earth. In conjunction with the change to these regulations, the legislation will also seize Bloodworth's well known gene weaving and incubation companies under imminent domain and transfer ownership of them to the Rothschild's Corporation.

"Bear with me! Here is the rainbow: I have spoken with Stephanie de Rothschild today, and Rothschild's Corporation is making a formal commitment, contingent upon the passage of this special legislation, to provide free gene weaving and incubation services to ALL natural born people in the Solar System whose fertility has been destroyed by the Bloodworth's virus. Every such natural born person in the Solar System will be able to have children again, up to two per couple, for no cost. You may choose to have basic genetic enhancements for your children or to forego them completely and have healthy children that are purely genetically natural, just like a naturally born child. Rothschild's will also allow couples to add-on extended genetic enhancements for their children, if they so desire, at regular commercial rates. Not only will this make our natural born population whole again, not only will it heal them, it also is a historic opportunity to bridge the divide between the economic underclass and overclass that has come to characterize our Solar System. This is a historic good that can be gleaned from such tragedy, solving a problem that seemed previously impossible to solve.

"Ladies and gentlemen, this action voluntarily being undertaken by the Rothschild's Corporation is a charitable commitment of many, many trillions of credits. It is also a miraculous and unexpected salve for the open wounds and agony that have so afflicted the Solar System in recent months. Rothschild's Corporation will be holding a press conference tomorrow morning, after the special legislation is passed, to make a public announcement of this formal commitment that they have undertaken, and will provide full details of the plan and answer questions at that time. But for now, please join me in giving them a round of applause. This is a miracle. I don't know how they can afford to do it, but Stephanie de Rothschild has assured me that they can. So please stand up with me to honor them. I have tears in my eyes. That's right. That's right. They deserve it."

He clapped his hands in the mirror before continuing with his speech. He still didn't know how Rothschild's could afford to do what they were proposing to do. It would use up virtually all of their known liquidity and almost certainly put them into debt. But Stephanie de Rothschild had promised him that they could and would. And Simon Okunle had told him that as well, which meant more. Simon Okunle was always true to his word.

TOM, THE CARGO FACILITY MANAGER in Magdalena City, blinked at the screen in front of him.

"We got trouble here," he said to Kevin, the assistant manager. "Did you find out anything about that new tanker pilot?"

"The company don't know anything about it," the assistant manager said. "The girl I talked to thought it was still the same pilot as always, but she didn't know for sure. The guy who would know doesn't come back until Monday."

"It says here," Tom said, pointing at his screen, "that there is an imminent attack threat to Magdalena and to be on the lookout for any suspicious vehicles, objects, or people who may not belong here. This is an urgent warning going out to everyone in Magdalena, on every card and every public channel."

"Is that for real?" Kevin slurped at his drink.

"Yes it's real, don't you know that war is coming? Just check your card. Shit. Get on the phone to security services right away and tell them about our tanker pilot."

"Right."

Kevin stared at his card, reading the emergency warning message.

"Well do it right now!"

"Right boss. I'm on it."

Tom stood up and crossed himself with his big, fat arms.

"I'm going to go take a closer look at this tanker."

Tom walked out to the hangar warehouse, switched on a big floating rack of tools and towed it out across the expanse of concrete and tarmac, toward the fuel tanker. Neptune's enormous solar reflectors were focused right on them at this hour and hot wind blew over the large field of ships, most of which were parked but a few of which were taking off or landing, moving hazily in the air.

When he got to the tanker, he walked in a careful circle

around its base. It was a big tanker, with a full cabin that would make it suitable for even inter-planetary jobs. It wasn't used for that, though. Just hops up into space to fill up when the mega-tankers were orbiting and little hops back and forth between Magdalena and Neo Vega. The ship looked normal as far as he could see.

He walked the perimeter of the ship again. Could it be a bomb? Should he leave? The imminent threat warning weighed on his mind, its message had seemed desperate. And he couldn't stop thinking about the tanker pilot he had seen, the man with the engineered eyes. How big of a bomb could someone plant in a tanker? He crawled along the ground examining some of the tanker's underside. It left his knees throbbing, but he didn't find anything.

A bomb the size of a tanker, if this tanker was a bomb, would blow up their whole facility and maybe hundreds of yards around it.

He called back to the office on his card.

"What did security say?"

"They said they'll send someone as soon as they can. They said try to get a picture of the pilot, or detain him if we see him. Or follow him. They're swamped."

"Ok. Keep me posted if they get here."

The pilot was long gone, Tom felt pretty sure of that. The more he thought about the man, the more suspicious the man seemed. But why would someone want to blow up the ship yard? It wouldn't serve much strategic purpose. You could land ships anywhere. Maybe there was an important ship in the yard. Or maybe the tanker wasn't a bomb, but had been converted into some kind of warship. A Trojan horse.

Or maybe it was just a tanker. He read the imminent threat warning again on his card. It seemed like the kind of warning you would get if the whole planet was in danger, like an imminent comet impact or something like that. It seemed desperate.

He climbed up the metal steps to the tanker's cabin door and rang its calling buzzer. Then he pounded very loudly on the door. After no response he tried to open the door, but it was locked and sealed. Growing impatient, he got a large force wrench from the tool rack and jimmied open the door. The steel of the bolts crunched and ground. Tools were good.

The inside of the tanker's cabin looked normal, except that it was too clean. There were no signs of it being lived in or of the pilot's personal effects. The bunk was empty and untouched. Well, the ship only made short trips anyway, that didn't mean anything. Maybe the pilot was fastidious. But the pilot did usually have to stay for a day or two when the ship came to Magdalena. And he wasn't authorized to roam the town. Although, who knows where the pilot had gone.

The manager sat down in the pilot seat of the tanker's cockpit. He flicked on the ship's computer screen. It was displaying a countdown timer that had 52 minutes left. 52 minutes, the seconds were counting down, 51 minutes. Tom's blood froze.

"Oh shit. Oh shit."

Why would there be a countdown timer? Was it a countdown to an attack? A detonation countdown? It couldn't be good, could it? Could it just be something innocent that the pilot was timing? Maybe he had meant to be back already and it was a reminder to him to call his girl.

Tom looked at the computer's active applications and saw that it was running Bloodworth's news feeds.

"Oh shit. Oh shit."

The countdown timer was down to 50 minutes. He called Kevin again.

"Is the security service here yet?"

"I haven't seen or heard anything from them. Did you find something new, boss? You want me to call them again?"

"No. I don't know. I don't know. I don't think it can wait."

He hung up the call.

There was an imminent threat. There was a suspicious tanker with a suspicious pilot. There was a countdown timer that was now down to 47 minutes. He had to find out what the tanker was carrying – if it was really fuel.

He went back out to the big floating tool rack and selected a large impact driver with a hard diamond bit. It was a driver that could easily punch holes in hardened steel. He walked a few dozen yards down the length of the tanker, away from the cabin, and hefted the driver up into position against the tanker's side. Even with its small pseudo-GCUs and inertial dampers the impact driver was unwieldy.

If he punched a hole in the tanker wall some of the fuel should spray out. But only some. Not much. All tankers in this class were required to be outfitted with an emergency force-shielding mechanism to contain the fuel and prevent disaster in the case of accidents or leaks. The tanker should reseal itself almost instantly – if it was full of fuel. And if the emergency sealing mechanism worked. But it should work.

He pulled the trigger on the impact driver and it began hammering through the thick tanker walls. A spark popped and fizzed against the steel of the ship's hull. What about sparks? Shit! He was too worked up. He set the impact driver down and pulled on a big, welding apron with arm sleeves and a welding mask. The fuel oil was formulated to be difficult to ignite, to prevent accidents, but if some of it hit a spark when it sprayed out, and if he was unlucky, it could light up and burn him like a human candle. The force shield mechanism would keep the whole tanker from going up. Assuming it worked. But, he didn't think there was going to

425

be any fuel. If there was, hopefully the welding gear would catch most of it. He picked the impact driver back up and resumed work. The machine kicked back at him, thump thump thump, with a machine-gun tempo and he leaned heavily into it with his chest, bruising himself. The rattle of diamond impacting metal was deafening. After about a minute the impact driver bit punched clean through the tanker wall. No fuel sprayed out.

Tom rested the impact driver on the ground and peered into the hole. It was dark. There was no hint of any fuel. He pressed two fingers as deep as he could into the hole, which was hot and burnt his hand – there was no seal. Grabbing a light from the tool rack, he peered into the hole again. No fuel was inside this tanker. He could see wires and what looked like some kind of machine.

He looked at the clock on his card – 12 more minutes had gone by, the timer had only 35 minutes left. He dialed his assistant manager, Kevin, again, hand tingling and shaking so badly that it was hard to press the keys on his card.

"Get security services here right away," Tom said. "There isn't any fuel in this tanker. I think it's some kind of bomb!"

"Boss, did you see the change to the warning bulletin? They think the threat is some kind of nuclear weapons that have been smuggled into the city!"

"Call them right now!"

Tom flicked the card off and grabbed the largest force wrench on the rack. His hands were steady again now. He used the wrench to tear the hole open further where the metal of the tanker body had cracked around it. With a strength and speed his body had never before had, he peeled back the thick steel of the tanker wall until there was a hole big enough to peer inside.

What he saw inside the tanker was a huge, segmented machine that seemed to fill the entire ship. The machine was composed of large, sealed, ball shaped structures in cubic frames. These structures were all joined and connected in a chain that appeared to run up and down the tanker's length. Each of the big, ball shaped segments was stamped "Bloodworth's".

"Oh shit oh shit oh shit oh shit."

The manager looked at the clock on his card again. The countdown timer would have about 30 minutes left. He could hear emergency sirens of security services in the distance. He called Kevin again, while running back into the tanker's cabin.

"This is one of those nukes, Kevin."

"What?"

"And it's on some kind of countdown timer with only 30 minutes left."

"I don't understand boss–"

The sound of the big tanker's engines starting up interrupted the conversation before fading into a dull background roar. Nearby emergency sirens droned louder and louder.

"I'm taking her up into space!" Tom said. "Start calling every cargo facility, hangar, ship bay and tell them what we have here. You have to call them fast! The other nukes are probably the same, on similar ships. They have to pilot them out to space right away!"

He looked at the countdown timer on the tanker's computer as the huge ship began rising. 29 minutes!

Back at the offices of the sprawling cargo facility, security services had finally arrived. Kevin was already connecting to a large cargo facility on the other side of the city. He put the call on hold and told the security services what was happening as quickly as he could. Then they all started making calls, and through the window behind them the big fuel tanker began to disappear in the sky. In less than ten minutes, the imminent threat messages being pushed out to all of Magdalena were updated to roughly describe the situation with the tanker, and instructed employees of all ship hangars, ports, and cargo yards to seize any similar suspicious ships and pilot them into space. Within ten minutes after that, five more large suspicious ships began to rise in the sky around Magdalena. And within five minutes of that there were three more.

As he rose up into space, Tom spoke through the ship's com to Magdalena authorities.

"There's some kind of big device filling up the tanker, not fuel."

"What does the device look like, Tom?"

"Ok, it's these big sealed balls, they look like chambers—"

"How big are the balls?"

"Maybe 10 yards in diameter. And they're held in sort of cubic frames, the frames are metal. And the balls are all connected together – it looked like they filled the whole ship. But I could only see a part of the inside of the ship, ok? I couldn't see the whole thing."

"Were there any hazard signs, or graphics that might give us a clearer idea what the device is?"

"The only thing I noticed was that the balls were all stamped 'Bloodworth's', like a big machine stamp, pressed into the metal."

"So where are you taking the ship?"

"Look, I'm not a pilot. All I can do is kind of steer her out into space. I figured, get her as far away from Triton as possible."

"That's good, Tom. That's what we're telling all the other ships to do, too."

"When I broke into the cabin and switched on the ship's monitor, the countdown timer was just there on the screen, already running. Now there's not very much time left."

"We're trying to locate the pilot who brought the ship in.

I want you to know that we all admire you, Tom; everyone here. You're a very courageous man."

"Lord help us," Tom said. "It seems bad, doesn't it?"

"It seems bad."

SCAMP AND LISA WERE AWOKEN by explosions in the middle of the night. Scamp was on his feet instantly and banged on Lisa's bedroom door.

"It's happening!" he said. "Get dressed, Lisa, we have to go."

Lisa got out of bed and started to put on a robe. More explosions filled the air, some of them far away and some close enough to shake the building they were in. She switched to putting on proper clothes, and got dressed as quickly as she could. In the corner of the bedroom was the backpack she had finally packed earlier at Scamp's insistence, which she had thought was so silly.

Scamp banged on her door again and Lisa opened it. He already had his own backpack on.

"There are destroyers in the sky," he said. "Grab your pack, we have to go."

Lisa picked up the pack and slung it onto her shoulders.

"Where will we go?"

"An evacuation shelter, or a bunker or something. We have to talk to our guards."

There was no one in the building entrance chambers, which were usually manned around the clock. Through windows in the main door, Scamp and Lisa saw the two duty guards standing outside looking at the sky.

Lisa opened the door to go outside and the din of war rushed over them like a flood. They crossed the threshold slowly and then stopped to look at the sky, caught up in the awe of the spectacle around them.

Battleships the size of palaces floated in every direction,

sparkling and crackling like giant electrical jellyfish. The battle-ships shot at each other, and at the ground, overloading every horizon with angry, flashing light. Around each battleship flew smaller ships, fighters and destroyers, that swarmed the bigger ships like feeding piranhas, or chased each other like battling minnow schools. Fires raged in many places on the ground, like sulfurous eruptions from an unstable seabed.

Overwhelming everything else, all-encompassing and in-escapable, was the sound of war. Booms that shocked the air and trembled bodies; piercing, other-worldly pings; crunching, grating, grinding sounds; sharp pitched electronic squeals; shouts and screams of fear, anger, excitement, agony. Lisa's ears rang and her chest shook, partly from the pressure waves that filled the atmosphere and partly from the beating of her heart. Her heart wasn't racing out of fear. Something had changed in her these weeks. It was exhilaration.

As she finally stepped forward to get the attention of the guards, a sound that diminished in tone as it increased in volume broke out from the din. Scamp lunged and tackled her to the ground. Dirt and mangled debris rained over them.

There was a moment of blackness. Was it a few seconds? Lisa was dizzy and couldn't hear. Something had hit her head – it was the ground. For a moment she couldn't think of where she was and pushed at Scamp violently. Then she remembered the battleships.

Scamp climbed to his feet and dragged her from the edge of a house sized crater back into the building. The bodies of both the guards were scattered in pieces. Beyond the crater, through drifts of smoke, Lisa could make out a woman with strawberry blonde hair and a sequined orange dress, bloody and stumbling. As Scamp flexed to close the twisted metal door she began to be able to hear the woman shriek.

CHAPTER 62

IN THE MOMENTS BEFORE ROTHSCHILD was attacked, Alexander Grumiaux rose from his seat in the Assembly to give his speech. His coppery face was solemn and the huge room was hushed. He chose to speak formally, at one of the speakers' podiums that dotted the 500 seat Assembly Stadium, rather than simply to stand and speak from his chair as was typical. His black delegate robe billowed around him as he walked up to the podium with a quick, measured stride.

The balconies that overlooked the bowl-shaped assembly floor were overflowing with more than their official 5,000 person capacity, and the people in them twittered softly, their voices accumulating into a vague murmuring sound that filled the air. The sound, and even the air itself, was shielded from the delegates below by a variety of transparent, mono-directional field barriers.

"This special legislation must be huge," a breathless journalist said to a competitor beside him.

"It's bigger than huge."

"You've seen it?"

"Only just. I haven't even had time to skim through it."

"I can't believe they've managed to keep it such a secret."

"Well even the delegates themselves only got the legislation two hours ago."

On the delegate floor, Arthur Grumiaux gazed around at his colleagues with a bearing of reassurance and authority, as if they, the audience, needed calming nerves, not he the speaker. Which was how it was.

"Yes, Delegate Grumiaux, you are recognized to speak," said the Chief Delegate from his table down in the center of the bowl, where he stood holding an elegant wooden gavel.

Alexander Grumiaux's eye followed the lines of gold beading that highlighted the Chief Delegate's robe. He himself could be Chief Delegate if he wanted, but he didn't need that status. The Chief Delegate was not one of his votes and would try to stop him. But wouldn't be able to.

"Thank you, Chief Delegate," Alexander Grumiaux said.

The sound in the delegates' chamber changed as he began to enunciate his next word. The air was abruptly larger, with more echo, and vague murmuring. In one of the front balconies, an average looking man in a dark suit, with neatly trimmed hair parted carefully on one side, stood up and held out his hand. Alexander Grumiaux's head exploded.

If there had not been instant pandemonium throughout the stadium, people on the balcony would have heard the man say 'sic semper tyranis' as he kissed a ring on his hand and became engulfed in a billowing cloud of smoke. If the smoke had not spread out to an enormous volume, practically filling the chamber in just a few seconds, witnesses would have seen the man leap 20 feet to the chamber floor below while donning a delegate robe in mid-air, and rush for the nearest chamber exit in the midst of the crowd of fleeing delegates. As far as anyone would be able to piece together again afterwards, the man simply disappeared, possibly in an act of self-immolation.

No one would ever be able to piece together Alexander Grumiaux's skull and face and brains again. His special legislation had failed.

IN SPACE ABOVE TRITON, ALREADY thousands of miles away from Magdalena City, Tom, the cargo facility manager, spoke to a holographic image of his wife's head and shoulders that was projected from his card. There were only a few minutes left on the ship's countdown timer and he ignored all the other calls ringing through, which were continuous and frantic.

"I love you, Trina. You tell the kids I love them too. I love them so much."

His wife's dark brown hair was styled in a neat bob; she had just had it cut that morning to surprise him. Her blue eyes would not admit a loss of hope.

"Don't talk like that, Tom. This isn't the end. Nobody knows that what's on that ship are bombs."

"It doesn't look good, honey."

"We couldn't make it without you, babe."

"You're strong. You're a wonderful mother. You'll make it."

"Why would someone do this to us?"

"I don't know why. There's evil in the world. We tried to get away from it, in our far corner of the Solar System, and just be left alone, but even then we couldn't get away. They even killed Samson Ford after he won their race. Even that."

"The Prophet said yesterday that these might be the end times. He said if these are the end times then the Messiah will appear to Magdalena soon."

"Yes, I hope so."

"God bless us, Tom."

"God bless us."

Tom stared at his wife's face and wondered what to say. He was glad that he didn't have to face death alone. He was certain that he would die. At least it would be painless.

"Don't come out of the basement until you know everything's ok."

"I won't."

"And tell Reggie that I don't want him to grow up being foolish like me, slaving away in cargo. Tell him I want him to get a good education and grow up to get a good job."

"Don't talk like that, babe."

"It's ok. God bless us. Tell Mary that I love her so much and that she's the most beautiful girl in the world and we're so proud of her, and I'm so glad that she will be there to help you get through this."

"Stop it, Tom."

Trina brushed at her hair and turned her head one way and the other.

"Do you like my hair? I thought I'd go for a bob. Do you like it? In a few minutes we are going to be laughing about all of this."

When the countdown timer reached zero, the tanker ship became plasma at the center of a 500 megaton nuclear explosion, and the image of Tom on the family holo-monitor turned into white noise.

CHAPTER 63

"SCAMP, YOU HAVE TO SAVE that woman," Lisa said, pointing to the bloody woman with the sequined orange dress stumbling around the edge of the crater outside.

"Ok," Scamp said.

Another blast obliterated the woman and blew out all the front windows and doors of the house. Lisa blinked distractedly and began picking bits of glass out of the skin on her arm. Scamp scooped her up in a bear hug, with his body between her and the window and carried her to a corner of the room that was sheltered by a section of concrete wall.

"DID YOU GET HIT WITH ANYTHING BIG?"

Lisa could see Scamp's lips move, but all she could hear was ringing. She touched his face and carefully pulled a wedge of glass the size of a golf ball out of his bleeding cheek. It bled more, but not dangerously. They both still had their backpacks on. They were both covered in small cuts and bits of glass. She held Scamp still and looked over his body where the blast had hit, for any large wounds. Luckily he was big, chunks of glass that might have cut her badly barely penetrated his thick skin. Scamp put his hands on her shoulders and turned her gently, looking her over for wounds as well. Her whole left side was a smeary mess of blood, but nothing that was deep or bleeding fast. They both crouched down against the wall.

"What should we do?" Lisa said, as she began to be able to hear again. The roar and thunder of battle shook the building constantly.

"I don't know! Hopefully someone from Rothschild's will come evacuate us!"

No sooner had Scamp spoken these words than a Rothschild's security agent sprinted through the blasted open doorway. The man was dressed in a dark suit and armed with an assault rifle.

"Are you two alright? Jesuschrist!"

"We're ok!" Lisa said.

"Just scraped up, nothing serious." Scamp said, nodding towards Lisa.

"We have to get to a bunker. Follow me!"

Scamp and Lisa scrambled to their feet and dashed after the man as he ran back out through the door. Just outside was a small, white, open-topped transport shuttle, and the man jumped into the driver's seat.

"Are you good with a gun?" he asked Scamp as the two climbed in behind him.

"Yes."

The man handed him the assault rifle.

"Shoot anyone that tries to shoot us."

"Ok."

Then they were off. The little shuttle leapt up and down through the air as the man piloted aggressively through the cityscape, but never very far off the ground. Fires and explosions and gunshots and screams sounded all around them and a dull, oppressive rumble smothered like a thick blanket over everything. Smoke and ozone and the dust of broken buildings filled up their noses and seeped into the pores of their skin. The great battleships in the sky, some near some far away, flashed at each other and the ground, exploding or causing explosions, floating tranquilly like jellyfish, surrounded by schools of darting electric minnows determined to bring each other or the big ships down. Scamp scanned the city for potential enemies as they passed, but nobody tried to shoot at them.

With a shriek and whoosh of inertial brakes, the transport shuddered to a stop in front of two small industrial buildings.

"We can link up with the palace evacuation tunnels here," the man said, and jumped out of the vehicle.

Scamp handed the man back the assault rifle and he led them to the side of one of the buildings where, concealed within a peculiar sculpture of thick concrete blocks, a metal staircase ran two stories straight down through a claustrophobic rectangular tunnel. At the bottom of the stairs was a heavy steel door that unbolted when the man scanned his palm and said his name.

"William Livesay."

He pushed open the door with a squeak of big steel hinges and they moved forward into a basement evacuation tunnel that was dimly lit with yellow blinking lights. The door closed and bolted itself shut behind them.

"You can call me Will," he said, then produced a small com that he clipped to his lapel. "This is Will, are you there still?"

"Of course we're here, what the hell have you been doing?"

"I've secured Ms. Maui and Mr. Maximus and we're proceeding through the tunnel below the currency administration building."

There was a pause of static before the reply.

"Great work, Will. There are battles in the tunnels, get through as quickly as you can."

"What?!"

"It's safer than outside! Even the Mistress might be down there somewhere, if you see her party do whatever you can to help them."

"Obviously," he frowned at the com.

"Well hurry up! Run!"

"Roger."

Will turned back to Scamp and Lisa. He was a distinguished looking young man with pale blue eyes and cloudy grey skin.

"Follow me. I'll talk for a minute as we walk, and then we'll start running. Can you both run?"

Scamp looked at Lisa.

"Probably," she said.

"Do you have another weapon?" Scamp asked.

"No. Ok," Will began walking quickly down the tunnel as he spoke, "there are bunkers and security stations below, where we'll be safe. These tunnels are like a maze. Some of them may be sealed off, especially since we're close to the palace. Follow me, try to keep up. I won't leave you behind."

He broke into a jog.

Over the next half-hour they came to many dead ends where tunnels had been sealed off by large blast-proof doors. At one of the dead ends they could hear the sound of blasts and violent conflict coming from the other side. They jogged and then walked and then ran and then walked. They could hear gun shots and screams echoing to them from some of the tunnels and at these points Will would break into a run and try to lead them away from whatever the conflict was. The path between dead ends and echoing violence brought them closer and closer to the palace itself, until they finally arrived at another exit to the whole bunker system. A ringing of gunshots and explosions seemed to be trailing along behind them now, getting closer and closer as they stood in front of a big bunker door that was identical to the one they had first entered.

"Shit!" Will said.

The three of them stood panting in front of the sealed door. Sweat dripped down their faces.

"They're coming this way," Scamp said.

"I know, but this door takes us back into the palace and the fighting is worse there."

"Well there's nowhere else for us to go!"

For the first time, Will realized that Scamp was terrifying. He had to consciously resist being intimidated.

"Hurry," Lisa said. "Let's go into the palace."

438

The shockwave of an explosion down the tunnel washed over them, then pitiful wails of someone hurt. Will started opening the door.

"If you get separated from me, just try to hide," he said. "The palace will be secured eventually."

The huge bunker door opened onto an alcove in a palace hallway that was much brighter than the bunker tunnels, but cloudy with smoke. Lisa coughed and choked. Blocking their vision majestically, at one corner of the alcove, was a big chunk of an ancient stone monolith, covered in hieroglyphics, that went up almost to the ceiling. Impressive artifacts and decorations were hung or displayed all along the hallway, some knocked over, some glass cases smashed. The sound of gunshots and clamoring footsteps filled the hall. A voice from the hall yelled to them.

"Lisa!! Come with us!"

And there, sprinting past, was Stephanie de Rothschild with a group of her security agents, who were engaged in a running gun battle with a mass of heavily armed pursuers. Two men at the back of Stephanie's group held portable force shields.

"Go!" Scamp said, and pushed Lisa violently forward.

Stephanie grabbed her hand and dragged her along as bullets whizzed all around the force shield edges. Lisa struggled to look back, then heard Scamp let out a tremendous yell.

"YAAAARRRRRRGGGGGHHHH!!!!!!"

He had leapt high into the space between the wall and the alcove's monolith, pushing against it with all his might. The top of the monolith started to move and then the whole thing fell over with a crash, crushing the front row of armed pursuers and halting the others in their tracks.

Lisa couldn't see what happened after that. She kept sprinting with Stephanie down the hall.

CHAPTER 64

ENIOR CHURCH MINISTERS AND A group of guards shepherded Samson through the immaculate, ornate halls of Magdalena Temple at night. The men were awed, confused, and terrified by Samson's presence. He could feel their thoughts and emotions. One of the ministers was deeply, completely reverential. True faith, without doubts. Two of the guards believed that he was an imposter. All of the men said little and avoided Samson's eyes. As they walked, the huge, echoing corridors of the outer temple gave way to smaller hallways, and eventually to the luxurious, carpeted chambers of The Prophet himself.

Samson met The Prophet in a small, circular chapel that had a single row of plush velvet benches arranged around an open central area with a domed roof. In the center of the domed roof, a set of ancient stained glass windows that depicted the resurrection of Jesus had been cleverly refitted and glowed softly against the night with lighting from below. The rest of the chapel ceiling, and the walls, were crafted from highly figured walnut planks and large beams, lined between with hand woven, jewel encrusted, silk brocade that depicted various religious scenes. The guards who had walked with them waited outside, but Samson noted three of The Prophet's own personal guard positioned inconspicuously around the edges of the chapel. The Prophet stood in the center of the chapel, in his full robes, under the glow of the stained glass. The church ministers entered with Samson and led him forward, but stopped in the shadows behind the circle of benches and waited nervously.

"Who are you, my son?" The Prophet said, as Samson walked down the aisle towards him. He looked older and frailer than Samson remembered.

Samson concentrated on reading The Prophet's thoughts.

He was flushed with adrenaline and felt relaxed. His mind had never been so crisp, his concentration never so exact. This quality, to become his most powerful self when under stress, was what had made him a great racer.

"I am Samson."

The Prophet was scared, confused, resentful. He was bitter, jealous, and ugly. But he was also more complicated than Samson had realized. He had genuine faith. He wondered if he might be wrong about Samson. What if Samson had returned from the dead, what if he had been resurrected? This scared him especially, and it made him angry, because he felt nearly certain that Samson was an imposter. He was worried about his image in front of the church ministers, he wanted to show them how he would deal with the imposter in a kind and deeply wise way. He wanted to reveal Samson, make him confess who and what he really was, and bring him into the fold of the Church. He could manipulate a traitorous spy, turn him into a good man, or at least a useful tool. Or he could find out, and destroy him. But he doubted himself. What if he was wrong? What if Samson was resurrected? Was this a test? Would he fail a test from God?

"Samson is dead," The Prophet said. "Who are you?"

There was something else in The Prophet's mind. A distant sense of dread that he was holding back. He had done something. If he were judged for it, if it was the wrong thing– It was something immense. The sense of it was vague, underneath all of his thoughts, but overwhelming. What had he done?

"Why do you doubt me?" Samson said.

"Why should I believe you?"

The Prophet began to think more concretely, of DNA tests and the whole genome sequence that he had on record for Samson, just as he had for every person in Magdalena, and for Stephanie de Rothschild since she and Samson had visited. Samson watched beads of sweat break out on the man's forehead and realized what he must do.

"You can run your DNA scan to confirm my body, child," Samson said, "if that will ease your heart."

The Prophet's lip trembled. His thoughts became more and more clear to Samson, more in focus.

"I know your thoughts. Your guard over there, Zechariah, have him bring down the machine and confirm the DNA."

"Y-yes," The Prophet said and turned and snapped his fingers in the air.

The guard, a broad, red-haired man, walked quickly down to them, stopping to kneel at the edge of the circle of benches, and scanned Samson's finger very carefully with his machine. He nodded his head reflexively to Samson, and then stopped and nodded to The Prophet, and then half-nodded again apologetically to Samson. And then stopped, looking confused. Samson tried to concentrate his senses only on reading the thoughts and feelings of The Prophet.

"It's a match," Zechariah said softly.

The Prophet nodded Zechariah away.

"You still doubt me, Benjamin," Samson said, snatching the name and its significance from The Prophet's mind. The Prophet gasped.

"No-nobody knows that name."

Samson drew deeply from within himself and stared down at the man before him, whom he had long hated, with genuine compassion.

"Do you know me?" The Prophet asked tremulously.

"I know even the number of the hairs on your head."

"He is risen!" The Prophet said suddenly and knelt to the ground, his cracked voice echoing around the chapel. All of the ministers and guards knelt without hesitation, crossed themselves, and repeated The Prophet's call, "He is risen!"

Their doubt evaporated to nothing, like desert mist before a dawning sun.

The Prophet prostrated himself abjectly on the floor, face pressed into the carpet, crying and now sweating profusely. The doubt and dread that simmered in the background of his thoughts had become overwhelming. And guilt. Dread and guilt. And faint hope and enormous doubt. The hope was that Samson was here to save him. The fear was that Samson was here to condemn him. And the thing that he had done. The thing that he had done. Option Omega. Option Omega. Was it wrong?? Option Omega. He didn't have a choice! Was it wrong???

"What is Option Omega?" Samson said.

The Prophet looked up at him nervously, his face was white.

"Mygod," Samson exclaimed as it suddenly came through in the other man's thoughts, "what have you done?!"

The Prophet pressed his face back into the carpet, and wailed.

From the notebooks of The Prophet, 20 years before:

"Option Omega –
Two of our scientists have discovered a way to destroy the Sun."

CHAPTER 65

A BEAUTIFUL, WELL ENGINEERED MAN stood on the beach with his children, in Northern California, and watched the ocean waves. The afternoon sky was clear and bright. He was wearing baggy shorts and a Hawaiian print shirt, with a thin gold chain around his neck. His skin was a glossy peach color, with faint red highlights, and the muscles in his calves and forearms rippled with perfect symmetry.

"When the tide finishes going out, in a couple of more hours, I'll teach you kids how to harvest muscles off of those rocks. We'll harvest seaweed too. And tonight we'll have a feast!"

The man's children, a boy and a girl, had platinum hair and skin that was like a darker shade of his own. They grinned with perfect teeth and bright green eyes.

"They don't have fresh muscles off the rocks at the restaurants in the city," the girl said.

"No, they don't."

"Is this the beach where you grew up, Dad?" asked the boy, who was younger.

"It is indeed."

As they waited for the tide to recede, the man and his children played games of tag, and dug a big hole, and built a sand castle. They became engrossed in the castle project as they built walls and towers, and dug a moat. The waves crept closer and closer, until the castle was almost overwhelmed.

"Wait, isn't the water supposed to be going out?" said the girl.

"It's going to wash away our castle!" said the boy.

The man jumped up and stared out into the ocean.

"But, it's supposed to be low tide now."

"Did you get it wrong, Dad?"

He got out his card and looked up the tide tables again. Then he checked the weather and the news.

"Did we miss the low tide?"

"No, low tide is supposed to be at 2 PM. I don't know why…" he gazed off into the ocean. "I don't understand."

The edge of the water began to lap at the front of their sand castle, filling the moat and pulling down one of their towers. The sky had turned a cloudy grey and suddenly looked stormy.

"What's wrong, Dad?"

Lightning flashed on the ocean, far in the distance.

"We'd better get off the beach," the man said, and ushered his children to quickly pack up their things.

A BARTENDER RODE HIS BICYCLE through one of Phillipeville's immaculate parks on a typically beautiful afternoon in that city. The air was fresh and clean. The shadow of a hawk passed over him and he watched the bird as it swooped across the sky and settled into a stand of oak trees that towered over a broad, shallow stream. In the stream, a beautiful woman was wading. She tossed back her long hair and held her hands up against the sun to watch the hawk as it landed up above her. The bartender watched the woman playing in the water as his bicycle whirred along. He loved this city. If she was still here when he circled the park again, perhaps he would stop and say hi to her. He could stop at the stream and eat his sandwich. He could watch the hawk in the trees and the fish in the creek. Perhaps the hawk would eat one of the fish.

He smiled as he pedaled on, with a relish for the cycling that belied his thick, paunchy frame. His skin was smooth and white, with red undertones, his eyes were bright and bronze, his spiky hair was pinkish-blonde. He sped up, pedaling hard and enjoying the wind rushing over his face. In twenty minutes he had circled the park again. The woman was still there, sitting on the bank of the stream with her feet in the water. He rode over near to her, stopped his bike and said hello.

In Phillipeville, you could say hello to anyone, that was one of the things he loved about it. There was no reason for you to be afraid of them, or for them to be afraid of you. Whether it was a small woman, or a big man, or even a child. Although there weren't many children, which was also good. But you didn't have to guard yourself, the city was safe. There was no trash.

"I was going to stop here and eat a sandwich," the bartender said. "Would you like company?"

"I don't mind it."

She had sharp features and startling blue eyes that had lines in them like star sapphires. He propped his bike up and retrieved the sandwich from his bag. The air blowing off of the rippling stream felt like paradise. The sound of the water was like music.

"My name's Frank," the man said, as he sat down on a boulder close to the woman. "I ride through this park almost every day, but I don't think I've ever seen you before."

"Would you remember me?"

"I think I would."

"Am I memorable?"

"You've got my attention so far."

The woman laughed a light, easy, gentle, friendly, sincerely carefree laugh.

"My name is Gladys," she said. "Don't you find this stream just wonderful?"

"I saw you watching the hawk before," Frank said. "Sometimes he swoops down and scoops up fish out of the stream."

"I was hoping he would do that," Gladys said. "*Buteo lineatus*, the red-shouldered hawk. He looks fat on these park fish. He's a beauty."

446

"They don't normally eat fish," Frank said. "Not often."

"Maybe crayfish."

"Exactly."

"But this is Phillipeville, after all," Gladys said.

"Exactly."

"They added thin blue stripes and subtle yellow highlights to his beak and wings."

"But you can only see it if you look closely," Frank said.

Gladys kicked her feet in the water.

"Of course," she said. "Otherwise it would be vulgar, like those horrible synthcats."

"Oh, I like the races," Frank said, glancing down at the bag holding his sandwich and starting to open it.

"They can be fun," Gladys said. "But I'd rather watch horses."

"Well, horses are different."

"Do you know I rode a wild horse once, in Wyoming? Untamed. It was exhilarating."

"Well they give those drugs," Frank said.

"Exactly, but they're still wild. And they're beautiful."

"Well, I think you're beautiful," Frank said. "Why haven't I seen you here before?"

Gladys cocked her head and glanced up at him with squinted eyes and a small, merry smile.

A beam of concentrated plasma, ten miles in diameter, shone down from the sky without warning and obliterated them. In a few minutes the beam had obliterated all of Phillipeville, transforming the city into smoke and gas and pools of liquid metal, and scorched and molten rock. Far out at sea, a few more minutes later, Phillipe Bloodworth's palace was also completely annihilated, down to the bedrock of the ocean floor.

Standing on the observation deck of a floating, city-sized

447

warship, which was completely cloaked, Phillipe Bloodworth watched the god-like beams of annihilating plasma with uncontained rage. He pounded his meaty fists against the armored glass.

"I'm not there, bitch!!!"

Dark clouds and smoke blew everywhere in the plasma's wake and the warship was soon engulfed in atmospheric mess. Lightning flashed again and again against the ship and incredible, driving rain pounded its hull. And for more than an hour, Bloodworth continued to slam his meaty fists into the glass.

Floating invisibly in orbit above Earth was the small, moon-sized planet Rothschild. Sunlight, and moonlight, and starlight shone through it as if it wasn't there. It was a small planet, a large city, an enormous space station, a strategic fort, a living warship, a homeland, a palace, a nation, a mobile world, and originally, at its structural core, the single largest weapon that humanity had ever constructed.

N A BUNKER APARTMENT DEEP inside Rothschild, Lisa sat curled up on one end of a couch and sipped fine whiskey with her grandparents. Her eyes were bright with energy, even sparkling. Her grandmother sat at the other end of the couch and her grandfather sat at a small table nearby, eating bacon and candied yams and smoking an oxygen pipe. The room shook occasionally and it felt like the whole planet was shaking, and perhaps it was.

"We've been moving through space and we've arrived somewhere," Lisa's grandfather said. "We must be orbiting one of the planets. It could be Venus, but I'm going to guess that it's Earth."

"Won't that throw Earth into chaos?" Lisa said. "I mean, with the tides and everything."

"Or Venus, most certainly it will."

The room shook especially violently and Lisa had to catch a small plate that rattled off the end table beside the couch.

"It was long speculated," Lisa's grandfather said, "that Rothschild is itself a giant weapon. The planet has something like a small sun at its core, powering it, giving it its gravity, or at least that is the theory, nobody really knows. But assuming that's true, that energy could be directed. And it could do things like obliterate cities. And that's probably what it's doing right now."

Lisa's grandmother frowned.

"The war has come to us," her grandfather said. "We didn't want it, but we have it."

The room shook again.

"Yes, but we don't have to speculate" her grandmother said. "Maybe the engines that push this giant thing around have developed a cough. We don't know what's happening."

"We don't. But we've definitely been flying somewhere."

"I know."

Lisa's grandmother gulped down her whiskey as Lisa watched her with concern.

"I feel different lately," Lisa said.

"We noticed," her grandfather said.

"You noticed?"

"We noticed," her grandmother said.

Lisa laughed.

"Well what do you think is different about me?"

"You have more energy," her grandfather said. "You're brighter, happier. Do you feel guilty about that? You shouldn't, by the way."

"We're lucky," her grandmother said, "we're old, retired. We don't have to do anything. We can just watch. Maybe that's why I feel so sour, but our work is done. Mostly. We don't have to fight this war."

"I don't feel guilty about it," Lisa said. "But I feel, energized."

"Inspired?"

"Yes!"

"It feels good to survive a battle," her grandfather said.

"Yes."

"But that's not why you feel so good?" her grandmother said.

Lisa sipped her whiskey. It tasted stringent and complex, and faintly sweet.

"Not really," she said. "I don't think so. I mean, Scamp was badly hurt. Although it looks like he is going to recover ok. Thank goodness."

"Scamp is a very unusual man," her grandmother said.

"He's unique."

"Is he a good man?" her grandfather asked.

"I don't know."

"Is it him that inspires you?"

Lisa thought about the question. Was it Scamp? She couldn't wait for him to move around freely again. She had realized that she loved him, and that she might be *in love* with him, although she wasn't sure about that part. It wasn't him exactly, but he was part of it. He wasn't the source of this new energy, this inspiration, but he was the vector that carried her to it.

"I don't know," Lisa said. "Not exactly."

"You have to be careful," Lisa's grandmother said, eyeing her very seriously, "when you go through traumatic events like that with someone you form emotional bonds that aren't always positive or healthy. At the end of the day you have to untangle that, find out what your bonds really are to that person and what was just the intensity of circumstance."

"Yeah," Lisa said. "I've definitely experienced some of that."

"But it's not about Scamp, is it?" her grandfather said.

"Not really. I mean, he's part of it. But it's more like, I know what I want to do and I'm excited about it."

"And what is that?" her grandfather asked.

"To fight the war."

"To fight?"

"Scamp and I will fight in the war together."

"You and Scamp will?"

"Yup."

"Like some kind of commando team?"

"Pretty much."

Lisa's grandmother looked aghast. Her grandfather carved up his last piece of candied yam and didn't say anything while he finished it off.

"I know what side I am on, and I know that I want to fight, and I know that I can feel good about it. Scamp is strong, he can help me, and I'm sure I can help him. I don't know how I know, but, I just know that I'm going to be good at this."

"Lisa," her grandfather said, licking his lips and dabbing at them with a napkin, "you know the work that I did."

"Yes."

"I haven't ever told you very much about the gene weaving that we did for you."

Lisa glanced curiously at her grandfather and gulped down the rest of her whiskey.

"You probably noticed," her grandfather said, "that you're good at things. Pretty much everything. You've never had any trouble keeping up or doing well at anything."

"That's true," Lisa said.

"We gave you many prototype genes. The best possible genes, better than what people can buy on the market. There are very few people in the Solar System with gene packages as advanced and valuable as yours was. And some of it was priceless stuff, genes that I had to personally custom manipulate on a case by case basis in order to integrate them, things that money can't buy."

"Then why aren't I the best at anything?" Lisa said.

"Well genes can guarantee a high degree of talent, but it still falls within a range, they can guarantee that someone will be highly intelligent, but not that they will be the most highly intelligent. They can guarantee someone will be strong, but not that they will be the strongest. It's as much art as science, and environmental effects also play a large role in the outcomes for each individual."

"You know what I mean, Grandpa."

Lisa's grandfather pushed the tips of his fingers together. The whole room shook again.

"We had an idea for you," her grandmother said.

"I also gave your father special genes," her grandfather

said. "Not only what I could do, and I was making big breakthroughs at the time, but your grandmother and I spent all of our savings on his gene package. We wanted him to have the best of everything, and to be the best of everything, and as he grew up he wanted that too. He was extremely driven. And your mother also had an expensive, exotic gene package and she was extremely driven too. And they were very unhappy people."

"Your father was often suicidal," Lisa's grandmother said.

"Why?" Lisa said. "Is that how they died?!"

"No, honey, no," her grandfather said, leaning across the couch and squeezing her leg. "It was just an accident."

"That's a suicide kind of accident."

"Well your father wasn't particularly unhappy at that time. And he wouldn't have done something to hurt your mother. There was never any indication that it was anything other than a freak accident. But listen, Lisa, I'm trying to talk about you."

"Yeah?"

"Well," her grandfather choked slightly and cleared his throat, "your parents had just passed and the gene machine was already set up to create you, and it was all up to your grandmother and I how to set up your gene package. We didn't want you to be unhappy in life like your father often was, and that's hard to control for because it's not simply a matter of your natural disposition, and a lot of the genes that are associated with high talent don't correlate well with personal happiness, so we had this idea and tried something different with you. We gave you no ambition."

Lisa watched her grandfather with a puzzled expression, and glanced to her grandmother who nodded at her with visible concern on her face.

"You are incredibly talented, you can do anything, learn anything, accomplish anything that you set your mind to and work for, but you don't have any ambition or drive to be the best. You don't care about that. We thought that in this way you could be whatever you wanted to be, make of yourself whatever you wanted to make of yourself, and still be happy and content with whatever that was or whatever it turned out to be. That's why you aren't the best at anything, because you don't care about being the best."

"And why do I feel so energized now?" Lisa asked.

"Because you've found your passion."

08/20

I'm finally starting to move around. Still in a lot of pain. I was in a coma for two weeks. It looks like everything is going to go back to normal, though. Nothing permanent. They said my thick skull saved me. It's half an inch thick. Everything's cleaned up now here on Rothschild, locked up and safe. Looks like we're going to Earth. Probably. I mean, we've arrived wherever it is, I'm pretty sure it is Earth. We've been blasting something. Probably took out Bloodworth's palace, maybe Phillipeville, who knows what all. Everything's locked down, and I'm still treated with suspicion, but they've also taken a liking to me and I get a lot of credit for helping to save Stephanie de Rothschild. But I'm still in bed mostly.

Lisa said she loved me. I was in the coma and I only have memories of it here and there, little bits of memories. She was sitting there crying and she said, "I love you, Scamp." She sat by my bedside a lot when I was in the coma. She said she loved me, isn't that amazing? It's not like it means romantic love or anything, but also it could. I mean, it could have been a dream, but I don't think so. She visits me here every day, we've become quite close. I feel like I'm bad for her, but I also feel like I love her to death, so. But maybe that's a bad way to say it. I really love her. I feel like

I can be a better man for her, and I am already, but I also can't erase my past. This is a crazy world. And if there's redemption here for someone like me then it's even crazier. Sometimes I think about Lucho, and I'm like, would it even be good for there to be redemption for someone like him? There shouldn't be redemption for someone like that. And aren't I the same? I'm not the same as Lucho, but I'm also bad. Objectively, I think. I can't say that I'm not a bad man. But I could be a different man than I was.

But now there is this war. I'll have to be bad again. Lisa said something like, as soon as I get better I can start teaching her how to fight. She thinks we're going to be some kind of commando team or something. I can teach her, and that will be fun, and we might as well while we're stuck here in these bunkers, but I don't really see how this will work out. She's very excited about it.

- Scampadorous Maximus

CHAPTER 67

Robert Ulysses Frazier gripped a dense, black, wooden baton in his right hand and slapped the business end of it into his left hand again and again. He hadn't cracked any heads open with it yet, but was sure he would. Round-up of the kinderfucks was always violent these days. Strapped to his left arm was a large, clear, plastic riot shield. The riot shield was good for smashing people, too. You wanted to get up to a good sprint and hit them with your full weight behind it, braced against your shoulder and thigh. BOOM! He'd gotten to practice against dummies on the grass of a big football stadium during his week of training. Boom! Boom! One of the dummy's heads had even come off. You could really hit them hard.

Underneath his riot helmet, Robert had thick, rose-hued hair, bright green eyes, and freckles. The freckles were an accident, his genetics package had gone a little bit wrong. His parents had been given a full refund, but decided to continue gestating him. Which he thought was stupid of them.

' Must have at least a beta-grade genetics package. NO NATURAL BORN! '

That's what the advertisement had said when he signed up for this job. His package had been alpha-grade, but of course when he went to the job interview they made him provide extra documentation. Because of the freckles. They laughed at him, but he didn't care. He had brought all the documentation with him in the first place and was given the job. What was the job? Just smashing people, really. Rounding up the natural born. Just smashing them and herding them into trucks and vans. Of course, the initial advertisement hadn't said that. It hadn't mentioned Bloodworth's Security Corps, it was vague. But he had liked the training and he was excited to be a corpsman. He hated the natural born.

The town they were marching through had streets that were lined with big trees, grass meadows, and fountains. Its buildings were colorful brick and seemed to all be unique, as if each one was some family's personal design and not part of an industrial blueprint or development plan. There were cute little cottages, eccentric small towers, quaint fueling stations, two or three big, imposing public halls. There were big canals that ran through the middle of town, with little boats on them. It was a lovely town, somewhere he would have liked to live. Maybe he could come back here and take one of the houses after the kinderfucks were thrown out. The town had an unusually high population of kinderfucks. That wasn't how such a beautiful little town should be.

The corpsmen all started jogging up the street and Robert followed along to orders from his helmet intercom. On his right was his friend Claude, and on his left his friend Sheena, all keeping close, shoulder to shoulder. They'd been getting to be good friends since the training had started, they had a good squad. Claude had a thing for Sheena and they were supposed to be finally going on a date that weekend.

In front of the charging corpsmen, a mob full of kinderfucks was marching down the street. The corpsmen didn't stop their run, but all raised their shields when instructed by the helmet coms, to deflect a rain of stones. A stone deflected off a shield behind Robert and hit the heel of his heavy boot as he ran, bruising his foot. Then they hit the mob. The people in the mob had signs and slogans, but Robert never had a chance to read them and didn't care. He was hurtled along by the storming boots behind him, the adrenaline, the slap and crunch of flesh and bones, the shrieks and screams.

You smashed any of the mob that was in front of you,

smashed them as hard as you could. Then you kept running. If anyone was putting up a fight you hit them with your baton as hard and fast as you could swing. If four people were already hitting them you hit them too, everyone did, until they lay still and stopped struggling. If someone was on the ground, you stomped them with your boot as hard as you could while you ran past, aiming for the face, neck, chest, groin, hand, in that order. That order of priorities was the training. You kept on running and smashing until the whole crowd was cleared, then you turned around and helped with the round-up. Anyone who looked natural born was pushed or thrown into the backs of the security trucks and taken away. No medical care, no mercy. If some of them were dead you didn't check to see, you didn't waste time.

Robert was surprised how exciting and satisfying it was. He felt like he was ten feet tall. He partnered up with Claude during the round-up phase and when they had to pick up and throw bodies into the truck they would try to see how far they could throw them. This was good exercise, better than weight lifting, and also fun. It was just the kind of thing that he liked to do, killing multiple birds with one stone, maximizing the efficiency of life and working towards a peak of performance.

"We won't need our gym workout today," Claude said, flexing his biceps.

Robert laughed.

Sheena was dragging one flopping body laboriously and they rushed to help her pick it up and throw it into the closest truck. He barely glanced at the obese, quivering, brown haired woman, no doubt a kinderfuck. Sheena grinned behind the visor of her helmet. They weren't allowed to lift their visors until after the clean-up was complete.

"This town is going to be nice soon," she said, winking at Claude.

"It will be a paradise," Robert agreed.

"Maybe you and me should come back here in a few months and take one of these houses," Claude said to Sheena.

"Oh, that's getting ahead of yourself."

"Is it very far ahead?"

"Well, you'll see."

Robert walked away and let them flirt. He hadn't heard from his own girlfriend in months. He took out his card and checked it reflexively. Little service. There was always little service lately, or none at all. The war was devastating. He didn't know if his girlfriend had dumped him, or simply hadn't been able to communicate, or if something had happened to her. They had been bickering the last time he had seen her, and then she had gone to Earth. So he thought that she had probably dumped him.

The first month of no communication had been brutal. Of course, you could hardly communicate with anyone. It wasn't only his girlfriend. He had been alone. He hated being alone. He was glad that Claude and Sheena were getting along. He would find another girlfriend again soon, too. Maybe one of the other cute girls in the corps, their whole group was getting to be like a big family. Although he wasn't sure if they would look past his freckles. But they would at least be friends.

He touched his face. He could grow his beard out to cover the freckles up a little bit, but that wasn't stylish, and it seemed to make people react to them even more.

Sometimes he thought about the time he had met Samson Ford. The king of the kinderfucks. That was when he was working as a bellhop, when he was in school, before Samson Ford had become really famous. It wasn't long ago, but seemed like it had happened in another lifetime. Samson Ford had told him that women would like his freckles. That was a laugh. Maybe kinderfucks were like that.

459

The thought of Samson Ford made him angry. There was no way that Samson had won the Solar Regatta without cheating. No possible way.

He got into formation again with the rest of the corpsmen and they proceeded with the house-to-house, building by building phase.

CHAPTER 68

ON MARS, A MAN NAMED Felix Choi stood by the huge glass windows of his Google sponsored high rise apartment and watched the street below. He was the Senior Manager in the Human Data, Acquisitions and Sorting Department, within the Psychological Biometrics Division. This made him the boss of about 5,000 Google employees, at any given time. It was a good job.

Huge mobs were fighting and rioting in the street below. Some were police or other security services. The well insulated walls and windows of the building blocked out most of the sound, diluting it to a vague rumble. Clashes of crowds on the street left people laying on the ground. Some of them didn't get up. Some were trampled over as fresh waves of human mob washed this way and that. What were they all fighting for? What was their objective? Who knew anymore. This had been happening for months.

Felix glanced at the glass where it reflected back the image of his bright silver hair and smooth, walnut skin, then his focus shifted to the wife and child sitting at the dinner table behind him. Felicia had silver hair too, but less metallic than his own and faintly blonde, and white, porcelain skin. She was beautiful, of course, as all the women were now. Or at least, the well engineered women, which may as well have been all of them to Felix. But he felt that she was particularly beautiful. And their seven-year-old son was beautiful. He had silver hair like his Dad's, and porcelain skin like his Mom's, and huge, beautiful, old-style blue eyes that they both loved. They had named him Henry, a traditional name.

The dining room was a raised area within the big, open floor plan of the apartment's main living space. There was also a sunken living room. Henry and Felicia were sitting in black stained wooden chairs on opposite sides of a luxurious, ebony-boarded dining table, underneath a huge and intricate chandelier hung with an assortment of ancient, incandescent light bulbs. The chandelier had been designed and crafted by a prominent local artist and was one of their prize possessions. It had cost a lot of money, and was worth more than money to them now. If that was possible.

Money was a funny thing, Felix thought. Was that the reason why the people down below were fighting? Just because they didn't have enough money?

No, it wasn't that.

Small explosions in the street left people scattered and wounded, and faintly vibrated the apartment windows. It was cold outside, but it was warm in the apartment. Everything in the room behind him was still. Henry and Felicia sat staring, silent, not eating their food. He wished they would relax more. Henry needed them to relax, but Felicia was so stiff. She hated conflict, she hated to see people get hurt, even people that she didn't know. They were just sitting there at the table holding their forks in the air, listening, staring. Felicia stayed at the table because he wanted her to, and because Henry needed somebody there with him. Henry wasn't allowed to watch out the window during the rioting.

"Just dim the windows!" Felicia said.

"I will, in a minute."

Felix watched the mobs fighting in the street. He felt vaguely sorry for them, but mainly he just found it fascinating.

What were they fighting for? Not money. Were all of them poor and desperate? Not all of them, or even most. Certainly the police and other security people weren't poor and desperate. But they were fighting, and killing. How long could things go on like this?

Maybe the real question, he thought, was whether things

could ever really be any different than this.

There were fires burning in the street down below, but the high rise had strong walls around it, they wouldn't be able to get any of the fires up against it to try to burn it down.

Fire was what man had always used. Fighting was what man had always done. This was the primal nature of humanity. People had always fought. They had always tried to control and destroy each other. They had always burned each other's buildings down. One brother had always stabbed a knife into the heart of another, since the very beginning, at least according to the ancient books. And science and history showed that was true. Was it inevitable?

Could humans, who had never not fought, ever not fight?

People didn't want to live in peace.

That was the thought that came to him.

People didn't want to live in peace.

These people in the street weren't poor and destitute. Maybe a few of them were. Maybe 10%, but not more than that. Probably a lot less than that. Yet they fought. They had good homes to go home too, didn't they? He thought that they did. Almost everyone did, even the natural born. Even if they got sent to another planet, they had decent homes there to live in. They would have. And most of them could go home tonight, if they wanted to, and sleep in a comfortable place, in a warm bed, a clean room, with climate control and running water, and good food. Maybe they didn't have an apartment with huge windows and a sunken living room, maybe they didn't have a beautiful chandelier, but they had something decent. Yet they fought, and killed, and died. He didn't blame the mob of idiots any more than the police and security people, the Bloodworth's Security shits and all the others. They were all a mob of idiots, really.

They didn't want peace, they wanted to fight. That was

their nature. Maybe that was just the nature of human beings, although he felt that he himself was an exception. Maybe it could be genetically modified out of them, although if it hadn't been already then maybe it couldn't. But technology would continue to improve.

Some people screamed and cried for peace, "Peace, peace, peace!", like pathetic little morons. That had never made sense to him, though only now did he finally realize why. Because people didn't want peace. Look at the mobs in the streets. It was obvious. Human beings, who had never not fought, could never not fight. To demand of them not to fight, would be like demanding that a monkey in a forest not swing on the trees. There were other human beings around, after all. Weren't there? So they would fight. And that's how it was.

He felt a little bit of blood rise into his throat and his hands clench slightly, though only a little. He could understand the will to fight, barely. Most people didn't think enough. But if he didn't have Henry and Felicia to take care of, if he wasn't at Google and in charge of 5,000 people, then maybe he would be down there fighting too. It would be exciting. There were bodies all over the street beneath him now. There was blood all over. It would be rich, it would be something to be in the middle of that, to have all your senses on fire, to have the gorge of the blood in your nostrils, the sting of the smoke and gas in your eyes, the heft and shock in your arm as you smashed a stick across some enemy's head.

All the windows of the apartment suddenly exploded inward with a tremendous "BOOM"! The only thing Felix could hear was ringing. He felt his face. It was wet and rough with bits of glass and smoky sediment. He scrambled up to the dining room table, to grab Henry, unsure if he had been on the ground or even what had happened. Henry's eyes were wide and shaking, his little face as taut as an instrument string,

464

and he seemed to be screaming. Felicia was trying to get between them, saying something, her whole body shook, she kept reaching for his face. Felix clutched Henry to his chest and gripped Felicia's arm, and ran with them as quickly as he could towards the safer, interior rooms.

None of them could hear the words that were mumbling faintly out of Felix's mouth. None of them could hear anything but ringing. Felix wasn't even aware that he was talking. Barely, unconsciously, under his breath.

"Not here. Not here! Not here. Not here. Not here."

END

AUTHOR'S POSTCRIPT

POSTSCRIPT

December 2022

Dear Reader,

Wow, it has been exactly ten years since I published *Blazing the Sun*. Thank you for sticking with me until now, and a big welcome to those of you who are just picking up these books for the first time. I hope that you've enjoyed reading *The Quick of the Sun* as much as I've enjoyed writing it.

Blazing the Sun was intended to stand on its own as a novel, but I always had percolating in the back of my mind the idea for a sequel. When the book was well received by readers that idea became a concrete plan, and not only to have a sequel but to expand the story into a trilogy of novels: the SAGA OF THE SUN. I've told more than a few of you over the years that a sequel would be forthcoming, and as year has passed on to year it has pained me to make you wait so long to read it.

Why the delay? According to my records, I wrote Chapter 59 of *The Quick of the Sun* in April 2017, so at that time I had nearly completed a full draft of the book. But then my wife got pregnant with our beautiful son and I started a new job to take care of the family and my health failed. Those events weren't necessarily connected. To make a long story short, only in the past six months have I managed to start doing a little bit of work again each day, most days. And that progress isn't mainly because my health has improved, it hasn't, but because over time I am gradually learning to manage it a little bit better. I wrote quite a bit about these health struggles in the most recent posts on my website, The Granite Notebook, if you are curious to learn more:

www.cameronlambright.com

You may find some other interesting stuff there, too.

Nevertheless, let me simply and unequivocally apologize for the long delay.

"Never mind all that," I hear you say, "what about the sequel to *The Quick of the Sun*? What happens next?" Indeed, the juggler has smiled at the crowd but there are several balls left up in the air! Let me set your heart at ease and assure you that I am actively working on the third and final book of the trilogy. I hope to finish it within the next three years.

"Hey, wait a minute, the last book took ten years and you're some sick guy," perhaps you are thinking. "I don't have that kind of time to wait, I could be dead by then or you could be!" All fair points. Three years is an ambitious target at this juncture, I will admit, but I think I can do it. Please look forward to reading the sequel to *The Quick of the Sun* in December 2025!

Before I conclude, I should probably note that everything about viruses in *The Quick of the Sun* was already written back in 2017, it hasn't been shoehorned in as a response to the recent SARS/Cov2 global pandemic. And so, it also wasn't conceived as a commentary on any events or circumstances related to SARS/Cov2. When I finally picked up work on the book again in the past year (2022), I realized how prescient much of it seemed, and felt enormous regret that I hadn't been able to finish it sooner. (I could have been a prophet!) I hope that these virus and pandemic story themes being now published in the wake of such real life events have not taken on a tone of irrelevance, absurdity, or impertinence. Hopefully they have rather seemed relevant, and pertinent.

Sometimes I think that we all have at least a little tiny bit of 'relativity sense'. Thank you for sharing the fruits of yours with me, in the form of your time and attention on this fictional journey, and I will continue to share mine with you as best I possibly can.

Yours sincerely,
Cameron Lambright

CPSIA information can be obtained
at www.ICGtesting.com
Printed in the USA
JSHW011954290123
37012JS00003B/13